D0343582

The Good Guy

Susan Beale

The Good Guy

JOHN MURRAY

First published in Great Britain in 2016 by John Murray (Publishers)
An Hachette UK Company

1

© Susan Beale 2016

A CIP catalogue record for this title is available from the British Library

ISBN 978-1-47363-033-8
Trade Paperback ISBN 978-1-47363-034-5
Ebook ISBN 978-1-47363-035-2

Typeset in Sabon MT Std by Palimpsest Book Production Ltd, Falkirk, Stirlingshire

Printed and bound by Clays Ltd, St Ives plc

John Murray policy is to use papers that are natural, renewable and recyclable products and
made from wood grown in sustainable forests. The logging and manufacturing processes are
expected to conform to the environmental regulations of the country of origin.

John Murray (Publishers)
Carmelite House
50 Victoria Embankment
London EC4Y 0DZ

www.johnmurray.co.uk

For Austen, Mitchell, Elliot and Samuel

Prologue
February 2008

Snowflakes swirled in front of the windshield. She had the wipers and defroster cranked up to the max and was leaning forward in her seat, peering intently at the road ahead, just like the little old lady drivers she used to mock. A 4x4 whizzed past in the left lane, sending up a spray of gritty grey slush that temporarily blinded her.

'Asshole,' she muttered, though the real source of irritation was herself. After sixty-three New England winters, she ought to know better than to set out for the coast in the middle of a February snow squall. What really galled, of course, was that she *did* know better. She knew, even as she scooped up her car keys off the kitchen counter, that the only place to be today was at home in front of the fire, with a cup of tea, her knitting and Larry who, though he hadn't expressly asked her not to go – as a rule, her husband avoided comment on anything remotely related to her relationship with her mother on the grounds that 'a man invites trouble when he meddles in things he does not understand' – had made clear he thought her a fool for doing so. And she was a fool, throwing caution, not to mention her better judgement, to the wind all because Mother sounded un-settled on the phone this morning.

She took the exit to her home town slowly so as to avoid touching the brake. Plough tracks lay half buried in fresh snow-fall. Main Street was deserted. The landscape was full of mystery mounds that might be cars, or bushes or wood piles. Take your pick. Her mother would give her an earful when she saw her.

'You are such a worry wart,' she'd scold, like always.

'Well, someone has to be,' she'd reply, like always.

Lord knows it wasn't going to be Mother, even after last week's tumble, which had left a multicoloured bruise the size of Rhode Island on her hip. The doctor had said she was lucky she hadn't broken it. Mother took her good health for granted. At eighty-five, she'd had a remarkable run, but it had to end at some point. Every minor incident made Penny wonder whether the inevitable decline was at hand. There were only two ways it could go: a disease of the body or one of the mind, and while neither had much appeal, the latter was by far the more frightening prospect, and that, finally, is what had got her out the door today. The unease in Mother's voice was so out of character. And anxiety was one of the early symptoms.

The car's headlights flashed on her childhood home as she pulled into the driveway. Barbara, the woman she paid to keep an eye on Mother (while pretending not to), met her at the door.

'Mrs Burgess,' she exclaimed, 'what are you doing out in this weather?'

'My mother called,' she started to explain, but then Mother appeared, shuffling toward her, sideways on account of the injured hip. 'Um, about some mail that arrived for me?'

Mother had, in fact, mentioned a letter this morning. It was a thin excuse to drive thirty-five miles in a blizzard. Barbara nodded.

Penny turned toward her mother. 'Shouldn't you be using your walker?'

'Damn thing's a nuisance.'

'What if you fall again?'

'Barbara is here. She'll catch me.'

'The doctor said—'

'Never mind that.'

Mother grabbed hold of her arm with both hands. The pressure was so light Penny imagined bones that were hollow, like a bird's. Nonetheless, the grip was surprisingly strong. She looked up at her with watery eyes.

'I'm glad you've come,' she said.

Penny's heart sank. This was not like her mother at all.

'Make us a pot of tea, will you, dear?' Mother called over her shoulder to Barbara as she steered Penny toward the parlour. 'And slice a few pieces of that angel food cake, too, while you're at it. Use the nice plates. We'll have ourselves a little tea party. Something to cheer us in this miserable weather.'

They headed for the table in front of the picture window, Mother's favourite place to play cards, and keep an eye on birds and her neighbours' comings and goings.

'That'll keep her busy a while,' Mother said, as though in confidence but at a volume that easily reached Barbara's ears. Mother refused to wear her hearing aid. She heard perfectly well, she claimed, provided people articulated.

Penny looked to Barbara, who smiled back – no offence taken.

'Just wait till you see what came,' Mother said.

Penny couldn't imagine the letter was legit. It had been nearly fifty years since she lived at this address. 'It's not from a Nigerian banker, is it?' she asked. 'Or someone from unclaimed properties? Because you know those are scams.'

Mother waved her hands dismissively. From the kitchen came the sounds of cabinets opening and shutting, of the good silver clattering against dishes and the low hiss of the kettle set on the stove to boil.

'And they prey on senior citizens.'

'No, no. This is personal, from a Jennifer somebody. Jennifer ...'

She slid a manila envelope out from beneath a pile of papers, smiling with a schoolgirl's sly delight at having thought to hide it in plain sight. She held it up close to her face. 'Lewis,' she announced. 'Jennifer Lewis.'

She began handing the envelope over and then stopped and pulled it back. 'Are you quite well, dear?'

'Fine, Mother.'

'Not nervous or anxious? Because you look a bit on edge. I don't want to give this to you if it's going to upset you.'

'If I sound anxious it's because you're making me so,' Penny snapped. She put her hand out and kept it there until the envelope was delivered into her open palm. The back flap was wrinkled and puckered.

'You steamed this open, didn't you?' she asked.

Mother looked away, pretending she hadn't heard. Too clever by half, Penny thought, irritated and yet also relieved. Nothing quite proved Mother's continued sound mind than this act of snooping and the ham-handed attempt to cover it up.

'Remember, dear,' Mother said. 'You don't have to do anything.'

Penny responded with an eye roll that would have made her fifteen-year-old granddaughter proud, and then she read the first sentence and felt as if she'd been hit by a sneaker wave. She had to go back and read it again. Twice. In confusion, she looked up from the page and saw that her mother was crying. How amazing that ink marks on paper can contain such power, she thought, and instantly remembered having had this very thought decades before. She stared at the handwriting, searching for clues about its writer – was she friendly, creative, a liar?

'She doesn't hate me,' Penny murmured.

In the kitchen, the kettle screamed.

September

1964

Chapter One

Ted McDougall stared into the bedroom mirror, smoking a cigarette and practising a smile that said, 'Why, sure, I entertain clients all the time.'

He sprayed Right Guard under his arms and put on a freshly laundered shirt. Sweaty salesmen are suspicious, Ted's boss Curtis Hale said, and, frankly, when the pressure was on, when getting things right really mattered, Ted was something of a sweater. The unseasonable warmth of the late September evening concerned him; temperatures had been declining steadily for weeks until today – out of the blue – they spiked over eighty degrees, so hot that Abigail had to bring the fans down out of the attic. His dark wool dress pants clung irritatingly to his legs and he'd only had them on five minutes. Spying the seersucker suit hanging in his closet, he wondered whether it was worse to be a sweaty salesman or an oaf who wears a summer suit three weeks after Labor Day. It was silly social convention and he would happily buck it if not for the fear that his dinner companion, Ken Schmidt of the Bedford Trucking Company, might fail to see the wilfulness in his gesture and, God forbid, mistake it for ignorance. A glance at his watch settled it. He would stick with the dark.

Perspiration bloomed at his hairline. This heat really was something, way beyond the norm, even for an Indian summer. That it should be so, and on today of all days, seemed somehow more than mere coincidence – a test of his mettle, perhaps, or a check on his ambitions; he'd know by evening's end which it was. He breathed deeply, rolled his shoulders and shook out his arms like a boxer preparing for a bout. His head churned with the main points of the deal he'd soon be pitching to the bulldog-faced Ken. It was important to stay focused, to keep his mind from drifting to how his life would be transformed if he closed the deal. Bedford Trucking bought fifteen thousand tyres a year. With a commission on an account like that he could pay the mortgage off early, fill baby Mindy's college fund, take Abigail on vacation to Europe. All of it could be his; *would* be his. At twenty-three.

So long as he didn't blow it.

He picked up the can of Right Guard and sprayed on a second coat.

The soft scuff of slippers on linoleum alerted him to his wife's approach and he watched, warily, as she appeared in the mirror, her pale blue housecoat billowing like a spinnaker as she passed an oscillating table fan. The quiet economy of her movements made the hairs on the back of his neck prickle.

'It's wonderful news,' she said, knitting her fingers together, 'wonderful. I'm just a little surprised, that's all.' She lowered her head and her face disappeared beneath a red paisley kerchief. 'I wish I'd known earlier.' She sat on the corner of the bed and seemed to deflate.

He buttoned his shirt. 'I tried to call this morning, soon as Curtis signed off on it,' he said. 'Nobody picked up.'

'Today is the third Thursday of the month,' she said to her lap before lifting her eyes to him.

'And tomorrow will be the third Friday,' he replied with a jaunty smile because he couldn't think what else to say and, clearly, she expected him to say something. But it was the wrong thing. The air in the room shifted in a way he had come to associate with her crying jags. He called them crying jags, but they weren't. Not really. His wife was not the dramatic sort. Though her translucent skin and tendrils of auburn hair gave her the appearance of a romantic heroine – a Pre-Raphaelite stunner in the words of Mr Holder, the English teacher cum drama teacher cum elocution teacher cum soccer coach at their tiny high school in New Hampshire – Abigail McDougall (née Hatch) was as solid as granite, a pillar of Yankee practicality and common sense. He had always admired her clarity and sense of purpose, the way she seemed to know not only where she was going but also the shortest, most efficient route to take her there. That's what made these episodes unsettling: seeing such a formidable girl utterly vanquished. And by what? She couldn't, or wouldn't, say. The stillness of her grief unnerved him. The way sadness seeped out of her suggested despair beyond anything he could fathom, let alone fix. Even when not preparing to strike life-changing business deals, he couldn't bear to see his wife so diminished. He held his breath, watching through the mirror for a telltale tremble of the lip.

'I made pot roast,' she said finally.

Relief swept over him and he exhaled in a great rush. It was only her New Englander's horror of waste.

'Put it in the fridge,' he said, giving her a wink. 'We'll have it tomorrow.' He lifted his arms and detected a worrisome tightness in the shirt.

'Of course,' she replied, nodding. 'Yes.'

'Honestly, honey, there is nothing I'd rather do tonight than enjoy pot roast with you. This is business. We've all got to make sacrifices.' He crossed and uncrossed his arms, certain, now, of a pinch through the shoulders. 'This deal could be life-changing.'

She clucked her tongue. 'You're selling tyres,' she said, 'it's not the lunar mission.'

The comment stung. He had been trying to be nice to her. Okay, tyre sales wasn't NASA, wasn't keeping the world safe for democracy, or even the Law that her daddy practised, but it put food on the table and a roof over their heads. Didn't she understand how nervous he was, how scared of messing up? He removed the shirt and pulled another from the closet.

Her eyes widened.

'It feels tight,' he explained.

'Did I ruin it?'

He knew that he ought to reassure her, but was too miffed to give more than an indifferent shrug. She flinched.

From the hall there came a thump, swish, thump, swish, as ten-month-old Mindy scooted toward them on her diaper-padded bottom. The sight of his daughter, with her pumpkin-stained face and wispy curls sticking to her skin in the heat, made him smile. He could not quite believe that she was his, that responsibility for her name, let alone her care and education, was entrusted to a clown like him.

'Ba-do,' she cried, scooting through the bedroom doorway, a half-eaten teething biscuit aloft in her fist like Lady Liberty's torch. She moved like a sculler rowing in reverse, thrusting her chest forward until her bottom lifted off the ground and then sliding swiftly to her heels, straightening her legs and then pitching her chest forward again. 'Ba-do.'

It was her favourite thing to say. What she meant by it was a mystery, although neither Ted nor Abigail doubted that it had meaning. Often it made her giggle, sometimes shriek with joy. God, she was cute, he thought, as she reached forward and grabbed a fistful of his trousers.

'Help, Abigail,' he cried. 'She'll get crumbs all over me.'

Abigail stooped to pick the baby up with a slowness that made it hard to recall that only a few winters ago she was skiing down mountains at breakneck speed. Really, his grandmother was more nimble these days. He brushed vigorously at a darkened spot left by the tiny clammy hand.

'When are you going to crawl, Mindy McDee?' Abigail said pleadingly.

'Why crawl when you can scoot?' said Ted, slicking back the sides of his hair, giving his tie a final straighten.

'Because crawling is normal.'

It was a point of dispute between them. Ted saw Mindy's unique mode of locomotion as a sign of uncommon intelligence. She had honed her technique to its most efficient form and moved effortlessly throughout the house, head erect, hands free to explore. Abigail worried that it was a sign of a deranged mind.

'She's normal.' Ted slid a finger across his upper lip, checking for moisture. 'She's perfect. Look at those curls, those dimples.'

'Ba-do,' said Mindy.

'Ba-do,' Ted replied.

'Today Frannie Gill told me she has a cousin who scooted. He dropped out of school and is now a trash collector.'

'He's a trash collector because he dropped out of school, not because he scooted.'

'It's driving me crazy, Ted.'

He bent down to kiss his daughter's cheek. 'Your mother is afraid you're going to be a blockhead like your old man, instead of smart like she is.'

Mindy smiled, revealing four small white teeth and an abundance of biscuit crumbs sluicing on drool. Such bright and curious eyes, kid's got to be a genius, he thought, snapping his head back just in time to dodge the slimy zwieback she pushed toward his mouth.

'Well,' Abigail said. 'I guess you'd better be off. Don't want to be late.'

He tucked his thumb under her chin and felt the tautness of her clenched jaw. Behind those pale green eyes was a mind churning with ideas. That was Abigail's problem: she thought too much. 'Take it easy tonight, hon,' he said. 'Put your feet up. Watch TV. Read a book.'

She swallowed. Her eyes began to fill. Don't cry. Please, don't cry, he thought. He didn't have time for tears right now. Later, when he got home, hopefully with the deal in hand, he would hold her and comfort her and tell her she was beautiful, but if he didn't get out soon he would be late for dinner and then he would lose the sale because, as Curtis said, 'Punctuality is the soul of business.' And if he lost the sale how long would he have to wait before Curtis gave him another shot at one? A low voice in his head whispered, *How could she do this to him?* And then, as he saw his big opportunity slipping inexorably out of his reach, Mindy shoved the soggy end of the teething biscuit into Abigail's mouth with a hearty, 'Ba-do!'

'Oh, Mindy,' Abigail cried with a small laugh and while she was busy wiping her mouth, Ted made a dash for his old DeSoto. Placing his feet gingerly around the rust spots in the floorboards, he began the delicate operation of starting the engine. The key had to be turned at just the right speed, a precise amount of pressure applied to the gas pedal. It was, he liked to joke, the perfect anti-theft device. Abigail came to the screen door and stood holding Mindy, who was still determined to feed the biscuit to her mother. Abigail gently batted it away each time and yet Mindy kept coming back. She was relentless. Ted watched with tenderness swelling in his heart. They depended on him and he took care of them. Now he was going off on his first business dinner, out to slay a contract for fifteen thousand tyres.

'Shouldn't be too late, honey,' he called as he backed out of the drive.

Abigail smiled and Ted was struck, suddenly, by how much she looked like Raggedy Ann. The housecoat, the kerchief, even the pigtails: how was it that he had never noticed? The thought bemused him as he steered – slowly, because children might be playing – along the gently undulating roads of Elm Grove, the tract housing development in which he lived, passing brightly coloured, slab-foundation ranches with cheerful names like Charmer, Monterey, Enchantress and El Dorado, owned by people just like Ted and Abigail: young families, husbands on the early rungs of their career ladders, wives at home with small children. They traded decorating and gardening ideas, borrowed tools; they gathered at cocktail and dinner parties. It was real life and yet it retained an aura of play. The props were bigger and sturdier, and nobody got called home for dinner, but otherwise Elm Grove wasn't much different from playing house in the lean-tos they used to build from fallen branches out in the woods behind the ball park in Wilsonville, back when he was a kid.

Out on Americana Boulevard (all the streets in Elm Grove were named after a variety of elm) Paul Jenks was tending to his fledgling rose bushes; Ted lifted his right hand in mock salute. Paul's shock at seeing Ted, in a suit no less, driving out just before the dinner hour, was priceless. Tomorrow Jean would drop by for coffee or to borrow a cup of sugar and ask Abigail where he'd been headed.

'A business dinner, at a steakhouse in Boston,' she would reply. 'A really big deal.'

That would give Paul something to chew on, old Paul, who thought living in an El Dorado made him lord of Elm Grove.

Yes, indeed, Ted thought, turning the car east on Route 9, toward the city centre and its promise of steak and martinis, deal-making and manly conversation. Light from the setting sun flooded through the car's rear window, so bright it was impossible to see where he'd just been.

Chapter Two

Abigail stood at the screen door even after Ted's car had disappeared and Mindy had wiggled free to scoot about the kitchen.

She would not cry. It was childish to cry over such things. Little unimportant things. Things that didn't matter in the world. Scolding herself this way only added to her wretchedness. Her chest filled with the weight of it. She would not cry.

She went to the oven and took out the pot roast, averting her eyes from the dirty dishes that filled the sink and spilled out along the counter. A blast of steam struck her face as she lifted the lid. She felt sticky all over. Cooking pot roast in this heat: what was she thinking? She'd wanted to make the evening special. She was still relatively new to cooking and didn't have many dishes in her repertoire that made the grade. Only two, in fact: fancy Yankee pot roast and chicken pot pie with buttermilk biscuits. Neither was particularly suited to warm weather. Her failure to master her mother's cold salmon and cucumber mousse recipe suddenly felt like gross negligence. The thought contained enough truth and injustice to fill her with morose satisfaction.

She knew darn well that this line of thinking was unlikely to improve her current frame of mind, but she also knew better than to try to halt it. Moods like this were like skiing on ice: once the descent had begun there was no stopping until she hit bottom and slowing down was far riskier than speeding up. Abigail responded the only way she knew how: she widened her stance and surrendered to the force.

The evening wasn't turning out the way she had imagined.

The house was supposed to be clean and tidy by the time Ted came home; Mindy would be fed, bathed and looking her most angelic, ready for a quick kiss from Daddy and then off to bed. And then Ted would make Tom Collinses while she swapped this hideous housecoat for a decent dress and the pearls that her father had given her for her sixteenth birthday, the ones she had stopped wearing because Mindy pulled at them; instead of house slippers she'd put on heels and they'd sit together on the sofa, sipping their drinks. Ted would tell a funny story or two about customers, or share some maxim of Curtis Hale's – 'A good salesman knows his customer's needs before he does' – and then he'd turn to her and ask, 'How did it go today?'

And she would pour out the whole sad, embarrassing story of how the members of the Elm Grove Ladies Culture Club had stopped listening five minutes into her big speech, 'Abigail Adams: Founding Mother', of how their restless shuffling, whispered chatter and muffled giggles had caused her to lose her place and how no one asked a single question afterward – whereas they'd all been falling over themselves last month when that Sanders lady had blathered on about flower arranging. She would describe the excruciating silence as she stood at the mantelpiece in Frannie Gill's living room beneath a large portrait of a sad-faced clown (Frannie collected clowns), red-faced from the heat, a perfect square, longing for the floor to open up and swallow her.

'But honey, there aren't any basements in Elm Grove,' Ted would say, teasing. 'If the floor *had* opened up, you would have been standing on a concrete slab.' From the warmth in his eyes she would know that he was on her side. Ted knew how to make her laugh at herself. And the moment she laughed, the awful feeling of failure would begin to shrink. She could tell him that the ladies of Elm Grove only put up with her because she was his wife. Saying the truth aloud to a witness would make it easier to bear, even if all Ted did was laugh and declare it was nonsense.

And they'd eat dinner in the dining room with a tablecloth and candles.

A loud crash sent a bolt of panic through Abigail. She whipped around and found Mindy beneath the breakfast table, face reddening, head thrown back in preparation for a wail, fists clutching the cloth that had, only moments before, sat atop the table together with the wooden fruit bowl that was a wedding gift from Aunt Mildred. The bowl now lay in two jagged, unequal parts on the floor along with the apples, oranges and walnuts it had held.

'You stupid, stupid, girl,' Abigail screamed as she ran to scoop her up. Mindy howled and shook, slimy threads of drool wobbling from her chin; scared, obviously, but uninjured so far as Abigail could see. Abigail pulled her close, shuddering at the thought of what would have happened had the bowl landed on Mindy's head instead of the linoleum – all because Abigail had been too busy wallowing in self-pity to pay attention.

With Mindy clinging to her like a little monkey, she went to the bathroom to draw the bath, kicking Ted's work clothes and wet towel into a pile. She was being a goose. A sane woman would want to forget the speech ever happened, not waste valuable time with her husband reliving it. It was ego, foolish vanity. She wouldn't have cared whether Ted remembered about the speech if it had been a success as, when setting out for Frannie's house this morning, she had been convinced it would be.

She had assumed the ladies would be as excited as she was to learn that one of the most respected minds of the colonial era belonged to a woman.

'Abigail Adams was one of her husband's most trusted advisers,' she pictured herself saying.

'Gosh,' they'd say. 'I had no idea!'

It hadn't seemed too far-fetched. Most of the ladies of the club had at least a few years of college and several had bachelor's degrees, which was more than Abigail had. She imagined proposing an excursion to the Massachusetts Historical Society, where John and Abigail Adams's letters were archived, offering to write to the librarian to request a tour.

'Oh, Abigail,' they'd say, 'you really are too good.'

Recalling it now made her cringe.

She had misread them, another error. Add it to the pile.

The house, far from being tidy, looked as if a bomb had gone off inside it. If there was a single bright spot in her whole day it was that Ted had likely been too distracted and over-excited to notice the mess as he sped through.

'Can't stay, gotta go!'

Mindy flapped her arms excitedly, her trauma forgotten at the sight of the running water. Abigail put her down and she held fast to the edge of the candy-pink tub.

She couldn't really blame Ted for being excited. The Bedford Trucking account was a big deal. It wasn't life-changing – hyperbole like that was just plain irritating – still, it was an enormous step forward for his career: his first business dinner. He would make the sale; she had no doubt about that. Ted McDougall could sell ice to an Eskimo. Naturally, though, he'd be a bit nervous. She couldn't remember now whether she had wished him luck; she had a horrible feeling that she hadn't.

She gathered up the clothes and sniffed Ted's work shirt on the off-chance it was clean enough to last another day; it wasn't, so she went to the spare bedroom across the hall to dig one out of the laundry mountain that a decent wife never would have let build up.

Mindy let out a joyful screech. She wobbled and swayed and pointed to the water, looking expectantly at Abigail, her mouth a perfect 'o' of amazement.

'Water,' Abigail said.

Mindy screeched and wobbled again.

'Water,' Abigail repeated, her voice devoid of enthusiasm. People were always telling her that Mindy's fascination with the world was a sign of cleverness. She wished she shared their confidence. Wasn't intelligence, in part, being able to predict the world and hadn't Mindy seen water coming out of a faucet often enough to be able to predict it? Abigail shut the tap off and dipped her

19

hand in the water to check its temperature – feeling a twinge of guilt for not using the elbow, as the parenting book advised. She stripped Mindy of her drool- and pumpkin purée-sodden top, and urine-soaked diaper, while Mindy kicked and waved her arms about in excited anticipation, like a jumping jack whose string was being repeatedly pulled.

'Hold on, now,' Abigail said. 'Hold on.'

The baby nearly slipped from her hands, it wriggled so much. Who would have thought something so small could be so hard to control? Kneeling next to the tub, Abigail dipped a facecloth into the water and squeezed it out over Mindy's head. She squirmed and did scissor kicks with her legs, laughing as the water trickled down her back.

In the presence of such unbridled delight, Abigail's outlook could not stay bleak. The speech was probably nowhere near the catastrophe she had made it out to be. Having put so much time into it, her perception of appropriate enthusiasm got skewed. What had seemed a long, awkward silence to her likely passed in two blinks of an eye to the ladies in the audience. And Ted was sure to remember eventually. After watching her devote every spare minute to writing it, filling the trash with crumpled-up balls of yellow legal paper from discarded drafts, how could he not? She left her research books on the dining room table so long that he had jokingly asked whether they were part of the new decor. He complained that the constant tap, tap, tap of her fingers on the old Smith Corona kept him awake late into the night. This very morning, in fact, she had apologised for packing burned oatmeal raisin cookies in his lunch, explaining, quite clearly, that it was because there weren't enough good ones to take to today's meeting. Probably, he'd remembered already and was sitting in the restaurant right now, kicking himself for having missed all the hints she'd dropped: 'Today's the third Thursday of the month' and 'Frannie Gill said today . . .'

'Now we wash your face,' she said, passing the cloth over Mindy's pink cheeks.

'We clean your hands,' she sang, wiping the stickiness from Mindy's palms, freeing the biscuit crumbs lodged in the rolls of her pudgy fingers.

'Fingers and nails,' she chirped, scrubbing the dirt out from beneath Mindy's nails.

She felt like an idiot.

Whoosh.

Mindy scooped water up. Her face was bathed in confusion, as if she couldn't understand why it dripped away. She tried again and again, pressing her hands together, closing the gaps between her fingers but the water always found its way out. Mindy's brow furrowed in frustration that Abigail understood perfectly. It was just like her battle with the housework – every day, an endless to-do list of cooking, cleaning, laundry and grocery shopping. She never stopped and yet always, at the end of the day, her hands were empty.

Abigail rested her cheek against the lip of the tub and let her hand dangle in the water. She was tired. That was the trouble. Hot and tired. The Culture Club ladies' reaction to her speech, and Ted's forgetting it, wouldn't have upset her half so much had she been well rested. She couldn't remember the last time she woke feeling refreshed, the last time she felt normal. Getting Mindy down for naps was a constant struggle; she seemed to be the only ten-month-old in the history of the world who didn't sleep through the night. Abigail felt as if she and Mindy were hooked up to the same energy source. The more Mindy consumed, the less there was for Abigail – and Mindy burned fuel at the rate of a diesel train. Even in the womb, she'd never stopped moving, often kicking hard enough to make Abigail's dress flutter.

'That kid's going to grow up to be a placekicker for the NFL,' Ted proudly announced.

How shocked they'd been when Mindy turned out to be a girl, and yet Abigail would not be surprised if Ted's prediction proved true, in the end. The worst part was knowing that it was entirely her fault. She was not a natural woman. What other woman spent her free time wondering whether the Louisiana Purchase violated the Constitution; if the land grants for colleges and universities would have passed Congress had the southern states not seceded? Not the ladies from the Elm Grove Culture Club, that's for sure. It was only logical, therefore, that she'd given birth to an unnatural daughter.

Mindy scowled down at the water and babbled at it in scolding tones and Abigail realised, with horror, that her daughter was mimicking her: this was what she looked and sounded like. How had she become this impatient, angry, frazzled shrew? Mindy was only one baby – and she didn't even walk! – whereas many of the mothers in Elm Grove coped effortlessly with three or even four children.

Perhaps she was never meant to be a mother. What if the difficulty she'd had getting pregnant wasn't, as the doctor suggested, due to anxiety that Ted would get drafted and sent to Vietnam but nature's way of telling her she wasn't up to the job? Certainly, there hadn't been anything normal about the delivery. The umbilical cord got wrapped around Mindy's neck and the doctor had had to perform an emergency caesarean.

'Spotted it just in time,' he told her when she woke in recovery. 'She was blue at first but she coloured up after a minute or two.'

Abigail would never forget the tone of censure in his voice, his look of disapproval.

The doctor wasn't the only one who seemed disappointed in her. Her parents and Ted's mother had the same strained expressions. The nurses and the orderlies avoided eye contact. The following morning, Ted told her that the president had been shot and the news, rather than explaining everyone's strange behaviour, only increased her sense of failure, as if Kennedy's assassination were somehow her fault as well.

'Mindy McDoo, your mother's a freak,' she said as Mindy leaned forward and blew raspberries into the water.

Once Mindy was in bed, Abigail promised herself, once she'd finished the housework, she could take a bath. She'd put on her baby-doll nightgown and the chiffon robe with the silk bows and puffy sleeves. When Ted came home she would be waiting on the sofa.

'How wonderful, darling,' she'd say, because of course the news would be good. 'I'm so proud.' And they'd have a nightcap to toast his success. He'd tell her all about what he'd eaten for dinner and the clever way he had tailored the deal to make it irresistible to the man from Bedford Trucking. She would compliment his business acumen. And then maybe, after the initial excitement had passed, he would remember to ask about the speech.

'Doe,' Mindy wailed as Abigail lifted her out of the water, feet kicking as if pedalling a bicycle. 'Doe, doe, doe.'

'Leave some for next time,' Abigail said, trying to keep her voice dispassionate. Why did everything always have to end on a sour note?

The only soup in the cupboard was her least favourite, cream of corn. As its viscous texture coated her mouth and clotted on her teeth, she pictured Ted at a table covered in a starched white cloth, a waiter whipping the napkin open with a flourish, cocktails arriving on silver trays. 'Is the steak rare enough, sir?' 'Can I get anything else for you, sir?' 'More sour cream for your baked potato? Why certainly, sir.' The soup left her bloated but not satisfied. There were pots and pans to scrub, the dishwasher to load, and the laundry to fold. The air cooled off as the sun went down, but the house held on to the heat and then the iron added to it. Stickiness became slipperiness on her forehead, the nape of her neck, and between her breasts as she pressed the collars of Ted's work shirts; her reward, when she'd finished, was rinsing the dirty diaper pail. It was quarter to ten before she picked up the Andrew Jackson biography her father had loaned her. Barely two lines in, the phone rang. Certain that it was Ted calling to say he was on his way home, she was startled by the sound of a woman's voice on the other end of the line.

23

'Abigail? It's Carol. Carol Innes?'

President of the Elm Grove Ladies Culture Club.

'Carol,' Abigail said, twisting the phone cord around her free hand. 'How nice to hear from you.'

'I hope I'm not calling too late. It's hard to know when's a good time.'

'Yes,' Abigail said, winding the cord tighter. 'I mean no, no it's not too late.'

'Well, good. Now look, Abigail.' Carol paused to clear her throat. 'I wanted to apologise for today.'

Abigail watched her fingertips turn white. 'Don't be silly, Carol,' she said, swallowing hard. 'There is nothing to apologise for.'

'Some of the ladies aren't as educated as you and I.'

You and *me*, thought Abigail.

'And, well, I feel bad. I think it was the heat. Don't you find it hard to concentrate when it's hot like that? The mind just begins to wander. But I saw how much work you put into your talk and it was really interesting.'

'Yes,' Abigail said. She had run out of cord to twist. Her hand tingled from lack of oxygenated blood. 'Yes, you said you found it interesting.' As in: *Well, that was very* interesting. *Goodness, I had no idea Abigail Adams was such an* interesting *person. I'm sure we'd all like to thank Abigail McDougall for that very* interesting *paper.*

'And I certainly hope you'll be able to come next month. Janice Gold is going to talk about quilting.'

Abigail knew then that she loathed Carol Innes; she loathed Frannie Gill and Janice Gold, loathed all of them, and yet more than ever she wanted to be liked by them, to be one of them. She shook her hand free. It throbbed in time with her beating heart.

'I'll try.'

She took the book with her to the bath. As she opened the taps, the faint sounds of fussing could be heard from behind Mindy's bedroom door. She ignored them.

'A child needs to learn to settle on her own,' Ted's mother, a nurse, had told her. 'You can't be always rushing to pick her up every time she murmurs.'

She stripped down, climbed into the tub, and opened the book, eager to escape into the narrative dream, but Mindy's cries grew louder and more insistent, rising up over the sound of rushing water. They would not let her be. Slamming the book shut, Abigail stomped out of the bath and strode, buck naked, across the hall and flung open the bedroom door. A putrid stench wafted into the hall; she gagged. Diarrhoea had exploded from Mindy's diaper, leaching through her sleeper and on to the mattress. Her body radiated heat. Abigail carried her to the bathroom. The air turned foul as she stripped off the sleeper; runny excrement was in Mindy's hair and down both her legs all the way to her feet and toes. Abigail dropped her into the bath water, realising only when Mindy bawled that it must be too hot. She turned on the cold water. For once Mindy was too distressed to notice the spectacle of it pouring from the faucet. The faecal matter was as acidic as it was rank. It had irritated every part of the skin it had touched; the cheeks of her bottom were raw and shiny. Abigail tried to be gentle with the cloth and soap, but bits were trapped in folds of baby fat and only scrubbing would get them out. Mindy thrashed in agony. By the time it was over, they were both in tears. Abigail gave Mindy baby aspirin. She rubbed Paregoric on her daughter's gums and then, in desperation, took a swig herself.

Mindy wanted her mother's arms. She howled when laid on the bed so that Abigail could put on underpants and one of Ted's dirty T-shirts, and did not stop until Abigail picked her up again and took her to the rocker. She snuffled and whined as Abigail softly sang, 'I'm a Yankee Doodle Dandy' until they both drifted off. When Abigail woke with Mindy's breath gently tickling her neck and the right side of her body numb, it was past twelve and the house was quiet.

Where was Ted?

Chapter Three

The Copley Plaza Hotel Oak Bar was like the first-class lounge of an ocean liner, Ted thought, and then wondered whether he had it the wrong way around. Were ocean liners designed to look like luxury hotels? Whichever it was, he was delighted to be there, delighted to be sitting among the opulent carved wood ceiling tiles and wall panelling, cut-glass mirrors, plush red carpets and heavy drapes. Over in one corner, a tuxedo-clad quartet played a mix of jazz and swing beside a tiny dance floor – an added benefit, present but unobtrusive, to be taken or left, as desired, because in this world of Boston high society and big business, every whim was catered to. Ted relaxed in the ample cushion of the armchair as Ken tossed back his fourth, or possibly fifth, Scotch and regaled a table full of air stewardesses with tales of Jimmy Hoffa.

'Nice guy, Jimmy. Taught me to eat veal scaloppini with a fork and spoon instead of a knife,' Ken said, and the stewardesses, knockouts, every one, sat wide-eyed with their mouths agape.

'Isn't he intimidating?' said a small bright-eyed one called Peanut.

'He's misunderstood,' Ken said. 'Sentimental, I tell you. The man cries at weddings.'

Entertaining as Ted found the Jimmy Hoffa stories, he preferred the ones Ken told about running low on gas while driving through Death Valley, or spotting UFOs at night on the Dakota plains. He was fairly certain they were all made up.

'Only two rules about bar talk,' Ken had said as they walked over from the restaurant. 'Rule number one, don't be boring.'

'What's rule number two?' Ted asked.

'Who cares?'

Who indeed? Not Ted, certainly, or the stewardesses gathered round the ugly man the way Ted's family used to gather around the radio to listen to *The Shadow*: 'Who knows what evil lurks in the hearts of men? The Shadow knows!'

Ted could get used to evenings like these.

'Pay attention, now,' Ken said to him as they opened their menus and the waiter placed warm crusty rolls on to their bread plates with long silver tongs. 'I'm going to show you how to order dinner on business.'

Cocktails and red wine from France, the most expensive steaks on the menu, baked potatoes, sides of buttered green beans and onion rings piled high in a basket. The T-bone that was set before Ted was the most marvellous piece of meat he had ever beheld. Ken lifted his martini and toasted to future business success together.

'So do we have a deal?' Ted asked, because he wasn't sure and, as Curtis said, 'Clarity affords focus.'

Ken's laugh was wide, expansive. He said, 'Would I be here tonight if we didn't?'

It was the only uncomfortable moment of the evening. Ted felt like an eight-year-old but the feeling soon passed. Tonight was a celebration. He was a winner: the victor laying claim to his just desserts, which tonight was the house specialty, Boston cream pie served with coffee poured from a silver pot.

'Another cup?' Ken asked.

Ted checked his watch. It wasn't even nine. He could offer to drive Ken home and still be back in Elm Grove before ten.

'Sure, why not?'

They stayed on for another thirty minutes of collegial conversation before rising from the table with little grunts.

'Can I drop you home?' Ted asked.

'Sure,' Ken said. He leaned in close. His cheek and forehead were glossy from the exertion of eating. There was a mischievous look in his small, beady eyes. 'But what's the rush? What say we go find ourselves some pretty girls?'

Ted's initial reaction was one of horror. He was sure that Ken, with that unfortunate underbite, was looking to grab hold of the coat tails of a handsomer man and Ted, who had been dating Abigail since seventh grade and had almost no experience talking to girls in bars, was going to disappoint. Another needless worry – like whether he would get the deal, or sweat in his suit (the restaurant was, of course, air-conditioned) – Ken was a pro. It didn't matter that his face resembled that of a dog that chased parked cars; his stories captivated.

It had been a point of pride to Ted that in high school and college he had never joined friends on their occasional boon-dogging trips across state lines to enjoy the society of girls who were not their steadies. Now he wondered whether he had missed an opportunity to develop his professional skills. He'd like to be able to tell great stories. He'd like not to be boring.

Tonight might be the best night in his life, Ted thought, and immediately felt guilty because, of course, the best night of his life was the night Mindy had been born. So maybe tonight was the second best night of his life.

It depended on the definition of best. If it meant the single best moment, then there was no doubt that seeing Mindy's tiny, swaddled form through the nursery window for the first time was it, but the plain fact of the matter was that the hours leading up to her safe arrival had been pure hell. The hospital was full of people crying over Kennedy. Rumours were flying – there was a conspiracy, someone had shot at Johnson's car on the way to the airport, it was the opening salvo of the Third World War – the air was full of tension and anxiety. And then the doctor coming out to the waiting room to see him, frowning and exhaling as he said the word: 'Complications.'

Twice he'd run to the toilet to throw up; that's how worried he'd been. Tonight, in contrast, was an unbroken string of good news, a staircase to the heavens.

'Do you work with the Teamsters, too?'

It was the little brunette sitting to his right, the one who looked a bit like Annette Funicello. Ted knew that he should say yes. It was part of the game: bar talk. He should invent a good story but, caught off guard and on the spot, he blurted out the unglamorous truth.

'I sell tyres.'

As if to confirm the rules Ken had taught him, the girl lifted her hand to hide a yawn.

'Sorry to bore you,' he said.

'Oh, gosh, no,' she cried, 'certainly not. I'm sure selling tyres is very interesting. Far more interesting than what I do, at least. I'm just tired, is all.'

Her expression was sincere, guileless.

'Was it a long flight?'

Her cheeks flushed. 'I'm not a stewardess,' she replied. 'My roommates are. I'm just tagging along, but none of these girls has to work tomorrow and I have to be at the office by nine.'

She pulled a cigarette from a slim enamelled case. Ted reached for his Zippo and lit it for her.

'So I guess we're the dullards in this crowd.'

'I guess we are.' She smiled. Yes, Annette Funicello, his favourite Mouseketeer.

Her name was Penny. She was a secretary at one of the larger insurance companies in Boston but she insisted that he did not want to hear about it. 'It's not worth talking about, honestly,' she said. But she did things that *were* worth talking about – seeing *The Nutcracker* at the Boston Ballet, art exhibits and plays, a jazz club called Lennie's and a Greek restaurant out on Route 1 where there was line dancing on Friday nights. Her life sounded so exciting. Why, he wondered, had he never thought to move into the city? It wasn't as if he'd reflected on the idea and then disregarded it. The thought had never occurred to him, even before Mindy was born. Now, of course, it was too late.

He looked over at the dance floor where a silver-haired

gentleman in an expensive suit was partnering a much younger woman.

'So you like to dance?' he asked.

'I love it,' she said.

Ted enjoyed dancing, too, though lately he'd had few opportunities to do so, not since leaving college nearly three years before, in fact. It was funny how life changed. All through his teens he could have danced every week, if he'd wanted. Even in dinky little Wilsonville there were balls, mixers, parties, tea dances and friends' weddings, but all that had stopped as soon as Mindy was born, or maybe before. He wasn't sure.

'Would you like to dance now?'

Her skin felt cool beneath his fingers. She smelled of honeysuckles, menthol cigarettes and something deeply feminine. She was petite, but their height difference wasn't noticeable once they started to dance. She responded to his lead as if they had been partners for years.

'You're good,' he said.

She looked up at him with that stars-in-the-eyes look Annette gave Frankie when they sang duets on the beach.

'I was just about to say the same to you.'

In fact, Ted had won best dancer back in high school, something that was bound to sound comically pathetic to a cosmopolitan girl like her. Competition for the title hadn't exactly been stiff – an ability to avoid treading on his partner's feet had pretty much ensured victory.

'Too bad the floor is small,' he said.

'I hear the one at the Ritz is bigger.'

'That's good to know.'

He stepped back and raised his left hand to lead her in a twirl; caught her, and slowly lowered her into a dip.

Ken insisted that they see the stewardesses home. All five of them piled into the back seat of the DeSoto.

'Jeez, what kind of a shitbox is this?' Ken cried as he fought

30

with the dented passenger-side door. 'Doesn't Goodyear pay you a living wage?'

'They pay me fine. This car has sentimental value,' Ted replied. 'It belonged to my late father.'

'I don't doubt it. Driving this? Poor guy must have been late all the time.'

'She's old but she's reliable,' Ted lied. The truth was that it was temperamental and drank motor oil like kids drank soda pop.

They dropped two of the stewardesses off at their hotel and then took the Sumner Tunnel over to East Boston where Penny and her two roommates lived.

'Guy like you, a salesman, ought to put his money where his mouth is: sports car, sitting atop the finest four wheels that Goodyear makes. Am I right, ladies?'

The ladies all agreed and helpfully shouted out suggestions that began in the realm of reason:

'Mustang.'

'Pontiac GTO.'

And soon became fanciful:

'Corvette.'

'Porsche.'

'Aston Martin.'

Penny wasn't saying anything.

'What do you think, Penny?' he asked.

'What's the cute little one with the grille in the front?'

'The Corvair?'

'Maybe,' she said. 'The convertible.'

He did not know East Boston and had to circle around the neighbourhood a few times because the streets all looked the same, some of them were one-way and Penny's roommates couldn't agree on the best route to take.

'Good thing they don't let them fly the planes,' Ken said.

In daylight the difference in size and stature between a Charmer starter home and a deluxe model El Dorado was clear enough, but at half past two in the morning, shrouded in darkness, they looked surprisingly uniform. Uniform and abandoned. Ted drove along Elm Grove's enclosed circuit without so much as a cat for company, the unsteady growl of the DeSoto's engine an embarrassment. The car was indeed a shitbox. He hoped he didn't wake anyone. Rounding the corner to home, he cut the motor and coasted the final yards into the driveway. He wasn't the least bit tired. The heat of the day was gone; the night air was delicious, mild with just a hint of dampness. Peepers chirped, drowning out the hum of cars on the Mass Pike, beckoning him to come and savour the best part of the day. He strode down the driveway, breaking into a jog that became a sprint. He charged from one streetlamp to the next, arms and legs pumping, his open jacket flapping, the hard soles of his shoes clack-clack-clacking on the pavement and when he reached the light he kept running, ignoring the rising tightness in his lungs, the growing heaviness in his legs, and the prodding reminders from his gut that it was busy digesting a large dinner. He powered on to the next light, lifting his arms as if breaking the tape at the Boston Marathon before doubling over, hands on his knees, mouth open, gulping in air, burping out gas and smiling. When he walked back toward his house he was strutting, marvelling at the night's sublime beauty and this feeling of total satisfaction.

He'd always known it would be this way. He used to whisper to his kid brother Danny about it, across the darkness of the narrow bedroom they shared. At the time, his view of the world was unduly shaped by the Westerns he watched Saturday afternoons at the Elizabeth Theater. Success meant being a cowboy, driving herds across the West; a ski patroller, leading daring search and rescue missions in the Rockies; or a Rough Rider (unaware that they'd disbanded). Thinking back on his boyhood logic made him smile. Still, he saw the common thread: to be a standout, universally respected by one's peers, a figure of inspiration. The belief that he was such a man endured despite middling to poor results throughout school. In sports, he did better, though he was by no means the best player in their small community. That made tonight's victory all the sweeter. He was sure that Danny, wherever he was, was watching and applauding. He lifted his head toward the sky.

'I did it, Danny,' he whispered to the night. 'I did it.'

He hadn't expected it to happen so fast. The job at Goodyear was only ever meant to last a few months. He and Abigail had come down from New Hampshire to work for a summer during college. The pay was better in Massachusetts, and they could stay at his grandparents' farmhouse in Lexington, where his mother and twelve-year-old twin brothers, Frank and Gene, had landed after Ted's father died. He made his first sale less than two hours after stepping on to the floor, to the Goldbergs, a nice Jewish couple with a Ford Galaxie. One minute they were telling him about their toy poodles, the next they were signing the purchase order for five premium radials – wouldn't entrust the safety of those prize-winning pooches to regular tyres, not even for the spare. Sales came so easy it didn't even feel like work, something that, sadly, Abigail could not say about waitressing at a Howard Johnson's on Route 9. She returned home with tender feet, looking a decade older. The greasy-sweet smell of fried clams and chocolate syrup clung to her hair and skin all summer long. When, in the second week of August, Curtis offered him the chance to stay on, full-time, he had not hesitated. Abigail was sore at first. They hadn't talked about it, but he knew she had her heart set on him going to law school and eventually joining her father's practice in Wilsonville. The idea of being married to a tyre salesman took a little getting used to. But Ted felt sure it was the right decision and every day since had brought fresh evidence to support his case. So what if he never became a lawyer? He was still the first member of his family to go to college, and the first to hold a white-collar job, even if the actual collars of the shirts worn by Goodyear salesmen were pale blue. Had he and Abigail stayed in school the three of them would now be cramped up in a tiny apartment in married housing, with barely two pennies to rub together.

He couldn't wait to tell Abigail about the deal. Mindful of how run-down she'd been these past months, he wouldn't wake her. Mindy could be counted on to perform that service and, with a little luck, he thought, as he gently pulled back the spring-loaded screen door, she'd get around to doing it before he went to sleep. Even if she didn't, he'd get up and keep Abigail company while she prepared a bottle, changed diapers or did whatever it was she did when Mindy woke.

He poured himself a Scotch on the rocks and took it to the living room to drink in his favourite armchair, a thoroughly modern design with a simple metal frame, wooden arms and leather cushions of equal size set together at an obtuse angle. They would buy more modern furniture; they would fill the house with it.

And a second car. He swirled his glass and took a sip. Whisky and ice was the perfect drink, the ice such a pleasant contrast to the liquor's warmth. Tomorrow he would ask Abigail if there was a particular model she preferred. They could go to dealerships; gather brochures. The sports car idea was a fantasy; a family car was what they needed: something sturdy, dependable, maybe a little dull. Ted was okay with that.

He was proud to be a good provider, the kind of man who bought a house in a place like Elm Grove. He almost hadn't. His mother said it was rash to make such a big financial commitment so soon after starting at Goodyear. At the very least, she said, get the two-bedroom model, the Charmer, instead of the three-bedroom Enchantress. Play it safe. He could always trade up or build an addition later. But there were no Charmers on cul-de-sacs, which was where Ted wanted his house to be. He took a chance and stretched himself. A gamble, perhaps, but it paid off. Prices in the development were up. A Charmer had recently sold for something approaching what he'd paid for the Enchantress. Had he waited, all the gains he'd made in his income would have been eaten up by appreciation. Instead, they were going straight into his pocket while the value of his investment increased. He was not the type to toot his own horn, but he had to admit that there was some brilliance in his thinking. Had he been truly rash he would have bought an El Dorado or a Monterey and even though he could afford either of those now – yes, Paul Jenks, even the El Dorado – he could not, with any certainty, have predicted that his career would advance as fast as it had. The Enchantress would more than meet his family's needs for the foreseeable future, and the open layout and modern conveniences gave it a large and luxurious feel.

From his chair he could see into the darkened kitchen, separated from the L-shaped parlour by a partition that doubled as a breakfast bar or, when entertaining, a buffet table. The kitchen had fitted cherry cupboards, Formica countertops and matching built-in appliances – oven, dishwasher and the Frigidaire icebox that had provided the ice cubes for the drink in his hands. In daytime, light poured in through a large picture window that faced the street and a sliding glass door in the back that opened on to the flagstone patio. Instead of old-fashioned steam radiators that clunked and banged and took up vital wall space, the house was warmed by water pipes built into the floor. Radiant heating was an ingenious invention, and more than made up for the lack of a basement. Who needed a cellar? It wasn't as if they had coal to store.

He swallowed the last of the Scotch and rubbed his cheeks. It was past three and fatigue was finally catching up with him.

Chapter Four

Abigail lay awake in the dark for more than three hours, beside the whimpering, thrashing bundle of discontent that was Mindy. Her nerves swung between extremes of sympathy and antipathy. Her rational mind understood full well that the chances of anything grave having happened to her husband were infinitesimally small and yet by the time one thirty rolled around, with no sign or word from him, her brain had composed an entire *tableau vivant* depicting his funeral. There she stood in a widow's black veil, before a coffin, holding tight to Mindy's little hand. There were flowers and fake grass covering the mound of displaced earth. The image provoked fear, but mostly a tender sadness. However, when another half an hour passed and he still wasn't home, she was grinding her molars and muttering, 'He'd *better* be dead.'

Still he didn't come. And then, at last, she heard the low rumble of the DeSoto. The light from its headlights floated across the bedroom wall. The engine cut and the handbrake was pulled; the car door opened and shut. She listened for the sound of his key in the lock and was shocked when what she heard instead were his clacking footfalls on the street. Her heart pounded as she waited for him to return home, and then even when he did, he did not come to her. The clink of ice cubes in a glass as he fixed himself a drink and sat in the living room. It took all her self-control to refrain from shouting or picking Mindy up and stomping out to him. She waited and waited some more until, finally, she heard the click of the wall switch, saw the band of light disappear from beneath the door, and footsteps in the hall came closer. She kept perfectly still, listening to the sound of the blood pulsing in her eardrums as Ted entered the room and began undressing. She was determined not to speak until he did. His tie made a soft *shhhhhh* as he drew it out from under the collar. When he carelessly let it drop to the floor, leaving it for her to pick up tomorrow, any thoughts of holding her tongue went out the window.

'Did you have a nice evening?'

'You're awake,' he said. The airiness of his tone made her want to scream.

'"Shouldn't be too late, dear,"' she said. 'That's what you said, wasn't it?'

His hands were on his shirt buttons. He froze as if hit by a stun gun.

'He wanted to go to a bar.'

'Couldn't you have just said no? Told him that you had a wife and a baby at home that you hadn't seen all day?'

He sighed as if she were a dim-witted child and said, 'Abigail, honey, the customer is always right.'

'Hogwash,' she replied. Bridled rage from the day's frustrations and indignities burst out of her and she popped up off the pillow like a jack-in-the-box. She remembered, just, to keep her voice low, so as not to wake the baby; the energy, which had to go somewhere, was redirected to the speed of her diction. Her words melded together into an unintelligible, hot and angry hiss.

Across the darkened room, Ted stared at her as if she were possessed and that made her even angrier. He waited for her to finish her diatribe, and allowed several long, heavy seconds of silence to pass before saying, in a quiet voice, 'I got the deal.'

More silence followed as they stared across the room at one another. Abigail crossed her arms tight against her body, resisting saying what needed to be said.

'Congratulations,' she muttered finally.

Mindy snuffled and flailed and Abigail saw from Ted's reaction that he had not realised she was there.

'Why isn't she in her crib?'

'She's been glued to me all night. It must be teething. I couldn't put her down.'

'You shouldn't let her sleep with you,' he said. 'Remember what Mother said?'

Abigail opened her mouth to explain, but what was the point? She lay back down on the bed.

'Feel free to move her.'

He picked up Mindy and left the room. Abigail counted the seconds until he returned. She got to four.

'Jesus, Abigail,' he said so loudly that Mindy startled and began to fuss. 'That place stinks. How could you leave it like that?'

No mention that the living room was neat as a pin or that the kitchen was spotless, just as, no doubt, tomorrow morning he would also fail to observe the clean and freshly pressed work shirt hanging in the closet ready for him to don. The only time the work she did was worth noticing was when she'd done it wrong.

Abigail knew that all she had to do was cry, shed a few tears and lament, 'How could you have forgotten my speech?' and Ted would be putty in her hands. But she was too angry to do it. Too proud. In Ted's arms, Mindy rubbed her eyes frowning in sleepy confusion. She'd spied Abigail in the bed and reached out to her.

'If you want her out, clean up her bed,' Abigail said. 'Clean it, Ted, because I'm not touching it. I've washed enough crap for today.' She opened her arms and Mindy lunged into them.

Chapter Five

Hank Burns looked up as Ted walked into the store.

'How'd it go, champ?' he asked, eyebrows arched in that smart-alec way he had.

Ted shifted his stride into a swagger befitting a man who had just closed a life-changing business deal. 'Headed to my desk to draw the papers up now.'

'Lucky bastard,' Burns said.

If only, thought Ted. Being made to scrape dried faeces from the bars of a crib at four o'clock in the morning could snuff even the greatest sense of triumph out of a man. He had come into the bedroom feeling like a king and his wife had made him feel like a peasant. The anger in her voice, the way she'd bolted up off the pillow, haunted him. What did he have to do to make her proud? How many tyres did he need to sell before she forgave him for not becoming a lawyer?

He went to his desk and pulled out the paperwork for Bedford Trucking. He had deliberately left blank the space allocated to the numbers of tyres sold, partly out of fear of jinxing the deal but also because he knew it would be more fun to do so knowing the commission for all those tyres was his. He wrote it in now, cramping all five digits into the small space provided, feeling no joy at all.

Ken came by just after eleven, looking bulldoggier than ever with bloodshot eyes, striding in to Curtis's office with his shoulders back, barrel chest out, square hand stretched out in front of him. Curtis, who was a head and shoulders taller than Ken, lifted partway out of his chair and leaned across his desk so that they were eye to eye. When Ken sat down he had a big grin on his face.

'Curt,' he said, 'can I call you Curt?'

'Call me anything,' Curtis replied, 'just don't call me late for dinner.'

There were no fantastic stories today, just the facts, going over the contract, dotting i's and crossing t's. Watching them was like getting a masterclass in sales. They looked for things to praise, they flattered, but never too much; they took their time, laid the groundwork, circled their subject and then, when it got to the point, they weren't afraid to ask for what they wanted.

'You won't be surprised to hear, Curt, that I shopped around for this deal,' Ken said. 'I had at least half a dozen young guns trying to pitch me their business, but something about Ted here made me want to choose him.'

'Ted's a hard worker. Got great follow-through.'

'Don't I know it. Don't I know it.'

Hearing two men – men he respected – say nice things about him, soothed his bruised ego. He was a hard worker; he did have great follow-through.

A few times during the day, he picked up the phone to call Abigail, but he always put it down again before he finished dialling. He didn't want the other guys to overhear him simpering. He didn't *want* to simper. There were enough customers for him to put it off in good conscience. When closing time came, however, he regretted not having cleared the air with her. He did not look forward to going home, to eating her dry, reheated pot roast and pretending that it was delicious, particularly with the memory of last night's steak still fresh in his mind; did not look forward to walking on eggshells, and the coaxing and cajoling required to tease his wife back into a good humour.

40

He especially did not look forward to playing along with the fiction that she was perfectly fine and not angry in the least. All the same, he declined an invitation to join the guys for beers after work, knowing it was better to go home and face the music. There was no reason to deny himself the pleasure of a beer, though, so he stopped off at a package store to pick up a case and thank God he did because it was only when sliding the bottles into the back of the car that he spotted the lady's glove lying on the floor. One of the girls must have dropped it. He knew instantly which one. Like its owner, it was neat and feminine, with a delicate trim of lace flowers at the wrist. He shuddered to think of the trouble he'd have been in had Abigail been the one to find it. Jesus, he could hear the fuss now.

'This isn't mine.'

He picked it up and was looking around for a trashcan when his nose caught a whiff of a minty-smoky-feminine scent and he was transported back to the dance floor. He recalled her Annette Funicello smile and the ease with which she followed his lead but, more importantly, the way he had felt. His success with Bedford Trucking was new and untarnished. He was proud of what he'd achieved and confident of his future. It happened less than twenty-four hours ago, but it might as well have been a lifetime. He buried the glove in the passenger-side compartment beneath a pile of maps and the car's registration and insurance papers: a souvenir.

Chapter Six

The loaf-shaped cake slid back and forth across the round plate in Abigail's hand in an equal and opposite reaction to the motion of the handbag swinging from her wrist. The lemon-flavoured icing would have held the cake securely in place had she only waited for it to cool before drizzling it on. Unfortunately, there wasn't time. She ought to have baked it last night, as planned, but when the last of the supper plates were cleaned, wiped and put away, the very last thing she felt like doing was messing the kitchen up all over again. Just one chapter, she thought, cracking open the Andrew Jackson biography. She ended up reading late into the night.

Not to worry, she told herself. She didn't need to be at Jeannie's until ten. Plenty of time to bake a cake, leave it to cool and then frost. She'd get up half an hour early and get it in the oven before anyone else woke. But when the alarm sounded, the bed was warm and soft, and Ted's sleep-filled arms were holding her with a firmness that said, 'You are dear to me.' She closed her eyes to savour it, only for a moment; when she opened them again it was twenty minutes later and Mindy was calling from her crib. The cake didn't get into the oven until after nine and the recipe said it needed an hour to bake. She turned the temperature up to save time. The edges got scorched, which might have been easily covered by the icing, had that not melted. Truthfully, it was barely presentable and she would have tossed it into the trash had she anything else to offer in its place. But she had nothing and going empty-handed would have been even more embarrassing, especially now that she was more than ten minutes late.

Liquid icing spilled over the lip of the plate and dribbled on to her fingers and wrist. Her other hand was fully occupied in keeping a squirming Mindy balanced on her hip. The stroller had seemed unnecessary; Jeannie's house was only a couple doors down. She hadn't thought about the accumulated weight of a small child and a cake on a plate plus a handbag, or the slickness of the sidewalk. Twice her feet slipped out from underneath her when her heels landed on one of the tiny wet leaves scattered from the neighbourhood's saplings. The second time, her courage flagged and she nearly turned back. She'd call Jeannie and say she had a headache. And then she remembered how nice it was of the ladies to reach out to her. Her speech to the Culture Club might have bored them – in fact, she knew it had – but they still thought enough of her to invite her to join their book swap. As Ted said, she had to make an effort. It was a comfort knowing that they were readers. Sharing books was bound to lead to discussions that would foster mutual respect, reveal common interests and, perhaps, give birth to new friendships. These thoughts carried her the rest of the way to Jeannie's front stoop where she realised, a bit belatedly, that she had no free hand with which to ring the doorbell. She shifted to one side and then the other, debating whether to pose the cake or Mindy on the wet stoop, go to another door, or perhaps the picture window where she might attract the attention of someone inside. Finally, arms trembling under the weight of their charges, she lunged forward and used the tip of her nose.

'Abigail!' Jeannie cried. The startled expression on her face made Abigail question whether she had misunderstood the invitation, but then Jeannie's face settled into its usual shape and she stepped back to let her in. 'Welcome.'

'Jeannie, hi,' Abigail said, pressing the plate into her host's hand and shifting Mindy on to her left hip. Her right arm throbbed. 'Sorry I'm late.'

'Not at all. You really shouldn't have gone to such trouble.'

'It was no trouble,' Abigail said. She followed Jeannie to the kitchen to wash the icing off her hands.

'There's a sink in the powder room,' said Jeannie, pointing unnecessarily. Every house in Elm Grove had a powder room off the front hall.

'This will do,' Abigail said.

Jeannie paused, lips parted, and then smiled. 'In that case, the gang is in the parlour.'

The gang, Abigail thought cheerfully.

Carol Innes, Frannie Gill, Janice Gold and Becky Johnson sat in the pair of matching brown Naugahyde sofas the Jenkses had recently acquired at Jordan Marsh. Coffee mugs and ashtrays cluttered an imitation Danish modern coffee table between them. The dining room table had been pushed back and toddlers and young children swarmed over an open toy box.

The conversation stopped as she entered; the ladies' faces exploded into smiles. Abigail felt as if she were walking on to a stage, with all the inherent pressures to do something worthy of the attention.

'Look who's dressed to kill,' Carol said.

Abigail shifted uneasily. She had assumed today would be like Culture Club – suits and dresses, hose and heels – but everyone was casually dressed in drainpipe trousers, sweaters and Keds. How was it that they all knew? Even Becky, who had only just moved to Elm Grove.

'And like mother like daughter,' Frannie added. 'How pretty.'

'Is that smocking?' Janice asked, pointing with her cigarette.

Abigail admitted that yes, it was. She'd dressed Mindy in her party clothes, a pink dress with a crinoline, white tights, Mary Jane patent leather shoes, a pink bow in her hair. This, too, had been an error. The other children were in corduroy overalls, dungarees and plain cotton pinafores.

The sofas were full, so Abigail took a seat in a chair opposite and placed Mindy on the floor next to her. The moment the child's bottom made contact with the floor her legs began their frog-like flails; Abigail restrained her long enough to remove her hat and sweater. The instant she lifted her hand, Mindy was off, land-rowing in the direction of the other children, her crinoline skirt riding ever higher up above her tights.

'Mommy, look what she's doing!' four-year-old Billy Gold cried.

'That's how she gets around,' Janice said.

'Go see Sarah, Mindy,' Carol called out over the couch. 'She'll teach you how to walk.'

'Oh, she's walking?' Abigail asked. 'How wonderful.'

'All my kids were advanced, but this one,' Carol said, tossing her head toward the dining room, 'off the charts for height.'

'Poor girl,' said Janice, blowing smoke toward the ceiling. 'Who's going to want to date a giraffe?'

'You know,' Frannie piped in, 'I've heard those height scales are out of date and not very reflective of actual heights, these days. The kids are getting taller all the time. In a hundred years they'll be giants.'

Presented with the choice of agreeing with either Janice, that her daughter's height was a disadvantage, or Frannie, that she wasn't so tall, after all, Carol chose to remain silent. Her mouth was downcast, defeated; her eyes declared that revenge would be hers.

Billy dropped to the floor and imitated Mindy.

'Ba-do,' shrieked Mindy joyously.

'Ba-do,' Billy repeated.

He had to swing hard with his arms to get enough thrust to lift off the ground and landed with a thud that shook the floor and rattled the good plates on display in the oak hutch.

'Billy Gold, you stop that this instant,' Janice cried. 'Don't encourage her. She needs to learn to walk.'

'That really is the weirdest thing I've ever seen,' Carol said, with a laugh that was like a cackle.

Abigail's shoulders started to curl inward.

'Did I miss the book swap?'

45

'It's over there,' Frannie said, pointing to a cardboard box on the floor next to the coffee table. 'Help yourself.'

What Jeannie had described as a book swap turned out to be more like a very small, informal lending library. It had not occurred to Abigail to bring more than one book. She hoped the ladies wouldn't think her mean or stingy. She had put a great deal of thought into selecting something she imagined the others would enjoy – after the Abigail Adams talk fiasco she ruled out history books and biographies – and she had considered what the book would say about her as a person, a possible friend. Apprehension turned to dismay as she looked over the titles. Apart from a battered copy of *Peyton Place*, all the books in the box came from the same series of dime store romance novels.

'What did you bring, Abigail?' Becky asked.

'*Olinger Stories*. I hope everyone hasn't already read it.'

'Never heard of it,' Carol said.

'It's by John Updike.'

'Who?' Frannie asked.

'He writes for the *New Yorker*,' Becky explained.

Abigail hardly knew Becky – her husband taught gym at the middle school, they had a boy of three or four and had recently moved to a Charmer – but she turned to her now the way a drowning person would turn to a life preserver.

'Look what Abigail made,' Jeannie announced, lifting Abigail's cake plate to general oohs. 'And it's still warm.'

They all sat up eagerly but after one look either froze or slumped back into their chairs. It no longer resembled anything like a cake. It must have fallen apart when Jeannie sliced it. The middle hadn't cooked through.

'It looks delicious,' Carol said.

It looked anything but. Crumbs and chunky pieces swam in the syrupy puddle that was opaque white at its edges. It could have been cornmeal mush smothered in lard. Everyone spooned small pieces on to plates and made polite shows of tasting it, making approving noises, and saying how delicious it was. Everyone but Janice.

'Honestly, I never bake any more,' she said, dumping packets of Sweet'N Low into black coffee. 'Who has time?'

'Fruit salad is my answer,' said Carol.

'Mine's Sara Lee,' said Frannie with an exaggerated laugh.

Janice inhaled deeply. 'Yes,' she said, lingering on the *s*.

Frannie put the plate down and rearranged herself into a smaller space on the sofa. The Naugahyde made a squeaky sound that could have been flatulence. She shifted around in the seat, trying to replicate the original noise. The Naugahyde squeaked plenty, though never as it had the first time.

'My Sandy walked at nine months,' she announced.

'Nine months is exceptionally early,' Jeannie said.

'Is it?' Frannie asked with a shrug of practised indifference. 'Well then, that's probably another reason we should have pushed harder for her to start kindergarten this year. The poor thing is bored at nursery school.'

Rattattattattat, a toy gun repeated through the air.

'Billy Gold, cut out that racket,' Janice cried.

Rattatattattattattat, said the gun.

'Don't make me come over there!' She lit a fresh cigarette off the butt of the old one.

A clatter: the sound of the plastic gun being tossed back into the toy box.

'Good boy,' said Janice, as the cigarette bobbed up and down in her mouth.

'When is Mindy's birthday?' Becky asked.

'End of November,' Abigail replied. She didn't like to say the date because people in Elm Grove practically genuflected at any mention of Kennedy's shooting. Admired in life, the thirty-fifth president was being canonised in death. It was just the sort of idolatry one expected from Catholics, though the Golds, who were Jewish, were just as badly afflicted. The assassination had horrified Abigail as much as the next person, more so, she liked

47

to think, as the use of violence to reverse the will of the people was particularly abhorrent to her. If asked, however, she would admit that she had thought him overrated, more style than substance, the beneficiary of good looks, a wealthy father and a fawning press. She and Ted were Republicans, like her parents and nearly everyone in Wilsonville. In the coming weeks she would cast her first ever ballot in a presidential race and she would do it for Goldwater in the full knowledge that he was going to get creamed by Johnson, whose signs bloomed in the yards of Elm Grove like a pernicious weed. It amazed her that moving a mere sixty miles south could so fundamentally distort the lens through which reality was perceived.

'Still plenty of time then,' Frannie said.

'What does your paediatrician say?' Jeannie asked.

'He says she's normal,' Abigail said.

'Does it even matter?' Becky asked. 'My Joe didn't walk until nearly sixteen months and he's fine – started hockey barely a month ago and already skates like he was born to it.'

'You're in for it then,' said Carol. 'If he makes travel team like my PJ, hockey will take over your life.'

'Oh, it matters,' said Jeannie. 'Gesell says very clearly that crawling is a fundamental part of motor development.'

Who's Gesell? Abigail wondered and, thankfully, Frannie asked.

'The Sigmund Freud of child psychology,' Jeannie said. 'Absolutely the source.'

'Experts,' Carol said with a roll of her eyes.

'Ted never crawled,' said Abigail. 'My mother-in-law says he scooted like Mindy does and then, one day, he stood up and walked.'

'Well, there goes that theory,' said Carol. 'There's nothing wrong with Ted.'

'You can say that again,' said Frannie.

Abigail's stomach lurched. So that's why they'd invited her. She hated being the baggage others accepted in order to have Ted around.

'The state college has a course in child psychology starting in January,' said Jeannie. 'I'm thinking of signing up.'

'If I don't sit in another classroom until the end of my days it'll be too soon,' Carol said.

'Amen to that,' said Frannie. 'Chalk dust makes me sneeze.'

'I like it,' said Becky. 'Pencil shavings, too.'

'Then take the class with me,' Jeannie said. 'It'll be fun – less scary – to go together.'

'That's a lovely thought, Jeannie, but I already have my degree.'

'Oh, well, what about you, Abigail? I've got the course description right here.' She hustled off and came back with a thick prospectus.

'You want to be a child psychologist?' Janice asked.

'Of course not.' Jeannie laughed and batted her hand as if pushing the thought away. 'I just want to be a better mother. It doesn't cost much and it counts toward my degree. Silly not to take advantage of it when the college is right down the street.'

'What do you need a degree for?' Janice said. 'You're already married.'

'Exactly,' Carol said. 'My degree is a waste of paper and four years.'

'I used mine,' Becky said with what Abigail sensed was an air of wistfulness. 'I taught third grade until Joe was born.'

'I would have been better off working in a shop or as a secretary,' Carol said.

'But you wouldn't have met college men,' Frannie said.

'I met Stan while selling scarves at Jordan Marsh over at Downtown Crossing,' Janice said. 'And I had much more fun than I would've had going to class all day learning to be a teacher or a nurse.'

'There's social work, too,' Abigail said, only because the list seemed so pitifully short.

From the other side of the room a child's voice rose up in a wail and all the ladies turned in its direction. The possibly, or possibly not, tall Sarah Innes was screaming her head off and her hand was stuck in Mindy's teeth.

Abigail jumped to her feet and hurried over. Carol followed close behind.

'Mindy, how could you!' Abigail cried, needing both hands to pry open Mindy's jaw.

'Savages,' Janice muttered as she lit a fresh cigarette.

'I don't understand,' said Abigail. 'She's never done anything like this before.' Mindy was still shrieking and lunging toward Sarah, hurling herself forward, reaching for a block that Sarah held in her other hand. It was identical to a pile at Mindy's feet.

'Is she hurt?' Abigail asked Carol.

Carol inspected Sarah's fingers. 'I can't see that the skin is broken. I assume Mindy's had all her shots?'

'Of course!'

'It's fine, then,' Carol said, though her upright carriage and clipped gestures said it was anything but. She led Sarah as far away from Mindy as she could get.

'Bite her,' Frannie said. 'That'll teach her.'

'Oh, I couldn't.'

'It's the only way she'll learn,' said Jeannie, the child psychology enthusiast. 'My kids all bit me once but, I'll tell you, none of them tried it a second time.'

Abigail lifted Mindy's fat little hand to her mouth and held it with her teeth but she would not bite down, not for lack of will, but for fear that she'd bite that little hand clear off.

From the picture window she spied the rooftop to her own home and felt an ache to be back there, in her housecoat, ironing, cleaning the oven, Lord, even rinsing out dirty diapers, anything not to be sitting in this room demonstrating, once more, her social awkwardness and feminine ineptitude.

'Could I see that course catalogue?' she asked.

'Of course,' Jeannie said, her voice rising on hope. 'You know, I'm just going to have one more little sliver of this cake, Abigail. It really is delicious.'

Abigail flipped past the child psychology course. She knew she ought to want to learn how to be a better mother, but the prospect of devoting more time to babies and small children made her want to lie in a warm bath and open a vein. She longed for something that would engage her mind, for questions that required hours of digging in a library and that led, ultimately, to more questions. The college offered a range of subjects: anthropology, education, English literature, home economics and, of course, history. American, Greek and Roman Civilisation, the Napoleonic Wars, the British Empire, all sounded interesting and several met in the evenings. She could get everything ready, settle Mindy, do the dishes, and prepare dinner. All Ted would have to do was serve it out; she'd be back well before bedtime. He would hardly notice she was gone.

'How far off your degree are you, Abigail?' Becky asked.

'Nearly halfway. I meant to enrol when we moved down here, but Mother Nature had other ideas.' This was not quite the truth. Her doctor had discouraged her from taking classes. He said that given the difficulty she was having getting pregnant, and the anxiety it was causing, she'd be foolish to add another source of stress, something he made sure to remind her of when, three months later and with an air of self-congratulation, he confirmed that she was pregnant.

'Speaking of school,' Jeannie called from the dining room, 'I think we've got us a couple of future botanists over here.'

Jeannie didn't mention names but Abigail dropped the catalogue and rushed over. Sure enough, Mindy and eighteen-month-old Patrick Gill were surrounded by overturned plants. In one fist she held mangled leaves, in the other, soil that she was in the process of stuffing into her mouth as she bounced excitedly, her legs rubbing loose bits of dirt into the olive-green carpet.

'Oh, Mindy McDoo,' Abigail cried. 'What a mess you make! Jeannie, I am so sorry.'

'Don't worry.'

'Patrick Joseph Gill, you are a holy terror,' said Frannie. She stood him on his feet, dusted him off, and then, with the hand that held a cigarette, calmly but forcefully slapped the back of each of his hands while pronouncing a stern 'No.' Patrick's face turned red and then he howled.

'All your plants!' Abigail said.

'Don't be silly, they're spider plants. I've been trying to kill them for years.'

'And the dirt on your lovely carpet. Let me brush it up.'

'Nonsense. It'll all come up with the Electrolux.'

'Mindy, look at you!'

'Does that dirt taste good, Mindy?' Carol called with another cackle.

Mindy smiled a dirt- and drool-filled smile.

In the safety of the powder room, Abigail let drop the forced smile she'd been holding since she entered the house. Her jaw ached. She washed the dirt out of Mindy's mouth, and brushed it off her tights and smocking while mentally totting up the mortifications she'd ratcheted so far. The list was impressive, and it wasn't even noon! She didn't know which was worse, Carol's subtle hostility, or Jeannie's exaggerated kindness.

'If we'd tried, Mindy, do you think we could have embarrassed ourselves any better?' she asked. She longed to stay in this powder room; heck, she'd climb into a box if it meant not having to go back out there, put on that phoney grin and pretend that she and her daughter hadn't made complete fools of themselves from the moment they arrived. She knew it was a pipe dream. If she lingered much longer, Jeannie would start rapping on the door and gently asking whether everything was all right.

'Pride comes before a fall.' That's what her mother would say. In her head, Abigail could hear her saying it, in a tone that was more a warning than a scold. Even in her demoralised state, she could not deny its wisdom. She needed to stop being ashamed of her imperfections and learn to laugh at them. So what if all the other women found housewifery a breeze and mother-hood the ultimate fulfilment? Trying to cover up her imperfections was only making them more obvious. These women were not ogres, they were her neighbours. She should reach out to them. There were things that they could teach her. It was time to stop being so shy, to stop putting the onus on others to draw her out.

She took a deep breath, rose and leaned in to the mirror to look herself square in the eye and tell herself, in no uncertain terms, to get out there and be sociable, and that's when she saw it, on the tip of her nose, where it had doubtless been ever since she rang Jeannie's bell: a dark smudge of dirt in an almost perfect circle.

Chapter Seven

For their new car, Ted and Abigail read up on all the relevant models. They reviewed their finances and set a budget; they visited dealerships and compared prices, read the literature and took test drives before settling on a Ford Galaxie Country Squire station wagon. Light blue, with faux wood panelling, it was a far cry from 'the finest thing on four wheels'. It wasn't even red. But its paint and chrome were shiny and the interior carpets and vinyl True Blue upholstering smelled like success. Ted felt a surge of pride every time he got behind its wheel which, admittedly, wasn't often. Common sense dictated that Abigail use it most of the time. A car opened up Abigail's world. Being free to come and go as she pleased would, he hoped, put an end to those terrible crying jags once and for all. Shitbox or not, the DeSoto would get him back and forth to work. Besides, driving a wreck by choice was completely different to driving one out of necessity. It said to the world that he wasn't overly concerned with material objects, that he rightly valued the safety of his wife and daughter over his own convenience. It said that the Bedford Trucking account hadn't changed him. And it hadn't. Ask anyone at the Goodyear store and they'd tell you that he still did his share of menial tasks, never dumped his paperwork on the secretary the way Hank Burns did. Ted believed that actions spoke louder than words. His actions declared him to be a man of principle, with his head screwed on straight, the kind of man who had willingly got out of bed at seven this morning to bring the family to church for the eight o'clock service.

If he had to go to church, and he knew without question that he did, he preferred going at ten o'clock. There was a grand processional and recessional, and a choir to lead the congregation in hymns and drown out the false notes. At ten o'clock the children sang during the offering and their sweet voices touched all that was decent in him. He gladly put his five dollars in the plate, regretting only that he could not give more. Afterward there was coffee in the hall and people their age to chat with. The eight o'clock had none of that, just the weekly dose of spiritual nourishment, served up neat, like a spoonful of cod liver oil. The atmosphere was as cold and shrivelled as the parishioners with whom they shared the pews. The blue-rinsed lady sitting next to him smelled of mothballs and geraniums. When he took her hand for the passing of the peace, her skin felt like parchment. He worried that it would crumble to dust in his hand. The sole thing to recommend the eight o'clock was its efficiency, delivering the required lessons in scripture and cleansing of the week's sins in under an hour. That left plenty of time to get to Abigail's parents' house for lunch at one, even if he observed the speed limit, as Abigail always insisted he do.

'Have you checked the oil?' she asked, as she climbed into the back seat with Mindy.

And he smiled at her joke. With the DeSoto, he'd always had to add more before they left, and bring along an extra quart to top up again before they came home. He sure didn't miss that.

They divided their Sunday afternoons equally between their respective parents. Ted's mother lived only twenty minutes down the road. The weeks they went to see her he could sleep in, go to the ten o'clock service, have lunch with the family and still be back in Elm Grove by three thirty. Wilsonville Sundays were all-day affairs.

At least the drive was easy. Once he got out on the Mass Pike it was straight sailing. Traffic was light.

'The engine is so much quieter,' Abigail remarked.

She was in a good mood, bouncing Mindy on her knee, singing

55

'She'll be Coming 'Round the Mountain' and 'The Itsty Bitsy Spider'.

They were bringing nothing but good news. He'd been named salesman of the month again, his seventh consecutive win, which, he guessed, was something of a record. Curtis Hale joked that they were going to have to rename it the Edward McDougall Salesman of the Month Award. Ted looked forward to Abigail telling her father about it.

Old Lincoln Hatch had been pretty cut up about Ted's decision to quit college, and he'd taken few pains to disguise the fact. Ted didn't blame him. Linc was concerned about his daughter's welfare, as any father would be. Ted suspected that he was nursing some personal disappointment, as well. For years he'd been complaining about how busy his office was and how he could use a partner to share the work. Obviously, he'd been counting on Ted to be that partner. It must have been a blow. All the same, it was more than three years ago, over which time Ted had gone from strength to strength. Ted had yet to hear the old guy acknowledge that Ted made the right decision, let alone admit he'd been wrong to second-guess.

As they neared the state line he watched Abigail through the rear-view mirror. She always smiled when they crossed over into New Hampshire. You could hear the excitement building in her voice as they drove through Wilsonville's Main Street, and then took the right on to High Street just in front of the McLean house, where the backyard apple trees bore a particularly tasty fruit. Ted and Danny used to climb the back fence to steal them.

'Almost there,' she said to Mindy as they neared the familiar bend in the road. 'Look, Mindy! Grandma and Grandpa's house!'

It was a nice place, Ted had to admit: three storeys, a dignified white with glossy black shutters and doors, a wide porch out front that wrapped around one side. Built at the turn of the last century, on the hill overlooking town, just down the road from the country club, it was Victorian in style, but a decidedly New England interpretation of the form, pared-down and tempered, with neither turret nor tower. Decorative trim was limited to the fly rafters and understated (none of that gingerbready ostentation), the roof pitched extra steep so snow didn't pile up, a house confident of its place in the community, like its owners who emerged from the front door as the Ford rolled up.

'Say, that's a smart automobile!' Abigail's mother Gretchen remarked, but only after she had taken Mindy in her arms with an, 'Oh, my darling, but you're getting so big!' They wouldn't accept his offer to go for a short drive, but they listened while he pointed out the various accoutrements – the radio that picked up AM and FM stations, the on-board cigarette lighter, the back hatch that could open out like a barn door or down like a drawbridge. Gretchen nodded appreciatively. Linc puffed on his pipe and chimed in with a few timely 'Ay-yuhs'.

Gretchen carried Mindy into the library and put her on one side of the braided rug, opposite a box of blocks; the baby scooted across to them.

'She's still doing it, eh?' Gretchen said to Ted because Abigail and her father were already deep in conversation about that biography she was reading. Personally, Ted preferred stories with action and suspense: adventures and whodunnits – he had an eye for spotting the killer well before the end of the book – or spy thrillers, like that James Bond fellow. He didn't see the charm in biographies. The subjects were usually already dead, so you knew from the start how it was going to end. He left them to it, unafraid of missing Abigail's telling her father about his latest success. She'd save it for a moment when she had their undivided attention. When they moved to the dinner table, Linc was hammering on about local politics.

'I'm worried about this cooperative school district they're pushing for,' he said between sips of broccoli soup. The first course was always soup, made from whatever vegetable happened to be growing in the garden.

'Yes, I saw your letter in the *Bulletin*,' Ted said.

Linc gave them a subscription to the local weekly newspaper every Christmas.

'If they get their way there'll be nearly three hundred youngsters in the high school. A travesty! The kids will be lost. And for what? Fancy science labs and more sports.'

'Three hundred isn't such a big school, these days,' Ted said. 'Over our way, they've got nearly three thousand high school-aged kids. They've had to build a second school.'

Gretchen, who was feeding Mindy puréed green beans, paused and shook her head sorrowfully. 'I dread to think of little Mindy having to find her way in such a place.'

'It's not like it's going to happen next week, Gretchen,' he said. 'Besides, more students mean more potential customers for me.'

He congratulated himself for concocting such a perfect lead-in for Abigail to mention his award, but instead she returned to the subject of the cooperative school district.

'Henry Benson's in favour of it.'

'He says it'll save us money,' Linc said. 'That's all they care about, these days, money, money, money.' He almost spat the word. 'But I say, you get what you pay for.'

'I saw Nancy Benson at the hairdresser,' Gretchen said. 'She got her hair cut short. It looks so cute. She says to stop by one Sunday, before you head home.'

'Oh, that would be fun, wouldn't it, Ted?'

'If we have time,' he replied. He'd disliked Nancy ever since grade school when she had mocked Danny for having a lisp.

Abigail frowned and looked away.

'I need to drop by the cemetery,' he explained.

'Oh,' she said, sounding suddenly conciliatory. 'Of course.'

He had to wait until they were halfway through the roast beef before Gretchen turned to him and asked how things were at work.

'Well,' he said, feigning reluctance, 'there have been some interesting developments.'

'Oh, what sort of developments?'

'What sort of developments would you say they were, Abigail?' he asked.

'Ted got salesman of the month again,' she said.

'Oh, congratulations, dear,' Gretchen said. 'That's wonderful news, isn't it, Linc?'

'Wonderful,' said Linc, who was cutting his meat and didn't look up.

'I think you told us about that last time.'

'That was for August,' Ted said. 'This is for September.'

'Every month,' Abigail said. And the three Hatches chuckled as if it were a family joke; Mindy joined in, which made them all laugh harder.

'I read something the other day, an interesting statistic,' Linc said, his voice taking on that lawyerly lecturing manner he had. 'America has seventy-five per cent of the world's cars. Seventy-five! Isn't that something? Three out of every four. And every one of them needs four tyres, five with the spare, and in some places a second set for winter. You tumbled into a good industry, Ted,' Linc said. 'Ah-yuh, you certainly did.'

Ted smiled to cover his hurt. His mother was no better, always urging him to tuck his commission money away for a rainy day, the implication being that his success was just dumb luck that was bound to run out. He wondered if they'd have thought the same if he'd been terrible at it. When he'd failed to get good marks in school adults told him it was his own fault. He was lazy or stupid or both. He didn't expect his family to understand the delicate dance of psychology and timing it took to convince people not only to spend their hard-earned money on his product, but to spend it with him. Still, it would have been nice if they recognised that it *was* a skill.

'I'll bring out the pie,' Gretchen said.

Like the soup and the roast beef, pie was a staple of Sunday lunch in the Hatch household. Delicious but thoroughly predictable, the only mystery being the kind of fruit that went inside it – apple today, with a wedge of sharp cheddar.

Abigail put Mindy down for a nap and then joined Ted for the short trip to the cemetery. The McDougall plot was near a large oak that offered shade in the summer and, at this time of year, a steady shower of acorns and dead leaves. Since his mother's return to Massachusetts, the job of visiting and tending to the family graves fell mostly to Ted. He was glad to do it. The physical act of clearing the ground around his father's head-stone and especially the small granite block commemorating Danny's twelve short years on earth soothed a conscience that remembered how, half an hour before his brother fell through the ice on Waskeegee Pond, Ted had ditched him to walk home from school with a group of older, cooler boys. Every pull of the rake was a silent apology for not having been a better brother.

When they returned to the house Mindy was sitting on the parlour floor, building block towers with Gretchen.

'No nap?' Abigail asked.

'She wasn't the least bit interested in sleeping, were you, Mindy? There's too much to see; too much to do, isn't there?'

'Ba-doo,' said Mindy.

They had coffee and then gathered around the piano for a singalong. Gretchen played and Linc showed off his baritone (*'Ol' man river, he jus' keeps rollin' along'*). The sun sank on the horizon and yet Abigail lingered, blind to the signals Ted sent her. Not until Mindy started to fuss did she reluctantly concede that it was time to get on the road.

'Before you've gone a mile,' said Gretchen, 'little Mindy will be off in dreamland.'

'Can we drop by Henry and Nancy's?' Abigail asked when they'd finished waving goodbye.

He winced, as if he really wished to go to the Bensons' but needed to own up to adult responsibilities. 'We ought to get back.'

She nodded glumly at the floor.

'You okay?'

'A little tired,' she replied.

60

Gretchen was wrong. Mindy was still awake after they'd gone a mile, two miles, five miles, ten, a thing that seemed to irritate the child nearly as much as it did her parents. Abigail tried everything to settle her: she rocked, she bounced, she sang, she played patty cake. Nothing worked. Mindy's cheeks glowed pink; she rubbed fiercely at her ears. Her whines became wails. Abigail sang louder, and higher, a war of the wills that went on for three-quarters of an hour. Abigail was the first to crack.

'Do something, Ted!' she shrieked. 'I can't make her stop.'

He pulled off at the next rest stop, got out and took Mindy from the back seat. She was hoarse and overheated from screaming, but the cold, damp air seemed to shock her and she quieted almost immediately, as in movies when a hysterical woman comes to her senses after being slapped. A bit of pacing back and forth across the parking lot was all it took for her to fall fast asleep. Carefully, he laid her down on the back seat and they continued on their way. He was proud of having solved the problem and expected Abigail to thank him. Instead, it seemed to have made her more miserable. She rode in silence up front, still as a statue, tears streaming from her eyes. Her misery stood in stark contrast to her earlier joy and the longer she went without saying anything the more he felt personally responsible for it.

'You know, honey, I've been thinking,' he said finally. 'Now that we've got the new car, you ought to drive it to Wilsonville on your own. You and Mindy could leave on a Friday morning. Spend the whole weekend up there, see Henry and Nancy and all the old gang.'

The next morning Abigail's mood was as grey as the sky outside. She said barely a word as she fixed his breakfast. A steady drizzle became a downpour just as he arrived at the Goodyear parking lot. Convinced it was a passing shower, he waited in the car, passing the time fiddling with his key chain and adjusted the rear-view mirror. He counted the change in his pocket, and then, remembering, he leaned over to the glove compartment and dug out the glove. The cotton was soft, cool and slightly damp, with traces of bright pink lipstick. He ran his fingertips over the small flowers sewn to the wrist and lifted it to his nose. The scent was faded but detectable, and it transported him back to that moment when he had felt like a winner.

Five minutes later, with the rain still pelting down, he made a dash to the store and in the eight hours that followed sold winter radials to seven separate customers, all credit for which he attributed to the glove, not because he thought it endowed him with any special powers – a man made his own luck. No, the glove simply reminded him of who he was. It motivated him and made him confident. And as Curtis said, 'A confident salesman makes sales.'

It became a ritual. At the start of each working day he took the glove out and held it as he collected his thoughts and reviewed the techniques that Curtis had taught him. His sales were better than ever. Gradually, his thoughts turned toward the girl to whom the glove belonged – Annette in his mind, though he knew her name was really Penny. He imagined the exciting things she'd got up to these past weeks, the carefree, fun activities that filled her free time while he was cleaning out gutters around his house, going to church, and spending Sundays with relatives. Every dark-haired young woman who came into the showroom made his head turn. He took Abigail to the Saturday evening show of *Muscle Beach Party* at the Shoppers' World Cinema and his pulse raced every time the camera zoomed in on Annette Funicello. The following morning he went out to buy doughnuts and when he opted to take the DeSoto over the station wagon, so that he might spend a few minutes with the glove, he knew his preoccupation had become unwholesome. His only option, he decided, was to return it to its owner.

But there was no question of doing so in its current condition. It was grey from manipulation, the fresh smell that had been its primary attraction had been overwhelmed by mustiness and motor oil. He took the long way from work and stopped at a dry cleaner's. He felt slightly embarrassed as he slid the glove discreetly across the counter to the attendant.

The man scratched his head with his pencil. 'Just the one?'

'Er, yes.'

The same guy was working when Ted went back a few days later to pick it up. He pulled the solitary glove, pinned to a wire hanger, enrobed in plastic twenty times its size, off the carousel before Ted produced his ticket. He handed it back to him with a sly smile.

He didn't think it would be difficult to find her. She had told him where she worked. He got the number from information and called the main switchboard.

'I'm looking for one of your secretaries,' he announced.

'Name, please,' said the operator.

'Penny.'

'Last name?'

He paused.

'Name please,' the operator repeated. Her voice had an abrasive, nasal quality.

'I don't know her last name.'

'Which department?'

'Insurance,' said Ted.

'Sir, this is an insurance company,' the operator said a little snootily.

Ted put down the phone.

Many would have given up at that point, but Ted was not a quitter. 'Success,' Curtis often said, 'is largely a matter of holding on after others have let go.' He arranged some afternoon sales calls in Boston so he could linger outside her office at the end of the business day. Lots of girls emerged from the brass and glass revolving doors, but not her. He drove around East Boston, staring out at street after street of three-deckers in a vain hope that one would trigger a memory. Each new dead-end only made him more determined to find her. It became a quest, like Sam Spade working on a case. He tried to recall everything they'd

63

talked about that night at the Plaza, searching for clues that might lead him to her. The breakthrough occurred when he wasn't even looking for it. Abigail called him at work one night to tell him to bring home a box of Bisquick. She was headed to her parents' house that weekend and she wanted to make a coffee cake. Why she needed to, when Gretchen baked all the time, he would never understand but he knew better than to ask. Apparently a first attempt had failed and now she was running low on key ingredients. That's how he came to be at the traffic light on Route 9, staring at the sign for Athena's Greek Palace when a light bulb went off in his head: line dancing, Friday nights on Route 1.

Abigail and Mindy set out for Wilsonville after breakfast so that they could make the journey unhurried, stop along the way, and still be there by lunchtime. She phoned to let him know they'd arrived safely. They reviewed the heating instructions for the leftover tuna noodle casserole in the fridge. After work, Ted joined a couple of the guys for drinks.

'To what do we owe the honour, McDougall?' Burns asked.

The other guys smiled into their beers.

'Normally you run out of the office like a man on fire.'

An unfair characterisation, Ted thought, though it was true that he normally tried to get home as early as possible. 'I like to see my daughter before she goes to bed.'

'A noble thing,' Burns said, sipping at the foam of his second round. 'I admire that,' he said, though his snide grin suggested otherwise.

Ted wasn't going to get upset about a little good-natured ribbing. He wasn't about to apologise for being a good guy. He dropped a few bills on to the bar – more than enough to cover the round – bid them goodnight and drove home to Elm Grove, but instead of turning on the oven to heat the casserole, he showered, put on a clean shirt, jacket and tie, and headed back out. He didn't know where on Route 1 this Greek restaurant was or even its name, but this didn't bother him. Perhaps it ought to have. Route 1 stretched sixty miles along the coast, from Boston all the way to New Hampshire, and was lined, on both the north and south sides, with novelty restaurants: one with a boat built into its roof, another in the shape of a Chinese pagoda; yet another with a totem pole. Ted's eyes darted back and forth between the red lights of the cars, all driving a foot from each other's fenders, and the neon signs on either side of them, flashing the words 'EAT', 'COCKTAILS', 'FAMILY FISH FRY', and 'LOBSTER DINNER' in yellow, blue and red. It was like playing pinball. Overwhelmed, he was looking for a place to bang a uey and head home when up ahead, on the south side of the median strip, he spotted the outline of the Acropolis glowing blue in the darkened sky. The parking lot was bigger than two football fields, overflowing with cars. Bingo.

It felt like August inside, so warm and humid was the air, and so full of people – there must have been hundreds – laughing and hollering above raucous folk music. Ted tapped his breast pocket, verifying that the glove was there, and stepped into the main dining room. A band stood on a dais in the most ridiculous get-up he had ever seen. Men in white pleated skirts, shirts with big blousy sleeves, fezzes, funny pointed shoes with pompoms on them, for Christ's sake – and yet nobody was laughing at them. They were too busy dancing and not just on the dance floor, either, but all over the restaurant. Most of them didn't even look Greek. Thoroughly normal Bostonians, men in collared shirts, blazers and ties, ladies in dresses and heels, were behaving like members of a primitive tribe. They traipsed around the restaurant with their hands on the backs of one another. Someone would shout out, 'Hayyyyyy-oh,' and the whole line would answer back, 'Hayyyyyyy-oh,' as they crisscrossed other lines and undulated around chairs and tables, bunching up in places, stretching out in others. It was impossible to say where the lines started or ended. It was a madhouse, a madhouse full of strangers, and standing there, taking it all in, Ted realised what a fool he'd been to come to this place, to think that he would find Penny here. There were at least five dining rooms. Even if he did find her in the crowd, what then? Would he just walk up to her and say, 'Here is the glove you left in the back seat of my car'? She might not even remember him. She could be here with a date, maybe her steady boyfriend. He'd driven miles, literally miles, out of his way to return a common, everyday, cotton glove, the kind available, in pairs, from any department store for less than two dollars. It was beyond silly. He should have thrown it away the moment he found it. He would throw it away right now.

He pulled at his tie, which felt suddenly, chokingly tight. He couldn't get back to his car soon enough, back to Elm Grove to eat the tuna noodle casserole cold from its earthenware dish. He turned and took a step toward the door, and then a quick step back, making room for a line of dancers approaching from his right. It was an instinctive move, an act of politeness and also prudence, the way one naturally stepped out of the path of a streetcar or an oncoming train. The faces of the people in the line glistened with perspiration. Hands reached out to try to pull him in but he stayed put, more determined than ever to flee. The line stretched back into the next room and beyond. He ought to have dashed ahead of it when he had the chance. He considered joining it as a means to get to the exit but he hesitated, unable to muster the courage. He stood with his hands on his hips, foot tapping impatiently until, at last, the caboose of this human train came into view: a small dark-haired girl in a red dress. Her face wore an expression of uncontained joy and the dress bounced and floated as she moved to the rhythm, giving a teasing glimpse of a fine pair of legs: Penny.

Chapter Eight

Penny Goodwin rode home from the Greek restaurant in an enormous Buick packed to the gills with travellers, most of them relatives of her roommate, Peanut, bound for Southie. Because they were getting out at East Boston, she and Peanut got to sit in front – a dubious honour, Penny thought while pinned sideways against the rattling passenger-side door, eyes squeezed shut, praying, at every turn, not to be thrown from the car. At least they hadn't made her sit on anyone's lap. Peanut was crammed in lengthwise, half folded like a jack-knife, head against the ceiling, her bottom resting on her brother Ronan, legs on cousin Eamon, feet across Penny, and she was in a mini skirt, no less.

The driver, Callum – another brother – bounced the car up on to the kerb in front of their apartment. Howls went up as heads connected with the roof; Penny let out an unladylike grunt as the combined weight of Ronan, Eamon and Peanut pressed her into the door. Amazingly, the lock held, but when the door was finally opened, the force of compressed bodies expanding sent her tumbling to the sidewalk.

Once inside their three-decker, Penny leaned on the banister as she climbed the central staircase to their apartment, taking pressure off her achy feet and being as quiet as she could be so as not to disturb her neighbours, efforts rendered meaningless when Peanut stomped noisily up the stairs ahead of her.

'Peanut,' she said in a pleading whisper. 'You know Mrs Rizzo is a light sleeper.'

'I've got to pee,' Peanut replied, not lowering her voice in the slightest. 'The old bat can suck a lemon.'

Penny cringed and walked the rest of the way extra softly, listening for the dreaded sound of a door cracking ajar. Peanut was already in the bathroom when she got in and Ellen, her other roommate, sat on the little sofa in her pyjamas, her size nine feet propped on the coffee table, next to a box of crackers and a tub of spreadable cheese.

'Is that dinner?' Penny asked.

Ellen spread cheese on a cracker. 'My flight got in late.'

'I can make you some eggs?'

'No thanks,' said Ellen. Her dark hair was newly washed and set in curlers.

'How was California?'

Ellen and Peanut saw more of America in an average week than Penny was likely to see in a lifetime. Much as she enjoyed their stories, she had no desire to be an air stewardess. So long as she needed to earn a pay cheque she preferred to do it with both feet on the ground, thank you very much.

'Beautiful,' Ellen replied, smearing cheese on another cracker. 'Cute dress.'

Penny did a pirouette.

'Easy as pie. I ran it up on the machine Wednesday night while you were on your way to LA.'

'Easy for you,' Ellen remarked, with a mouth full of crackers.

It was true that the dress itself was not complicated. The things that made it special – the way it hugged her figure, its daring, above the knee, hem, the soft bows she added to the shoulders – were Penny's own confections.

Peanut came out of the bathroom in her pyjamas and sat down next to Ellen. 'Ask Penny who she met this evening,' she said, as she helped herself to cheese and crackers.

'Ah-hah, a man,' said Ellen. 'That explains the glow.' Ellen offered Penny a cracker that she waved off in favour of a cigarette.

Penny blew her match out as she exhaled. 'The one from the Copley Plaza,' she said.

Peanut snapped her fingers. 'I thought he looked familiar. The good-looking one, Ellen, not the old troll. He bought her dinner. They were together the whole night. He cut right in on my poor cousin Declan, who was left crying in his beer, God love him.'

'Oh, hush, Peanut.'

Penny was too embarrassed to mention that 'poor cousin Declan' leered at her and groped her bottom any chance he got.

'Mind you, you'd be a fool to fall for young Declan. He'd either break your heart or put you in a cold-water walk-up in Southie.'

'Hard to say which is worse,' said Ellen.

'The cold-water walk-up, no question,' Peanut said. 'A broken heart will heal, but a cold-water walk-up in Southie lasts for ever.'

Peanut was always putting her old neighbourhood down. Penny suspected she did so out of fear that, without a steady stream of reminders, she might forget why she left it.

'Oh, I don't know.' Penny thought she could do without hot water if she were married to a man she loved. That man was not Declan, however.

'He could do both,' Ellen said. 'Simultaneously.'

'Or consecutively,' Peanut added, laughing. 'Take my advice, steer clear of my cousin.'

'Which one?' Penny asked.

'All of them.'

'That's half of Southie,' Ellen said.

'As a matter of fact, why not make it all of Southie but never mind that. Tell us more about the man!'

These late-night chats with her roommates were what Penny loved best about being a single girl in Boston: the only child's dream of life with sisters come true. Beneath all the banter and the teasing was real affection. Ellen and Peanut were street smart and had saved her a fortune in both dollars and indignities, but they intimidated her a little. They knew so much more than she did. It bothered her that the things she did for them – things like mending and altering clothes, tidying up, making sure they ate balanced meals – required neither skill nor talent. Had they been real sisters, she would be the baby, the one everybody protected and laughed at.

Peanut took a cigarette from Penny's pack. 'How funny that you should run into him.'

'That's the thing. It wasn't funny, you see. He went there to find me.' She explained about the glove.

'Why was it so important to return it?' Ellen asked. 'It's just a glove.'

'Beats me.' Penny shrugged.

'How did he know you'd be there?' asked Peanut.

'He didn't. He couldn't have. I didn't know myself until this afternoon.'

'That evening at the Plaza was ages ago,' said Peanut. 'Has he been looking for you all this time?'

'Sounds a little creepy, tracking you down like that,' said Ellen.

'At least you got your glove back,' Peanut said.

Penny made a sheepish face. 'I threw the other one out. I didn't have the heart to tell him. He had it laundered, look.'

'How strange,' Peanut said.

Penny preferred to think it romantic or fate.

'Would have been stranger if he'd laundered it himself,' said Ellen.

'That wouldn't have been strange. It would've been a miracle,' said Peanut.

'Did he ask for your number?' Ellen had a knack of hanging on to the thread in any conversation.

Penny blew smoke toward the ceiling, taking her time, acting nonchalant. 'He wants to take me dancing at the Ritz.'

'Ah, how romantic,' said Peanut.

'Did he try to kiss you?'

70

'Wait till I tell you.' Penny stubbed out the cigarette and put her hands up, small palms facing outward. 'He helped me with my wrap and then he kissed my hand.' A warm shiver went through her veins as she recalled his lips brushing against her skin.

'A charmer,' Peanut said, shaking her head. 'Definitely a charmer.' Peanut was wary of charmers because, she said, her father was one and she'd seen what loving him had done to her mother.

'He sounds too good to be true,' said Ellen, whose father had walked out on the family when she was ten.

Penny and Peanut exchanged smiles and Peanut said, 'Next you'll say he could be the Boston Strangler.'

'Well, he could be,' Ellen said, as the other two laughed. 'You don't know! Think about it. He hasn't attacked since January.'

They were all fixated on the Boston Strangler. Ellen, particularly.

'Yeah, that's it, Ellen. The Boston Strangler has been biding his time, selling tyres and line dancing in search of his next victim,' Peanut teased.

'Nobody knows what he's been up to. It would be foolish to believe he won't kill again.'

'He can't be the Boston Strangler,' Penny said. 'He's from New Hampshire. He only moved to Massachusetts a couple years ago, after college.'

'That's what he says,' said Ellen, with a sceptical purse of her lips. 'And anyway, Boston is an easy drive from New Hampshire.'

This sent them into fits of giggles.

'Oh really, Ellen,' Penny said. 'You're too much.'

'Laugh if you want. I'll bet Mary Sullivan laughed before she was raped and strangled in her bed.'

'For heaven's sake, you're giving me chills,' Peanut said. 'There must have been a hundred people who saw Penny dancing and eating dinner with him tonight. And at least a dozen of us who

71

were at the Plaza the night they met and he told us where he works. If Penny is found dead in the coming weeks, the police will nab him in a second.'

'I can't tell you how much better that makes me feel,' Penny deadpanned. She didn't know Mary Sullivan personally, but they both came from Cape Cod which, given the grizzly circumstances of her death, made it feel uncomfortably close to home.

'You can never be too careful. Don't let him, or any man, into the apartment when we're not here.'

'I wouldn't dream of it, Ellen.' She knew that Ellen only had her best interests at heart. Still, she resented a little this tainting of the nicest, most delightful man she had met in months.

'As if she could get him past Mrs Rizzo,' Peanut said.

Their downstairs neighbour kept a close eye on their comings and goings. Her complaints were so frequent that Ellen and Peanut had stopped listening to them; they had all switched to slippers after she moaned about them walking around in shoes, and then she grumbled that the scuffing sounds drove her crazy. Penny was the only one who still tried to stay on her good side.

'The old bat may have her uses after all,' Ellen said. 'Make sure you have your screwdriver with you.' The screwdriver was Ellen's preferred tool of self-defence.

'I never leave home without it,' Penny promised, opening her purse to reveal its bright orange handle.

While Peanut and Ellen got into a debate about whether crime in the city was going up or down, Penny turned her thoughts to Ted. She wondered how long she'd have to wait before he called; she felt a flutter in her stomach – not the scary kind that came when there was a big test at school, but the happy kind she felt during the run-up to Christmas or her birthday. There was something familiar about him that put her at ease. She kept these things to herself, because Ellen and Peanut would tease her about being lovesick already.

Neither of them was in the market for a husband. Ellen swore that she never would be; Peanut was willing to consider marriage, with the right man (a modern one), but only, she said, after she had been around the world and knew Paris and Dublin as well as Southie. Since the airline where she worked, Eastern Airways, only flew to cities on the Eastern Seaboard, that day was still a ways off.

'Don't you worry that if you wait too long all the good ones will be gone?' Penny asked her later that night, lying in her bed in the room they shared.

'Sometimes,' Peanut confessed. 'But I'm more worried about living my mother's life.' Peanut's parents had married when her mother was sixteen. Their first child was born nine months and a day later; six more followed in quick succession.

'But what about, you know' – Penny lowered her voice – 'sex. Aren't you curious?'

'You don't have to be married for that, silly.'

When Peanut said such things, Penny felt naive and prudish at the same time.

'There is no way I would *not* sleep with a man before I agreed to marry him. Would you buy a car without taking it for a test drive?'

'How many test drives is a girl allowed?'

'As many as it takes.'

'Peanut O'Reilly, that is just a lot of loose talk. I know you're still a virgin.'

She could hear her giggling in the next bed.

'I saw you take communion last week.'

'Stop, Penny, you're killing me. What I don't get is why you aren't more cautious when it comes to marriage.'

There was no need to play dumb. Her roommates knew about her mother's divorces.

'Some people have bad luck,' Penny said, though she knew that wasn't the whole story. Not by a long shot.

'Bad luck? Twice?'

'The first time doesn't really count.' Her parents, Bill and

Rose, married in the early days of the Second World War, barely three weeks after they'd met, and divorced when Penny was two. Penny never saw her father again.

'The second is still a mystery.'

Her mother's second husband, Cliff Goodwin, was decent and kind, if a bit of a milksop. He had insisted on adopting Penny and fulfilled the role of father in every respect, right up to helping her move into the secretarial school dorms, but when she came home for Thanksgiving that year his hat was missing from the hook in the hall, his toothbrush gone from the holder in the bathroom. In the four years since, she hadn't heard a word from him, not even a card at Christmas or her birthday.

'I still can't believe your mother never told you what happened.'

'I asked where he was and she said he'd left, and when I asked where he'd gone she said Connecticut.' A year or so later, her mother mentioned, offhand, that he'd remarried.

'Your mother is so strong,' Peanut said with admiration. 'She doesn't need a man.'

'It's true,' Penny agreed. Her mother *was* strong, the type of plucky career gal who drove the heroes in books and movies crazy until they realised they were madly in love with her. She was pig-headed, impossible to control, and men were drawn to the challenge. But Penny had seen how living day-to-day with such a woman wore a man down. A wife ought to be a helpmate, not a sparring partner. She believed she had the perfect temperament for the job. She was a nurturer, a booster of egos, who devoted as much energy to avoiding arguments as her mother did to winning them. The reason her mother's experience hadn't shaken her confidence in the institution of marriage was simple: she was nothing like her.

Her roommates thought her a hopeless romantic, but Penny was more of a realist than she got credit for, and she worried that, for all their superior intellect and drive, Peanut and Ellen were setting themselves up for unhappy lives. They couldn't be stewardesses for ever. Most airlines kicked girls out at thirty-two.

74

Possibly, they'd let them work until thirty-five, which still left thirty years until retirement and no prospect of finding a husband except, possibly, some sad, decrepit widower. Being a single girl was fun in your twenties, but it was bound to seem old hat, pitiful, even, at forty, when all your friends were married and had families. Ellen and Peanut laughed at Mrs Rizzo and complained about her nosiness. They couldn't see how much of it stemmed from loneliness or that they might end up just like her – a doddering biddy, living alone in a tiny apartment, surrounded by strangers.

Chapter Nine

Ted took a cube of bread from the basket and skewered it with the long-handled fork.

'That's it,' Maude Hale replied, taking a large swallow of her drink. 'You want to anchor it.'

Anchoring the bread cube was what he had failed to do the first time. It had slid off his fork, carried away by the melted cheese and Curtis had laughed and announced, in the same voice that rose above the din of the Goodyear store garage, that Ted owed everyone a round of drinks. Ted felt self-conscious until he noticed how much his clumsiness had brought tired, dumpy Maude out of her shell. His boss's wife had barely uttered two words throughout the crab salad, downing iced Manhattans with morose determination; but the sight of Ted blushing, empty fork in hand, must have tapped her maternal instincts. If having someone to lecture on the dos and don'ts of fondue fulfilled Maude, Ted was happy to oblige. He applied some of the sales techniques Curtis had taught him: he asked lots of questions and followed her slurred recommendations with regard to the proper grip with which to hold the fork. When he ran out of questions he made stuff up to keep her engaged.

'Is it better to stir clockwise or counter-clockwise?'

'Ever tried this with Wonderbread?'

The effect was remarkable. Maude's vacant stare had yet to disappear altogether, but there were definite signs of life beneath the bloated mask – traces of the pretty woman she must once have been – as she impressed upon him the importance of gradually covering the paraffin to prevent the cheese from burning.

'I love your home,' he told her, a remark that filled the sweet spot between flattery and truth. It was the kind of house that stood out. The glass, stone and dark wood used in its construction were a welcome change from the clapboard and shingled Colonials. It was a house of the future, full of natural light and open space. The clean lines of the furnishings – not an overstuffed hassock or a Tiffany lamp to be found – complemented the architecture. Why, even the Hales's dishes were modern, with a bold orange and olive-green pattern that, depending on how you looked at it, could be either interlocking circles or the sun's rays. They were full of hidden meaning, unlike the old-fashioned red and white ones that Abigail had inherited from her grandmother. The only thing Ted didn't like about the Hales' home was the way it made him feel about his own. Here was the original to which his Enchantress was but a cheap knock-off.

'Lift it up now,' Maude instructed. 'That's it. Now roll it. Roll it up like you're reeling in a fish.'

Ted popped it into his mouth. A thin thread of trailing cheese stuck to his chin. He made no attempt to remove it, waiting for Maude to notice and then feigning puzzlement when she tried to bring it to his attention. To her, at first, subtle and then increasingly vigorous brushing of her own chin he responded with a polite smile and furrowed brow until Maude leaned over and wiped his chin clean with her napkin. Her action and words expressed exasperation, but the laugh on her lips conveyed delight.

Taste was secondary to the experience. Fondue was another step along the road to becoming a cosmopolitan, like sampling Greek food. Looking around the table now, he had to smile. The women in their shiny evening dresses with their hair done up fancy, and the men in their suits and dark ties, dipping long, slim forks into pots – they were like people in a magazine. Abigail, Ted was proud to see, was the prettiest girl of all, and not only because she was the youngest. It was a relief to see her out of that miserable housecoat. The dress hugged her shape in a way that made the weight that had settled on her hips since Mindy's birth look voluptuous instead of dowdy. Her curly hair was piled high on her head and corkscrew curls fell around her ears. It thrilled him to see Curtis giving her so much attention. Though slightly concerned that she'd bore him with talk about one of the Founding Fathers or whomever it was she was reading about now, he wanted Curtis to see that, in addition to being pretty, she was also uncommonly intelligent.

It had not escaped his notice that he was the only salesman from the store invited to this intimate – he might even call it exclusive – dinner party; he and Abigail had been placed to their hosts' right: the guest of honour position. The other couple, Mike Cook and his pleasant but forgettable wife Marie, were old friends.

'This here is Ted McDougall,' Curtis had said to Mike when making introductions. 'Best wingman I've ever had.'

'Pleasure to meet you, sir,' Ted had said as they shook hands. They were standing in front of a large picture window, Mike's bald pate glowing with the rosy light of the setting sun.

'There'll be none of that "sir" business at my house,' Curtis said, handing him a large Scotch in a tumbler of crushed ice. 'This evening is strictly social.'

'A toast,' Curtis said. 'To President Lyndon Baines Johnson, and nuclear war averted.'

'We dodged a bullet this week, didn't we?' said Mike.

Ted raised his glass together with the others. How could anyone be in favour of nuclear war?

'So how do you two know one another?' Ted asked.

'Back from our hungry days as junior salesmen,' Curtis said.

'Those were the days,' Mike said.

'All of us just back from the war, wondering whether there'd be jobs for us, eh, Mike?' Curtis sucked air through his teeth. 'I remember the first commission cheque I got. It was for two dollars and eighty-seven cents. It could have been a million dollars as far as I was concerned.'

'Five thirty-three, mine was.'

'All right, Mikey, no need to boast.' He gave him a playful slap on the back. 'That's why this guy works at corporate and I'm still just a lowly salesman.'

Ted's respect for Mikey, already significant due to his being a friend of Curtis's, rose still higher. In company lingo, 'corporate' meant working for Old Joe Fielding in the regional sales office over on Route 128. It was mostly the preserve of guys with fancy business degrees; only a few made the leap up from the stores.

Mike rocked back on his heels and nodded at the floor. 'You, a lowly salesman? Right, that's a good one.'

Uniformed servers, brought in especially for tonight, cleared away the fondue pots, the bread baskets, and other condiments. Curtis leaned on the table with both elbows and swirled the drink in his hand. The crushed ice made a shushing noise. It was, Ted thought, a marvellous way to get people's attention.

'Two billion tyres sold, worldwide, last year. Who can tell me the secret to our success?' He looked at his dinner companions, one by one. 'I'll give you a hint. It isn't just the huge, and I do mean huge, expansion of the highway system over the last thirty years.' He swirled his glass some more, took a slow, deep sip, a hit off a cigarette. Oh, the command, Ted thought, the majestic power of his personality.

'No, the number one reason for our success,' Curtis said, pausing to stub out his cigarette, 'is women.'

Surprised titters rippled around the table. Curtis held up his hand.

'It's no joke. Like it or not – and I mostly don't – more and more women are behind the wheel, and not just occasionally, mind, every day. Mothers, dropping the kids off at ballet class or piano or hockey, boy scouts or girl scouts.

'Hey, Maude,' he called, 'how many miles you drive last year?'

Maude shook her head and made indiscriminate waving motions with her hand.

'She has no idea. Women have no idea how many miles they drive, but I can tell you, it was over fifteen thousand. Fifteen thousand miles and most of it was just back and forth to the grocery store, Shoppers' World and Annie's swim lessons. Often it's at night, in bad weather. Women want to feel safe. They want their children to be safe and we men want to know they're safe and that's why we give them the Life Guard Safety Spare. The spare within the spare means Maude can roll over anything and keep on driving, right, Maudie?'

Maude nodded as she gripped her drink with both hands. 'You ought to see the lifeguard who gives Annie swim lessons,' she said slowly, her eyes gleaming. 'I'd roll over him any day.'

Silence fell across the table. Abigail furrowed her brows at him. Marie squirmed and flustered in the seat next to him while Maude smiled the way a cat might.

'So it's the technology,' Mike said, as if Maude had never spoken.

'No, Mike,' Curtis replied. 'The technology is every bit as good in our commercial line. But business is dominated by men, who are rational. Retail, on the other hand, is dominated by women, who are emotional.'

'So then it's advertising,' Abigail offered.

Curtis turned in surprise. 'Partly correct, Gail.'

Ted glowed with pride that Curtis acknowledged his wife was half right.

'It's Abigail,' his wife replied.

'I'm sorry, sweetheart,' Curtis said, reaching over to give her hand a pat. 'Abi-Gail.'

Ted's cheeks prickled with embarrassment. Why couldn't she just let it go? He blamed Linc for indulging her all these years.

'You've got your hands full with this one, Ted,' Curtis said, with a roar of laughter. 'Knows her mind. I'll bet you could do with a straight-talker like that over at corporate, right, Mikey?'

'We sure could,' Mikey said with a patrician chuckle.

Ted laughed, too. And then the lights went out. There was some more confusion and then the servers rolled a flaming dessert in on a trolley.

'Ladies and gentlemen,' Maude slurred, the diamonds on her fingers catching the light of the flames as she made more waving gestures with her hands. 'Baked Alaska.'

Cigar smoke always reminded Ted of the fetid breeze that used to waft into his bedroom window on hot summer nights from Wilson's dairy farm, but when Curtis offered him one to go with the after-dinner whiskies they were enjoying down in his wood-panelled den, he took it gratefully and with every intention of liking it.

'I want to apologise for Abigail,' he said.

Curtis waved the cigar dismissively.

'Let me tell you something, Ted, women are like horses. Some, like Mike's Marie, are workhorses. Not the sleekest of models – am I right, Mikey? – but dependable and steady. Other women are thoroughbreds – beautiful but nervous and erratic. Maude used to be like that. Had a temper on her like nobody's business and when she's angry, plates fly. I used to walk into the house with my briefcase in front of my face for protection.'

It was hard to picture his docile dinner companion as a plate thrower. The doubt must have showed on his face.

'You wouldn't know this,' Curtis said, 'but Maudie was vale-dictorian of her class at Barnard; editor of the school paper. Let me tell you, the woman had opinions. I like a feisty woman. Takes a toll on their systems, though, not to mention the dishes. The doctor has these pills he gives her, hasn't thrown a plate since.'

'Talk about feisty,' Mikey said. 'Remember that girl at the sales conference in Atlantic City, way back? What was her name? A beauty: blonde hair, blue eyes and a bosom that you could get lost in.'

'For days,' Curtis added with his eyes a-twinkle. 'You'd enjoy the sales conference, Ted.'

'How do I get invited?' He had no interest in big-bosomed girls, but he wanted to be on the inside, a member of whatever club it was that Curtis and Mike belonged to.

'Store managers only,' said Mike.

So he was not a success yet. Success wasn't being an assistant manager, with a nice little commission cheque and a threebedroom Enchantress in a neighbourhood full of them. Success was a custom-built house, with a full basement to use as his den, an acre of manicured lawn, and a pair of cement lions standing guard at the top of the drive; it was having his own office, and attending sales conferences and meetings with the guys from corporate. It was two weeks' vacation in Acapulco every winter, and dinner parties where the guests were served food and drinks they'd never tried before by uniformed professionals hired in for the night who did the cleaning up so Abigail didn't have to.

'Bitsy!' Mike shouted.

'Bitsy, that's it,' said Curtis. 'Most inappropriate name ever.'

'Nothing bitsy about her,' Mike said.

'Good times, remember? With Buddy and Frank and Lefty.'

'Ah, yeah. Lefty,' Mike said, a sudden hint of nostalgia in his voice. 'We were all young guns then.'

Curtis leaned forward to tap his cigar in an ashtray. 'He's a good guy.'

Mike looked down, shook his head.

'Hal Baron,' Curtis explained to Ted. 'Got the nickname Lefty after his right hand got mangled in the Battle of the Bulge. A good man: decent, honourable and a real hero. He's just not a salesman.'

'That he is not,' said Mike.

'He's been running our store over in Lynn. Not sure if you know much about the city, around the size of ours.' Curtis looked to his left and right, as if checking to make sure they were alone. 'They do about half the business we do.'

'Wow,' said Ted. 'That's a . . . pretty significant difference.'

'I'll say. What with the economy humming along like it is? The company's profits have grown about thirty per cent in the last five years but in Lynn – now, I only heard this through the grapevine, Mike, so correct me if I'm wrong – the word is that the Lynn store's numbers are actually down.'

'I couldn't comment, officially – off the record, though, they're not what we hoped.'

The men shook their heads and tapped their cigar ashes in the cut-glass ashtray.

'Can you imagine how much that store could sell if there was a true salesman running the show there?'

'Huge,' Mike said. 'Why don't you take it over?'

Curtis smiled. 'There is nothing I'd like better than to get in there and turn that place around. You know how I love a challenge but . . . I'm attached to my little store. If I were to move all the way over to Lynn and start anew, well, I don't think Maude would be too pleased about it.' He arched his eyebrows and looked up at the ceiling. The wives were in the living room, directly above them. 'You need a young gun. Someone who's hungry. Someone like Ted here.'

Desire caught in Ted's throat. Curtis gave him a friendly shoulder punch and asked if he could freshen his drink. 'Freshen' sounded so much more sophisticated than 'top up' or 'refill'. The conversation switched to the odds of the Celtics repeating as NBA champions or whether, come springtime, Tony Conigliaro was going to hit anywhere near as good as last year. Ted sucked on the cigar, astonished that when blended with enough raw ambition, even cow manure tasted sweet.

'A store manager's position is going to be opening up in the next couple months,' he told Abigail on the ride home, electing, for her sake, not to bring up her dinner table gaffe. 'I think I might put in for it.' Saying it aloud made him want it more. He'd wear a suit and tie instead of a work shirt. He would be somebody.

'Where?'

'In Lynn.'

'Will we have to move?'

83

'No, I think I could drive it.'

'Lynn is clear on the north side of Boston. You're going to drive all that way in the DeSoto?'

'I'll get a new car.'

From the corner of his eye he saw her eyebrows flicker upward – a tiny gesture that contained one thousand nags.

'We can afford it, okay?' he said. 'Store managers make big money. Look at Curtis.'

'What does he think about the idea?'

'He suggested it.'

Her eyebrows flickered again. 'Why would he do that?' she asked.

'Maybe he thinks I'd be good at it.'

'Maybe,' she replied, staring at the road ahead. 'If he truly values you, though, I'd think he'd be trying to do whatever he could to keep you.'

The only word in the whole sentence that mattered to Ted was 'if'. Why did Abigail think Curtis had asked them to dinner if he didn't value him?

'Maybe he likes to see his people advance.'

Abigail pushed air dismissively out her nostrils. Ted gripped hard at the wheel, reminding himself that, for all her reading and cleverness, she didn't understand business.

And neither did his mother, who was babysitting Mindy and whom Abigail consulted the moment they got home.

'Shame to move so soon after settling here,' she said.

Why did every woman think they'd have to move? 'I can drive it.'

'Lynn is far.'

'About thirty miles, I expect.'

'That's halfway to Wilsonville. You're right around the corner from work now,' she said, thrusting her chin forward the way she did when she was against something. 'And that old jalopy isn't going to make it that far, twice a day, every day.'

'I'll get a new one.'

His mother pursed her lips together. 'Mind you don't stretch yourself too thin.' She didn't believe in buying on credit, even large purchases like cars or houses.

'I wouldn't.'

'Without the Bedford commission?' Abigail seemed determined to quash his advancement.

'The Bedford commission is nothing compared to what I'd get if I had my own store,' he replied.

'A bird in the hand, Teddy,' said his mother with another jut of the chin.

'The store manager gets the plum accounts,' he explained. 'And five hundred dollars at Christmas.' He could have added the bonus for hitting sales targets, but why waste his breath? They were determined to oppose him. They'd be perfectly happy to have him go through life never reaching the top, never being the man he could be, so long as he never took a risk and scrimped and saved everything for a rainy day. Well, too bad. They'd see, in the end, who was right and who was wrong, he thought, as he helped his mother into her coat and walked her out to her car.

His mother's lack of confidence in him was a longstanding source of hurt. She seemed always to be expecting him to fail. Admittedly, he had been a pathetic child – terrible at school while Danny earned top marks. But Ted was a man now, and real life wasn't like school. He'd been right about buying the Enchantress. Couldn't she see that he was good at this? He opened the car door for her and she took the wheel.

'Drive carefully, Mother.'

'I always do.'

Yes, that was true. His mother was careful in everything she did and had engrained her carefulness so deep in him that he felt its visceral pull even now, when he knew it was hooey. His father had been careful, scrupulously setting a little from his weekly pay packets aside for a rainy day. That day came when he suffered a stroke at thirty-nine. Twenty years of savings disappeared in two years of nursing care. Success didn't go to the don't-bite-off-more-than-you-can-chew, a-bird-in-the-hand-is-worth-two-in-the-bush types. It went to men who were bold enough to take risks and grab opportunities. Had his father taken a risk or two, his mother might not have had to move in with her own parents and return to nursing after his death.

He watched her back slowly out of the driveway, diligently checking all three mirrors and turning back to make sure there was nothing in her way even though the street was empty. His irritation toward her softened. He had to give her credit. She'd managed pretty well.

Through the window, he saw Abigail sitting at the kitchen table, bent over a book. 'I'll just finish this chapter,' she would say if he asked when she was coming to bed. Her wariness was harder to understand. She had always lived comfortably. The Hatches weren't rich, by any means, but even a town the size of Wilsonville generated a sufficient number of deaths, deeds, personal and business disputes to support a life of relative gentility for Linc and his family, with a housekeeper, a lakeside cabin, and membership at the local country club. The only possible reason she could object to his going for the job was that she didn't think he was good enough. Moments like this reminded him that his mother wasn't the only one who'd loved Danny best. Abigail and he were classmates and childhood buddies, always found in the Wilsonville library, sitting knee-to-knee, reading history books.

Ted stood for a few moments, letting the cold air seep through his dress shirt; burn his hands and the tip of his nose. There'd be frost tonight. If the weather held, the ponds would soon be covered with a thin film of ice. He stuffed his hands in his pockets and strode toward the door. No point speculating on what might have been.

Chapter Ten

Abigail was not in the habit of making long-distance phone calls and could think of lots of sensible reasons why today should be no exception. A call was likely to alarm her mother, to whom telephones existed for emergencies only. It would arouse her suspicions and lead, perhaps, to pointed questions that Abigail would prefer not to answer. Also, if past experience was anything to go by, Gretchen Hatch was not the best person to turn to when she was feeling blue. No one was more aware of Abigail's shortcomings, or more willing to point them out. Reaching for comfort and understanding could easily end in a lecture, but the childish desire to hear her mother's voice and feel its soothing power would not be quieted. When all was said and done, she had no one else. After she put Mindy down for her late-morning nap, she picked up the phone and dialled.

She needed to hear a sane human being. Dinner at Ted's boss's house had been the final straw. The Hales were like villains from a B-movie – Curtis, so slippery and self-satisfied and Maude with her glassy eyes and dirty jokes. Ted said after that she takes pills to calm her nerves; well who wouldn't with a husband like that? She had tried to give Curtis the benefit of the doubt, but he had no interest in conversation, he wanted an audience. It was hard enough listening to him drone on about tyres and cars, as if anybody gave a care. She was willing to grant he knew a thing or two about the subject. But he seemed to think expertise in one area made him an expert on every subject. Abigail held her tongue when he claimed that 'Old Ironsides' fought at 'the battle of the Boston Tea Party'. She hadn't contradicted him when he repeated the foolish fear-mongering about a Goldwater presidency, but when she'd glanced toward Ted in the expectation of exchanging a knowing look, she found her husband hanging on the blowhard's every word. An almost unthinkable prospect entered her head. Could Ted, her Ted, have voted for Johnson? She couldn't bring herself to ask.

At the other end of the line, the phone began to ring, a slower peal than the phones in Massachusetts, which were tinny and somehow less authentic. She imagined it ringing in the foyer, on the small cherry table, sitting beneath a white doily that her mother had crocheted, and then her mother walking toward it from the kitchen, wiping her hands on her apron as she approached.

Abigail didn't trust Curtis. He would take advantage of Ted if it suited him, and Ted, intoxicated as he was by the idea of being a successful salesman, would be easy prey. He didn't see the Hales and their friends sneering at them: the poor New Hampshire country folk who had never tried fondue. As if bread and melted cheese was terribly exotic. What was wrong with a roast? Of course, the whole dinner party had nothing to do with taste and everything to do with novelty. Abigail had peeked beneath a vase and found a price tag from Jordan Marsh on it. They probably walked into a showroom in Shoppers' World and bought everything in it.

'Hatch residence.' The voice was deep, the pause between the two words lasting a fraction overlong.

'Daddy!' Abigail cried. 'What are you doing home?'

'Abigail? Is that you? What's wrong, child?'

'Nothing,' she replied. The familiarity of his voice brought a lump to her throat. 'Nothing's wrong, Daddy. I just called to see how you were.'

'We're fine here. Why waste your money?' Few words but each one was infused with affection. 'Is Mindy all right?'

Her nose was running. She sniffed as quietly as possible. 'She's fine, Daddy. Napping. She's got two new teeth.'

'Does she, now?'

'And she jabbers all day long.'

'Sure am looking forward to seeing her.'

'Thanksgiving is next week.'

'How are things down there in Massachusetts?' He spoke as if she were in a foreign country; it often felt like she was.

'Just fine, Daddy. I'm thinking about going back to school.' She didn't know why she mentioned that. She hadn't even discussed the idea with Ted. 'There's a course on Colonial Boston that looks interesting.'

'That would be interesting. What else would you take?'

'Probably just that one. The state college has lots of night classes. No minimum course requirements.'

A pause and then, 'That's wonderful, Scrib.'

It was his pet name for her, short for Scribbler because, as a child, she used to carry around a notebook in which she scribbled down her thoughts. 'Just wonderful. Why don't you take a full course-load? I'd be happy to pay for it.'

'It has nothing to do with cost, Daddy, honestly. I worry about being away from Mindy.'

'A few hours away from her mother each week isn't going to damage her. Any fool or book that tells you otherwise is just plain wrong.'

'A full course-load would add up to more than a few hours, Daddy.'

'All the same, you need to finish that degree and go on to law school. Come up here and lend me a hand. I'm not getting any younger.'

'Oh, Daddy.'

She heard her mother's voice in the background. 'Don't go putting ideas in her head.'

'Fiddlesticks,' her father replied. 'There's a paper in the law journal written by a lady lawyer.'

'She's a wife and a mother,' Mother said. 'Have you asked after her husband?'

'How is your husband?' he asked.

'Good. Really good. His boss invited us for dinner the other night.'

'Did he now?'

'Yes. They have a big house a couple towns over. Very modern.'

'Those tyres still flying off the shelves?'

'Ted might get his own store.'

'Say now, that's something.'

'Yes, well, nothing is confirmed yet, of course. We'll have to wait and see.'

'Ah-yuh, wait and see.'

In the background, the old grandfather clock chimed the hour. Abigail closed her eyes, picturing where it stood in the hall, at the base of the stairwell.

Thanksgiving was Abigail's favourite holiday. She loved its simple authenticity – families and friends coming together, everyone bringing something to the feast – and its history, seeing in that original gathering of starch-collared Puritans and buckskin-clad natives a spirit of equality that was, she firmly believed, the inevitable result of true freedom. The previous year she had eaten Thanksgiving dinner off a hospital tray, under the pall of national tragedy. Her expectations for this year were even greater than normal. She and Mindy drove up to Wilsonville in the station wagon on the Wednesday morning. Mother and Mable, the housekeeper, had both Mindy and the meal preparations in hand. Abigail only had to set the table and then was free to spend the afternoon with her father, sitting by the fire in his study, talking. The cooperative school district was going ahead, despite Linc's objections. They speculated on what Martin Luther King Jr might say when he accepted the Nobel Peace Prize in a few weeks; and the coming week's launch of the Mariner 4 spacecraft.

'Imagine, Scrib,' he said, 'in a few months we could be seeing pictures of Mars!'

There were many exciting things to discuss, but from the moment Ted arrived, late that evening because of traffic, and throughout Thanksgiving Day, all he wanted to talk about were tyre sales and the store manager's position. Her mother tried to humour him – she had always been partial to him – but he began so many sentences with, 'Curtis Hale says,' that even she smiled when, as they were eating pie, Daddy asked what Curtis Hale would say about the crusts. Ted fell into a sulk. During the post-dinner singalong, his lips barely moved and later, when everyone else picked up a book, he wanted to be watching football.

'Linc,' he asked, 'why is it you don't have a television?'

'Never seen the need, I suppose,' Daddy replied, eyes not stirring from his page.

Ted grew restless. He paced about the room and stared out the window at the darkness, sighing. Not long after she'd got Mindy settled he announced that he too was calling it a night, and they all fell over themselves to say how perfectly understandable it was: such a long day and an early start planned for tomorrow.

'Poor boy doesn't know how to relax,' Daddy remarked once he'd gone, and Abigail felt the need to defend her husband.

'You're not going to join him?' Mother asked, as she picked up her crocheting.

'Let her be,' said Daddy. 'It's a holiday. Abigail doesn't get much chance to read uninterrupted.'

Too late. The notion that it was disloyal to remain downstairs after Ted retired took hold, stealing attention from the book in her hands. She stared at the open page, her eyes taking in nothing. A short while later she followed Ted upstairs, despite not being tired. He was already asleep, sprawled diagonally across the bed. Her bed. She twisted and contorted herself into the remaining space. Tomorrow he'll be gone, she thought, and the house could return to normal. It was a despicable thing for a wife to think, and between the steady barrage of self-recriminations such a thought produced, and Mindy's fussing, she got little sleep. She dragged her unwilling body out of bed at five-thirty the next morning, determined to be nicer to him. The lights in the kitchen hurt her eyes. Her neck had a crick in it. Mother was already up, busily packing a picnic basket with Thanksgiving leftovers, something, Abigail realised, that she ought to have thought to do. Instead she sat with Ted at the kitchen table, searching for a way to break the ice.

'Did you check the oil?' she asked.

He gave a stiff nod, as if responding to a nag rather than concern for his welfare and then he quoted something Curtis Hale said about preparation and she wanted to scream. When he placed a hand on her back as he bent to kiss her goodbye she recoiled. Minutes after the DeSoto had puttered out of the driveway, she was filled with remorse and regret that it would be three days before she could make amends.

'Go back to bed, dear,' her mother said. 'You look exhausted.'

She was exhausted, though it hurt to know she looked it. Upstairs, Mindy shrieked into a new day.

'I'll get her,' her mother said, wiping her hands on her apron.

Abigail knew that a good mother didn't fob her baby's care off to others any more than a good wife forgot to pack her husband a picnic basket. She shuffled back to bed, weighed down by her deficiencies.

Chapter Eleven

Penny's eyes scanned the room as she lifted the champagne coupe to her lips. It was hard not to ogle. The lady next to her wore a necklace of matching pearls the size of malted milk balls. In the powder room a short while ago, she had shared a mirror with an exotic creature with a dragonfly brooch made of white, yellow and pink stones that sparkled like diamonds. Ted gave her a conspiratorial wink. She smiled and took another sip of the cocktail, her third. Giddy. That was the word for how she was feeling. Giddy, and a tad light-headed. Two cocktails would probably have been enough.

The Ritz was a place she passed every day on her way to work without ever venturing inside. It had always seemed inaccessible, cordoned off by an invisible shield of wealth and privilege. And here she was, sitting at its oak-polished bar on a Saturday night, sipping champagne cocktails alongside Brahmins and members of the jet set. And the truly astonishing thing, so astonishing it made her want to laugh out loud, was that nobody could tell that she was a humble secretary, out with a tyre salesman.

In the powder room, the creature with the dragonfly brooch had eyed her dress with admiration. It *was* beautiful. The grey satin material, painted with large pink flowers, was clearly of the finest quality. Who would guess that she had picked it up for next to nothing in an end-of-bolt sale? Its strapless princess neckline flattered her figure; the fitted bodice and a full skirt made her tiny waist look even smaller. For a final dash of flair, she had added a petticoat of pale pink tulle that showed whenever she twirled. Peanut had helped her do her hair up like Audrey Hepburn in *Breakfast at Tiffany's*; Ellen had loaned her a pair of opera gloves that came up to her elbows.

When Ted called out of the blue yesterday morning to invite her dancing tonight, she knew what she ought to say, especially to a man who'd left her dangling for over a month: *Thank you for the kind offer. Unfortunately, I have a previous engagement.* But there was no such engagement, and after two days at home she was ready to grab any excuse to get out. Thanksgiving had been a gloomy affair: just her and her mother, declining food and taking turns coaxing the other to eat. Ted's willingness to phone long distance spoke well of his intentions, as did his success in charming her mother's phone number out of Ellen, with whom he'd spoken when he called the apartment. The nervous, almost bashful, way he requested her company for the evening won her over. One would think he'd never asked a girl on a date before. Besides, how could she pass up such an ideal opportunity to wear her new dress? She hopped on the next bus back to Boston.

So far, things were working out fine and this pleased her as much as the pretty dress and the fine company. She wanted to believe in a world where, with the right man, a girl didn't need to play games, could break a cardinal rule like, *Thou shalt not be available at the last minute,* and not just get away with it, but be rewarded.

The band started up 'Moonlight Serenade'; they finished their drinks and Ted led her to the parquet floor. It was nice not to be pushed around like an old mop, not to have to worry about getting her toes trodden on. Ted's feet were always exactly where they were supposed to be. They foxtrotted beneath the rosette-carved rotunda, his palm resting on the fabric of the dress; his fingertips lightly brushing her skin. The hard sinews of his biceps were evident beneath his jacket as he held her securely and led her in a twinkle. They danced on, rising and falling together through rumba and cha-cha, mambo and waltz and then back to the foxtrot again. Other couples started to make way for them, like they did for Fred Astaire and Ginger Rogers in the movies Penny used to watch on Saturday afternoons at the old Park House Theater when she was little, her feet tapping along on a floor sticky with spilled root beer and crushed Juju Beans. Tonight was like a dream. If not for her aching feet, she would not have believed it was real. Tonight, aching feet were the most marvellous thing.

When the band took a break, Ted proposed a stroll through the hotel. They headed first into the oak-panelled lobby, but the fire in the fireplace threw out too much heat. The large sunroom at the back of the building was cooler and more private. Their clicking footfalls echoed on the tiles as they moved to a window to admire the city's skyline. Ted stood close; the heat from his body contrasting with the cold air seeping in through the leaded windows made her shiver. He wrapped his arms around her and she leaned against his chest. Outside, the weather beacon atop the Hancock Tower was shining blue, signifying a high pressure system.

'Steady blue,' she said.

'Clear view,' he replied.

He nuzzled her neck and she shivered again. Softly, he laid a trail of kisses the length of her neck, across her cheek, then with his hands on her shoulders, he gently guided her around to face him. As she had on the dance floor, Penny surrendered to his lead. His mouth tasted of cigarettes and bourbon.

'It's wonderful here,' she said.

'You're wonderful,' he said, drawing her close. His shirt had the clean peroxide smell of Oxydol, the same safe, comfortable detergent her mother used. She felt his heart pounding and was touched that a simple kiss could invoke such a profound response.

'Isn't it strange how Thanksgiving felt almost normal this year?' she asked with a sigh. 'Last year I thought the holiday was ruined for ever.'

'Yes,' he murmured. 'It felt that way.'

95

'Where were you when you heard that Kennedy was shot?'

She had said something wrong. His whole body tensed; he took a step back. She watched, bewildered, as the muscles in his face went slack, tightened, and then went slack again. His lips parted long before he spoke and when, at last, he did his voice sounded different – its rhythm altered.

'I was at the hospital . . . holding my newborn daughter.' He looked away.

Penny's heart dropped to her toes in a great rush.

'You have a daughter?' Her breath was suddenly shallow.

Facing her seemed to take great effort but eventually he managed. 'A beautiful daughter,' he began. His voice was uneven, at first, but smoothed out as he went along. 'Her name is Mindy. She's got dimples and a head of strawberry-blonde curls and she just celebrated her first birthday.'

Penny's mouth was dry. She was dizzy – too many champagne cocktails.

'And your wife?' she asked. How strange her own voice sounded: thin and reedy.

He looked her squarely in the eyes. It felt like an eternity although it was probably not more than a second or two. His Adam's apple bobbed up and down as he swallowed once, twice.

'Complications in childbirth,' he said in a hoarse whisper.

She covered her heart with both hands, feeling his pain as if it were her own. How shallow of her to think she had suffered last year when she'd pitied Jackie and those sweet, fatherless Kennedy children; shedding self-important tears over her own lost innocence. True sorrow was standing before her now, with its lips pursed firmly together, jaw jutting out, trying to hide its anguish.

'You poor man,' she said, reaching out to put a hand on his cheek. His arms fell around her. 'You poor, poor man.'

'It's been difficult,' he admitted with understatement that raised him still higher in her esteem.

'You must have loved your wife very much.'

'Yes,' he whispered. 'I do love her.'

Her breath caught. No wonder it had taken him so long to call! No wonder he had been so moved by a kiss! It had probably been years since he'd kissed any woman other than his wife – possibly, he'd never done so before. Oh, what guilt he must have felt! Life had taught Penny to prize loyalty in a man above all other things. A handsome man whispering heartfelt words of affection for a departed wife and infant daughter stirred up previously undetected passions. She was not a forward girl. She believed it was the man's place to lead and a girl's to follow, or not, depending on the circumstances and her own inclination. But in that moment she took his face in both hands and kissed his lips and then he cried and she cried, tears of exultant anguish and pain.

As they walked back to the dance floor, he said something in a low voice that she didn't quite catch.

'What is it, darling?' she asked, trying out the word and liking it.

He smiled. 'Nothing at all, sweet pea.'

Chapter Twelve

Ted woke from a night of intense dreams with his dick throbbing like a stubbed toe. Sunlight slanted through the window of the bedroom he shared with Abigail, diagonally bisecting the bed that, together, they had selected. His body was wrapped in bedding drawn from his wife's hope chest; his head resting on a pillow that had been a wedding gift. He was content, his conscience as placid as a still lake, the only ripple of guilt due to his decision to skip church this week.

A little dancing and a bit of kissing was small beer compared to what most men got up to. He was thinking of Curtis and Mikey's stories about the sales conferences, but also the guys he'd grown up with back in Wilsonville.

In retrospect, he could see that something like last night was bound to happen. He'd never so much as kissed any girl apart from Abigail. Inevitable that curiosity would get the better of him. He probably should have taken Darlene Bouchard from math class for a spin back in high school – she'd made it crystal clear that she liked him plenty and everyone knew Darlene put out. A little extramural experience would have given him perspective (wouldn't have hurt his sorry wedding night performance any, either). Integrity was his undoing. He never so much as looked at another girl, not even at college. Until he and Abigail married he'd hurried back to Wilsonville every weekend to sit in Linc's parlour like a well-trained lap dog and clean greasy pots and pans at the diner to pay for Abigail's engagement ring. If there were such things as fidelity credits, surely he'd banked enough for half a dozen affairs.

Not that he was looking to have an affair. He was a happily married man. He loved Abigail; had always loved her, *would* always love her. Last night was a harmless dabble in fantasy. He knew where to draw the line, how to keep the situation from getting out of hand. He and Penny had had a wonderful time dancing and then he'd driven her home, walked her to the front porch of her apartment on Paris Street – was there a more perfect street name for a stylish, beautiful, cosmopolitan young woman to reside? – and gone on his way. Their final goodnight kiss was a doozy. Penny's red-lipsticked mouth rising to meet his, full of desire and shyness at the same time. He felt how much she wanted him and that made him want her even more. Had she invited him upstairs, he might well have lost his senses. And that, he thought, was why Penny was the ideal girl with whom to spend his one night of adventure (he wouldn't go so far as to call it a fling). Obviously, she was safeguarding her virginity for her wedding night, which meant that, even had his moral defences crumbled, hers would have held. He'd watched to make sure she got in, and then driven back to Elm Grove with balls as blue as a pair of cobalt aggies, embracing the discomfort as a fitting penance.

He was proud that he had not lied to her, replying to her question about where he was when he'd heard Kennedy was shot the same as he did when anyone asked it, despite knowing that her next question would be about Abigail. Even then, he had not, strictly speaking, lied. Abigail *did* have complications in childbirth; he *did* love his wife.

He could have been more explicit, of course, but what would have been gained by that? An emotional scene in the middle of the ballroom: Penny would have hated that. Possibly, she would have stomped out on him and he could not have borne the thought of her travelling across the city, late at night, all alone, with the Boston Strangler and God-knew-who-else on the loose, and with just that silly screwdriver in her purse for protection. Had anything happened to her, he never would have forgiven himself.

What was the point of ruining a perfect evening? Thanks to his discretion, they each had the memory of it intact and unsullied. He knew he would always cherish his; he hoped that she felt the same. They were meant to be dance partners. She wasn't one of those backseat-driver types, challenging him for control. There was no push-pull. They rose and fell together as if riding the same wave. When he lowered her into a dip, his hands mapped the arc of her back. And as the evening wore on, a funny thing happened. The fictional history that he'd never actually articulated, merely implied, took root in his imagination and flourished. He saw it unfolding in his mind's eye like a movie in Technicolor: himself as the lonely widower, sad but resolute, soldiering on with little Mindy, and pretty soon he was wearing this persona like a new suit. Penny stared up at him as if he were a tragic hero while he led her around the floor and his heart swelled with the sweetest kind of melancholy.

She confided her shame about her mother's two failed marriages, and her personal sadness at losing contact with both of her fathers. He told her about his father's illness and death, and admitted that his mother's move south with Gene and Frank had been entirely due to economic circumstance. Baring his soul to her was liberating, exhilarating.

The evening wasn't only doom and gloom. He made her laugh so hard she said her belly ached, with stories about the awful student he'd been, and the hijinks he'd got up to when he was a kid. That's when Danny's name came up.

'Wait,' she said suddenly. 'You have a third brother?'

'Well,' he explained, 'Danny was born two years after me so technically, I guess, he'd be my first brother.'

'Where is he?'

And it seemed to him that the evening already contained enough tragedy and so he told her that Danny was an airman, stationed out in Colorado.

What did it matter? He was high on bourbon and dance and an intensity of feeling previously unknown to him. Penny had a way of looking at him as if she saw straight into his soul, and though he hardly knew her and would never see her again, he felt incredibly close to her. In their goodbye kiss, on the front step of her apartment, he'd wanted to swallow her whole. But there was no risk. She wouldn't dream of inviting him upstairs. She wasn't that kind of girl.

Supposing that she was, though? Supposing that she was one of those rare but magnificent, mythical creatures who gave every appearance of being virtuous while being, deep down, dirty, dirty girls? He reached down and began to jerk off as he imagined her leading him by the hand, her hips gently sashaying beneath that full skirt to her bedroom; unzipping that silky grey dress – slowly and masterfully, the way James Bond did in *Goldfinger* – her body pressing up against him so close he'd be able to feel it trembling. She'd be scared out of her mind, but she wouldn't want to stop. She wouldn't want to stop. Ecstasy pooled in his groin. He tightened his grip and stroked faster, picturing his hands disappearing under the pale pink petticoat, grabbing at undergarments that were white and girlish and soaked through with desire. Desire for him. He arched his back and let out a little moan. His eyes fluttered opened, only for an instant, but long enough for him to see, lying on a chair, directly in his line of vision, Abigail's Raggedy Ann housecoat and though he immediately shut them again, he couldn't unsee what he'd seen. Shame drove him from the marital bed – his reflection in the mirror was an embarrassment, a throbbing purple penis poking obscenely out of his pyjama bottoms. He headed for the shower. The warm water awakened his arousal. He recalled Penny's mouth, that luscious, beautiful mouth! He turned the dial to hot and with one hand braced against the wall, he used the other to beat himself raw as the shower's spray fell all around.

Once the usual disgust at his self-abuse had passed, he felt an inner calm. The pressure of pent-up lust had been relieved, quietly, discreetly, and soap and water had washed it all away. He walked from the shower a new man, a man ready to devote the afternoon to all the little jobs around the house his wife wanted done. He took down the screens, put up the storm windows. He spread mulch around the flowerbeds.

Abigail was delighted and not just because of the work he had done. Mindy was walking!

This totally predictable event was remarkable to Abigail, who, despite being very clever, had convinced herself it would never take place.

'Daddy held out an apple slice and she walked over to get it,' she said, marvelling at the genius Linc had shown in thinking up such a trick.

'I'm so sorry you missed it, Ted,' she said, her voice full of feeling.

After dinner, she chased Mindy to bed while he poured himself a Scotch and turned on Ed Sullivan. His daughter had been walking for less than a day and already catching her was proving difficult. Be careful what you wish for, Abigail, he thought with a chuckle. He had just freshened his drink when his wife reemerged wearing the negligee from their wedding night, the one that was forever linked in his consciousness with premature ejaculation. When he got up to pour one for her she turned the television off without asking. They sat close together on the sofa, their intermittent observations – how nice it was to have a quiet moment together like this; how wonderful that Mindy was walking – punctuated by extended stretches of silence. Later, in bed, when the offending piece of clothing had been removed, he grabbed hold of her thighs in the place where stretch marks had given the skin the texture of orange peel, and reminded himself that he had always admired their fullness.

Chapter Thirteen

The men of Elm Grove believed they were shapers of their own destinies, captains of their own ships, kings of their respective castles. They understood, however, that even kings had certain obligations and one of them was to accompany their wives on shopping excursions. An occasional afternoon of trudging from store to store, two paces behind the missus, like a pack mule, toting bundles that grew heavier as their wallets grew lighter, was as inevitable as death and taxes, a thing to be endured grimly and without complaint, like a trip to the dentist or a visit from the in-laws. The lucky ones got ten minutes to wander the tool department in Sears and made it home in time to watch the game on TV.

It was a source of solidarity for them, guaranteed to invoke a wry smile, a sympathetic shrug of resignation. Ted had perfected an expression that declared, 'I know what you're going through,' but the truth was that when he and Abigail headed out on their shopping expeditions, he was the one striding ahead and she the one reluctantly following. He loved to shop, was quite happy, even, to do so on his own, especially at Shoppers' World.

Shoppers' World was a temple of plenty, with over one hundred stores on two floors, surrounded by a parking lot with space for nine thousand cars. When Ted strolled along its walkways – conveniently covered to shield patrons from rain and snow – he felt something close to perfect contentment, a sense that there was no question he could not answer, no need he could not meet, or void he could not fill with something available for purchase within its awesome, seven hundred and eighty thousand square feet of retail space.

It was more than just a bunch of stores; it was a community centre, with a movie house, the Cinema, that was also a fully operational theatre. A couple of years ago they'd added a second screen so if you didn't like what was playing in one, chances were that you'd like what was playing at the other. The centre courtyard had a kid-sized amusement park and the amazing 'Dancing Lights' water fountain. Seasonal plantings kept the place looking nice. There was a little train that took customers around. A motorcycle riding school operated out of the parking lot and autocross races had been held on the premises. Celebrities visited, the Lone Ranger came, back in the fifties, when the television show was at the height of its popularity, and in the coming year Flipper the dolphin was scheduled to drop by. Ted had no idea how they'd build a tank big enough to hold a dolphin but he was sure the guys at Shoppers' World had it all figured out. They were an ingenious bunch.

Something was always going on at Shoppers' World, particularly at Christmas time. Stores competed with one another to create the best holiday display. The courtyard was transformed into a toy land with eight-foot-tall toy soldiers in ceremonial red coats with golden epaulettes and braiding and presents as big as garden sheds. Children could sit on Santa's lap and pet the real reindeer in front of the Jordan Marsh anchor store.

When Ted arrived for his annual, solo gift-buying trip, he spent a few minutes gazing at the scene from the upper floor. The sight of so many people bustling about with their bags of packages wrapped in brightly coloured paper and ornamental bows caused the blood to flow quicker in his veins. The sound of carols and Christmas songs piped across the public-address system made him sentimental. Well, who wouldn't be moved? He defied anyone to look upon such a display of prosperity and generosity and not be stirred. If only the electric typewriter he'd come to buy for Abigail inspired similar feelings. It was ugly, boxy, utilitarian and unromantic. It hummed like a car idling at fifteen miles per hour. When the sales assistant, a dour man with grubby hands and a sour smell, touched the keys it sounded like the report of an automatic rifle. Ted pictured it sitting on his dining room table – an industrial carbuncle in the midst of his modern domestic paradise – and reluctantly conceded that if it was what Abigail really wanted, then he should buy it. It was heavy, though, and there was no point lugging it from shop to shop. He decided to get the other presents on his list first and pick it up on his way back to the car. There wasn't much chance that the shop would sell out of them.

He headed for Jordan Marsh, Shoppers' World's mother ship, a flying saucer of a department store, with an unsupported dome bigger than the Capitol in Washington. He loved its open plan: two floors of three hundred sixty degrees of consumer goods. He could wander from department to department: furniture to electric goods to toys to children's clothing to men's to leather goods, and at this time of year it had an additional buzz of energy, glittery trees made of tinsel and gold-coloured balls and enormous red velvet ribbons. So many lovely things: mannequins in elegant winter coats with large buttons and matching fur-trimmed collars, stylishly cut dresses in solids and bold prints. In the toy section he bought a doll for Mindy and model planes for Frank and Gene. At the perfume counter he purchased a bottle of his grandmother's favourite scent, and then moved on to the men's section to pick up a box of linen handkerchiefs for his grandfather. From there he strolled into leather goods, where handbags were displayed in cases beneath glass as if they were precious goods. Enquiring the price of a bright green one, he found that they were, in fact, precious, costing nearly the same as an electric typewriter. He asked to see it, just to know what a handbag that cost as much as an electric typewriter felt like. Solid, was the answer. The patent leather was shiny and perfect, the clasp opened and shut with a decisive snap that said quality. It was lined with yellow silk instead of nylon, and had lots of small compartments including one with a zip. There was a matching change purse, the sales person said, and a wallet in the same style.

'I'd like to see them,' he said.

'Certainly, sir.'

He turned the bag over in his hands. What kind of husband bought his wife a typewriter for Christmas? Abigail should have something pretty and extravagant that showed how much he cared for her. His pulse quickened. If he was going to blow so much money on a handbag, he should probably choose one more tailored to Abigail's understated and sober tastes. He was about to ask if the style in his hand was available in black or brown when it struck him that the whole point of Christmas gifts was to buy things that people wouldn't normally buy for themselves. What Abigail really needed was a frivolous bauble.

'I'll take the whole set,' he told the assistant, and she wrapped it up for him with shiny silver paper and an enormous gold bow. It was a beautiful box and he walked with a spring in his step over to the glove department, determined to employ the same strategy for his equally pragmatic mother. Instead of buying a pair of leather gloves in predictable brown or black, he asked the girl behind the counter about the range of colours. Her eyes lit up with admiration.

'Colours are the height of fashion,' she said, laying out two sets of five-fingered rainbows on the glass top between them, one in cashmere, the other wool. The cashmere ones were softer and, when compared directly with the wool, the obvious choice. He bought a pair of light blue ones, thinking they would complement his mother's navy winter coat.

'In large, please,' he said. 'And the matching scarf.'

Why not splash out? He could afford it.

The assistant smiled. 'I'll wrap them up for you,' she said and she took a step away.

'A pair of the pink ones, too,' he added. 'Size small.'

Chapter Fourteen

Abigail could tell by the shape of the box and its oversized ribbon that it wasn't the IBM Selectric. Ted presented it with a flourish and looked on hungrily, his face full of eager anticipation, fingers twitching with the urge to help as she fumbled with the ties and the thick paper. The pressure to show enthusiasm and gratitude commensurate with his expectations was heightened by self-knowledge: she was a terrible actress. Trepidation morphed into mournful resignation once the present was revealed because not even Julie Andrews could have feigned excitement in the face of such disappointment. Obviously, the bag was expensive. It looked like something a high fashion model or a movie star would carry. Shiny patent leather in a shade of green so bright that it probably glowed in the dark. Not in a million years would she ever have chosen a bag like this.

'The surface will be easy to wipe clean,' she said, searching for something positive to say, adding, as his eyes took on the expression of a wounded Labrador's, 'and I'm sure I'll never misplace it.'

The bag felt over-bright in her hands, as if she were carrying around a billboard that said 'Cocktails!' or 'Welcome to fabulous Las Vegas!'. It clashed with most of her clothes. Nonetheless, she loyally took it with her everywhere; it was much praised. Carol Innes was particularly effusive, remarking more than once that Abigail was lucky to have a husband with an eye for fashion. Her own mother (who would not have been caught dead carrying anything so gaudy) stressed the thoughtfulness that the gift represented. Every compliment confirmed Abigail's fear: her feelings were not only ungracious, they were *wrong*. The bag became her hair shirt, the symbol of her sins. Her spirits teetered on the edge of a deep funk. The only thing that kept them afloat was knowing that her course was starting in the second week of January. The day was circled in red on her calendar and it pleased her to see it creep a bit closer every day. The week before, she drove over to the school to confirm her registration and pick up the reading list. She went straight to the college bookstore and bought everything on it, even those that weren't required, merely suggested, and she dipped into them in the evenings and whenever she had a free moment. The night before the first class her sleep was shallow and full of vivid dreams. She was in class. The professor was giving a lecture but she couldn't understand a word he said, as if he were speaking some unintelligible foreign tongue, except the other students weren't having any problems. They nodded along, answering, in English, the questions he posed, and then the professor turned toward her. The room was silent; all eyes on her. She tried to ask him to repeat the question but her mouth wouldn't form words; when she opened it to speak, no sound came out, the way Ted's father had been after the stroke. It was terrible.

That evening, she set out early from home, in case she got lost, but the campus was well marked and she had no trouble finding the designated classroom. She was the first to arrive and took a seat in the second row, one place to the right of centre, so as not to look like a suck-up. About ten minutes later people began to trickle in, acknowledging one another with slight nods and nervous smiles. Everyone, she was glad to see, was older. Some had clearly come straight from work. A few men, it appeared, were already acquainted.

'How's it going, Dick?' said one, a couple rows up from her.

'Back for more punishment, eh, Al?'

'Damn distribution requirements. It was either this or the Romantic poets.'

There were exaggerated laughs. 'How'd you do on the final?' said a new voice.

'C minus.'

There were whistles.

'Yeah, he raked me over the coals. What'd you get?'

'B minus. Lowest grade I've had.'

'That probably makes you valedictorian. This guy is a hard-ass.'

Abigail's heart sank. She was used to getting As. A girl slipped into a seat three away from her. She was significantly older, maybe even in her thirties, with cat's-eye glasses dangling from a black beaded chain, no wedding ring. They exchanged wan smiles. At seven thirty precisely, the professor walked down the steps carrying a large pile of papers. Apart from being younger than she expected, he looked exactly as a professor should: rangy, with a slight stoop, wearing an old wool blazer and threadbare corduroy trousers in olive green. He went to the chalk board and wrote with his left hand. *History 315: Colonial Boston, 1630–1776, Prof. David C. Crocker.* The letters slanted back on themselves, as if blown by an easterly wind. He turned to face the class and his right foot began to tap.

'Good evening,' he said. His wavy brown hair was shaggy around the ears and the nape of the neck. 'I am Professor David Crocker. That is Crock-*er*,' he said and he took the chalk and underlined the last two letters of his name, 'not to be confused with Davy Crock*ett*, "king of the wild frontier". Nineteenth-century American history is another course.'

She started to laugh, but checked it when the men who had called him a hard-ass failed to react. The room was quiet, apart from some discreet throat clearing. The professor's foot-tapping accelerated. People shifted awkwardly in their seats.

'This is Colonial Boston 1630 to 1776,' Professor Crocker continued. 'We will begin with the city's founding by the Puritans and discover how its citizens went from being proud and loyal British subjects to rebels leading the fight in the Declaration of Independence.'

As he settled into his discourse, his foot-tapping slowed and then disappeared.

'We will explore the aspects of religion, social hierarchy, economic structure, agriculture, education, as well as the effect of immigration and increasing ethnic diversity, also battles with the natives including King Philip's war and . . .'

Abigail scribbled as fast as she could, a smile spreading across her face. She felt the way she used to on the first few runs of a new ski season, a little stiff, slightly flabby, but back in the groove and ready to cope with whatever lay around the corner. It had been two years since she had been in a classroom, but the brain was a muscle like any other, and it remembered. The required reading would be a joy. She'd do it in the evenings when Ted watched television and in the afternoons when Mindy napped. She'd take Mindy to Wilsonville for weekends to prepare and write the three required papers. Mother would love the chance to look after Mindy and Father would gladly share his study.

'And so without further ado,' Professor Crocker said, 'let us begin our first lesson: *City upon a Hill*. Does anybody recognise this statement?'

Abigail looked around and waited for one of the men to answer.

'Anyone? Fletcher, what about you? What does "City upon a Hill" mean to you?'

'I don't know, sir,' said the man who claimed to have been raked over the coals.

Everyone was looking down, staring at their desks to avoid eye contact with the professor. Abigail was surprised that none of the men knew the answer to such an easy question. She stared at her hands folded in her lap. The continuing silence strained her nerves, especially when the professor resumed his manic foot-tapping. When she could bear it no longer, and it seemed certain that none of the men would answer, her hand shot into the air.

'Yes, Miss . . .?'

She almost answered Hatch, but caught herself, and said her married name.

'All right, Mrs McDougall, to what does "City upon a Hill" refer?'

'To John Winthrop's sermon aboard the *Arbella* before landing at Boston, sir. He believed Massachusetts Bay Colony would be a religious utopia.'

The look of pleasure on Professor Crocker's face satisfied like a glass of cool water on a hot day.

Chapter Fifteen

Goodyear's regional headquarters for New England, aka corporate, was a five-storey building in a complex off Route 128's famed Magic Semicircle and District Manager Joe Fielding's office occupied the entire top floor. If the architecture lent itself to the contemporary, the decor was strictly traditional. A large, grand oak desk dominated the space like an aircraft carrier on the sea and behind it sat Old Joe himself, captain of the New England ship, in an equally substantial leather chair with a high back, wings and decorative nailhead trim. He had the phone to his ear, not talking, listening, when Ted was ushered in by one of the three secretaries. He gave a slight nod in Ted's direction and then looked away, just before Ted nearly fell on his face, tripping over the extra plush carpet.

Ted stared at the walls around him, pretending to be engrossed by the photos, awards and Goodyear memorabilia so as not to give Old Joe the impression he was eavesdropping. His eyes, however, drifted back to the desk. What deals had been signed there, he wondered, worth how many millions of dollars? He pictured himself seated at such a desk, in such an office – too preoccupied with business matters to acknowledge the young gun waiting patiently before him: the poor slob with the sweaty brow and twitchy legs, disturbed by the plushness of the carpet beneath his feet.

'Send it over,' Joe Fielding said finally, in a voice that was clear and direct, without much warmth. 'I'll have a look later today.' He hung up without saying goodbye.

'I suspect you know why you're here,' he said to Ted. 'The Lynn store's performance hasn't been what I'd have hoped. I need a man to put things right. Word is that you're the one to do it.'

'I'm honoured for the chance to, sir.'

Old Joe stood and came around to Ted's side of the desk.

'Make the Goodyear Corporation notice the Lynn store for the right reasons, Ted,' he said, clasping Ted's hand, while patting his shoulder with the left. 'And, I promise you, Goodyear will notice you.'

The sound of his name on Old Joe's lips sent a surge of energy through Ted and he pumped Joe's hand with both of his. 'Yes, sir,' he said. 'I won't let you down, sir.'

Out of nowhere the secretary appeared at Ted's elbow to lead him out.

There was a lesson there: the power of Joe's silence. He tried to emulate it when he got back to the store. He said nothing; met no one's eye, just sat down and went about his business. And it worked. The room went quiet.

'Well?' said Burns eventually.

Only then did he let the smile creep across his face. 'Guess I'll be seeing a little less of you chumps.'

'You old sonofabitch,' Burns said as whoops and hollers went up across the sales area. Someone threw a crumpled piece of paper at him; soon paper balls were flying from all directions. Curtis pulled a bottle of Jameson out of his drawer and got his girl to fetch some cone-shaped paper cups from the stack next to the water cooler in the repair shop.

'To the rising star of Goodyear Tyres. Try not to forget us, McDougall.'

Forty minutes later he was at the Chevy dealership asking a salesman with a mustard stain on his shirt about the Corvair Monza.

He froze when he saw her sparkling like a jewel in the noon-time sun, the two-door convertible, red exterior, beige interior:

the exact model and colour of his dreams. Surely this wasn't a coincidence. The crisp, clean styling, the taut, athletic lines, the front grille and four small headlights filled him with boyish longing. His hand went out and touched the glossy hood.

'Thoroughly modern car,' the salesman said as he ran through the features. Before he was halfway through his pitch, Ted told him he'd take it.

The Monza's power was evident, even moving from traffic light to traffic light on Route 9. It was quick off the line when the light turned green; she stopped on a dime and handled with ease. Out on the Mass Pike, though, that's when she really showed her stuff. He slipped the stick into fourth and pushed down on the gas pedal. The car surged forward and Ted felt it deep in his belly, something animal. The thirty-mile trip to Lynn and back every day was going to be a treat. He'd buy a pair of sunglasses for riding with the top down this summer.

That evening he drove through Elm Grove slowly, looking for neighbours to wave at; he hung on the horn as he pulled into the driveway and waited for Abigail to come to the kitchen door.

'Guess what, honey?' he called, loud enough for Paul Jenks, out tending his roses, to hear.

'You got the job,' she replied. Her voice was flat and devoid of admiration, not at all the way he'd imagined.

'Hop in. I'll take you for a spin.'

'Are you on a test drive?'

He smiled broadly. 'Nope.'

Her eyebrows didn't just flicker, they flamed. 'You bought a car? We didn't discuss this.'

'I wanted it to be a surprise.'

'For whom?' she cried.

Whom. It seemed to Ted that everything that was wrong with Abigail was contained in that tiny word: her straight-laced, conventional correctness; her inflexibility; her dour, Yankee frugality.

'Look, Abigail,' he said, bringing his voice down a notch,

keeping the lid on his rising anger. 'I don't need your permission.'

She shook her head. 'The house, Ted, and the station wagon, my tuition . . .' She trailed off, as if to imply there were other things that she wasn't bothering to add and Jenks was hearing every word.

'Honey,' he said, laughing, as if this were a pretend argument. 'I can't be driving all the way to Lynn and back every day in that old DeSoto.'

She stared at him blankly.

'I got the job, Abigail!' he said, and then louder, with his hands cupped around his mouth like a cheerleader, broadcasting it to all of Elm Grove. 'I got the job.'

'This is counting chickens before they hatch, Ted,' she said, mouth pursed like she was sucking lemons. 'And nothing good ever came of that.'

Why did she always expect him to fail?

Chapter Sixteen

Penny was in the kitchen preparing a supper of egg noodles and a kind of stroganoff out of chicken and a can of mushroom soup. The window was open a crack, letting in cool, fresh, nearly spring air. March was a fickle month. Less than a week ago she had been slogging to work through five inches of snow. This evening, not only had the snow disappeared, there were buds on the old pin oak near the entrance to the T, buds that she swore had not been there when she passed by on her way to work this morning. Soon it would be time to swap her pink cashmere gloves for cotton ones.

The doorbell buzzed and Peanut, happy for any excuse not to help with supper, rushed out to answer it, clomping down each step like a Clydesdale, all the way down and then all the way back up again, now calling to Penny to grab her coat.

'But dinner is almost ready.'

'Never mind that,' Peanut said, tugging at her arm. She wouldn't let go, pulling and prodding her down the stairs, past Mrs Rizzo who was hollering, 'Why all this rumpus bumpus?' and out the door to where Ted stood, holding open the passenger door of the most darling red convertible sports car.

Penny's hands went up to touch her hair. She hadn't combed it, hadn't even removed her apron. How could Peanut let her go out looking like this?

'You look fine,' Peanut said, reading her thoughts. 'Come on!' They hurried over and scrambled in. Ted started up the engine and as they pulled away from the kerb Penny saw the lace curtains on Mrs Rizzo's sitting room windows twitch.

'You got the job!' she cried.

'I start Monday. I just met my team – swell bunch of guys.'

'Oh, Ted, that's wonderful! Was Curtis upset about you leaving?'

'He was great; shook my hand and said, "Looks like you're the rising star, McDougall."' His face glowed with pleasure.

'I'm so pleased,' she said, thinking that he looked even more handsome than usual. 'I'm sure you deserve every compliment.'

'Rising star,' he repeated softly.

Peanut leaned in from the back seat. 'So did you buy this car, Ted? Or am I chaperoning you two on a *test drive*?'

The stress she gave the last two words was full of innuendo. Penny's face began to burn.

'I bought it.'

'It's beautiful,' Penny said, stroking the cream-coloured vinyl on the door, averting her head so that he wouldn't see her blush. 'You didn't waste any time.'

'Ha-ha,' he replied. 'Did it on my lunch break. Should have seen the salesman's face.'

'You made his day, I'll bet,' Peanut said.

'It's not something I'd advise anyone to do. As Curtis says, an over-eager buyer over-buys. I was a little surprised the guy at the dealership didn't push for a better deal, but they had exactly what I was looking for and I knew my price. He came round to it pretty quick.'

'He could tell he was dealing with a pro,' said Penny.

Ted tilted his head as if she had made a valid point. He pushed on the gas pedal and the car surged forward.

'Golly,' she said.

'Fastest acceleration in its class,' he said. 'The air-cooled flat-sixes engine is all aluminium. The weight to power ratio is unbeatable.'

'Gosh,' she replied. The words were gobbledegook, but Ted was delighted; that was all she needed to know.

'You should see how she handles on the highway,' he said.

'I can't wait.'

He smiled. 'How about next Friday? There's a Japanese steak-house I heard about. They cook the food right in front of you.'

'Wonderful,' she said, though this Friday would have been more wonderful.

The night they spent dancing at the Ritz had been followed by nearly three weeks of silence, an eternity for Penny, who feared she would never see him again and not, she knew, due to any lack of attraction on his part but rather the surplus of it, or, to be precise, because of the guilt brought on by the force of his feelings. That he *felt* conflicted was proof of his excellent moral character, which only increased his appeal and, by consequence, her own pain at the prospect of being denied him. The situation had enough drama to elevate the budding romance to a potential True Love Story. Penny fell head first into the sharp and exquisite suffering of her first romantic fever. When he phoned just before Christmas she had nearly wept with joy.

Since then, the time between dates had shortened significantly. She would have liked it to be shorter still but, understanding the responsibility he had to his daughter and his burden of guilt, she was willing to be patient. They went dancing, often at the Greek place, or ate dinners at exotic restaurants. On their second date, over shrimp toast in Chinatown, he had said he wanted to eat his way around the world and Penny had said she was game. Their dates were always arranged well in advance on account, she assumed, of his daughter's schedule and needs, but he'd taken to dropping by the apartment unannounced – to fix the drippy faucet in the kitchen, or with little gifts, the latest issue of a fashion magazine or the 45rpm record of a hit song, inex-pensive things that were thoughtful but didn't put her under any sense of obligation.

'So, turns out they had the Boston Strangler all along. I guess you girls are happy.'

'I know, isn't that something?' Penny said. 'I guess it explains why there hasn't been an attack.'

'Have you taken the screwdrivers out of your bags?'

'Are you kidding? Ellen won't let us.'

'She out west?'

'San Francisco.'

'Not with the pilot, I hope?'

On a previous trip, one of the pilots, an attractive man who Ellen respected and admired, had confessed to being trapped in a loveless marriage and expressed a desire to know Ellen better.

'No, Ted. She ended it,' Penny said. 'Thanks to you. What you said really opened her eyes.'

Ted nodded. 'A married man will never leave his wife and children.'

'She didn't want him to,' Peanut said.

'That's what she says now,' he replied. 'Things change.'

Penny did not doubt that he was right and was glad that he was around, looking out for them.

'So, tell me, Peanut,' he asked, 'how was life as a blonde?'

Peanut had read an article that claimed men hit on blonde girls four times more often than brunettes and had decided to test the theory. A regular on her Boston–Newark flight loaned her some top-of-the-line wigs made with real human hair.

'A hoot!' Peanut replied. 'We went to four bars and I've never been so popular in my life. I'm considering bleaching my hair. It'll save me a fortune. I'll never have to buy another drink.'

'Don't you dare, Peanut,' Penny said. 'Your hair is adorable.'

'You should have seen Penny, Ted, she looked so cute.'

'Penny always looks cute.'

'Blondes definitely have more fun,' Peanut said.

'The wigs were all different shades so we didn't look like we'd shared a bottle of peroxide between us,' Penny said. 'Different styles, too. Mine was a bob, Peanut's was a bouffant and Ellen had a beehive.'

'You don't mind, do you, Ted?' Peanut asked.

'Why would I mind? It was just for kicks, right?'

'And the free drinks,' Peanut said. 'Penny practically had to fend them off with sticks. How many guys asked for your number, Pen?'

'Hush, Peanut. Don't exaggerate. It was only two.'

'And did you give it to them?'

She squirmed in her seat. 'They were so polite. I didn't want to hurt their feelings.'

Ted went quiet and stared out at the road as if it required his full attention.

'But I wrote the number wrong.'

He slapped the steering wheel and roared with laughter.

When they got back to the apartment, Ted ran around to open their door and hand them out. Penny invited him to stay for supper, of course, but he said he needed to be getting home, which was just as well because the noodles were dreadfully overcooked.

'Did you notice how worried he looked when he heard those men asked for your number?' Peanut asked.

A pleasant warmth started in Penny's belly and spread throughout her body.

'You shouldn't have told him you wrote the number down wrong,' Peanut said, piling mushy noodles on to her fork. 'Men behave better when they think they've got a little competition.'

'I couldn't,' she replied, picking around the noodles for bits of chicken and mushroom. 'It would be too mean, after all he's been through.'

'Mmm-hmm,' Peanut agreed, her mouth full of stroganoff. 'Still, it's not as if you owe him anything. It isn't as if you're going steady, or anything.'

The thought of a man such as Ted using childish, high school words like *going steady* made her want to laugh. 'We're taking things slow.'

'You aren't seeing anyone else, though.'

'Ted's such a gentleman,' she said, with a one-shoulder shrug. 'It's a nice change not to have to be always thinking up ways to fend off roaming hands.'

'Sounds boring,' said Peanut.

'God help any man who tries to take advantage of you, Peanut O'Reilly,' she said, because she could not put into words how thrilling it was to hold Ted's hand, sitting quietly while her insides did loop-de-loops. 'Sometimes, I confess, it's all I can do to keep my hands off him.'

'Who says you have to?'

'Really, Peanut. What would he think?'

'That you're a modern, sexually liberated woman.'

'Sexually liberated, honest to God, Peanut! I'm just happy that things are working out for him. A new store to manage, a new car, you know? It's a fresh start.'

'Hmm. It can never be a truly fresh start, can it? Not when he has a daughter.' She shovelled more stroganoff into her mouth.

'No,' she agreed. 'His wife's death devastated him. He can barely speak about it.'

'Don't get me wrong, I think Ted's a great guy. He appreciates that we girls have our own lives. Most men seem to think that when they're not around we just twiddle our thumbs, waiting for them to return. But would you really want to be the second wife?'

'It wouldn't be my preference, all things being equal, but they aren't equal. Having a man who respects me is worth a lot.'

'But would you want to be a stepmother?'

'She's just a tiny thing. And a darling.'

'Have you met her?'

'I've seen pictures. Ted's face lights up whenever he talks about her.'

Peanut raised her eyebrows suggestively and mimed gripping the wheel of a car. 'Vroom, vroom!'

121

'Hush, Peanut,' she said, as her face reddened again. She pointed to Peanut's now empty plate.

'I can't believe you ate those noodles.'

Now it was Peanut's turn to feel self-conscious. 'That's because you didn't grow up eating dinner with six hungry brothers. In my house, if a person didn't eat whatever was put in front of them, and quick, they'd starve.'

Chapter Seventeen

Abigail was enjoying her course on Colonial Boston more than she had any right to. Professor Crocker wasn't the most dynamic speaker, but he had a comprehensive understanding of the subject matter. He made her think. Her classmates were a little rough around the edges, but they were conscientious, for the most part, and listened respectfully to everyone's opinions, even the girls'. Abigail walked away from every class feeling that she had not only learned something but also that she had contributed meaningfully to the discussion and while that was all well and good, the grade she received at the end of the semester would be based on the quality of the term papers she turned in. The first was due the last week before the spring vacation; she approached the assignment with apprehension. It had been a long time since she'd written an essay, apart from the one on Abigail Adams that she would rather forget. She had high expectations and wanted very much to impress Professor Crocker. She took Mindy to Wilsonville for a weekend well in advance of the due date and locked herself up in her father's study with books and essays about King Philip's War of 1675 and returned feeling the essay was well under control.

And then a few days later Mindy came down with an ear infection that progressed to croup. The hours Abigail intended to devote to finishing the paper were instead consumed by the needs of a fussy toddler; four straight nights sitting in a steamed-up bathroom with Mindy barking like a distressed seal left her too tired to function. Frustration brought whispers of resentment that were promptly smothered beneath a blanket of guilt and denial. She bundled Mindy and the Smith Corona off to Wilsonville again the following weekend, but wasted the bulk of her time catching up on lost sleep. With the deadline looming and the work still half finished, she made the choice to go for a third straight weekend, which even her mother felt the need to comment upon.

'Of course we love having you,' she said, 'but doesn't your husband miss you?'

Perhaps it was excessive, but necessary. She only finished the last of the typing an hour before she left for class.

She used the vacation to catch up on all the cleaning she had let slide – floors, walls, drapes, oven and closets, pausing only for a Culture Club meeting in which one of the new gals from Dutch Road spoke about macramé. Her mind frequently wandered toward her term paper. Counter points to the arguments she'd offered kept popping into her mind, undermining them. She'd imagine Professor Crocker reading her words, shaking his head at her ignorance, and scrub harder at the grease baked into the stove, or the mould in the bathtub. She prepared elaborate meals, apart from the two nights that Ted had business dinners. They talked about inviting the Hales for dinner some time soon, but not immediately because Ted still had so much to learn about running his own store.

On the Tuesday that class resumed, she was too excited to eat. She put Mindy to bed half an hour early and laid the table for Ted's dinner as the casserole warmed in the oven. She waited with her coat on, rushing out the instant she heard the Corvair in the drive. Professor Crocker's lecture on the Salem witch trials was not at all what she had expected. She would have predicted a quick recap of the facts followed by comparisons to McCarthyism and Miller's *The Crucible* and though all these were mentioned, the primary thrust of his talk involved asking the class to imagine the Revolution and what the Constitution might have looked like had there been no witch trials.

'Might we have had a Puritan theocracy?' he asked. 'Would an America that had not suffered the trauma and shame of what happened in Salem in 1692 have been as concerned about due process? Would it have been as wary of its leaders' human fallibility?'

'Are you saying that hanging people for supposed witchcraft was a good thing?' Dick asked.

'Not at all, Mr Fletcher. I'm trying to point out the dangers of studying any historical event in isolation. Experiences have a profound ability to shape us. This is true for nations as well as for men. Maritime safety regulations were much debated up to the *Titanic*'s sinking. Elaborate equations were devised to figure out the number of lifeboats a ship needed. After *Titanic* the equation became simple: a place for every soul aboard.'

'Same was true for fire and building codes after Coconut Grove,' said Tony, who was a fireman.

'Precisely, Mr Sebatti. Our failures cause us to react much more vigorously than our successes.'

The evening passed in a flash, with Abigail scribbling ideas as fast as she could, afraid of losing even one word. It wasn't that she forgot about her term paper, but it was pushed to the back of her mind until the end of class, when Professor Crocker began handing them back. Harry, seated to her right, smiled when he got his. He balled his hand into a fist and flexed his arm muscles in a victory salute; Gloria glanced briefly at the last page of hers and then stuffed it into her bag and quickly left. Abigail sat and waited. Professor Crocker didn't look at her when he handed it back. Her palms stuck to the pages. She peeled them apart with care, as if she feared something would escape.

'B plus,' Harry said, leaning toward her. 'How about you?'

Her eyes scanned the page and her stomach lurched. There was no grade, just a small note in red ink: *'Please see me.'*

*

Her mouth was dry as she sat in Professor Crocker's drab grey and white cube of an office. She stared at the metal brackets that held the bookshelves behind his head. The metal-framed desk between them echoed like a tin drum when her knee accidentally bumped it.

He smiled. Up close like this she could see how crooked his teeth were. One of the front ones was severely chipped.

'What is your view on the American Revolution, Mrs McDougall?' he asked.

Abigail cleared her throat. 'I guess I'd have to say I'm an Imperialist.'

'An Imperialist?' The question blasted out of his mouth the way it did in class whenever he suspected (correctly, usually) that someone hadn't done the required reading.

'I mean, in the sense that Charles Andrews is an Imperialist.'

One side of the professor's mouth turned up. 'And what, if I may ask, is Charles Andrews's definition of the Imperialist School of American revolutionary history?'

'Basically, ah, it's a bit like the thrust of your argument this evening. That is to say, we can't understand colonial history without understanding English history.'

'In what way?' The intensity with which he looked at her almost caused her brain to stall.

'Er, it wasn't just British tyranny. They were, um, at times, tyrannical, but mostly they were inflexible; ignorant, also. They didn't realise that colonies had become autonomous functioning political bodies.'

He nodded. 'Interesting,' he said.

The same word Carol Innes chose to describe her speech to the Ladies Culture Club.

He peppered her with a few more questions on the subject and then leaned forward. His sweater had a moth hole on the shoulder. The collar of his shirt was frayed.

'How many college-level history courses have you taken, Mrs McDougall?' he asked.

'Four, I think,' Abigail said, though she knew precisely. 'Western Civilisation, Seventeenth-century France, Tsarist Russia and England under the Tudors.'

'Never American History?'

She shook her head. 'Not since high school, no. But it's been a hobby of mine ever since I was a little girl.'

'Your paper was very interesting.'

There was that adjective again. Was she really such a bore even to a history professor?

'I have graduate students who can't advance an argument that well. Hell, I couldn't advance arguments that well when I was a grad student. It was, and I don't use this word lightly, remarkable.'

She wanted to jump from her seat and shake her fist as Harry had done – to raise both arms in a victory salute and scream, 'yes!' Instead she smiled down at her feet, quietly enjoying the sensation of undiluted joy seeping through her veins. 'Thank you, sir.'

He nodded. 'And I have a proposition for you.'

Abigail shot him an astonished look and saw, immediately, that his surprise was even greater than hers. His professorial authority dissolved; every bit of exposed skin, from his shirt collar on up, including the earlobes, flushed a deep crimson.

'I am so sorry. Please forgive me. I meant nothing untoward, Mrs McDougall, really . . .'

She could not hold back the laugh that rose within her.

'I'm working on a project, you see. A book, in fact,' Professor Crocker said, the blush clearing slowly. 'It's a big project. Very complex, and a research assistant with your knowledge and skills would be invaluable.'

'Really?'

He clawed absentmindedly at some papers on his desk.

'The pay isn't much. It's not glamorous, I'll warn you. Lots of reading and typing up summaries. I, I, assume you can type?'

'Of course.'

He grinned; his chipped tooth gave him a child-like appearance. 'Great, that's great. Now, the only catch, I'm afraid, is that you'll need to register as a full-time student.'

Chapter Eighteen

Ted knew that continuing to see Penny was wrong.

Then again, it wasn't *that* wrong, not like sneaking-off-to-cheap-hotels kind of wrong. Hardly. They were almost never alone. Nonetheless, he meant to break it off, just drop out of sight, stop calling. There were a number of sound, logical reasons why he put it off. First and foremost, Penny was a good dinner companion. As a salesman, he needed a variety of restaurants at which he could entertain business clients. Only a fool would take a client to a restaurant he hadn't previously dined at – as Curtis said, 'Success is preparation' – and he hated eating alone. Taking Abigail on these trials meant getting a babysitter; it meant driving all the way into the city and then all the way back again, robbing her of precious study time, and she didn't even enjoy foreign food. Penny, on the other hand, loved exotic dishes, and lived and worked in the vicinity. He could meet her for dinner at six, and be home by nine.

Furthermore, he enjoyed line dancing at the Greek restaurant. When Abigail and Mindy were in Wilsonville for the weekend, there was no reason he shouldn't spend his free evening engaged in an activity he enjoyed, especially now that he was working only ten minutes away from the establishment. To call Penny beforehand was just common sense. Imagine the embarrassment, the potential for hurt feelings, if they ran into one another unexpectedly! Sometimes they agreed to meet there; other times she'd invite him to dinner at her apartment. In such instances, he felt it would be rude to refuse. They watched television, played cards or listened to records. It was no different from when Art and Carol Innes invited him to dinner, the last time Abigail was away.

For the most part, he behaved himself – a little smooching, sure; his hand sometimes lingered on her bottom when they danced, and once, while watching an evening news report about the Gemini 3 launch, he had briefly fondled her right breast through her blouse, but that was all. Compared to the debauchery he'd witnessed at the three-day regional sales meeting in Atlantic City, it was a model of chastity (which wasn't to say that it lacked erotic power – the hardening of her nipple beneath his fingertips had brought forth from his lips a spontaneous, whispered moan), but theirs was above all a friendship. They got on well. He loved spending time with her, loved hearing about the things she and her roommates got up to. They could stay out dancing until three in the morning and then sleep until noon, if they wanted, so long as it wasn't a work day. Their unfettered freedom captivated him, and caused him to question certain assumptions.

Growing up in Wilsonville, the unspoken goal was to find a steady at the earliest opportunity, and certainly no later than the Homecoming Dance, sophomore year. Having a steady cemented one's social status. This was true for girls and boys alike, though for different, almost opposite, reasons. To the girls who received them, the gift of a class ring or a letterman's jacket signalled a boyfriend's respect, love and devotion. To the guys who gave them, they were marks of ownership, walking billboards of their sexual prowess. The myth that even nice girls granted sexual favours in exchange for these gifts was accepted as gospel by young males and none of them, least of all a boy with a steady, was ever going to set the record straight. Having a steady had numerous immediate advantages; its singular drawback was evident only in retrospect. It set one on a course that, once begun, was almost impossible to slow down, let alone reverse. You couldn't not give your steady your school ring and, as soon as people saw her wearing it, they'd start asking her if you were pre-engaged. After a little while she'd start bugging you about it; soon you talked of little else until finally you decided that, yes, you were pre-engaged, and once people heard you were officially pre-engaged, they'd start asking when you were going to get engaged for real. It was a vicious cycle and many were caught up in it. Tom Wakefield was the first to take it to the ultimate conclusion when, in the last week of September, Ester Childs came to school flashing a diamond solitaire. The girls went gaga. Within a few months, about half a dozen other guys, Ted included, had followed suit. There was an element of competitiveness to it, an undeclared race to see who could amass the trappings of adulthood the fastest. Looking back, he wondered why the rush.

He doubted he would have noticed any of this if he hadn't been spending time with Penny and her roommates. She opened up a whole new vista on the world. He was used to everyone around him knowing everything about him. With Penny, it was as if he had been presented with a blank canvas and, keeping in mind Ken Schmidt's admonition not to be boring, he eagerly covered it in bold strokes and bright colours. The Ted Penny knew had travelled to more places, read more books and knew more interesting people. He had put himself through college at the University of Colorado, playing football and working for ski patrol; spent time in the service and done a stint in Vietnam with the CIA. And the truly amazing thing, the really *beautiful* thing, was how real it felt. His pulse raced as he described out-skiing an avalanche in the Rockies, or walking through a swamp on patrol over in Nam. When he told her about ice fishing trips up north with his father – trips that he had no doubt *would* have taken place since, before the stroke, his father had often talked of doing so 'one day' – he felt the cold air on his cheeks and the stiffness in his frozen toes and fingers, saw his father's steely gaze and Danny's mischievous grin because Penny's Ted had a brother Danny who was alive.

Every fib put a little layer of insulation between regular Ted and Penny's Ted until, in his mind, they became distinct and separate. Life was simultaneously fuller and less complicated.

He couldn't explain it, but knew in his bones it was so; he believed it had made him a better husband. Abigail hadn't had a crying jag in months. His marriage vows, and Penny's hymen, were both intact. Everything was well within his control. When Abigail took Mindy up for an extra-long weekend in mid-May for a gala dinner at that Wilsonville Country Club in honour of Linc's fiftieth birthday, Ted begged off, claiming that he was still getting to grips with his new job. He took Penny dancing at the Greek restaurant on Friday and went to her place after work on Saturday. They ordered in pizza and played canasta. Ellen mentioned that Stan Getz was playing at Sonny's jazz bar and so, at midnight, they went out to hear him. Ted got home at four, slept until eleven, and then went back to pick Penny up for the Sunday afternoon Sox game against the Oakland A's. He was teaching her baseball.

He got the cheapest tickets, in the bleachers, and told her they were comps from his pal, Tony. The Sox weren't doing much this year, but Tony Conigliaro was hitting even better than he had in his rookie season. Ted looked forward to seeing Penny's eyes light up when she saw Conigliaro's name on the boards.

'Is that your friend Tony?' she'd ask.

Given the way Tony C was swinging, the odds were better than even that he would hit one out to the bleachers in at least one of his at-bats. Ted would tell Penny it was meant for them, and she would give him the look of awe that made him feel as if he were Superman. The game started at one. Abigail and Mindy wouldn't be back before six. There'd be plenty of time to drop Penny off at her apartment, zip on to the Mass Pike, and be home before five.

Storm clouds were gathering on the horizon when he drove in to pick her up. The first raindrops fell as they were parking the car; by the time they got to Lansdowne Street, the game had been called.

'I know a place we could go,' she said.

'Lead on.'

'You might be sorry,' she teased.

'Not a chance.'

She tied a kerchief around her head and they hurried off, arm-in-arm, down Jersey Avenue, leaning into the rain all the way to the Back Bay Fens. They dashed across the park, leaping over puddles, and when they came out the other side they were standing in front of a mansion. Penny led him through its heavy wooden doors. Inside there were arches and marble columns and an atrium garden, with a glass roof on which the falling rain sounded like brushes on a cymbal. It looked like the palace of an Italian prince, but Penny said it was actually a museum.

She removed her kerchief and shook it. Water collected at their feet.

'Wow,' he said, looking around. That was the great thing about Penny. He would have walked straight by, never knowing it existed. Because of her, he was becoming more cultured, more refined.

'You want to know the most amazing thing about this place?' she said, guiding him toward a wide set of stone stairs. 'One lady bought everything in it.'

Ted whistled. 'She must have been loaded.'

Penny pointed out portraits of her – there were several – hanging around the museum. The woman obviously had an ego. The imperial way she held her chin reminded him of his mother.

'I wouldn't have crossed her,' he said.

He followed Penny up a set of stone steps into a gallery that could have been a living room. She walked up to the largest painting in the room – of a dishevelled girl, falling off the back of a bull – and stood there, staring up at it.

Ted raised his eyebrows. 'She needs to grab that bull by the horns.'

'It's Jupiter.'

'Who?'

'The king of the Roman gods. The girl is Europa. Jupiter fell in love with her so he disguised himself as a bull and pretended to be tame so she'd climb on to his back.'

'Like the fox and the gingerbread man.'

'If the fox wanted to rape the gingerbread man.'

'You're kidding, right?' He looked at the woman's face. 'Does she know?'

Penny stared at the canvas. 'She knows.'

'She doesn't look all that upset.'

Penny tilted her head to one side. 'She doesn't, does she?'

Her mouth fluctuated between a frown and a smile. Her eyes never left the painting.

'I came here with my secretarial school, once,' she said. 'The teachers wouldn't let us look at this.' Her voice dropped to a whisper. 'So I came back on my own. I've never been able to figure out why she looks the way she does. I mean, it's obvious that she's scared, but also sort of like she's enjoying it, the way her eyes are rolling back. Look at those cupids chasing her.' She pointed with her finger. Her voice began to waver. 'Her bosom exposed, ready for the arrow to pierce it.'

Ted looked at the painting and then back at Penny.

Her teeth began to chatter. 'Take me home, Ted,' she said. 'Now.'

As he ran back to get the car, he told himself that she wasn't saying what he thought he was hearing. She was soaked to the skin from the rain and the museum was cold. He was imagining things. Their breath steamed up the car's windows.

She put the keys into Ted's hands because hers were shaking.

Her tennis shoes squelched as she pulled them off her feet. The normally neat girl left her sodden coat and kerchief on the floor where they fell. She hurried to the bedroom she shared with Peanut. She left the door wide open, and turned to face him as she began undoing the buttons on her shirt.

He took a step into the room. 'Are you sure? Are you sure?' he asked, though he could not swear that the words did anything more than echo around his head, so loud was the clamour of the wanting and the disbelief at his own fantastic luck as she stripped in front of him. The stark innocence of her plain white undergarments almost overwhelmed him and he stared, mouth agape, as these, too, were removed and she stood before him, shivering, her arms slightly out to the sides as if she did not quite know where to put them.

He took another step toward her. 'Are you sure?' Was the question for her or for himself?

The moment his hand touched her breast he lost all restraint. He was Jupiter, lifting her up on to the bed – a girlish single with a pink dust ruffle – and she submitted as the rain beat a percussive riot on the roof overhead.

The storm was followed by a dense fog that rolled in from the harbour. Ted lay with Penny in a moist tangle of limbs and bed linens. He wondered at the time, aware that, whatever the hour, it was too late. Much too late. He felt filthy and disgraced and he wanted, more than anything in the world to be out of this bed, out of this apartment and back home where he belonged.

He extricated himself and stood to dress. Penny rolled over and lit a cigarette, a coy smile on her lips, loose locks of dishevelled hair falling seductively across her face. Watching her play the sexpot for his benefit was odious, this nice girl that he had spoiled.

Don't do this, he shouted in his head. *I'm a creep and a liar.*

Instead, he whispered that she was not to worry, he'd see himself out. She wouldn't hear of it. In a nod to the girl in the painting, she fashioned a loose toga out of the top sheet – exposing, in the process, a small bloodstain on the under sheet that they both took pains to ignore. They walked together to the door and, as they embraced in a farewell kiss, she casually loosened the toga and let it fall. Caressing her for what would most certainly be the last time, he quaked with yearning. Self-loathing was the only thing that kept him from carrying her back to bed.

'Give Mindy a kiss for me,' she called when he was halfway down the stairs and his brain flooded with the image of his daughter sitting at the breakfast table on Thursday morning in her one-piece pyjamas, putting her ear down to her breakfast bowl, listening to her cereal 'talk'. His foot nearly missed the next step.

Outside, the air was close and eerily quiet. The dashboard clock told him he should be home already. The trip down Meridian Street to Porter was like driving through a cloud. Streams of condensation dripped from the car. Inside, the air was humid and sweet with the mix of honeysuckle, menthol cigarettes and femininity that was unmistakably Penny. He lit a cigarette, turned up the bi-level, opened the vents and the window a crack, and yet the scent remained. The car's roof appeared lower than he remembered. If only he could ride with the top down. He had to get rid of Penny's scent before he saw Abigail.

Abigail!

He was halfway down Soldier's Field Road when he saw the snake of red tail lights blocking his path. The traffic around him slowed to a crawl and then stopped dead. He sat for a minute and then a minute more. He lit another cigarette with trembling fingers. The on-ramp to the Mass Pike was right there, but two hundred yards of cars sat bumper-to-bumper in his way and showed no signs of moving.

In Wilsonville, today, the Hatch family would have sat down to Sunday dinner at two thirty sharp: soup, followed by a roast and then dessert – strawberry pie, he'd bet, given it was in season. By three thirty they'd have retired to the living room for coffee and conversation. Linc's latest letter to the *Bulletin* would be complimented. At four, Gretchen would have gone to the piano to lead them in songs. In his head he heard Abigail's voice warbling on the high notes and something caught in his throat. Why, for God's sake, hadn't he gone to join them after work yesterday?

By no later than four thirty, Linc, so irritating and yet at this moment lovable in Ted's eyes, would have announced with patrician concern that Abigail ought to be getting on the road. They would have got Mindy cleaned up and loaded the car with produce from the garden and whatever New Hampshire staple the Hatches believed unobtainable sixty miles south. Ted pictured Lincoln and Gretchen waving from their front porch to Abigail and Mindy who, at this very moment, were motoring toward home at a mile a minute while Ted sat helplessly parked in traffic.

He gripped the steering wheel with both hands and knocked his forehead against it. 'Aarrggghh!'

His nostrils were still full of Penny. She was on his skin, clinging to the fibres of his clothes. The cigarettes did nothing to mask the taste of her. How would he ever get it out?

What if . . .

A blood vessel in his forehead began to pulse not quite in time with the tic of the second hand sweeping its way around the dashboard clock. He could not bring himself to finish the thought. Minutes passed and then, behind him, the sound of sirens and red lights. In his rear-view mirror he saw a police cruiser creeping through the traffic jam; cars inching aside to make a path for it and the pair of tow trucks it was escorting. It was another aeon before the traffic began to move. Ted was terribly behind schedule when he finally shifted the Corvair into first. The drive to the on-ramp was made in fits and starts. The guard at the toll booth counted out dimes for Ted's change with maddening slowness. When, at last, the barrier lifted, Ted shot into the left lane and put his foot to the floor. The car kicked up spray from the wet road as it accelerated: sixty-five, seventy, seventy-five, eighty . . . He swerved around other cars, passed on the inside, and skidded close to the rail when exiting, certain that he'd clawed back minutes of lost time, but when he looked at the clock he saw that it had made next to no difference. He was still late; and sorry, so very, very, sorry.

Elm Grove was a little more than half a mile north from the Pike, off the old post road, and there was hardly any traffic. He could have covered the distance in less than a minute if not for the lights dispersed every hundred yards that seemed deliberately set against him. Every time the one in front of him turned green, the next one turned red. Stop, go; stop, go; he advanced intersection by intersection.

'Come on!' he screamed, pounding the steering wheel with his fists. 'Come on!' His fingers tapped an impatient rhythm.

The eighth and final light turned green and he pulled into the intersection for a left turn, waiting for the southbound cars to pass. There was a line of them, spaced just far enough apart to prevent him from crossing. Fuming, he gazed toward the horizon, looking for a break in traffic, and saw, in the distance, at the end of the long line, a powder-blue Ford station wagon with wood-panelling: Abigail.

He stepped on the gas. The Corvair hurtled out into oncoming traffic, between a black Pontiac and a green AMC. A horn blared; brakes and tyres squealed. Ted closed his eyes and waited for the impact that didn't come. The slow drive through Elm Grove was painful. He manoeuvred around a pack of kids on bicycles, stopping to let the boy who'd flubbed an easy catch retrieve his ball from the road, knowing that Abigail was gaining on him every second.

His breath was shallow and quick when he pulled into the driveway. He hopped out of the car and rummaged with his keyring, frantically searching for the one to the kitchen door and when, at last, he found it, the key didn't want to fit into the hole; he fumbled like a drunk. Sweat trickled from his forehead and armpits, blending with Penny's scent into something cheap and base.

The key turned in the lock. He pushed hard on the door and it flew open, banged against the wall and swung back, nearly hitting him on the nose; he sprinted across the kitchen, past the living room, down the hall to the bathroom. He twisted the shower knob on full, pulled off his clothes, dropping them on the floor only to snatch them back up when he remembered they were infected with Penny's smell. He burrowed into the dirty clothes hamper, burying them beside smelly socks and the T-shirt he'd worn to do the yard work. He jumped into the shower,

yelping as the cold water hit his skin; took the bar of soap
between his hands and rolled it into a froth, white and pure,
that he rubbed furiously over his body. He opened his mouth
and let the water splash inside. He ran the soap across his tongue;
it stung and pricked. He sneezed; his eyes watered. The door to
the bathroom flew open.

'Ted?'

'Grawl,' he said, his mouth frothing like a rabid raccoon's.

'You left the door open. And the keys in the lock.'

'I only just got home, hon,' he said, spitting soap.

Through the smoked glass of the shower door, he saw her
arms folded tight across her chest.

'No point trying to hide, Ted,' she said.

Every muscle in his body froze. It seemed a minor miracle that
water continued to flow from the shower head. He should have
known he'd never fool her. Abigail must have picked up Penny's
scent in the kitchen, followed it through the house into the bathroom. Why, he smelled it now, through the steam and the soap.
'Forgive me,' he wanted to say, but soap had numbed his tongue.

'I saw you cutting across the traffic like a maniac,' she said.
'You're going to kill somebody someday.'

Chapter Nineteen

As soon as Ted was gone, Penny's nakedness embarrassed her. She hurried back to her bedroom and put on a pair of dungarees and an old sweatshirt. Her limbs felt hollow. She couldn't keep still. Like a hummingbird, she flitted about, tidying: picking her coat up off the hall floor and hanging it in the shower to dry; mopping water off the floor. Her underpants kept soaking through; she changed them three times. She stripped the sheet off the bed and soaked it in cold water with salt. She fixed her hair with a tease comb and lots of hairspray. When it was all done she made herself sit on the sofa. She lit a cigarette.

'Forgive me, Father, for I have sinned,' she said aloud, and laughed a small laugh followed by a deep pull on the cigarette. She chewed on a fingernail and checked the clock. Peanut wouldn't be home for another two hours, an eternity to wait for the reassuring words that she yearned to hear: that this was no big deal; that she had not crossed the Rubicon or that maybe she had, but on the other side lay not shame and sin, but maturity and womanliness. Doing the deed, that's what they called it, as if it were something to be endured. It hadn't hurt at all. The feeling – submitting to someone she trusted, respected and loved and who she knew loved her back just as much – was bliss.

How soon, she wondered, before he proposed? What setting would he choose: a fancy dinner or a beautiful natural setting? It would be wonderful to be proposed to on the Cape, just as the sun was setting. She hoped he wouldn't approach it too rationally or practically. It might be a second wedding for him, but it was her first; she wanted the fairy tale: down on one knee, holding out the velvet jewellery box (Tiffany blue, preferably) containing a diamond solitaire, set in platinum, the bigger the better.

She wiped down the counters and cupboards in the kitchen and put away the dishes on the drying rack. On a notepad that they used to write grocery lists she wrote, in her neatest hand:

Penelope McDougall
Penny McDougall
Mr and Mrs Edward McDougall
Ted and Penny McDougall
Merry Christmas from the McDougalls
Mrs Edward C McDougall.

She felt sneaky, as if she'd been granted membership to a secret society. She was glad that she and Ted hadn't waited until their wedding night. She fully intended to wear white, though. People would kiss her goodbye, thinking that she was on the cusp of a profound experience, unaware that she was fully educated. A spring wedding would be her preference, when the cherry blossoms were in bloom, though she appreciated that this could be hard to time. Well, they'd plan for late May or early June and hope for the best. She already knew exactly what she wanted for a dress: a simple design, in satin, cut along the bias, something that showed off the smallness of her waist. She wanted a fingertip veil held by a small, sequin- and bead-encrusted crown, and a delicate bouquet of lilies of the valley. She wanted her father to give her away and for Mindy to be a flower girl with a basket full of rose petals to sprinkle as she walked down the aisle. She couldn't wait to meet her.

She took the sheet out of the water, added it to her dirty clothes basket and carried it to the washer and dryer in the basement. On her way back up the stairs she saw Mrs Rizzo standing in her doorway in a black dress and house slippers.

'Your boyfriend leave?'

The brusque tone and stern look made her sheepish. Mrs Rizzo knew he was here. 'Yes.'

Mrs Rizzo nodded. 'I make coffee. Come.'

'Oh, Mrs Rizzo, I'd love to but—'

'Come, I got cake.'

'I just put laundry on.'

'So you have half an hour to spend with an old lady. Come.'

She pivoted and made a beckoning motion with her arm as she walked toward her sitting room with her head down. Reluctantly, Penny followed.

'Sit.'

Penny sat down in one of a pair of armchairs. Mrs Rizzo disappeared into the kitchen. She fidgeted like a schoolgirl in the principal's office – or, more precisely, as she imagined a girl who'd been sent to the principal's office would fidget. She had no first-hand experience. She did not want this moment spoiled by a lecture about the need to safeguard her reputation. It seemed a long time before Mrs Rizzo returned with a tray loaded down with china cups, a silver coffee pot, and an elaborate layer cake with cream frosting, sprinkled with toasted almond slivers.

'Rum cake,' Mrs Rizzo said, cutting a slice with a long knife. 'You like?'

'I've never tried it. It looks delicious.' Penny took a spoonful. Her mouth filled with the tastes of vanilla, chocolate, cream and rum. 'You made this from scratch?'

Mrs Rizzo nodded. 'Old family recipe.'

'Gosh, it must have taken all day.'

Mrs Rizzo shrugged. 'What else I got to do with my time? It was my Tino's favourite. Today his birthday. He woulda been sixty-eight years old.'

'Is that him?' she asked, pointing to a sepia photo of a stocky man dressed in breeches and gaiters with a folding cap set at a jaunty angle on his head.

Mrs Rizzo smiled. 'In his uniform.' She reached over and picked up its silver frame, with a little grunt. 'A soldier in the Great War, before they knew there would be a greater one,' she said. 'Ten days before the end, he die.' She shook her head. 'We didn't know until two weeks after. We celebrate, "Hurray, war is over! My Tino gonna come home." But,' she sniffed, 'he already in his grave. In Belgium.' She kissed her fingertips and then touched them to the photo. Penny forced a mouthful of cream and cake over a large lump in her throat. She pictured Ted marching off to war. The months of uncertainty and then celebration as the end to hostilities was announced and then having the army chaplain knock on the door. Her eyes filled.

'I had no idea,' she said, reaching out and putting a hand on the old lady's gnarled knuckles. 'I'm so sorry.'

'Ah,' Mrs Rizzo said, wiping away her own tears with the back of her hand. 'Ah.'

Chapter Twenty

For the next week Ted felt like a condemned man standing on the gallows, the noose around his throat, waiting for the floor to open up beneath him. He startled easily, measured Abigail's every word, examined her every gesture. He felt so materially changed it was impossible for him to believe it didn't show, that there wasn't a physical stain. 'The lies are written all over your face,' his mother had told him when he was nine and tried to deny having stolen candy from DeWitt's store. How was it that adultery left no trace?

He became a model husband. He took the garbage out without having to be asked, mowed the lawn once a week, kept the flowerbeds weeded, and made sure the station wagon was always sparkly clean, inside and out. He bought Abigail bunches of daisies or violets, wrapped in brown paper. He fully supported her taking the research assistant job, and going back to school full-time next fall.

Other husbands complained when their wives fell behind in the housework, but Ted pitched in to help, washing dishes, scrubbing the blackened bottoms of pots with iron wool; folding laundry in front of the television in the evenings after Mindy went to bed, while Abigail did her school work at the dining room table. On Sunday mornings, he took Mindy with him to buy doughnuts so that Abigail could sleep in.

In only one respect was he not a model: he kept seeing Penny.

It's not that he didn't try to cut things off. Many times, he vowed to end it, promises he generally kept a day, perhaps two; by the third, he'd be missing her and feeling the itch to call. He would dial her number with the intent of breaking up, only to have his resolve melt at the sound of her voice. Face-to-face attempts proved no more successful. She would look at him, so open and trusting – she was a great gal, Penny, a real gem – and all he could think about was how much she was going to suffer and that she hadn't done anything wrong. Making love to her changed the equation. He had taken her virginity. Only a cad would use a girl in such a way and then dump her. Ted would never claim to be a perfect man, but he was not a cad. The lines governing morality and respectability were not, as he had been taught, clearly delineated, concrete and immutable. They were drawn in sand, vulnerable to changing winds, the movement of the tides and a myriad of other things beyond man's control. Some things in life could not be labelled right or wrong.

When he'd stolen the candy from DeWitt's, somebody – a neighbour or maybe old man DeWitt himself – had probably seen him do it. Wilsonville was so small everybody knew everybody else's business. Had he ever taken Darlene Bouchard for that metaphoric spin, word would have got back to Abigail in less than a day. But Abigail and Penny lived more than twenty miles apart and had no common friends or associations. There was no chance of either finding out about the other and, therefore, no chance that either would get hurt, so long as he took care not to mix the worlds, and he did. Scrupulous care. Apart from the first time, in her little bed, Ted never thought of Abigail when he was with Penny; likewise, when he entered the house in Elm Grove, Penny disappeared into a back closet of his brain.

A double life was remarkably simple to maintain. Abigail's universe was Elm Grove and school, Shoppers' World and north to Wilsonville. Penny's was Boston and south to see her mother on Cape Cod ('down the Cape,' as she charmingly said). They didn't just move in different circles, they occupied wholly independent worlds.

As the threat of discovery receded, so, too, did the guilt. Spring gave way to summer and his life became an amusement park ride, full of thrills but no real danger. In the mornings he rose eagerly from bed, knowing that each new day would bring moments that left him breathless. He walked taller. His jaw seemed squarer, more pronounced. There was a glint in his eye that hadn't been there before. No man, he was certain, had ever felt like this.

At home he was a doting father and a caring husband, so proud of Abigail's A in history that he bragged about it at cocktail parties and pinned it on the refrigerator.

Time with Penny was the treat for which he laboured all the other days of the week. He could not bring himself to call it an affair. Affairs were vulgar and indecent. What he and Penny had was deep and meaningful; it transcended everyday life. They connected on a level most people only dreamed about. She was a special soul; he was addicted to her smile, to the way she hung on his every word, to the gentle sway of her body beneath the palm of his hand when they walked together side by side. He was addicted to the man he was when he was with her. Penny's Ted was a true romantic, the kind of guy who called his girl up to let her know he was counting the minutes until they were together again, the kind of guy who bought a book of postcards of the city where he worked and sent her one every day, with a line from a love song scribbled on the back.

The kind of guy who never signed the cards because he didn't need to.

The Goodyear Tyre store in Lynn, Massachusetts, was a ten-thousand-square-foot glass and metal cube, harshly lit with fluorescent ceiling rods; the name, Goodyear, writ large across its storefront. Built to specifications handed down by the head office in Akron, Ohio, the design was supposed to look space-age in suburban shopping mall parking lots, and to shine like a beacon of modernity beside superhighways. In downtown Lynn, however, dwarfed on all sides by nineteenth-century red-brick shoe factories, it appeared not so much modern as small and breakable.

146

From his tiny office tucked into one corner of the sales department, a glass box within the box, Ted daydreamed about Penny sitting on his lap to take his mind off quarterly sales figures that showed none of the revenue gains he'd assumed would flow naturally from his appointment as store manager. Improving sales at the Lynn store was going to be harder than he thought. He'd implemented techniques learned from Curtis, things such as keeping the door to his office open except during meetings.

'An open door,' Curtis liked to say, 'tells your team that you're always ready to listen, and also, that you're always listening.'

Ted's door was open now, but a fat lot of good it was doing. Jack Bernardi had his feet up on his desk. Louie Delucci, who as assistant manager ought to be setting an example, was working on his stand-up gig, slowly unspooling his favourite joke about a drunk in South Boston during Holy Week. And Al Harris, still acting like the new dog on the sled team despite three months on the job, wore a polite smile as he pretended to be entertained by a joke he must have heard Louie tell at least three times. With nearly two hours left until closing, the only one doing any actual work was Sally, the secretary, pecking steadily at her typewriter.

Ted pushed up from his chair and walked the two steps into the frame of his office door, quietly satisfied with the way he filled it.

'Don't any of you fellas have work to do?' he called.

Al jumped in his seat and began purposelessly shifting papers around on his desk, but neither Jack nor Louie flinched.

'Showroom's empty, boss,' Jack said.

'What about paperwork? Did you get the details about the Hendrick's deal over to Sally?'

'I just closed it this morning. What's the rush?'

Jesus, if that didn't typify what the men at corporate said about this store: lazy foot-draggers.

'Get it done,' he barked.

'Right-o, boss,' said Jack, removing his feet from the desk.

Ted turned to Louie. 'What about you?'

'Sally's typing up my orders now. Aren't you, Sal?' He gave her a wink.

'What about the old lady I saw you talking to just before lunch?'

'Mrs Lacey?'

'The one with the Lincoln, asking about winter tyres.'

'Yeah, that's Mrs Lacey. I gave her the whole spiel. She says she'll think about it and get back to me.'

'Did you take her number?'

'She said she'd be back.'

'How many times do I have to tell you guys? Take the phone numbers so you can follow up. You're letting potential sales slip through your fingers.'

'I'll follow up.'

'How are you going to do that when you don't have her number?'

'I'll look it up. I'm telling you right now, though, she's not going to appreciate me being pushy. Diamond District people don't take kindly to the hard sell.'

'It's not the hard sell if you do it right.'

'Okay, boss, I promise. If she doesn't come back here in a week or so, I'll give her a call. Listen, if you don't mind, I gotta push off a couple minutes early today. I got a package to send and the post office closes at six.'

'What a shame; we close at six, too.'

'Yeah, but it's for my kid brother, Joey, the one in the service.'

'Why didn't you send it at lunchtime?'

'I forgot. I've got to get it off today, though. His birthday's coming up and it takes weeks to get there – out in Okinawa.'

'Have a heart, boss. It's Louie's kid brother, Joey. Besides, nobody's going to come in now, are they?' Jack said.

These guys had been selling tyres in this store for more than a dozen years. Ted thought back to what he'd been doing twelve years ago. He was in dance class in the Wilsonville Town House, trying to get partnered with Abigail Hatch.

What if he was still here twelve years from now? Still driving half an hour each way between Elm Grove and this sorry industrial city every day? He'd be thirty-six: middle-aged. By then there'd be no point changing jobs. He'd be stuck here for another thirty years. The thought terrified him.

Jack or Louie didn't seem bothered, just as they didn't care whether they sold one set of tyres a week or thirty. Both had fought as teenagers in the Second World War. Jack marched across Europe with Patton and Louie hopped islands in the Pacific. Brave stuff. They had nothing to prove. Ted envied them that. If he had one regret about having grown up in the peace and prosperity of the past twenty-five years, it was that it had deprived his own generation of an overarching struggle against which to define itself. His father's had had the Great Depression; Jack and Louie's had made the world safe for democracy. The wars since, Korea and now this thing in Vietnam, were too small to matter much. The prospect of thermo-nuclear war was a challenge, to be sure, but one that, by its very nature, would be short. Nothing much an individual could do about it.

He let Louie go. His personal lack of military service rendered him powerless to impede a veteran's plans to do something nice for a kid brother stationed in Japan. He kept the others there right until the end, though, and declined Jack's invitation to join him for a few cold ones at Arno's, despite Curtis's teaching that such moments were important for fostering a casual rapport between manager and salesmen. He was steamed.

He'd expected some resistance to his leadership. Louie, he figured, would be sore not to have been named manager. But resistance wasn't the problem. These guys lacked ambition: Lynn boys, born and bred, just like the mechanics who worked out back. Aside from Ted, the only one who didn't live within walking distance of the store was Al, who probably had the most potential of the three, but needed a lot of hand-holding. He never would have believed it, but he missed Hank Burns. How was he going to turn the place around with this cast of clowns? The best thing would be to fire them and start anew. They'd been around too long for that, though. Besides, what with them being locals, the store might find itself on the receiving end of community resentment, which certainly wouldn't push sales numbers northward.

America was booming, but the city of Lynn simply wasn't. Its greatness was in the past – one of America's first truly industrial cities, a centre of shoe manufacturing since the late 1600s. There were still plenty of brick factories clogging up the downtown area, crowding out the sea view, but the industry was under pressure from overseas competition. Despite the jobs the GE jet-engine plant had brought in, the city's population was shrinking. Those with the best jobs, engineers at GE and the directors of the shoe factories, were doing the same as Ted: living in suburban communities west of Boston and commuting in. Lynn's housing stock was all wrong for modern times: big and draughty shingled Victorian-era mansions out on Lynn Shore Drive and tenements and three-deckers over in the Brickyard. The latter was close to the shops and factories so people had little need for a car, which was just as well since they had little means to buy one, and even less space to park one. It was a world away from the car ports and double garages belonging to the families that made up his bread and butter clients at Curtis's store. Crime had risen sharply and the city's reputation was well summed up in the popular North Shore ditty:

> Lynn, Lynn
> The city of sin.
> You'll never come out
> The way you went in
> What looks like gold
> Is really tin
> The girls say 'no'
> But they'll give in.
> Lynn, Lynn
> The city of sin.

Chapter Twenty-One

Abigail could just as easily swing past Becky's on her way back from the college, but she preferred to go home first, drop off her books, and collect Mindy on foot. The short walk helped to clear her head of French verb tenses and trigonometry formulae, and readjust her thoughts on to a domestic plane. No one had forced her to take two courses over the summer. On the contrary, Professor Crocker had said it would be fine to wait until September, but Abigail insisted, fearing he would change his mind and find someone else to be his research assistant. A few summer courses would prepare her for the jump to a full course-load in the fall, and get a few distribution requirements out of the way at the same time. Having made the decision to return to school, she was impatient to make up for lost time. The girls with whom she had started college – those, at least, who hadn't dropped out either to marry or have babies (a fair few, admittedly) – had graduated this past June.

As she approached the Johnsons' Charmer, she heard young voices making truck noises: the rumble of engines, shifting gears and the squeak of hydraulic lifts.

'Knock, knock,' she called.

'Come on in.'

Mindy and Joe were driving Joe's collection of bright yellow bulldozers, excavators and dump trucks through piles of oatmeal on the kitchen table, ploughing paths through it, scooping it up and moving it.

'It makes a mess but it keeps them busy. They've been at it since you left,' Becky said.

'I'm not surprised. I want to play.'

'Coffee?'

'Love some.'

Abigail withdrew a white envelope from her purse and set it on the counter where Becky could casually sweep it up and tuck it into the back of a cupboard. They were like spies exchanging secret documents. At first, Becky had refused to take money for looking after Mindy – as if watching an eighteen-month old for three hours, twice a week were one of those things that neighbours did for one another. But Abigail had pressed her to agree to a sum. She hated being beholden to anyone and most especially dreaded the prospect of having to reciprocate. The discussion was brief and, once concluded, never revisited. Neighbours trading services for money is always a delicate thing. In a place as homogenous as Elm Grove, small differences in status got magnified and there was lots of potential for wounded pride. Abigail didn't even know whether Becky had told Rob about their arrangement. Judging from how far back in the cupboard she stashed the envelopes, Abigail rather doubted it. Silence suited her just fine.

'I'm amazed at the ways you think up to keep the children occupied.'

'It's the teaching, I guess.'

Becky often found a way to mention her teaching.

'You must miss it.'

'I do,' she said, with feeling. 'Not that I don't love being a mother. But I was a good teacher. I know I'm not supposed to say so, but I was.' Her face lit up and then dimmed. 'Sometimes I think I would have been better off not knowing how much I liked it.'

'You can always go back. Not now, of course, but when Joe is older. He'll be in school in a couple years.'

Becky shook her head. 'Rob would never approve. He didn't like me teaching after we married. He worries people will think he doesn't earn enough to support us.'

'Well, that's just silly. He's a school teacher. His salary is public information.'

Becky smiled. 'Lots of gals would say Rob was being silly, but only you, Abigail, would cite that as the reason.'

'It's perfectly logical.'

'Since when is there anything logical about male pride? I'll bet Ted hates that you're back at school.'

'Not at all.'

'Won't it bother him if you're more educated?'

'I've always been more educated than Ted.'

'I believe that,' Becky said with a laugh. 'You're a lucky gal.'

It felt nice to speak freely without worrying that it would be taken the wrong way.

'Is it really true? About Rob's salary being public information?'

'Of course. It's listed in the town accounts just like the salary of the fire chief, and the men who work for the DPW.'

'When did they pass that law?'

Abigail tried to hide her disappointment that the person she liked best in all of Elm Grove, the person who was the closest thing she had to a friend, knew so little about local government.

'It's always been that way.'

Becky bristled. 'It seems so un-American.'

'On the contrary. We provide the taxes that pay their salaries. We have a right, I might even say an obligation, to see that our money is spent wisely.' Her voice was rising together with her passions. She paused to clear her throat and, she hoped, recalibrate her tone to something less strident. 'How can we do that if we don't know what things cost?'

'I guess I never thought about that,' Becky said. 'But don't people have a right to privacy?'

She had to resist the urge to cluck her tongue. Ignorance like that was fine in a dictatorship. They probably gave medals for it over in Communist Russia, but an educated population was the cornerstone of a good functioning democracy.

'Rob gave up the right to keep his salary a secret when he decided to work for the town.'

Becky shook her head. 'I always learn something from you. But here's something I suspect you don't know.' She lowered her voice. 'Something scandalous.'

She made a show of looking at her watch and gasped with faux alarm.

'My gosh! It's time for *Bozo the Clown*!'

Joe dropped his truck as if it were a hot brick and ran to the living room, calling, 'Yeeeaaaaayyyyy.' Mindy followed behind, swept up in the moment. When the television blared, Becky resumed in a low tone.

'You know how I hate to gossip, but' – she raised her eyebrows suggestively – 'the Golds are on the rocks.'

'What happened?' Abigail asked, secretly unsurprised. Living with Janice couldn't be easy.

'He's been having an affair. With his secretary.'

Abigail didn't think she was the kind of woman who enjoyed gawking at other people's dirty laundry but, undeniably, the news lit a spark within her. Affairs with secretaries were the stuff of dime store novels, high society scandals and the soap operas her mother listened to on the radio when Daddy was at work. It seemed incredible that a man she knew personally, a neighbour, would be engaging in one, especially Stan, with his paunch and thinning hair. 'No!'

'It's true.' Becky's eyes gleamed. 'Janice was over at Jeannie's the other day, crying her eyes out, poor thing. From what I gather . . .' She cut her voice and mouthed the final words: 'He's thinking of leaving.'

Abigail gasped. 'The children!'

Becky nodded, solemnly.

The Golds' daughter couldn't be more than nine and little Billy wasn't even in kindergarten.

Chapter Twenty-Two

This year's Elm Grove Fourth of July festivities were under the direction of Carol Innes. She had promised to get a programme of events and a list of tasks and responsibilities out to the neighbourhood a week in advance, but then, on the last day of school, eight-year-old Ben broke his arm climbing the backstop at the ball park. Between worrying about damage to Ben's growth plate and making sure he didn't get the cast wet, she had lost track of time. Her husband, Art, ended up running around the neighbourhood with the overdue documents and apologies, in the sultry hours of the early evening of the 2nd.

The McDougalls were in the kitchen. They had just finished dinner and the sun shining through the partially drawn shades gave everything a golden aura. Abigail was wrapping the leftovers; Ted reading the paper. Over by the window, Mindy was repeating her name into an electric fan to hear the vibrato. Abigail studied the three-paged mimeographed brochures, replete with drawings of shooting stars, exploding fireworks and a crude depiction of Old Glory flapping in the wind.

'There's going to be a bicycle parade down Americana Boulevard in the morning,' she announced. 'With Uncle Sam.'

'That'll be Jenks, I bet,' Ted said. 'I'll pull Mindy in her wagon. She'll love it.'

'And a potato sack race,' Abigail said, 'and three-legged race and wheelbarrow race.'

Ted stood and read over her shoulder, 'Egg cup race, ring toss, horseshoes . . . and fireworks at night, jeez.'

'It's going to be a long day.'

'What'd they put us down for?'

Abigail turned the pages for their name. 'Tonic and hotdog and hamburger buns,' she read, stunned. She let the paper flutter to the floor in disgust.

'You look upset.'

'I am.'

'Don't know why,' said Ted. 'Seems like you lucked out.'

'I told them I'd bake a pie.'

'Saves you from slaving over a hot stove in this heat.'

'Miiinnnnddyyyyyy.'

'Even Carol is making something. And she's been dealing with a medical emergency.'

'So make a pie.'

'Miiiiiiindyyyyyyyyyyyyyyyyy.'

'I can't now. Obviously. Stop, Mindy.'

She dreaded the thought of spending all day with these people who obviously mocked her behind her back. 'Do we have to go, Ted?' she said. 'Can't we just drive up to the lake, spend the holiday with my parents?'

'Yyyyyyyyyyyyy. YYyyyyyyyyyy. Mmi . . .'

'That's enough, Mindy McDoo,' she snapped.

'Of course we have to go, honey. It's a neighbourhood tradition.'

'Tradition?' she scoffed. 'This place was home to nobody but cows five years ago.'

Ted volunteered to go to the grocery store but Abigail would not hear of it, even though she had a vocabulary list and some exercises on the homonyms *on* and *en* to prepare for tomorrow's French lesson. It was bad enough that she couldn't bake; how pathetic would it be if she couldn't shop? On the drive over, warm air blew in through the open windows, spinning her hair into a rat's nest while doing little to shift the trapped heat. At least the store would be air-conditioned.

The place was a zoo. Everybody, it seemed, had decided to do their holiday food shopping at the same time. She had to park at the opposite end of Shoppers' World and walk across the sun-baked lot, the tops of her thighs rubbing irritatingly together with every stride. The coolness of the store took a momentary edge off her frustration, but then the grocery cart she got had a wayward front wheel that rattled and turned and required constant attention to be made to go in the desired direction. Steering the uncooperative cart in such a crowded store meant that by the time she arrived in the bread aisle, her knuckles were white. She grabbed a pack of hamburger buns and threw it into the basket. And then another, with more force, and another. One for Carol Innes, one for the Culture Club, one for her lousy baking skills, one for the damn, stinking heat.

'Why hello, stranger.'

She looked up and saw Maude Hale approaching in a blousy chiffon skirt and a tight, low-cut top. Straight off, Abigail could tell she'd been drinking.

'Oh, hello, Maude. How have you been?'

'As if you care.' Maude took a tottering step back on red kitten heels and grabbed hold of her carriage to steady herself. She stared at Abigail with glassy eyes.

Abigail blushed. It had been eight months since the Hales had had them to dinner and they had yet to reciprocate. 'Of course I care, Maude. Don't be silly. We've been meaning to have you over. I've had a lot of school work and Ted's busy learning the ropes at the Lynn store.'

'That's okay. I don't care about you, either.' Her head bobbed downward, toward Abigail's cart. 'That's a lot of buns.'

Too many. She'd lost track of how many she was supposed to buy. Well, too bad; she was damned if she'd start putting them back now. She smiled. 'Neighbourhood party.'

Maude nodded. 'Don't you just hate the Fourth of July? All that phoniness: "Great to see you!"; "Isn't this fun!"' She began twirling her hands the way she'd done at dinner. 'Smiling when the creepy guy from down the street gropes you when what you really want to do is kick him in the nuts.'

Abigail's eyes widened in shock, and then she recalled Paul Jenks playing Santa Claus at the neighbourhood Christmas party, beckoning every lady in Elm Grove to come sit on his lap.

'And the food,' Maude continued. 'I swear, if I have to make another God-damned red, white and blue gelatine I'm going to go out of my fucking mind. God Fuck America.'

Passing shoppers shot alarmed looks at Abigail, as if she were responsible for Maude's crude language.

'So nice running into you,' Abigail said, taking a step back.

'The fireworks,' Maude continued, with an exaggerated roll of her dull eyes. 'Every man's projection of his own dick. Bang!' She tottered again, and had to grab hold of her cart for balance. 'Kerpow!'

Laughter swelled in Abigail's chest. It tickled her throat and stung her eyes and she knew that the harder she tried to keep it in, the harder it would fight to get out. She pursed her lips together and swung the cart around, pulling extra hard to overcome the wayward wheel and only just avoided ramming it into an elderly lady, 'Oh, I beg your pardon,' she said, struggling not to smile. When the elderly lady looked at her with disdain, Abigail's shoulders began to convulse.

'See you again soon, Maude,' she called, her voice warbling with repressed laughter as she hurried around the corner and down the frozen food aisle, intent on getting as far away as possible before the fit of giggles overtook her. Maude really was too much. To think that vacant-eyed mess of a woman was once editor of a college newspaper! Abigail tried to picture a young, unbloated Maude, juggling a staff of reporters and photographers, writing editorials and meeting deadlines. She remembered the pills Ted said rendered Maude 'calm as a kitten' and the urge to laugh vanished; when a shiver ran down her spine, she knew it was only partially due to the cold emanating from the open freezers.

Chapter Twenty-Three

Penny invited Ted to bring Mindy down to her mother's house on Cape Cod for the Fourth of July.

'We'll have a barbecue on the beach and in the evening there's a big fireworks display. They light them off a barge. The view is fantastic.'

'I wish I could, sweet pea,' he said. 'Unfortunately, I already agreed to take Mindy to see her grandparents in New Hampshire.'

'Come the next weekend, then,' she said.

He accepted without hesitation, and not just because her mother happened to live on Cape Cod. That was swell, but his primary reason for saying yes was to make Penny happy. There was no chance of hanky-panky. Penny's mother would be there, and he'd be sleeping on the parlour sofa. All the same, it required the invention of a regional meeting for new store managers down in Rhode Island. It was the first outright lie he told his wife and it turned his stomach sour. The pains grew particularly acute on Saturday morning as he prepared to leave the house.

'It's awfully mean to make you work Saturday night,' Abigail said, handing him the bag he'd packed with casual shirts and his swimming trunks.

He muttered something about scheduling difficulties and staggered to his car. All the way down the old post road it felt as if a knife were twisting in his gut. But the bellyache eased a little with every mile he put between himself and Elm Grove. By the time he arrived at work it was a bit of intestinal gas, expelled with a fart. Leaving work early that afternoon, he felt only childish excitement. He was going to the Cape: land of warm breezes and melodic, rolling surf. The weather was postcard perfect. He rode with the top down, his sunglasses reflecting the glare. Traffic was lighter than he expected and he made a speedy job of the Southeast Expressway through Boston, rolled past Dorchester toward Milton, where Route 1 became Route 3, the Pilgrims Highway. At Braintree, he confidently navigated the confluence of traffic brought on by the merger of Route 3 and I-93 South – a place, he had heard, that others found confusing – and from here it was a clear shot. A little beyond Weymouth, he pulled off for gas. A pimply teenage attendant in desperate need of a haircut came to fill the tank.

'Can I wash the windows for you, sir?' the kid asked, ogling the car with eyes as big as hubcaps.

'That'd be fine.'

'Check the oil for you?'

'Sure, that'd be swell.'

'How's she run?'

Ted smiled. 'Like a dream.'

The kid's restraint broke and a torrent of words rushed from his mouth as he darted around the car: questions about acceleration rates, suspension and handling, and how Ted managed to keep the car so shiny and clean; compliments on Ted's choice of red and of the convertible Monza over the hardtop. The bill came to two thirty-five. Ted threw the kid a five.

'Keep the change, son,' he said, lowering his glasses so that the boy could see him wink. 'Put it toward your own Corvair.' He gave the engine an extra rev as he returned to the highway.

The radio was playing 'Hang on Sloopy'; the sun warmed his head and shoulders. He put his foot on the accelerator and turned the radio up, humming along to 'Sloopy' and all the tunes that followed. Much too soon, he began searching the horizon for the Sagamore Bridge, one of the pair of steel and concrete rainbows that straddle the Cape Cod Canal. He felt like he was eight years old again, trading punches with Danny in the back seat to release his excitement. 'Are we there yet?' It was ages until the bridge appeared on the horizon. There was a little congestion at the rotary. He waited patiently. No point trying to sneak in or be aggressive. He slid into the line of cars coming up in the outside lane. Just as they reached the summit, a pick-up truck that had been chugging along ahead of him moved into the right lane, leaving the road wide open. Only one word described the view: magnificent. The water in the canal sparkled bluey-black. Visibility was clear, right out to Cape Cod Bay, a couple of miles off. The Cape was the first American soil the Pilgrims had touched, and fittingly so because the peninsula was an amalgamation of the entire continent, an arm-shaped jumble of rocks and earth left behind when the glaciers receded during the last ice age. His father used to say it was the New World shaking its angry fist at corrupt Europe. He headed down Route 6, the Mid-Cape, the central artery that went all the way to the very tip, though he'd only be taking it as far as the elbow.

He took the exit and headed straight for the town where Penny's mother lived. Architecturally it was a mix of Capes and Colonials, a white clapboard Congregational church, red-brick school and town hall, and a library built in the Greek revival style – same as Wilsonville, and yet somehow different. Maybe it was the pine trees, smaller than at home, and gnarled, or perhaps the sandiness of the ground? The saltiness of the air? Penny's mother's house was on a road near the centre of town, a neat white Cape with a small L extending out the back.

Penny must have been listening for his car because she came out to meet him as he turned into the driveway.

'You didn't bring Mindy?' she asked.

She was wearing a top he didn't recognise, a halter in an outrageously bright Indian print of orange, saffron and pink. The sight of her made his gut ache.

'She's got the sniffles,' he said. 'Must have picked something up at the lake.'

'Oh,' Penny said, looking down.

'You look fantastic,' he said as he stepped out of the car. He wondered if she was wearing a bra. He suspected not.

'Why thank you, Ted.'

He leaned in to kiss her cheek, letting a hand rest on her bare back. Nope, definitely not wearing a bra. 'New top?'

She nodded.

'Something you made yourself?' He slid his hand over until his fingertips touched the hem.

She tilted her head and smiled. 'How did you know?'

'It looks too good to come from a shop.' His fingertips caressed the fabric's edge. It would be so easy to slide his hands inside.

She took his other arm and squeezed it. 'You sure know how to flatter a girl, Edward McDougall. I'll bet you're hungry from the drive.'

'Famished,' he admitted.

He noticed the child's beach pail and shovel just inside the kitchen door. Penny introduced him to her mother.

'Where's the child?' Rose Goodwin asked.

'She's caught a cold,' Penny said.

'Nothing like salt water for a cold,' Rose said. 'Clears the nose.'

'I didn't want to risk it,' Ted said. 'I'm a bit of a mother hen, I'm afraid.'

Penny's mother was a trim lady of middle age. To look at her was to understand where Penny had got her sense of style. She laughed easily, while displaying an intellect that said she was nobody's fool. Ted liked her instantly. In anticipation of his arrival, Penny had set out chicken salad with home-made mayonnaise (Ted didn't know such a thing even existed) and tarragon fresh from the garden. There was coleslaw and freshly baked rolls that were toasted on the outside, airy on the inside. Mother and daughter begged him to eat as much as he liked. They asked what else they could give him: salt and pepper, pickles, sliced tomatoes? And beamed when he took more, four sandwiches in all – they were small – and two portions of coleslaw, washed down with cold beer.

After he had eaten his fill, Penny threw a blanket and some towels into a canvas bag and they headed to the beach. Her blue and white striped swimsuit had a little skirt that made it both demure and sexy. The weather was gorgeous; his belly was full. He was stepping on to the sand, hand in hand with this beautiful, stylish woman. They walked the length of the beach, straight to the waterline to look out.

'My father did this every time we went to the beach,' he told her. 'He'd point to the horizon and declare that, out there, far across the water, lay Glasgow, "City of me birth," he would say. "And it's better on this side, aye,"' he bellowed, mimicking his father's brogue.

'You are the best storyteller I've ever met,' Penny said.

'Did I tell you about the time Danny ate the hermit crab? We were at the beach. He was about two, maybe – around Mindy's age, I guess – saw one crawling around, picked it up and popped it in his mouth. You should have seen the look on his face – he had the sweetest face, angelic – and those tiny claws wiggling out between his rosy lips.'

She laughed. 'I can picture it.'

'Hard to believe that kid is now telling pilots where to park their jets.' Whenever he spoke of Danny he'd get a picture in his mind's eye of him all grown up, standing on the airfield in his blues and flight cap, squinting into the sun. He spoke of him often.

'I'd love to meet him.'

'He'd love you.'

Ted dived into the surf. The coolness of the water made his scalp tingle and he let out an involuntary but still, he thought, quite manly, yawp. He felt alive, invigorated, and he gambolled about like a dolphin in the surf while Penny laughed from the blanket because she didn't like to go deeper than her ankles. He swam for a long time and then went to where she sat and shook all over her like a dog; she squealed as the cool droplets of water splattered on her sun-warmed skin.

For dinner Rose baked scrod and served it with silky mashed potatoes and green beans. Dessert was a flaming crêpe Suzette made by Penny.

'*Les crêpes Suzette, ooh-la-la*,' he said.

'Do you speak French?' Rose asked.

'*Non, madame*,' he replied. 'Danny does, though. He speaks three languages fluently: French, Spanish and Dutch, I think, though maybe the third is German. He's the clever one. I'm the blockhead.'

'Ted is being modest, as always,' Penny said.

'And your daughter is being sweet, as always, Rose.'

'If you were a blockhead, the CIA wouldn't have sent you to Vietnam.'

'Penny, please,' he said, lowering his voice to just above a whisper. 'It's not something we talk about.'

Rose's eyes flickered with interest.

'You were a spy?'

'I, I couldn't possibly comment, ma'am. Officially, I mean.'

'Johnson's right. We've got to take the fight to the Commies,' Rose said, punching the air with her fists. 'Cut this snake off at the head. How long were you there?'

'Not long. My – uh – skin reacted to the swamp water and so they sent me home, thus ending my glamorous life as a spook.'

'What's it like?'

'Exotic.' He described a jungle of unfathomable verdant darkness in which snakes hid in trees and gracious, humble people lived with quiet dignity in heart-breaking poverty.

'Sounds romantic,' Penny said.

'It might have been,' he said with a chuckle. 'If not for the Viet Cong lurking in the darkness, waiting for a chance to slit my throat.'

'Ah, but when you know you could be dead tomorrow, that's

when you're really living, aren't you?' Rose said. 'It was like that for a time, right after Pearl Harbor. There is nothing more exciting.'

'Yes,' Ted said. 'You're right there.'

Rose went to the kitchen and came back with a bottle and a pair of glasses.

Penny beamed. 'She likes you, Ted. She doesn't bring the whiskey out for just anybody.'

'Ice?'

'Please.'

'You're my kind of man.'

She told stories about working in the armaments industry during the war, the parties and the dances. When she went to bed, Penny took him for a barefoot walk on the beach. The stars were bright in the dark night sky. In a secluded place between the beach plum bushes, his hands slipped inside her halter top and his body slipped into euphoria. The next thing he knew they were making love, his toes digging into the cool, luminescent sand. Afterward, lying on their backs staring at the stars and the small sliver of a moon, he whispered to her his dreams of a little cottage, right on the water and the small sailboat that they could pull up on to the shore in the evenings and push straight into the water the following morning; and how Mindy and perhaps, someday, her brothers and sisters, would grow up with hair and skin golden from summers in the sun.

'Not all with golden hair,' she said. 'Surely there'll be at least one brunette in the bunch.'

The living room sofa that Penny made up for him wasn't built for sleeping – an old-fashioned mission style, with cushions sitting in a wooden frame. The bottom cushions kept sliding apart; the back ones tipped forward on top of him. He didn't care. He wasn't tired. A parade of snapshots from the day's events flickered in his mind's eye, each one more lovely than the last: chicken salad with tarragon, Rose pouring the whiskey, telling him, 'You're my kind of man,' the coolness of the sand and, most especially, the soft warmth of Penny. His body hummed with the memory of hers, and the knowledge that she lay no more than ten feet away, separated from him by only a thin door. He imagined her tucked into her childhood bed, dreaming of him.

He slept lightly and was fully alert the instant she lifted the latch on her door early the next morning. They tiptoed out to the garage for buckets and shovels and headed to the tidal mudflats. In a floppy canvas hat and pedal pushers turned up to reveal a pair of slender calves, she showed him how to spot a clam's tiny air holes in the fine wet sand, and to dig quickly before they burrowed deeper. They collected two bucketfuls. Penny and her mother steamed the small ones, and shucked and minced the larger ones for chowder made with diced potatoes with the skins left on, chunks of salt pork, onions and clams in a milky broth that they ate with crunchy oyster crackers and cracked black pepper. It was the most delectable thing he had ever tasted, a world away from canned.

'Come again,' Rose said as he and Penny prepared to leave. 'I have a friend who keeps pots. We'll do a lobster bake. And bring that little girl of yours.'

They rode home with the top down, his hand resting on the inside of her thigh.

Penny went from being the highlight of his life to the centre of it. He'd rearrange his schedule to meet her for lunch at Coletti's, where they shared plates of spaghetti and meatballs the size of tennis balls (and afterward, garlicky kisses). He'd leave the office a few minutes early and drive to her apartment to sit on the porch with Mrs Rizzo, sipping iced tea, watching Penny walk up the sidewalk at the end of the work day. He invented end-of-week store-manager meetings so he could take her for romantic dinners in the city. For every hour of work he skipped, he vowed to work two later.

Even though the mere thought of Penny was enough to get his body buzzing with desire, he never took her out with an express idea, let alone a plan, of ending up in her pants and each time it happened he was surprised anew. They were moments when opportunity and need entwined: in the apartment, when her roommates were out, and once, memorably, in his car at the end of a desolate road. Each one was a gift that came, if not from God, then from some higher, erotic spirit that filled them with urgency and banished modesty into a far corner and he felt those times to be sacred. There was a sound she made when she released herself to him, a sort of moan, soft and low. He would open his eyes to see her face altered by delirium. *She likes this*, he'd think, gratified. *She wants this as much as I do*. It had been naïve to believe he could keep things from getting out of hand. Undeniably, he loved her, loved the man he was when he was with her: brave widower, college football scholarship winner, rising star of tyre sales. He hadn't planned it; he hadn't seen it coming. It was simply stronger than he, or any mortal, could fight.

He'd conducted a careful, exhaustive study of Penny's character and could not find a single fault. She was beautiful, sexy and supportive, a clever seamstress and an excellent cook, and so thoughtful! Hardly a week went by that she didn't give him some little gift for Mindy – a hair bow, a tiny stuffed Scottie dog, a pair of ankle socks with frilly lace – gifts that were promptly disposed of, though never without regret. No detail about Mindy was too trivial to hold Penny's attention and like any proud father (and storyteller), Ted was happy to regale her with tales of her progress from walking to running, climbing and jumping, and lists of words recently added to her vocabulary – cup, shoe, book – though somehow avoiding mention of her current favourite: study.

Chapter Twenty-Four

'Mommy duddy.'

'Yes, Mindy, Mommy has to study.'

In the back of the station wagon, Mindy nodded in agreement, brows furrowed thoughtfully.

'We are taking a short trip to school to pick up some papers from Professor Crocker and then to the grocery store for food, and then, after we do all those things, we can go home and you can play in the paddle pool.'

She hoped that Mindy wouldn't hold her to the last bit. There wasn't time. Ted had no clean work shirts; they were out of eggs and bread and even toilet paper. She had no idea what to make for dinner, except that it ought not to be hotdogs. They'd eaten far too many hotdogs this summer, with sweet pickles and potato salad from the supermarket deli because it was nicer than macaroni and cheese in hot weather. Cooking this summer had been all about ease. She had sat her final French exam on Monday and the one for trigonometry yesterday. For the first time in weeks, there were no assignments to prepare, no quizzes looming on the horizon and her plan had always been to devote the next two days to catching up on all the housework, to making the Enchantress enchanting, before they left on vacation. This job David wanted her to do – some notes that needed transcribing – was only a tiny wrench in the wheels. So long as she started right away, she'd have both the notes and the housework complete before they left on Saturday morning. Of course, she couldn't do that if Mindy was in the paddle pool. But how could she say no to David? And anyway, Mindy had all next week to paddle and swim.

The rhythm and habits that had previously made Abigail an excellent student had returned quickly. When engaged in her lessons and working with David, she felt alive, brimming with untapped energy, able to work long hours without fatigue. But those hours had to be drawn from the same twenty-four allocated to each day and the deleterious effect it had on her homemaking was impossible to deny. This was a source of irritation, like an eyelash stuck somewhere in the back of the eye and the really shameful thing was that Mindy often bore the brunt of her frustrations; at times, even Ted did, and this concerned her as she looked toward the fall semester. If two courses upset her schedule this much, how would she cope with four? Paradoxically, this was yet another argument in favour of saying yes to David today: she'd have to do the work eventually, anyway; better to do it now than when she went full-time.

Her mother said it was foolish to stretch herself so thin. 'Get a housekeeper and be done with it,' she said.

But Abigail resisted adding such an expense to their household budget. Much as she disliked housework (detested it, in fact), she accepted that it was her responsibility. Moreover, it was something she felt *ought* to be within her ability. Hiring a housekeeper was like admitting defeat. None of the other ladies in Elm Grove had housekeepers. They might think she was putting on airs. Ted's support of her going back to school – in not just words but deeds – only made her more determined to do the rest of the work herself. If he could pitch in with the dishes and the folding of laundry while learning how to be a store manager, how could she refuse to do her part?

A week spent rowing around in the little boat, playing horseshoes, picnics and, maybe, possibly, a late night skinny-dip, would put everything right. In New Hampshire she breathed better; she slept better. It didn't hurt that going away over the Labor Day weekend meant missing one of those horrid neighbourhood parties. Ted needed this vacation as much as she did. She wondered whether he had known before he took the manager's job, how many extra hours it would entail. She worried he was wearing himself out with all that driving to and fro, even on Sundays, sometimes, to catch up on paperwork when the store was closed. He hadn't visited Wilsonville since early spring; hadn't been to a Sunday dinner at his own mother's since late June, though she and Mindy generally went. It seemed like a great deal more work in exchange for about the same amount of pay – a transitional situation, she hoped, same as hers with school. Once fully trained, he would be home more, and over time he would make deals, secure commissions and all the upheaval would be worthwhile.

'Well hello, there,' said the history department secretary. 'You've certainly got your hands full.'

'I'm sorry, Betty,' Abigail said, putting Mindy down but holding firmly to her hand to prevent her wandering off. 'I wouldn't have brought her; it's kind of last minute.'

'You look very pretty.'

'Oh, this?' Abigail said, glancing down at her new gingham dress.

'Your hair looks nice that way.'

Abigail put a hand to the French twist that had taken her twenty minutes to fix.

'Just, you know, to get it out of my eyes. Is Professor Crocker in?' Her voice lifted just a tad higher than normal.

David bounded out of his office. He was in need of a haircut. His short-sleeve shirt had sweat stains under the arms and a faded blue spot on the pocket where a pen must once have leaked.

'Abigail! I'm so glad you could make it,' he said, placing a jumble of loose papers and notebooks on to the secretary's desk. 'I'm sorry to dump this all on you. I'm taking the early bus to Philadelphia tomorrow and it would be marvellous if you could have these notes transcribed for when I get back in two weeks.'

Abigail picked up a notebook and thumbed through its pages, filled with his now familiar spiky, east-wind scrawl. There was no way such a job could be finished before she left for New Hampshire.

'Of course,' she said.

'Thanks, I knew I could count on you.'

She smiled. He was like a mutt – making up for his lack of beauty with earnest enthusiasm and good temper.

'Oh, and, by the way, excellent analysis of Bailyn's argument.'

'Makers of history are always stronger than makers of empire,' she said.

'Exactly.' He strode eagerly around to the front of the desk and almost bumped into Mindy.

'I'm sorry. I didn't realise you brought someone with you.'

'This is my daughter, Mindy,' Abigail said, swinging Mindy's arm. 'Mindy, this is Professor Crocker.'

David didn't tap her on the head as if she were a cat or a dog. He didn't pull her curls or call her 'princess' or 'little cutie'. He extended his hand as he would to a real person and said, 'Hello, Mindy. Pleased to meet you.'

Mindy pulled her thumb out of her mouth and gave him her soggy hand, smiling shyly.

'Let me carry these books to your car.'

Chapter Twenty-Five

Penny's mother's friend who kept lobster traps was having the best year he could remember. Every time he lifted a trap from the ocean floor, it seemed, lobsters were inside. The bounty exceeded the appetites of his extended family and network of friends (many of whom, it must be said, also kept traps). 'Not lobster again,' the kids and grandkids had begun to groan when they sat down to the table for Sunday dinner.

'Imagine,' Penny remarked to Ted, 'groaning because you have to eat lobster!'

It wasn't often that Penny had a story to tell. She tended to be more of a listener, uncomfortable demanding attention, but this was such a good story, and she was so confident that Ted would find the end worth the wait, that she wanted to draw it out for as long as possible by adding interesting but, strictly speaking, irrelevant details, such as how, already in July, the man's wife had grown bored of all the traditional ways of preparing lobster and started adding the meat to any dish she could think of: lobster potato fritters; lobster and rice casserole; lobster macaroni and cheese, lobster à la king, for goodness sake! And still the lobsters kept walking into the man's traps, faster than they could be eaten. The spare refrigerator in the basement was crawling with them.

'Literally, of course,' she said with a small laugh.

The man's family started coming up with excuses to dodge Sunday lunch. His wife – whose ability to pick a lobster carcass clean was the source of the family nickname 'the Seagull' – complained that she was beginning to hate it.

'"And if you make me hate lobster, Warren," she yelled,' Penny said, making her voice go gruff and craggy, '"so help me, your life won't be worth living!"'

Knowing that his wife wasn't bluffing, the man pulled all his traps out of the water, calling an early end to the season. But the problem of what to do with the lobsters in the fridge remained until, hearing this tale of woe over coffee and warm cinnamon rolls at Costa's Bakery yesterday morning, her mother had generously offered to take them all off his hands.

'She's having a clambake on the beach across from her house this Saturday. The works: boiled lobsters, steamers and chowder, baked potatoes, corn on the cob and linguica,' Penny said brightly, 'and she wants you to be her guest of honour.'

She waited for his eyes to light up, for his mouth to spread into a broad grin. Instead he winced.

'I have to go to New Hampshire Saturday,' he said. 'If only I'd known! I would have rescheduled.'

'There was no way of knowing,' she said, allowing sharpness to enter her voice. An image had taken hold in her mind, of them walking together on the beach just as the early evening sun painted everything pink-gold, of sneaky smiles exchanged when he realised they were only a stone's throw from the secluded spot among the beach plums, of leading him around the fire pit, introducing him to her mother's friends, and seeing those dry, stoic Yankee ladies reduced to giggling schoolgirls by her boyfriend's smile and charming, 'how do you dos', of being one half of a young couple in love. A late summer weekend was the perfect setting for a proposal and when that image, so clear an instant before, vanished, the shock was rude. 'Getting a refrigerator full of live lobsters isn't something a person plans.'

His body went limp with disappointment and she was sorry for having lashed out. It wasn't his fault that she would be spending yet another evening listening to her mother's friends' long-winded tales of their children's domestic bliss, a few perfunctory enquiries about her life as a 'single gal' tossed in before picking up where they left off.

'Come Sunday, then, for leftovers. Bring Mindy.'

He gave a grim little shake of the head. 'We'll be up there all week.'

A whole week? 'You didn't mention that.'

'Didn't I? I'm sorry,' he said.

Always Mindy. His fierce commitment to his daughter was one of the things she loved best about him, but right now she hated it and she hated herself for hating it because what was that hating, after all, but jealousy, and how could she be jealous of a little girl, a baby, really, who had lost her mother? She wanted to scream. Ted moved closer, tried to embrace her; she pushed him away.

'Come on, Penny, don't be sore. Mindy needs to see her grandparents.'

'But why do you have to go?' she cried, sounding like a baby herself. 'Can't you just drop her off with them?'

'I've been away a lot lately, what with getting to grips with the store and' – he paused before adding – 'everything,' and Penny understood that by 'everything' he meant the time he was spending with her and this made her madder still. 'She needs me, Penny.'

I need you, too, she wanted to say, but what came out was a churlish, 'Go then. What do I care?'

'Don't be like that.'

'We never spend holidays together,' she said, realising, as the tears started, that she had put her finger on the problem. He reached out for her. She resisted, at first, making him work hard for the privilege of comforting her. When eventually she relented he rocked her back and forth as if she were an infant, whispering soothing words about future holidays shared, of vacations to national parks and Disney World.

Chapter Twenty-Six

With the first flash of Penny's temper, the earth shifted below Ted's feet. How could he have been so blind? Penny would not consent to continuing for ever the way they were now. She was bound to get frustrated and restless and then she'd cut things off. And, make no mistake, a good-looking girl like Penny would not stay single for long. His perfect life was nothing more than a mirage. How much longer could it last? A year? A season? A month? Panic rose up within him. He wanted to race to her side, to make the most of every second. He could go to the lake any time; this might be his only chance to experience an authentic Cape Cod clambake. He blamed Abigail, which is why he felt within his rights to withdraw into himself on the drive north as Mindy sang the first verse of patty cake over and over in the back seat. He pretended not to hear her calling his name, waiting for her to repeat it four times before he looked her way.

The Hatches were waiting on the porch when they got to the lake. Linc had just checked his watch. His left arm was straightening at the elbow, his head turning back toward the water in a gesture that, to Ted, implied judgement. The old picnic table was set with a red and white checked cloth. The air was heavier and more oppressive than he expected, the sky was the colour of dirty dishwater.

'What are your plans?' Gretchen asked, spooning out chicken salad without fresh tarragon.

'I have some work I need to finish,' Abigail said.

'Work? On vacation?' Gretchen said. 'Nobody likes a greasy grind, dear.'

Ted muttered something about trying to do a little fishing. He couldn't bear to look at them.

'You really are a good sport, Ted, to put up with it,' Gretchen said.

'I hope you brought a book or two,' Linc said, pointing with his pipe to a bank of clouds far out over the Wapack Range. 'Looks like a storm rolling through this afternoon.'

'It'll hold off,' he replied, more to push back against his father-in-law's confidence than out of any certitude.

Linc drew a pouch of tobacco from the breast pocket of his jacket and filled the pipe.

'You think so, do you?' He put the pipe in his mouth and lit it. 'Hmm. For your sake, I hope you're right.'

The pipe whistled; a plume of fruit- and nut-flavoured smoke engulfed the table like a wreath. Ted had bought a pipe once. The habit didn't take. He preferred cigarettes.

The first, plump raindrops speckled the dirt drive as Linc and Gretchen headed homeward, Linc at the wheel of the Ford, smiling smugly, the hands of both lifting in unison to wave. Mindy cried. She wanted Grandma to stay and play. Abigail hauled the type-writer out and went to work directly, her fingers klack, klack, klacking on the keys, leaving Ted to play patty cake with an increasingly grumpy Mindy, who wouldn't sleep in an unfamiliar place while thunder echoed off the mountains, shaking windows. In the moist air, the fireplace stank of smoked hickory. He thought of Penny sitting around a fire at the beach, eating clam chowder and fresh lobster meat dipped in drawn butter. The kitchen counter was piled with zucchinis and summer squash from Gretchen's garden. Some were as big as baseball bats.

'We've got them coming out of our ears,' she had said.

On Cape Cod, people gave away lobsters. Here it was zucchinis.

*

The storm had cleared by first light, taking most of the humidity with it. They went out in the boat. He rowed while Mindy and Abigail sat in the stern; Mindy watched the water with fascination, trying to make sense of the boat's movement. Abigail let her hand dangle in the water. It was pleasant for about three minutes until Mindy got bored. Soon she was standing in the boat, pointing toward the cabin, saying, 'There! There!'

He had thought he would teach her to swim. She loved playing in the bath and in her inflatable pool, but she disliked the muddy sediment at the lake's edge, lifting one foot and then the other out of the muck, whining and looking at him expectantly. He lost patience and snapped at her, and then she cried and he carried her back to Abigail. It was hard not to be resentful; he felt quite let down by her.

In the mornings, Abigail got up early to hammer on her infernal machine. After breakfast they'd go out on the boat and then swim until lunchtime. In the afternoons, they'd hike around the lake and over the mountain trails. Abigail kept her hair in braids, wrapped around her head like a Swiss milkmaid. She wore old plaid cotton shirts with the sleeves rolled up, over a faded red bathing suit and cut-off blue jeans revealing legs made manly from years of hiking and skiing. He was slightly disturbed that he found them so alluring; moreover, it bothered him that she didn't think he was worth dressing up for.

When Mindy napped, Abigail went straight to the typewriter. To get away from the sound, he'd take the boat out. He'd row to the middle of the pond, pull in the oars, lie on his back and stare at the sky as his mind slowly retraced the perfection of Penny's body, recalling their lovemaking in precise, glorious detail. He whispered her name just to hear it spoken. He wondered what she'd been up to these past few days. Suddenly, rivals for her affections were all around: the men she worked with over in the insurance company, that red-haired punk, Peanut's cousin, what was his name? Or those guys in the bar who'd asked for her number the night they'd worn the blonde wigs, a stunt that, in retrospect, seemed more provocative than fun. No wonder Peanut was surprised that he hadn't minded. He did mind. In fact, he minded very much. He pictured her getting off with someone else, her body going loose the way it did with him. It was gutting, but also weirdly arousing, and he jerked off, spraying his jizz across the centre bench near the spot Linc normally occupied.

He tried to remember why he used to love it up here. There was nothing to do. A cabin at a New Hampshire lake couldn't compare to a house on Cape Cod. Forget television, even radio reception was fuzzy out here. Their only neighbours were on the other side of the lake. They came across them occasionally on the water; exchanged perfunctory greetings before paddling their separate ways. Evenings after dinner were the worst. If only there was a good jazz club somewhere, or a decent Chinese restaurant. Abigail typed and he took a beer out on the porch to sip while he looked at the stars and thought of Penny, wishing there were something that would tie her to him for ever.

Thursday night, Abigail cleared the remains of the hotdog and zucchini fritters. She put Mindy to bed and sat down at the typewriter. He didn't think he could stand more klacking.

'I'm running low on cigarettes,' he said. 'Need anything at Clauson's?'

'We could use some milk,' she said, waving him off, her head full of colonial Boston or was it revolutionary history? He could never remember.

He drove slowly down the long bumpy dirt road as the sun dipped below the trees. The days were noticeably shorter and though still warm, the sultriness was gone. The temperature was, in fact, as close to perfect as it could get. The night his father died had been like this. When he got out on to the highway he hit the gas, wishing he was in the Corvair. Trees banked the road on both sides for miles in every direction. The white lights of Clauson's were a cold artificial oasis carved into a dark forest: two gas pumps and a white clapboard building that served as a gas station, grocery store and post office. Ted bought the milk and the cigarettes and a fifth of Jack Daniels, paying with a ten. He asked that a dollar's worth of the change be in dimes and went to the payphone at the edge of the parking lot and called Penny.

Ellen answered. Penny wasn't home, she said. Something about her voice made him suspicious.

'Who is she with, Ellen?' he blurted out.

'She's with Peanut.'

It seemed to him that the response was too quick, that it must have been rehearsed. 'I've always been nice to you. We're friends. Please! I need to know what's going on.'

'Ted, I don't know what you're talking about. She's with Peanut. They went to see *The Sound of Music*.'

Why would Penny want to see the same movie they'd seen a week before?

'She liked it so much she wanted to see it again,' Ellen said, but Ted hadn't asked the question.

'Be straight with me, Ellen. There's another guy, isn't there?'

'No!'

'Does she love him?'

'Honestly, Ted, Penny would never two-time you.'

He hung up, embarrassed by his aggression and the desperation it revealed. He sipped from the bottle and took his frustrations out on the car and the unlit, winding, forested road. Every song on the radio reminded him of Penny: 'Hold What You Got', 'How Sweet It Is (To Be Loved by You)', even 'California Girls', which was stupid because Penny had never been to California. He had no reason to believe she was cheating on him. The realisation that he was destined to lose her one day had convinced him that the day was at hand. It ate him up inside to think that another man would have the privilege of enjoying her special chicken salad and clambakes on Cape Cod, of making love to her whenever he liked.

He skidded to a halt on the dirt drive and cut the engine,

179

surprised to hear only the sound of peepers calling and not Abigail's typewriter. He figured she'd gone to bed, but then he saw her outline on the porch, hugging her knees and staring at the night sky. He sat down beside her and offered her the whiskey. She took a swig.

'The stars are brighter out here.'

'Yes.'

'Do you remember the first time we came here?'

'Of course.'

It was their wedding night. The first whiff of cedar and damp still stirred the coltish excitement he'd felt when carrying her over the threshold.

'I was so nervous,' she said, looking toward the lake and smiling. 'Excited, but so nervous. I was afraid I was going to do it wrong.'

He chuckled. 'Me too.'

'We were pitiful.'

'I think you mean me.'

She gave a laugh that ended in a snort. 'I asked you whether it counted. Remember? Oh, God, that was me in a nutshell. Not, "was it good?" but "did it meet the scientific criteria?"'

She stood and put her hand out. 'Let's go for a swim.'

She started to unbutton her shirt. In the place where he expected to see her old bathing suit there was only pale, luminescent skin.

'Race you,' she said, and he was still half dressed when the moonlight caught the perfect sphere of her bottom in the instant before it was swallowed by the water.

Chapter Twenty-Seven

On their last morning at the cottage, Abigail forced herself out of the warm bed despite internal protests that it was too early, that only farmers and roosters got up at this hour, that this was no way to spend a vacation. She ignored them all, determined to make the most of this last chance to get some work done. Her muscles were slow to respond; she took extra care as she dressed and crept to the main room. She put a towel under the typewriter to muffle the sound; rolled a fresh sheet of paper into the machine, and stared, bleary-eyed, at David's spiky scrawl until she found the place where she had left off the night before. She began to type.

To almost all Americans – from the Calvinists in New England seeking God's will in scripture, to the rationalists in Virginia studying nature for evidence of His infallible divine foreknowledge – everything around them was the work of providential design . . .

She smiled at the syntax, so clearly David's, speaking in what she now thought of as his lecturing voice, the one that gave hard consonants an extra edge and paused at unexpected places in a way that forced listeners to sit up and pay attention. It was the voice by which she had first known him. The only time she heard it these days was when transcribing his notes. The men from class would never believe how informal he could be, that beneath that crusty professorial persona lay a jokester, the kind that replied, 'Okey, dokey, artichokey,' when she asked him to verify her schedule for the upcoming week, or said, 'See you later, alligator,' when leaving for the day.

'In a while, crocodile.'

Men could, and frequently did, dispute what the message meant, but they did not dispute there was a message.

Outside, the first rays of sun skimmed across the lake. She imagined how the early settlers would have reacted, coming upon it for the first time. Talk about a divine message! What a change it must have been from England's crowded slums. So much land for the taking, and such bounty: rivers and lakes teeming with fish, the woods full of deer and rabbits and wild turkey.

To those who believed they were settling the New World in the service of God, prosperity was an inevitable manifestation of His irresistible grace; part of the eternal order.

David would love it up here. The table was large enough for a pair of typewriters with space left over for books and notebooks. The thought set off a chain reaction in her head; she felt the need to explain, to herself, the innocence of it. She had merely meant that the cabin was a perfect example of how the early settlers could believe they had been singled out for the unmerited favour of God. The chance to work in concentrated solitude out here, free of distractions, would allow him to progress on the book far more quickly than he could at his office. What wide-ranging conversations they'd have! But of course, such a thing could never happen. She could never ask Ted to spend his vacation being seen not heard while she worked with her professor. And who would look after Mindy? As if on cue, stirrings began at the back of the cabin, soft murmurings of 'Mama? Mama?' She typed faster, racing to finish as many sentences as possible before bowing to the inevitable. A couple minutes later the door opened and Ted came in carrying Mindy. Her cheeks were pink and tear-stained.

'She's been calling and calling for you,' he said.

'Good morning,' she said.

'And you just ignored her.'

He put Mindy down; she ran to Abigail.

'Pee-yew, Melinda McDoo,' Abigail said. 'You stink.'

'Pee-yew!' said Mindy with a laugh.

'Yeah,' said Ted, scraping back a chair and sitting down at the table. 'She needs a change.'

Abigail took Mindy to the bathroom, feeling annoyed with herself. One would almost think she resented putting her family first, when everyone knew that being a wife and mother was a woman's most basic source of fulfilment. What was wrong with her? She washed and dressed Mindy in a fresh diaper and rubber pants, and a striped pinafore with a fish appliquéd on its front that Mindy pointed to.

'Fish,' she said.

'Fish,' Abigail repeated. She really needed to show more patience.

Ted was in the kitchen, whisking eggs and milk in a bowl.

'How does French toast for breakfast sound?'

'I can make it,' Abigail said.

'Nah, I'll do it. Get your typing done.'

He whistled as he stood in front of the griddle, knowing just when to flip the eggy slices of stale bread so that both sides got a uniform golden brown. Hers always ended up undercooked on one side, burned on the other. After breakfast they went for a final swim and packed up the car. Her parents came to see them off, bearing a fresh supply of zucchinis and a few tomatoes.

The wind blowing in from the car's open windows made conversation difficult on the ride home. The engine's steady drone put Mindy to sleep, wiping out any chance that Abigail would get any more typing in before this evening. To keep from falling into a funk, she made a mental list of all the things she had to look forward to in the coming weeks: working with David, of course, but also calculus, anthropology and two history classes. And it helped. She was almost happy to be back in Elm Grove.

Frannie Gill came over before they'd even got all the zucchinis out of the car and, after the briefest enquiry about their vacation, dropped the bombshell that Stan Gold had left Janice.

'Drove out of here on the Friday before Labor Day, happy as a clam. Well, you can imagine the state Janice is in.'

Abigail did her best to look surprised.

'It cast a pall over the block party, I can tell you that.'

'Well, sure.'

'It's just so very sad, him thinking he can snap his fingers and start over with someone new. Mark my words, it will all end in tears. As Paul Jenks said, "Eddie Fisher thought he could swap Debbie Reynolds for Elizabeth Taylor and look how that turn—"'

'Knock, knock,' Carol Innes called. Her face was lit with excitement that dimmed when she saw Frannie. A few minutes later Paul Jenks came over and repeated the comment about Eddie Fisher. Everyone wanted to talk about the Golds. Their hearts went out to poor Janice, such a blow, and of course, most especially, to the children, who were bound to carry the scars for ever. All agreed that it was shocking; simply shocking. So shocking, that for the next several weeks no one in Elm Grove spoke of anything else.

Chapter Twenty-Eight

The first time Penny threw up she assumed it was due to the leftover chicken she'd eaten for dinner the night before. The taste that lingered in her throat seemed to indicate it had sat overlong in the refrigerator. When she threw up again the following morning, a touch of flu became the more likely culprit, or potentially motion sickness because the feeling got worse on the ride to work. The carriage was crowded with schoolchildren laughing, shouting and swinging their clunky metal lunchboxes. She clung to a pole, burping discreetly into her palm as the T lurched along. Sick rose up her throat and into her mouth and she had no choice but to swallow it; it burned in both directions. The nausea calmed when she got out into the fresh air, and then returned again on the ride home. When Ellen suggested she could be pregnant, she was shocked; also a little offended.

'You've been throwing up for a week.'

'I know. I just can't seem to kick it,' she said.

'Does he use a rubber?'

Her face burned. Ellen could be so crass.

Mother's only advice regarding sex had been to think of it as being like a car: men were the gas pedal; girls were the brake, and the idea was to maintain a speed that was both *reasonable* and *proper* (emphasis hers) at all times.

Plenty of people claimed to know how to manage birth control, but with doctors and medical professionals unable to discuss these matters without violating the state's Crimes against Chastity,

Morality, Decency and Good Order, it was difficult to separate fact from fiction. Penny stuck to what she believed was most true: she was a nice girl and nice girls didn't get pregnant – a theory that gained credence every month. Trumping all was her unshakable faith in Ted, who was a man of the world and would never do anything to hurt her. She was sure he would not allow her to get pregnant unless, deep down, that's what he wanted her to be.

But Ellen wouldn't let it go. When, she asked, had she last had her period?

Penny tried to recall. 'Remember, Peanut, when we went to the art festival on the Esplanade and I didn't dare to wear my white shift?'

'That was in July,' Peanut said.

Could it really have been that long ago?

From that moment on, every little abdominal twinge convinced her that her period was on its way. When she wasn't rushing to the bathroom to retch, it was to check her underpants for stains. Twice she strapped on a belt and a pad, so certain was she of its arrival. But when another week passed with continued sickness and no period, Ellen gave her the name of a doctor over in Longwood.

'Protestant?' Penny asked.

'Jewish,' Ellen said. 'Dr Bitteman.'

She nodded. Anyone but a fellow Catholic.

She wore her grandmother's wedding ring and gave them her mother's maiden name, but she could tell she wasn't fooling anyone.

'How long you been married?' asked the nurse who took her blood.

'Not long,' Penny replied, as her face flushed deep red.

Such humiliation seemed punishment enough. She didn't want to be one of those girls who threw a wedding together at the last minute and then had a baby six months later. She dreaded the barrage of sly winks and remarks at her good fortune in having a healthy baby three months early. A pregnancy meant no springtime wedding, no cherry blossoms. It was unthinkable. She didn't mention the doctor's visit to Ted.

'I want him to ask me to marry him because he loves me; not because we have to,' she told Ellen.

'Not everybody gets that luxury,' Ellen replied.

Penny couldn't care less about anybody else. She wanted her romantic dream. She felt she'd earned it.

'What if it turns out to be nothing? I don't want him to think I'm trying to trick him into marriage.'

'Are you?' asked Ellen.

'Ellen!' Peanut said. 'For the love of God!'

'Of course not,' Penny said, and yet a part of her did wonder, oh, not on any conscious level, but it was true that she wanted to be Ted's wife, wanted it more than she'd wanted anything in her life, and it was also true that her behaviour of late did not exactly fit that of a girl who didn't want to get pregnant. Instead of looking for ways to keep Ted's natural urges in check, she'd been actively seeking ways to excite them. She said the words, but without conviction. The last time she'd urged him to 'be good' she'd had both hands wrapped around his penis.

'I thought we'd be engaged by now, to be honest.' She shook her head and took a thoughtful drag on her cigarette. 'Not that I blame him,' she was quick to add, 'after all he's been through.'

'With that little girl to raise, I should think he'd be eager to remarry,' Ellen said. 'Girl needs a mother.'

'He feels guilty about bringing in another woman to take Abigail's place. He loved her very much and it hasn't even been two years.'

'That hardly sounds like a man about to propose,' Peanut said.

'But he's always talking about the things we'll do when we're married: "We'll have a cottage down the Cape"; "We'll take Mindy skiing in Colorado" and "We'll have the best parties in the neighbourhood." He's just cautious. And I respect that. His

187

mother and grandparents are helping him take care of Mindy. There's no need for him to rush.'

'There might be one now,' said Ellen. 'If it turns out you're PG you've got two months. Three, if you dress and eat carefully. I'd say that the sooner and quieter you do it, the better.'

'It's his second wedding, so people won't expect a big to-do,' Peanut added. 'A nice suit from Bonwit Teller or Talbots in cream or light grey, a size or two bigger than normal, and go on down to City Hall or have a justice of the peace at your mother's house. Get it over and done with.'

'Maybe,' said Penny, who had been dreaming of the Happiest Day of Her Life since age ten. Through the years it had undergone several alterations and amendments, but nowhere in any of its many inceptions had a grey or cream suit, City Hall or a justice of the peace ever featured.

On the day that her results were due, she slipped out of the office just after eleven thirty, before any of her fellow secretaries in the pool had even started thinking about lunch. Instead of heading to the deli across the street, she went to a small, out-of-the-way place, a couple blocks away.

'The Reuben's good,' said the man behind the counter. He had a friendly face and a pair of furry caterpillars for eyebrows.

God, not cornbeef, she thought.

'Hot pastrami's popular.'

Penny shook her head. 'Something cold, I think.'

'Sure, I got ham, tuna, chicken, crabmeat, roast beef . . .'

'Tuna,' Penny said, out of habit, and then hesitated. 'Make that roast beef on rye.'

'Pickles?'

'All right.'

'Mustard or mayonnaise?'

The thought of either made her want to gag. She shook her head. 'Is there a payphone?'

'Out back,' he said, indicating with his chin.

The phone hung on the wall of a wood-panelled corridor, opposite the washrooms. From her purse, Penny withdrew a scrap of paper, a pencil and three dimes. Her hand trembled slightly as she placed a dime into the coin slot and dialled Dr Bitteman's number.

A nurse picked up on the first ring.

'Yes, Mrs Wood, I have your results right here,' she said brusquely. 'The test is positive. Congratulations.'

Was that sarcasm?

'Uh-huh,' said Penny.

'The doctor has estimated a due date of May 23.'

'Uh-huh.'

'He'd like to schedule an appointment with you for November 4, that's a Thursday, at five o'clock, if that's all right with you?'

'Uh-huh,' said Penny. Those two syllables appeared to be the only sound her mouth was capable of making. She was still saying them when the line went dead, and the dime fell into the phone's belly with a metallic kerplunk.

She stared down at the scrap of paper on which was written half a word: *Pos*. She crumpled it in her fist and then she returned to work in a daze.

She spent the afternoon typing letters her boss had recorded on the Dictaphone. Her fingers flew across the keys, hitting the letters and bars to make words and sentences and paragraphs. The process was automatic, quite removed from thought. If asked, she could not have said what any of the letters were about.

Her brain was too preoccupied. After the initial shock and disappointment that the marriage proposal of her dreams was not going to happen, she was quickly discovering a bright side. A fall wedding wasn't the end of the world. There would be no cherry blossoms, it was true. The ground would be frozen, the trees bare, but the inn on the water near her mother's had a large stone fireplace in the main room. Root vegetables made the tastiest soups and everybody was happy to eat turkey at that time of year, and it was cheaper than roast beef. An evening ceremony, with lots of candles, would be beautiful. Her mother would help her whip up some nice bridesmaid dresses on short notice. Something simple. She had a few ideas in mind. Pink was out of the question, but Peanut and Ellen would probably prefer dark green, anyway. She would make a floor-length cape to keep warm for the trip between the church and the reception. And the baby would be born in spring, which meant they would always have something to celebrate at that time of year.

The first tiny buds of excitement appeared. Maybe this was for the best. She and Ted were both such careful people; perhaps they were always going to need a little push. It was daunting to think that, within a few months, she would be a wife and mother to a little girl that she had not, as yet, even met, and that by the middle of next year she would have a baby of her own.

No, she must not think like that, must not use words like 'own' when referring to the baby she was carrying. Dear little Mindy would hear that and feel bad.

Chapter Twenty-Nine

Pregnant, Ted thought, and then spoke the word aloud to the stop-and-go traffic headed toward Boston. 'Pregnant.'

His heart thumped in his chest as his feet did a syncopated two-step on the pedals, clammy hands slipping on the wheel and stick as he shifted into first gear, to second, to neutral and then back again to first. It seemed impossible that his skin could contain the boiling mass of panic rising within him. He was going to explode. Right there in his car, on Route 2 southbound in a light afternoon drizzle. A vessel in his brain would burst, just like his father's had. He put on the radio for distraction but snapped it off at the first crackle of static. The wipers filled the silence with their rhythmic *s-q-u-e-e-e-a-a-a-k, thump; s-q-u-e-e-e-a-a-a-k, thump*, a sound at once so predictable and so annoying that Ted believed it might just kill him.

How could Penny be pregnant? They'd only done it a handful of times, a dozen at most, and he'd pulled out before he came practically every time.

Well, almost every time.

He'd definitely pulled out sometimes.

He thought of the awkward conversations he and Abigail had had with doctors, the humiliating tests, the fooling with thermometers, blocks stuffed under the foot of the bed. It didn't make any sense. It was ridiculous; it was obscene.

And it was going to be costly. The cheapest option, making it go away, was also the most daunting. He didn't know the first thing about finding someone who did that kind of procedure. It wasn't as if he could ask around the neighbourhood. 'Say, Jenks, any idea where I can find a really top-notch abortionist?' He needed someone good, too; he wasn't going to send Penny to a butcher. Had he been a real scoundrel, he'd probably have had half a dozen names and numbers in his Rolodex. The thought brought a glimmer of comfort at this desperate hour: his useless-ness proof of his essential goodness.

Curtis was probably his best bet, but Ted worried about losing his old boss's good opinion. He remembered how taken he'd been with Abigail. Would he think less of Ted for screwing around? For not taking steps to safeguard against this very thing? 'A good salesman,' Curtis always said, 'is prepared for any even-tuality.' Ted had been caught unprepared and had no idea what to do.

The traffic in the other direction was fluid. It would take nothing to turn the car around and head for the interstate. He imagined easing the clutch into fourth, putting his foot to the floor and feeling the miles pile up between himself and this life-sized problem. He could head out west and get a job with ski patrol in the Rockies; leave this whole mess behind him. Hard physical work and clean mountain air would cleanse him of his sins, make him new again. Such thoughts were tantalising and a weaker man would probably have given in to temptation. As he inched toward Boston and what was bound to be the most unpleasant conversation of his life, it was reassuring to know that he was not this weaker man.

He wondered whether anyone back at the store had noticed the effect Penny's call had produced in him. The alarm in his eyes was plain enough, the sight of his face in the rear-view mirror had startled him. For once he was glad that his sales team had the collective IQ of plant life. Sally might have picked up on something – he detected a slightly raised eyebrow as he left – as for the rest of them, he was sure that the episode had flown over their heads. If only it could fly over his. Why was this happening to him? Lots of men had one-night stands with girls they romanced in bars and brushed aside afterward. He was better than that. Penny could never doubt that his affection for her was deep and real.

'Oh, Danny, what have I done?' he asked the empty seat beside him. 'What have I done?'

He would come clean. It was the only thing he could do. Lay all his cards on the table. Penny would be angry and hurt – beyond hurt, devastated – but the sooner she knew the truth, the better off she would be in the long run. She would despise him and there probably weren't enough words in the dictionary to convey the condemnation Peanut and Ellen would heap on him. Rose, too. Fair enough. He deserved their scorn.

'Oh, hurry up. Hurry up!' he shouted as the traffic crawled along. The echo of his voice reverberating off the windows hurt his ears. He honked his horn at a driver nudging his Olds in ahead of him. The guy flipped him the bird and Ted only just managed to keep from ramming him or leaping from his car. He imagined his fist making contact with the guy's jaw. Oh, the sweet release!

'I'm sorry I misled you, Penny,' he'd say. 'I'm thoroughly, utterly ashamed of myself.'

He was ashamed. Ashamed that he let the situation get so far beyond his control; ashamed at ever having let it begin. Oh, why couldn't she have kept hold of her damned gloves?

He saw her up ahead, pacing outside her apartment in her trench coat, looking fragile and vulnerable. What was she expecting him to say? He tried to think back to the phone call. Had he said anything apart from, 'I'll be right there'?

'Are you okay?'

She gave him a weak smile. 'I am now that you're here.'

'Let's walk.'

He did not want to have this conversation within earshot of Peanut or Ellen or, God help him, Mrs Rizzo. He took her hand

193

and steered her toward the harbour where there was lots of open space and, in the spitting rain, few people.

'You've seen a doctor? A real doctor, I mean. He gave you a test?'

Penny nodded. 'I'm due at the end of May.'

'That doesn't leave us much time.'

'It doesn't,' she agreed, 'especially with the holidays.' She sighed. 'But it's not wedding season so I don't think we'll have any problem reserving the church. If we do, or if you'd rather not wait, we can go to City Hall or have a justice of the peace at my mother's house.'

'Penny,' he began, 'please—'

'Wait, Ted, there's something I need to say first. I know you're scared. How could you not be? I'd be scared, too. Heck, I am scared, but I want you to know . . .' She paused and took a breath. 'I want you to know that I'm going to be the best mother ever to your little girl. I will love Mindy with every ounce of my flesh.' The emotion rose in her voice; her eyes filled. 'She will be mine every bit as much as this baby is mine. There will be no difference.'

She was the sweetest girl in the world and he was not worthy of her. How could he walk away now? Just leave her on her own when she was carrying his child? Only a monster would do that. He might be a skunk and a cad, but Ted McDougall was not a monster.

'I'm so . . .' 'sorry' Ted meant to say, but sobs choked his speech.

When she reached up to wipe the tears rolling down his cheeks, he threw himself into her arms.

'It's okay, Ted,' she said. 'We're going to be okay, you'll see.'

Her faith in him was unbearable. 'You'll hate me,' he gasped. 'And you should hate me. God knows I deserve it.'

'I could never hate you.'

'You haven't any idea. You're a sweet, gentle, nice girl.'

'Not that nice. I'm an unwed mother,' she joked.

194

Ted broke from their embrace and took a step back. 'My wife didn't die in childbirth.' There, he said it.

'Well, then how did she die?' She spoke the words slowly. The last of them were still leaving her mouth when her expression changed. The transformation was fascinating, confusion turned to horror before his eyes.

He was ready to tell her everything, the whole, sad, horrible story of his deception and fantasy, but how to make her understand that it had all been done out of love? To protect her? Standing there, she looked so fragile, so vulnerable. He got the sense that, at the present time, in her delicate condition, the truth might be more than she was capable of handling, this poor girl who had no father, no brother, no man to lean on apart from himself. He could not destroy her. It would be wrong. It would be cruel. He opened his mouth and words tumbled out.

'I was embarrassed to tell you the truth. She left, took off, back to her parents in New Hampshire.'

'When?'

His head reeled. 'A month, maybe two, after Mindy was born. I forget, exactly. It's all kind of a blur.' He would most certainly go to hell for this.

Penny shuddered. 'What sort of a woman leaves her newborn baby?'

'Don't blame Abigail,' he said, determined to hold on to some shred of his integrity. 'We were kids when we married; engaged before we left high school.'

'Even so, to leave a baby! She'd have to be crazy.'

Yes, that was true, he thought. She would. 'To be honest, she isn't very stable, mentally, I mean. She suffers from nerves, thinks I'm out to get her.'

'How awful.'

'It is awful,' he said. 'And I was afraid that, if you knew, it would scare you off.'

She began to cry. Her face was slick with tears and the rain, her eyes searching to make sense of what he was saying, and he wanted so much for it to make sense, to reassure, to explain, to ease her mind.

'I had no idea, at the time, you see, how important you'd become,' he continued, speaking rapidly, 'how much I'd come to love you. And, honestly, Penny, I do love you. I love you more than life itself.'

'I love you, too, Ted!'

Her love for him was a knife twisting in his heart. 'I figured everything would work out okay; that my divorce would come through long before we were ready to marry.'

It was amazing how fast the colour drained from her face.

'You aren't divorced?' A whisper. She began to tremble. It was unremitting, uncontrolled and unbearable, and when he took her in his arms her shivering echoed in his own body. He needed to make her stop by any means possible.

'We're separated,' he said. 'Legally separated.'

'But how can we marry if . . .?' Her teeth began to chatter.

He lifted his hands in desperation and turned his tear-stained face towards the sky. 'I wish to God I knew,' he cried. 'I thought it would be done when I went to New Hampshire. I didn't want to tell you before, but that was my reason for going, to light a fire under my lawyer. He's had the papers for months, only he hasn't served them.' Righteous indignation rose within him and he began to shout. 'He's always coming back to me saying he needs one more paper, one more signature. Excuses. Her father is a lawyer in town; he holds a lot of sway. He wants to make the divorce my fault but I won't have it. She walked out on me.'

'Of course you wouldn't want to take the blame. But does it really matter? I mean, so long as you get divorced.'

'It matters,' he said confidently as his brain searched for a reason why it mattered. 'They could take Mindy away from me, don't you see?' He saw it clearly. It made perfect sense. 'What judge is going to grant child custody to a man who's admitted mental cruelty to that same child's mother?'

'What judge is going to give a child to a mother who has abandoned her?'

He anticipated the question and was ready with an answer. 'Her parents want custody.' Linc would, too. 'They blame me for what went wrong and, who knows, they may be right, but I'm not going to let them take Mindy. I'm not going to sign away my rights to my little girl. I can't let that happen, Penny. It would kill me.'

'Of course not, Ted. And I'm sure no judge in his right mind would take that little girl away from a loving father who is so well supported. It isn't as if she is being neglected.'

'I've ruined it.' He sighed. 'Even if my divorce came through tomorrow, I can't remarry in Massachusetts for two years. I could kick myself for not taking care of this before.'

'We can marry out of state.'

He shook his head. 'It wouldn't be recognised here, not even after the two years. Massachusetts is spiteful that way, and Abigail's parents will use it against me – they'll say I'm living in sin and . . .'

'Then we'll run away, head out west to where Danny is.'

'You wouldn't want that. Besides, Mindy is here; so is my job.'

'But where does that leave us? And our baby?'

She looked at him, wide-eyed, expecting to hear how he was going to make everything all right and it seemed to him that everything he loved most about her was encapsulated in that single expression: her beauty and innocence, her goodness and her complete and total belief in him.

'We'll do whatever you want. If you want to go to one of those homes, I'll pay for it.' His Christmas bonus ought to cover anything she needed. He'd sign it all over to her. 'If you have a relative you can stay with, I'll get you there, even if it's across the country. I'll buy you a plane ticket. I'll pay all your medical bills and I'll be with you every step of the way.'

The sound that came out of her mouth was difficult to describe. It wasn't a cry, exactly, more like a wail or even a howl. It was primitive and automatic and quite literally the most horrible noise he had ever heard a human make. He hugged her close and rocked her back and forth. 'I won't abandon you, Penny.'

Chapter Thirty

Normally Abigail spent Tuesday morning in anthropology and then American constitutional history, but it was the Columbus Day holiday. The men were back at work, but there was no school. She intended to spend the day cleaning the oven – a plan she was happy to put on hold when Becky phoned and invited her over for coffee. When she got there, Carol and Frannie were already seated at the kitchen table with mugs of coffee, sharing a pack of cigarettes and a plate of Pepperidge Farm's Milano cookies.

'She's getting so big,' Frannie remarked.

'How old will you be next month, Mindy McDoo?' Carol asked, cackling at Mindy's deadly serious response:

'Mindy McDoo two.'

'Joe and the kids are watching *Captain Kangaroo*,' Becky said.

Mindy's eyes lit up. She wound up like a cartoon character preparing to make a speedy departure: swinging her arms forward, kicking her free leg back across her body, and then uncoiling in a sprint toward the living room.

'So cute,' Frannie said.

'We hardly see you any more,' Carol said.

Abigail pulled up the fourth chair; Becky handed her a coffee. 'School keeps me pretty busy.'

'Abigail is helping a professor write a book.'

'How exciting,' Carol said. 'Our neighbour, the lady author.'

'I'm just the research assistant,' Abigail said. 'I enjoy it, though.'

'Better you than me,' Frannie said.

'We were just talking about Janice,' Becky said.

Of course they were.

'I ran into her at the school and I nearly gasped,' Carol said. 'I've never seen someone so changed. Her skin was positively grey.'

'Thin as a rail,' Frannie added.

'She sits in that house with the drapes pulled, in her bathrobe, smoking,' said Carol.

'At least she's not hitting the gin,' Becky said.

'So far as we know,' said Carol.

'I wouldn't blame her if she did,' Abigail said.

'I know she wasn't the easiest person to live with,' Frannie said, 'but she doesn't deserve this.'

'How old is she?' Becky asked.

'I'm going to say around thirty-three,' Becky said.

They looked at one another and silently shook their heads.

Frannie reached for another Milano.

'Chuck ran into Stan at Sears. He said he looked about ten years younger.'

'God, it isn't fair.'

'Hair cut all neat; lost his pot belly.'

'How old is his secretary?'

'Barely twenty-five,' Becky said. 'Wears mini-skirts to work.'

'I made sure Paddy's secretary was old and ugly,' Frannie said. 'I'm not taking any chances.'

'What's Ted's secretary look like?'

'Sort of middle-aged. She's been at the office for twenty years.'

'You're safe then.'

'Ted?' Frannie asked. 'He's the perfect husband.'

'Doesn't he do the dishes?' Carol asked.

Abigail nodded and took a bite of a cookie. 'Folds laundry, too.'

'How did you train him to do that?' Becky asked.

'He just does it. He used to work in a diner.'

'I'm going to send Al over for lessons,' said Carol.

'Apparently, she may need to go back to work,' Becky said.

'As if the poor woman doesn't have enough troubles.'

'She's afraid she'll lose the house,' said Becky. 'It's those kids I feel for, the poor dears, getting pulled in every direction. I guess there isn't room for them to stay over at the little apartment he's renting. He takes them for a few hours after school on Tuesdays and all day Saturday. He doesn't know how to cook so they go out for hamburgers and pizza which, of course, makes him a hero in their eyes.'

Carol turned toward Abigail. 'You seem different.'

'Do I?' Abigail asked.

'Hmm. She's right,' Frannie said. 'I can't put my finger on it.'

'More relaxed, maybe?' Carol said.

Frannie snapped her fingers. 'Yes. That's it.'

'More relaxed?' Becky called. 'She runs around like a chicken with her head chopped off.'

Illogical as it sounded, Abigail understood what they meant. Her workload was greater than ever, and yet somehow she had more energy. She wasn't more relaxed, she was more at ease. With her brain full of school, she didn't worry so much about what the outside world expected of her. That's not what she said to Carol, though.

'Maybe it's because Mindy's getting older. I'm finally getting some decent sleep.'

'Time for another, then,' Carol quipped.

God help me, Abigail thought. 'We'll see.'

Chapter Thirty-One

Ted pulled a sock out of the basket and set it aside. He always saved the socks for last. He was folding laundry while watching *The Man from U.N.C.L.E.* He loved the show's premise: the notion that a secret world of espionage could be operating right under people's noses, that inconspicuous shops might really be shells for super-secret agency command and control centres. He wanted to believe that, for all the bluster between Johnson and the Soviets, the superpowers could still pull together the way they had in the Second World War if faced with a big enough threat. Napoleon Solo was a pretty cool customer. He never got hassled, never lost control, not even when the guys from T.H.R.U.S.H. had him cornered. The Ruskie, Illya Kuryakin, was a bit soft, but he and Solo made a good team. 'Open Channel D,' they said, speaking to one another with their special agency phones disguised as cigarette packs, last season, and cigarette cases, this one. This season wasn't as good as last year's. They were doing more gags, going for laughs; it was better when they played it straight.

They were shooting it in colour. It said so in big, fat letters in the intro, so folks with crummy black and white sets knew what they were missing.

'Wouldn't it be great to have a colour television?' he called to Abigail.

'Hmm?' she said, head buried in notes for her professor.

'We'd be the first in the neighbourhood.' He took a bath towel and folded it in half lengthwise and then in thirds. 'That would be something.'

He wasn't sure she was even listening but then she said, in that artificially calm voice she used with Mindy, 'Colour televisions cost a fortune.'

Less than his Christmas bonus, he thought, before remembering that his bonus was already spoken for.

'You could always give up your courses,' he said, picking up a pillowcase and stripping off a sock stuck to it.

She slapped her pen down on the book.

'It's a joke, Abigail. Take it easy.'

'My father would be happy to pay for my courses.'

'Not a chance,' he said. There was no way he was going to be in Linc's debt. 'But if your father wants to give us a colour television set for Christmas, I have no objections.'

On TV, Solo and Kuryakin walked into the U.N.C.L.E. control centre in the basement of Floria's tailor shop. Ted tried to picture an U.N.C.L.E. office in Elm Grove. What better place to hide a secret office than in the basement of a suburban home that wasn't supposed to have a basement? Ted looked around the living room and thought of the adjustments necessary to transform the Enchantress into a top-secret spy headquarters. The reproduction still life on the far wall could slip down to reveal a map; the high-boy in the corner would convert into a communications centre at the touch of a hidden button. Which of his neighbours would be the agent? Jake Somerset over on Dutch Avenue was pretty shady. But, no, U.N.C.L.E. was smarter than that. They'd have someone who slipped completely under the radar, a person who looked the opposite of how a spy was supposed to look, somebody like that wimpy Phelps guy who claimed to be an engineer but couldn't explain what he did, at least, not in any way that Ted could understand. He imagined himself as more of a guest star, an innocent, average Joe, swept up into the action after being mistaken for some top-level spy with whom he shared a passing resemblance. The men from T.H.R.U.S.H. would take him to their interrogation room.

'Where did you hide the Henderson plans?' they'd ask and he

would reply, 'I haven't the foggiest idea what you gentlemen are talking about. I don't know any Henderson, let alone anything about his plans.' His voice would sound polished, and vaguely British. He had a hunch he would acquit himself well. The guys at U.N.C.L.E. would be impressed, so impressed that maybe they'd offer him a job at their agency.

Saving the world from evil forces bent on enslaving it, staying calm even when one's life was in danger: now that was adventure! If only the challenges he faced were like that.

He dumped the socks on to the coffee table and began to pair them. The key was to keep busy, avoid thinking. Fortunately, the Enchantress provided an almost limitless supply of distractions. As soon as the show was over he'd head to the kitchen and scrub a casserole dish that he'd left soaking there. Tomorrow, after church, he'd take down the screens and put up the storm windows. Next week he'd bring in the patio furniture, sand and paint each piece with fresh linseed oil and stow them on the rafters in the garage.

Neighbourhood get-togethers were another form of escape. Last week they had gone to a potluck dinner at the Jenks's where, over plates of Swedish meatballs and chicken à la king, talk of the second phase of building in Elm Grove finally displaced the Golds' divorce as conversation topic number one. Plans recently printed in the local newspaper called for it to double in size, with split-levels instead of ranches.

'It's going to look like a foreign country,' Frannie Gill lamented.

There was palpable anger at the proposed street names, the general consensus being that these new people were getting better ones.

'Liberty Avenue, Great Road: why couldn't we have had those?' Jenks asked.

Much concern was voiced about standards and whether the new residents would be 'the right sort' of people.

'The white sort is what they mean,' Abigail had joked on the way home. 'I said to Art, "If black people can afford to buy here, why shouldn't they be allowed to?" He almost choked on a party wiener.'

'You didn't.'

'I did! They were all in favour of civil rights. Did they think it was only for the south?'

For his part, he could not remember a more enjoyable evening. He relished the chance to sound wise, and above the fray.

'To be honest, I would have loved to live on Liberty Avenue, but Treaty Lane isn't so bad,' he told Carol, and, 'Of course, we all have a material interest in making sure that Elm Grove remains a desirable place to live,' he'd said to Fran or was it Jeannie? For a while he could trick himself into believing that these trivial matters were the biggest problems he faced. The shared responsibility was delightful. He wasn't alone, grappling with an intractable problem. They were together in this – all of them – equally invested in a common goal: the success of Elm Grove. In contrast, this thing with Penny was like carrying around an invisible backpack full of rocks. Nobody noticed how weighted down he was. This should not be happening to him. He was a nice guy. A good guy. Dependable. A loyal son, a good older brother, a hard worker. He had great follow-through.

However much he suffered, though, he never forgot that Penny had it far worse. For a girl like her to be with child, and not even engaged . . . well, he wasn't surprised she was dragging her feet about contacting adoption agencies. He listened thoughtfully to each new scheme she proposed, ideas torn straight from the pages of celebrity gossip magazines, involving extended stays in Mexico, Utah or a Nevada dude ranch.

'If it were only a matter of getting a divorce, I'd get us on the next plane,' he told her, explaining, yet again, the mandatory two-year wait.

'Think of the child,' he said. 'Remember *The Scarlet Letter.*'

'Of course,' she'd say, and then a couple days later she'd mention that Ingrid Bergman had a son with that Italian director while still married to her first husband.

He didn't blame her for dreaming. The law, however, was unyielding and perfectly clear. His hands were tied, until a bright and frosty morning a week before Thanksgiving. He was on his way to work, humming along to the fade-out of 'Unchained Melody' when the news came on.

In a move some are calling shocking, the Massachusetts State Legislature voted yesterday to abolish the two-year wait for divorcees seeking to remarry. As of today, any divorced person in the Commonwealth can obtain a marriage licence upon presentation of a certified divorce decree. State Congressman Bernie Latham of Hingham, sponsor of the bill, says the change is necessary because the law is not working as intended and has become an undue burden on individuals.

His stomach dropped. 'God damn you, Bernie Latham,' he said as the first beads of cold perspiration dripped from his armpits. 'God damn you.'

Chapter Thirty-Two

Penny first saw it on the front pages of the newspapers carried by her fellow travellers on the T. She read snippets of the story over people's shoulders and when she arrived at her stop bought her own copy of the *Globe* just to be sure she wasn't imagining things – that it really meant what she thought it meant.

Mildred, who sat at the next desk over, shook her head, and asked, 'Is nothing sacred?'

It was a struggle for Penny not to smile. She called Ted the first chance she got.

'Have you heard?' she whispered.

'Caught it on the radio coming in.'

'Isn't it marvellous? I knew it would all work out.'

'Let's not get ahead of ourselves.'

'Is everything all right?'

She hoped he wasn't angry that she'd called.

'It's fine,' he said, with a cool professionalism that led her to understand others were within earshot. 'A little busy at the moment. Can I call you back?'

At any other moment, the tone of his voice might have made her anxious, but she was too elated to admit to a single cloud on the horizon. Or, more to the point, a single *extra* cloud; difficulties remained. Ted's lawyer still had to serve Abigail with the divorce papers, and then they'd have to wait for the court to schedule a hearing and then another six months before the divorce was final, but those difficulties, though substantial, were nothing like the impossible situation they were in yesterday. Her greatest fear had been that Ted would be forced to choose between Mindy and her, which was bound to put a terrible strain on any relationship. Thanks to the change in the law, her mind was at ease. They were going to be able to keep their baby!

At lunchtime she bought a bridal magazine to peruse as she sipped vegetable soup. She flipped past the more traditional gowns in search of something short and chic for a City Hall wedding. How far she'd come. The girl who, only months ago, pouted at the thought of a wedding without cherry blossoms was going to be a mommy before she became a wife and she didn't care. So long as they married soon after, everything could be hushed up. She would lose her pregnancy weight quickly and look normal in the photos. They'd move to a new neighbourhood and, if anyone asked, say they'd married a year earlier. Her mother would have to be told the truth, of course. Penny would let her decide how to explain things to people at home. She didn't care if they saw through the white lies, she didn't even care what the priest thought. If he hemmed and hawed about baptising her baby, she'd go to one of the Protestant churches. It wasn't a bluff, either. She would bear any inconvenience, fight any battle, right up to the gates of hell, to keep her family together.

When Ted didn't phone back, she was surprised but not alarmed. He was probably working on a big deal, something that would contribute to their financial security. She was glad that now he wouldn't have to leave all his hard work behind and start from scratch in some other state, far from home.

She was slicing carrots for dinner that evening when he appeared at the door, face ashen.

'There is something you should know,' he said. His Adam's apple bobbed up and down when he swallowed.

Her hands gripped the back of a chair. 'Tell me.'

'Abigail's father signed her into a mental hospital.'

She closed her eyes and took a deep breath. 'When?'

'Last week. I didn't want to upset you. I thought she might stabilise in a few days and be released.'

A strange sound, a sort of *pifft*, escaped her lips as her lungs emptied. The room swayed. Ted caught her in his arms. His coat was cold against her skin.

'I'm sorry,' he whispered as he led her to a chair. He knelt before her and held her hand in both of his. 'I didn't think she was that bad. If I were paranoid, I'd say that her father cooked this whole thing up just to thwart me.'

'Thwart you how?'

'Stop me from divorcing her.'

'No parent wants their child to divorce, but to go so far as to have his daughter committed just to—'

'I didn't say it was unnecessary. She's been heading downhill for some time now, but the timing of it seems too perfect to be a coincidence. You have to admit, it couldn't be worse. It's almost as if he knew about us.'

'How could he, though?'

He stood and began to pace.

'Hire a private investigator. Of course! Why didn't I think of it before? You haven't noticed any suspicious people around, have you?'

'Suspicious?'

'Maybe there's a man you pass every now and again on the way to work or when you're out shopping? Have you seen anyone standing out on the sidewalk who doesn't seem to be headed anywhere?'

She didn't know. She hadn't been looking.

'That old codger! He's been laying a trap for me. He's probably had a guy tailing me for months.'

The idea that some Sam Spade in a fedora and a grimy trench coat had been following them with a camera gave her the chills. She recalled the naughty things they had done when she believed they were alone, the stolen kisses by the Charles, the times she'd let him rub up against the back of her in a darkened corner of the Greek restaurant . . . the time in his car at the end of the isolated road? What if they hadn't been alone?

What if someone had been following them, watching, taking pictures . . .?

'Oh, dear God.'

'It's absolutely essential that no one finds out about your – er – condition,' he said. 'If word gets back to her father, I'll lose Mindy.'

'Yes,' she mumbled. 'Yes, of course.'

'I blame myself,' he said, and he talked about the training he'd received in counter-surveillance while inside Penny's head a court-room drama played out, featuring dignified men in three-piece suits peering at eight-by-ten glossies of her performing lewd and indecent acts. She had the sudden urge to vomit.

'But, Ted, what will we do?'

'I'm taking Mindy up there over Thanksgiving. Maybe I can make her father see sense.'

'You're going to spend Thanksgiving with them?'

'Abigail wants to see Mindy. It might be just what she needs to get healthy.'

'Even so! I wouldn't let them get within fifty feet of my child, not after the way they've treated you.'

'You catch more flies with honey than with vinegar, sweet pea,' he replied.

She could only marvel at his magnanimity – the generosity in the face of such open hostility – and trust that his more virtuous plan was also the wisest. Little could be gained from alienating his soon-to-be-former father-in-law; quite the con-trary. The man might feel provoked to attack, exposing Penny to potential embarrassment and shame. As long as a chance remained that this delicate situation could be settled amicably, Ted was willing to swallow his pride and bend over backwards to see that it was. She was amazed that he could keep such a cool head. She knew he was every bit as impatient as she was to get his divorce and keep the baby. He was truly one of the best men she had ever known and, for his sake, she would try to be brave and not add to his burden with her worries.

But she had no problem sharing these with Ellen, once he had left.

'It feels as if the world is conspiring against us.'

Ellen cleared her throat. 'There are things that can be done.'

Blood drained from Penny's head.

'I know somebody. It would have to be quick, though. The later you wait, the harder it is.'

She pictured a darkened hallway, people with faces covered in masks, sharp instruments. A tremor travelled up her spine.

'He's a doctor – a real one. You'd be safe.'

She shook her head. 'I could never.'

'Well, if you're not going to *do* something about it,' Ellen said, 'you'll have to do *something* about it.'

Everyone knew about the homes, places where unmarried girls from nice families went to have their babies in secret, even if the secret inevitably got out. When Shirley Webber left high school in the middle of sophomore year, ostensibly to care for a sick aunt in Wisconsin, the whole town knew she was really in a Florence Crittenton home in the western part of the state. Poor Shirley. When she returned for junior year, people treated her like a leper. No one would sit with her at lunch or be her lab partner in science. The girls were especially unkind. The bolder ones made teasing references about the power of Wisconsin cheese to transform a woman's figure.

'I hear the cheese in Wisconsin makes women shapely.'

'I wish my bust was bigger.'

'Eat Wisconsin cheese!'

Looking back, Penny was aghast at their collective cruelty, their total absence of compassion, herself included. Why had they been so mean? Plenty of girls went for tumbles in the backseats of their boyfriends' cars. Shirley's crime wasn't that her morals were looser, it was that she had got caught. Meanwhile Wes Connors, the boy rumoured to have been her partner in the caddy shack, got elected class president and then went to Brown.

Penny went home for Thanksgiving on Wednesday afternoon, intent on telling her mother everything, but returned to Boston early Friday, having said nothing. She was too ashamed; too scared. Saturday morning, alone in the apartment, she looked up maternity homes in the phone book. She was surprised how many there were. Florence Crittenton and the Home for Little Wanderers were most familiar to her. Out of a lingering sense of, totally misplaced, moral superiority over Shirley Webber, she decided to call Little Wanderers.

'I need to talk to somebody about adoption,' she told the woman who answered the phone.

'I see. Are you interested in adopting?'

'No, I need to talk about . . .' Her hand went down and touched her abdomen.

'Are you in the family way?'

'Uh-huh.'

The line went quiet for a moment and then another voice.

'Admissions.'

'I'm sorry. I think there's been a misunderstanding. I'm just calling for information. How does a girl . . .'

'Most of our girls come in their seventh month of confinement.'

Confinement, like prison.

'I see, well, I'm not as far along as that.'

'We charge one hundred dollars a month plus there's a fifty dollar hospital fee. Of course, all bills related to the birth are the responsibility of the patient.'

'So expensive?' Penny asked.

'Well . . .'

If the woman didn't actually say 'actions have consequences', her silence conveyed the message to a tee. 'The price is all-inclusive: room and board, towels, bedding, clothing . . .'

'Clothes?'

'Yes.'

'Like a uniform?'

'No. They're regular clothes.'

'Can a girl bring her own if she chooses?'

The woman's short, tight laugh told Penny she was being silly. 'I don't know. No one's ever asked that before. The girls and their families generally appreciate not having to pay for clothes they'll wear only a few months.

'We have a staff of certified high school teachers.'

'I've already graduated,' Penny said.

'Oh,' the woman said, and paused briefly. 'There are activities for older girls, too, classes in sewing, arts and crafts, cooking.'

Penny's mind was stuck on the issue of clothes. It had never occurred to her that she wouldn't be allowed to bring her own.

'Do you want to reserve now?'

'Oh, no thank you. Nothing is settled yet.'

'Don't wait too long, dear,' the woman said before hanging up. 'We're already full through January.'

Penny lit a cigarette and adjusted the tie to her bathrobe. She pictured life at the home, being the oldest girl, surrounded by teenagers except when they were in class and she was left to sit around like a beached whale in borrowed clothes, her days a mix of inane adolescent chatter and abject loneliness. Now that she thought about it, Little Wanderers was a stupid name for an institution. Who was it that was supposed to be wandering? The mothers? The babies?

She longed to talk to someone who understood her predicament, but there was no one. Ted was in New Hampshire with Mindy. Peanut wouldn't be home until this evening and Ellen not for three days. She picked up the phone and called her mother.

'I'm in an awful fix,' she said and began to explain, speaking rapidly, cramming the air with specifics about the sequence of events and long, meandering tangents about all the ways in which fate or circumstance or some combination of the two was keeping them from their goal, which was, of course, marriage as soon as possible. She made sure to include every important detail, along with several irrelevant ones, because as long as she was talking her mother couldn't declare her disappointment, or say she never wanted to see her again. On and on, she talked, until she was out of breath and there was nothing left to say and she had to sit back, allow the silence in, and wait for Mother to pronounce her verdict. She took her time, so much time that Penny began to think she'd hung up.

'Come home,' Mother said at last. 'We'll get through this together.'

Penny handed in her notice on the following day.

'You girls,' her boss remarked. 'As soon as we get you trained up, you all find husbands.'

Penny twisted her handkerchief. 'My mother had a health scare recently,' she said, repeating the words she had been instructed to say. 'I'm moving back to the Cape to keep an eye on her.' But her boss had already stopped paying attention. To him she was a cog in the wheel, easily replaced. Was it wrong of her to have expected a bit more?

The girls in the secretarial pool gave her flowers and a silver letter-opener monogrammed with her initials. Mother drove up and Ellen and Peanut helped load the car as Mrs Rizzo looked out through her lace curtains.

Once home, Penny threw herself into preparations for Christmas. On daily walks in the woods she gathered pine cones and fir branches that she wove into a pair of wreaths, one to hang on the front door, the other for the centre of the dining table. She found the box containing the Christmas decorations. For a fleeting moment, she considered hanging her father's stocking for Ted, but then decided she'd knit one for him, a snowflake pattern, using cranberry and cream-coloured yarn from her mother's stash. And a second one, if she had time, in reverse colours for Mindy.

From her father's old chair in the den she knitted the day away. The pattern required her full attention, which kept her from brooding. She listened to the radio, preferring the local station with its reports on the high school senior class's Christmas tree sales and the St Mark's Church annual bazaar to the national broadcasts of inner-city riots and increased troop deployments to Vietnam. The baby needed good news. It made her happy to be doing something for Ted, who was under so much stress. He felt duty-bound to act in a way that served not only the best interests of themselves and their baby, but of little Mindy, and even Abigail who was, as Ted said, still his wife, in name if not in deed, and who was clearly suffering a great deal. Despite all the trouble Abigail's parents caused him, he always responded with charity and understanding. It was only natural, he explained, for a parent to want to blame someone else for their daughter's mental breakdown and he was the obvious candidate. Penny was humbled by the force of his empathy; reassured, too, for it convinced her that Ted would never let their child be put up for adoption. When the time came, he would not be able to bear the prospect of losing their child. One had only to look at his determination to keep custody of Mindy. In less than a year she would be knitting a third stocking in a snowflake pattern.

She planned a special treat for when he came on Friday evening, a full Christmas dinner: roasted duck with cranberries cooked in sweetened orange juice, potatoes au gratin and fine green beans with almond slivers. For his pleasure, she set the coloured lights on the mantelpiece, hung mistletoe in the front hallway, and strung yards of popcorn to drape around the tree. She filled the finished stockings with candies, chocolates and an orange for good luck as well as something special for each: a teddy bear with movable limbs for Mindy because, as a child, Penny had always wanted one, and for Ted a jar of beach plum jelly, in a subtle reference to their spot on the dunes.

Chapter Thirty-Three

Ted had an inkling that Sally, his secretary, was on to him. She had a talent for recognising voices and Penny called often enough – too often for it to be business. Sally was making comments that felt like dropped hints.

'Any calls?' he'd ask, when returning from lunch or a meeting.

'A few. None from your wife,' she'd reply, stressing the word 'wife', and then she'd hand him a stack of messages and there'd be one or more from Penny.

He wasn't worried that she'd say anything – she would never be so unprofessional – but he didn't like the thought of her judging him behind his back.

He was doing the best he could. He felt like a wad of salt-water taffy, stretched in every direction. Thank goodness Abigail was distracted by end-of-semester school work and that book her professor was writing. He didn't think she had any suspicions. But he knew, too, that his wife wasn't the type to lob blind accusations. She'd keep her questions to herself and, quietly but thoroughly, investigate. The first he would know of them would be when she hit him with irrefutable proof, which is why his heart went into freefall when she returned home from a weekend in Wilsonville and announced, 'We have to talk.'

He had been anxious to begin with, trying to make it appear as if he had not only just come back from Penny's apartment. His arms went limp at his sides and his throat turned dry. He was on the verge of blurting out, 'She meant nothing to me,' when Abigail asked whether the Corvair had ever tucked on a corner.

The question so confused him that even after he had asked her to repeat it, he only managed to babble incoherently. And then she handed him a copy of *Time* magazine. It turned out some guy called Ralph Nader had written a book on car safety – specifically, the lack of it. The Corvair got its own chapter.

'No, not once,' he stammered.

'I'm worried, Ted,' she said with her brow furrowed.

He was touched by her concern.

Demands on his time would only grow now that Penny had moved back to the Cape – not that he was anything but grateful to Rose for having taken her in, but it was more than a two-hour drive from both work and home. He dragged his feet about visiting, putting it off, even though Abigail went with Mindy to Wilsonville every weekend after Thanksgiving so she could write term papers and prepare for final exams. He dreaded facing Rose. They hadn't met since that perfect weekend back in July – a time that now seemed to belong to another era. He valued Rose's good opinion and regretted losing it, but understood that she had every right to be angry and this was uppermost in his mind as he prepared to go there to make a flying visit on the Monday before Christmas. He tapped his breast pocket to feel the five one hundred dollar bills, his entire Christmas bonus, his armour, his circular shield, like Captain America.

He headed out of the Goodyear parking lot with a knot in his stomach. He would make no excuses; he would admit responsibility, apologise, humbly and profusely, and submit to whatever harangue Rose chose to hurl in his direction. A few blocks into his journey he passed an appliance store, advertising colour televisions, and swung in. He wanted to see one up close. It cost nothing to have a look. They had a large selection of televisions, including the same Bright Rite model he had at home, state of the art when he bought it two years ago. Already it looked tired and a tad old-fashioned next to the colour sets. He had never seen such yellow; the greens were greener than in nature. He couldn't look away. The sixteen-inch Magnavox was on sale for three hundred and forty-five dollars – fifty bucks off. It was almost as big as his Bright Rite. He laid his hand on the oak veneer case. He could buy it right now – in cash! But he wouldn't, of course.

He didn't have to. The salesman explained that he could put half the money down and pay the rest on the instalment plan for just a tiny bit more. If he set five dollars aside from his weekly pay cheque, a sum so small he wouldn't even notice it, he'd pay the TV off before the year was out. The idea was sinking in when his eyes fell on an RCA Victor posed on a platform like a king on his throne. A Victor beat a Magnavox any day of the week. Top of the line, twenty-inch screen – large enough to be seen from clear across his living room – in a solid walnut case. It came with a two-year warranty, compared to one year with the Magnavox, for just a hundred dollars more, ten dollars a week instead of five, hardly anything at all. He'd bring his lunch to work; change the oil in his car himself. There were thousands of ways he could make up the difference. And he'd still have three hundred dollars to give to Penny. Three hundred dollars was a lot of money. He didn't think he'd paid much more than that when Mindy was born. Surely it didn't cost more to have a baby that you gave away than it did to have one you kept.

'I'll take the Victor,' he told the salesman, and ten minutes later he was motoring south with a smile on his face. A little way before the bridge, he stopped at the Howard Johnson's, for gas.

'That swing-axle suspension give you any trouble?' the kid working the pump asked.

'You don't believe a mamma's boy like Nader, do you?' Ted replied.

'Dunno,' said the kid. 'Why would he make stuff up?'

Ted put one of the two quarters he was holding for a tip back in his pocket on account of the kid's sass. And then he went over to the restaurant and had a few highballs to take the edge off his irritation. He arrived at Rose's an hour late.

'Mrs Goodwin,' he said, head bowed, hat in his hand. 'So nice to see you.'

'It's Rose, Ted.' Her tone was not hostile and yet not exactly warm. 'Same to you.'

'Thank you for allowing me to visit.' He shuffled his feet and proffered the bottle of Jameson he'd brought for her. 'I wouldn't have blamed you if you had refused.'

'I'll admit I considered it,' she said. 'But Penny needs you now. Besides, what good will it do for us to get on the wrong side of one another? You're going to be my son-in-law, soon enough.' And then she poured him a gin and tonic.

He imagined the same scene playing out with the Hatches. He would have had to prostrate himself before them, crawl on his belly, simper and grovel for the rest of his life.

The little house was warm and cheerful. It was decked out for Christmas; Bing Crosby was playing on the stereo.

'I'm so glad you're here,' Penny said. Not a word about his lateness. She glowed the way expectant mothers were said to glow.

She set out salted nuts, pretzels and cheese and crackers to nibble. He had a second gin and tonic and then wine with dinner. The duck melted in his mouth. There was Christmas pudding with brandy butter. Rose opened the whiskey and afterward they exchanged presents. His fingers traced the stockings' weave. How many hours had gone into their creation?

'It's too much,' he said, his voice cracking. 'You've done too much.'

The scarf and glove sets that he had brought for them – red for Rose, lilac for Penny – looked pathetic in comparison.

'Don't be silly,' she replied. 'What else am I going to do with my time? Will Mindy like hers?'

'She'll treasure it.'

'I'd be delighted to knit a sweater for her. What's her size?'

'I . . . I'm not sure. She grows so fast these days.'

'Bring her for a visit and I'll measure her myself.'

She should have wanted to claw his eyes out; instead, she had knitted stockings for him and his daughter. What a terrific mother she would make. She could teach Mindy to sew and cook and be a real lady; she would never be impatient or frustrated the way Abigail sometimes was. He wasn't so drunk as to think a judge would grant him custody of Mindy, but he was sufficiently drunk to believe that Abigail, clever and practical as she was, would see that it made no sense to pay Becky to look after Mindy when Penny was happy to do it for free. They could come to an arrangement that would allow Abigail to pursue her courses and research and whatnot, and see Mindy whenever she wanted.

'We'll have duck every Christmas,' he said, carried away by the mood and booze. 'It'll be our tradition.'

He woke at four thirty the next morning to the sounds of bacon sizzling. He walked four steps to the kitchen and Penny handed him a mug of coffee.

'You like your eggs sunny side up, right?' She returned to the stove and picked up the metal spatula.

He sipped the coffee, hoping it would clear his woolly head. 'That would be great.'

She tossed a pat of butter into the pan and then broke two eggs on top of it. 'When does Danny get here?'

'Christmas Eve.'

'You must be looking forward to it.'

'You bet.'

'He'll have some great stories to tell.'

'Knowing Danny, that's for sure.'

'I can't wait to hear them, every detail.'

'Of course.'

'I'd love to meet him.'

'I'm not sure there'll be time, sweet pea.'

She nodded, working the eggs loose from the pan with the spatula. 'I forget, sometimes, that he doesn't know I exist.'

He put his arms around her from behind and kissed her neck. His hands rested on the hard bump in her abdomen. She put her head against his chest. 'He knows everything about you.'

'Call when you get to work,' she said. 'I want to know you're safe.'

Things were busy at the store and he was sluggish from the early start and the previous night's excess. He got back to Elm Grove late, but it didn't matter since Abigail and Mindy were in Wilsonville. There was nothing enchanting about the Enchantress. It was dark and cold. The Christmas decorations sat in a box in the hall. The tree Abigail bought last weekend was propped against a wall in the garage, probably drying out and losing needles. She said she'd get to it between handing in her final paper tomorrow morning and the Gills' Christmas party in the evening. Ted was sceptical, even though she'd be without Mindy, who was staying with Linc and Gretchen. They'd drive her down when they came on the morning of the 24th.

There wasn't much food in the house. He opened a can of clam chowder that tasted nothing like Penny's home-made stuff. The spoon travelled methodically between the bowl and his lips; his body was hollow as a cave.

The thing was he loved Abigail, but he was not *in love* with her, never had been, actually. He married her because he thought she would be good for him. She was like eating spinach – something a person did, not because they liked it, but because Popeye said it would make them big and strong. Penny was like drinking champagne – intoxicating and bubbly. Was he really supposed to spend his life eating spinach when he could be drinking champagne?

The next day he walked into a jeweller's on his lunch break and asked to see the engagement rings. He knew exactly what he wanted and paid for it with the remainder of his Christmas bonus. He skipped out of the store early and drove with the needle at ninety nearly all the way to the Cape, pausing at the flower shop on Main Street to buy a dozen long-stemmed roses. The shop was out of them, and so he bought a poinsettia instead. The look of surprise on Penny's face was priceless.

'Did you forget something?'

He put the poinsettia on the table, took her hand in his, and got down on bended knee. Minutes later he was back in the car and barrelling toward home, smiling. The dainty ring had fitted her small hand perfectly, as he knew it would. He felt joyful – euphoric. Having at last showed the courage of his convictions, he had broken the yoke of confusion and indecision that had been dragging him down. The next few months wouldn't be easy – he had no illusions there – but his deep, deep love for Penny and the certainty that he was doing the right thing would buoy his spirits. She was the perfect girl for him. Together, they would have the perfect life.

Chapter Thirty-Four

Abigail drove from Wilsonville straight to the college to drop off her two final papers and then back home to get cracking on the Christmas cards. She needed to bring the neighbourhood ones to the Gills' party tonight and get the others in the mail for them to stand any chance of arriving before the holiday. She sat down at her desk and looked at the list. It was surprisingly long, given how few friends they had, filled with distant relatives and friends of their parents, childhood buddies they never saw any more, and people Ted knew from work. To these she had to add everyone who had sent cards, in itself a puzzlingly large number. 'Merry Christmas and a Happy New Year from Ted, Abigail and Mindy McDougall', she wrote for the first two dozen and then, as her hand tired, she shortened the message to, 'Merry Christmas from the McDougalls'. She didn't feel very merry. Of the more than one hundred families she was writing to, there weren't more than a handful to whom she would have chosen to extend tidings of joy. Sending cards to all these people she didn't care about, and who, in all probability, cared just as little for her, meant she had no time to write letters, or even personal notes, to the few that she did care about. And yet she must display all these cards on the living room mantelpiece – proof to those who had sent them of how much she valued them; proof, too, of her own popularity. Carol Innes had festoons of cards strung all the way around the living room.

After she'd written the final address and affixed the final stamp, she went to the kitchen and made a peanut butter sandwich with grape jelly and as it seeped through the industrial white bread like a bruise, she realised that she hadn't thought to write one to David. She went back to her desk and took out another card. *Dear David*, she began, *Thank you for*, and she paused, her pen hovering over the paper, with no idea how to continue. Her original thought, *giving me something to look forward to*, was, upon greater consideration, entirely inappropriate, not to mention easily misunderstood, but every alternative she tried – *bringing joy to my life*, *always being there*, *making my life worth living* – was much the same, if not worse. *Thank you* on its own would have done nicely, but now that the *for* was written she couldn't very well cross it out. She must find something to follow it. After a great deal of thought she settled on, *giving me a chance to witness true scholarship*. It wasn't very festive, admittedly, but it was heartfelt.

She went to a gift shop at Shoppers' World and bought a tin. It was white, with toy soldiers printed on the front, and she filled it with cookies from the selection her mother had given her to take home. 'You'll need something to serve company and I know you haven't got time to bake.' There were almond snow-balls and gingersnaps; lemon squares and peanut brittle. She stuck a red bow on top of it and took it to David's office.

The door was slightly ajar. His back was to her, leaning over his desk. She knocked softly.

'Come in,' he said. When he saw her he sprang to his feet.

'Abigail,' he said 'I, I thought you were one of my students.'

'Oh, I'm sorry. Am I interrupting?' She turned to go.

'No, no!' he called. 'You're not interrupting at all. No one ever comes during office hours.' His hands fell limp to his sides; he dropped into his chair.

'A little something for the holidays.'

'That wasn't necessary,' he said, but she could tell he was pleased. He held it with both hands. 'This is so nice, Abigail. Thank you.'

'It's nothing.'

'How you ever find the time while doing such excellent work for me and, I know, in your classes, well, I'm—'

She felt the colour rise in her face. 'I didn't bake them.'

'Oh, I'm sorry. My mistake. They look home—'

'No, they are, just not by me. My mother is a great baker.'

'Well, of course you wouldn't have time, would you? It's very nice of you all the same. I don't get many gifts from students.'

'I suppose you're the wrong sort of teacher for that.'

He looked confused.

'My mother always baked something for my teachers at Christmas.'

She could not believe she had said something so monumentally stupid. She considered clarifying for him that the idea of giving the cookies had originated with her, but no. She had already made enough of a fool of herself.

'Yes, the cookies are better at elementary school. Unfortunately, I love history. I wanted to share it with other people, not that it's worked according to plan.'

'Looks to me that it's worked exactly to plan.'

He nodded his head to the side. 'My courses are just ticks in the box for my students' distribution requirements.'

Abigail recalled the conversation she'd overheard her first night in class.

'I don't blame the night school people. Most of them are juggling work and families, trying to improve themselves. I respect their efforts. The full-time students are more frustrating, especially the ones who live here on campus. You can't imagine how demoralising it is to lecture for an hour when no one's listening and half are asleep.'

'I think I can,' she said, thinking of the Culture Club. 'You're brave for trying.'

'I'd probably throw in the towel,' he sighed, 'if not for you, Abigail.'

He took her hand in both of his and stared down at it, as if it were something wondrous. When finally he lifted his eyes to hers, she was certain that he would stand and take her in his arms, and equally certain that she would not stop him. She waited and watched, frozen like a statue, staring into his brown eyes, too mesmerised even to breathe and then, suddenly, he let go of her hand, and looked away.

'Thank you again.' He cleared his throat thoroughly and began shuffling papers on his desk. 'Ah – Mrs McDougall, I mean, Abigail. Your professionalism and your scholarship are appreciated more than you can know.'

'It's been a pleasure . . .' she muttered, unsure, suddenly, how to address him, settling finally on a quiet, 'sir.'

'Why don't . . . uh.' He picked up a pen and held it in both hands. 'Why don't we plan to meet again in the New Year, hmm?' He gave her a bland smile. It was excruciating. 'Have a wonderful holiday with your family. And we can discuss what, if anything, ah, we need to do next.'

She left the office without a sound and did her best to act natural when she said, 'So long,' and 'Happy holidays,' to Betty and then walked to her car in a daze.

Back at Elm Grove she took up the housework with a penitential zeal, scrubbing the bathroom of soap scum, wiping weeks (months?) worth of dust from every surface. About an hour in, while mopping the kitchen floor, the fever that had taken hold in David's office eased and she began to feel quite foolish. She had entirely misread the situation; romanticised it. David was grateful for her assistance; that was all. Theirs was a professional relationship. The suggestion that there was anything improper . . . and she . . . well, she *admired* him, of course, as a scholar. Working with him had taught her a great deal. It was just a silly . . . there was nothing untoward; she was a married woman who loved her husband. Adored him; couldn't wait to see him, in fact. She put the cards on the mantel, giving the one from Curtis and Maude Hale pride of place in the centre because she thought Ted would like that. She brought the tree in and strung it with lights; she unpacked ornaments and tossed them higgledy-piggledy on the branches, set the white porcelain nativity scene up on the buffet that was still too high for Mindy to reach. She gave herself a good scrub in the now sparkling tub and was slightly surprised that Ted wasn't home by the time she got out. Surprised, but not concerned. Things were hectic this time of year; traffic was bound to be bad. She dressed with care. Getting things done was certainly easier without Mindy underfoot. She chose a fitted turtleneck and a long skirt of Black Watch tartan and put her hair up the way Ted liked it, high on her head with corkscrew curls falling around her ears. She was spritzing perfume on her pulse points when she heard his car.

'Traffic heavy?'

'You have no idea.'

He seemed distracted. He didn't remark on the Christmas decorations.

'Do you want to walk or drive?'

He checked his watch. 'I need a shower. We'll drive.'

They were the last to arrive.

'Ah, there you are, Abigail,' Frannie said. 'Don't you look pretty! We haven't seen you for ages. Got that nose in a book, I'll bet.'

'Why you do it I'll never know,' said a ghostly pale Janice Gold as Abigail joined their conversation circle which, it turned out, was in the midst of a very animated discussion about floor wax.

Chapter Thirty-Five

Ted awoke on Christmas morning to the smell of fresh coffee and something wonderful – warm and yeasty, spicy and sweet.

'Cinnamon rolls?'

'Almost done,' Gretchen said.

They were his favourites, made from Gretchen's secret family recipe: the size of softballs, dripping with cinnamon and cara- melised brown sugar and topped with a fluffy cream cheese frosting. He was polishing off his second when his clan arrived a little after nine.

'It's positively balmy,' his mother, Fee, announced. A warm front had come through a few days earlier and everyone was overheating in their winter-weight clothes.

He led Grandma and Granddad to the pear-green sofa with the clean lines and needle legs that they had bought at Jordan Marsh.

'I don't remember this,' Grandma said.

'It's new,' Ted said.

'Very nice,' Grandma said.

'Doesn't look too sturdy,' Granddad said. 'Not much padding.'

Ted had intended to tell Abigail his plans to leave and marry Penny the moment he got back to Elm Grove, but as he settled in to the drive and the headiness of the previous twenty-four hours began to fade – right around Westwood, when I-93 was becoming Route 128, and traffic got heavy – it occurred to him that this was perhaps a bit hasty. Selfish, even. The Gills' party was in less than an hour. The whole neighbourhood was going to be there, and Abigail's parents were coming the day after tomorrow. A big Christmas dinner had been planned, with his family as well as hers. He couldn't throw all that into disarray. Much as he believed Abigail would appreciate his playing straight with her, doing so two days before the biggest holiday of the year would look insensitive, if not downright cruel. Not even Stan Gold would do such a thing, and he was a Jew. There would be plenty of time to sort out the particulars once the holidays were over. Whether he filed for divorce December 22 or January 3 was immaterial. It wasn't like he and Abigail were at one another's throats. On the contrary, they got on well. He retained an enormous amount of affection for her and he hoped that one day, once this whole convoluted business was over, they could be friends, all of which argued in favour of holding off on making any big announcements.

He was glad that he hadn't done anything rash. This Christmas would stay in his mind for a long time. The previous year Mindy had been too young to take much notice of things, but this year she was enchanted by everything: her stocking, the tree, the lights, the presents, the carols. Frank and Gene gave her sock puppets and she squealed when they took them up and made them spring to life. Who could watch such enchantment and not be infected by it? Not Ted, certainly. Linc had carved a wooden rocking horse for her. It had glass eyes and a mane and tail made of real horse hair.

'Beautiful, Linc,' his mother said. 'Such attention to detail.'

And yet Ted was certain that his gift would trump them all. He'd had the store deliver it last night when everyone went to watch the Christmas show at Shoppers' World. It was tucked far in back, the biggest box of all, buried by other presents, and he insisted it be left for last, when all the handkerchief sets and the musty old books had been distributed: 'Jonathan Edwards's biography! Daddy, how did you find it?', 'A tie, Mother. That will come in handy,' and 'A subscription to the *Bulletin*, Linc? That's swell.' He wanted no distractions when it came to the unveiling.

Mindy got the honour of tearing off the wrapping. She was taken with the oversized ribbon that adorned it, and paraded around the room with it raised up high. She had to be called back to remove the paper.

'Such extravagance, Teddy!' his mother said. It was more of a scold than a marvel.

'You bought a colour television?' Abigail said.

'Top of the line,' he said. 'Look at that screen – twenty inches!'

'Hot dog!' Gene said. 'Ted bought himself a Christmas present.'

'It's for all of us: a family present.'

'Cool!' said Frank.

'Not you, wormwood,' he said.

'Language, Teddy,' his mother said.

'I don't watch television,' Abigail said.

'You will, and Mindy will like it, too. You'll see, pretty soon everything will be in colour.'

'I see those kids staring at the television over at the Winthrops' house,' Linc said. 'Zombies, they look like.'

'Zombies,' Frank said in a low, monotone voice. He and Gene jumped to their feet and walked around the room with their arms stretched out in front of them. 'Zombies, zombies.'

Mindy giggled, which was all the encouragement they needed to exaggerate their movements even further.

'You two are a fine pair,' Linc said.

'Can we plug it in?' Frank asked.

'Sure,' Ted said. 'Be careful, though. It's an expensive piece of equipment.'

He expected Abigail would appreciate the television's value once she saw its vibrant images, but she wasn't there to see them. The women headed to the kitchen as soon as they'd cleared the wrapping paper out of the living room, and they stayed there until dinner was ready.

When people think of major milestones on the path to adulthood, it's generally the obvious things – driver's licence, high school graduation, marriage, first job and the birth of a first child. Little attention is given to the more obscure, but no less significant, events such as the first time a man hosts his family for a major holiday. Nothing quite announces one's arrival at the adult table better than a seat at its head. It was profoundly pleasing to hold the carving knife, and pour the wine. The pinnacle was when Granddad turned toward him partway through the meal and said, 'This is a fine home you have here.'

He thought he'd burst with pride, until he recalled that it wouldn't be his home much longer.

He'd still be paying the mortgage, though; alimony and child support, too. It would eat up nearly all his salary. He and Penny would have to live entirely off what he earned in commissions. That didn't seem so bad, at first, and then he did a quick calculation of how many tyres he'd need to sell each month in order to afford a second Enchantress and got a number higher than any Goodyear salesman had ever managed in a single month, let alone for an annual average. He tugged on the knot of his tie to loosen it.

'Delicious ham, Abigail,' his mother said. 'So moist.'

'Thanks, but it was my mom.'

'Oh, hush, Abigail. I just lent a hand,' Gretchen said. 'A holiday dinner is hard. I remember the first one I did.' She laughed. 'I cooked the turkey with the giblets in it.'

'I once made a pumpkin pie with no sugar,' his mother said. 'You should have seen people's faces when they bit into it. Frank, give Mindy that last potato,' she called. 'Cut it up for her, nice and small – no, let him do it, Abigail. You deserve a break. Now Gene, dear, take this dish out to the kitchen and fill it up.'

'Don't get me wrong, stop lights are fine for a city,' Linc said, 'but in small towns like Wilsonville I prefer a four-way intersection. It encourages friendliness, common courtesy. Drivers have to look at one another, make accommodations, the way pedestrians on the street do. If we start putting machines in charge of when we stop and when we go, we stop being human.'

'I couldn't agree more, Linc,' his mother said.

'How do you think you did this semester, Abigail?' Frank asked. 'All As?'

'Probably an A-minus in calc.'

'A-minus in calculus?' Gene said. 'That's fantastic! What did you get in calc, Ted?'

'I can't recall,' he said. He'd flunked pre-calc.

'I've always known you were bright,' his mother said, 'but I must say you're surpassing even my expectations. All As and with a baby.'

'Ted helps,' Abigail said, as she shifted food around her plate.

'Well, I would hope so,' his mother said. 'And you still find time to work on that professor's book. How's that coming along?'

'Um, good, yeah,' Abigail said. 'He's about two-thirds done.'

'Fee, you've got to help me convince her to go to law school,' Linc said. 'Come and work with me.'

'Oh, not this again, Linc,' Gretchen said.

'Wouldn't that be something,' his mother said. 'To have a lady lawyer in the family.'

'Marvellous,' said Grandma.

'Neat,' said Frank.

Yes, Ted thought, Abigail *was* family, a feature in Frank's and Gene's lives for as long as they could remember. She was present at their first communions and their confirmations, their school plays and field days. She'd helped with their math homework and book reports. Wives weren't like sofas – you couldn't just swap a new one in.

There had never been a divorce in the family.

'This heat sure is something,' Grandma said.

'Sure is,' said his mother.

'I think it's the bomb,' Granddad said. 'It's changed the world. We're all going to bake.'

The thing was, there was no guarantee that he could get a divorce. He had no cause to file for one – Abigail wasn't guilty of adultery, he was. He assumed that she would want to file as

232

soon as she learned about Penny, but she might decide not to; might opt to draw things out, let him stew in his own foul juices. Even if she filed right away, it would be six months before he'd be free to marry Penny. The baby would be here by then. Word would get out and when it did, things would get hard for Penny. At the Gills' party, there had been plenty criticism of Stan Gold circulating along with the Mai Tai pitchers and platters of pigs in blankets, but the most biting remarks were reserved for the girlfriend. Polite society simply could not accept a woman who lured a man away from his wife and family. Penny was innocent in that regard, but who would believe that? Was it fair to put her through that kind of judgement? Was it fair for a baby to go for months without a name? Was it even allowed? Even if they eventually married, the kid would be stained by illegitimacy for the rest of his life.

'At this rate, the Old Reservoir won't freeze over until February,' Frank said.

'Never mind pond skating. The MDC rinks are fine,' his mother said.

'They don't allow sticks on the ice,' Frank added.

'Or pucks,' said Gene.

'You can't trust the ice around here,' his mother said. 'Not like in New Hampshire.'

'People have been known to fall through the ice in New Hampshire, as well,' Gene said, with a smart alec's grin and a single eyebrow sardonically raised (a muscle isolation trick he'd practised in the mirror for weeks). Gretchen gasped and his mother, quick as lightning, reached across the table and slapped his face so hard the sound echoed through the house.

Gene's expression went from cocky to stunned. He looked at his mother and then quickly down at his plate when he saw her red face and the daggers shooting from her bright blue irises. Four finger-shaped scarlet plumes appeared on his left cheek.

Mindy left her seat and crawled on to Ted's lap for safety. She laid her head against his chest and stuck a thumb in her mouth.

'Fatherhood suits you,' Gretchen observed.

He nodded and leaned forward to kiss the top of his daughter's head. It smelled like caramel. It didn't matter that Gretchen was just trying to change the subject and smooth the mood. The truth was that it did suit him. Sweat bloomed at his hairline. What the hell was he thinking? No judge in his right mind would let him see his daughter ever again. A small trickle of sweat travelled around his ears and down the back of his neck.

'You okay, Teddy?' Frank asked. 'You don't look so good.'

'The heat,' he said, dabbing at the sweat with his napkin and then he blurted out, 'I miss Danny.'

As soon as the words left his mouth he wanted them back. He looked toward his mother but she averted her gaze.

Abigail placed her hand on his. 'Me too,' she said.

His mother jumped to her feet. 'We'd better get a move on,' she almost shouted. 'They play "O Come All Ye Faithful" first. I don't want to miss it.'

It was sixty-five degrees, warmer than it had been at Easter, and yet they all put on their winter coats before leaving the house. They filled a pew in the church. Gene wore the imprint of his mother's fingers on his face that night and for several days after. Ted held Abigail's hand throughout the service, and when the congregation stood for the confession, his voice rose up above the inarticulate mumbles, giving weight to every word.

Chapter Thirty-Six

There was never any question of Penny living openly as an unmarried woman in the family way. Heaven forbid! The Goodwins were known in the community and, despite Rose's two divorces, considered respectable. It was therefore imperative that news of Penny's condition be contained to the handful of people already in the know. The best way to do that was for Penny to stay out of sight. After the New Year, she kept indoors during the work week when, so far as anyone in town knew, she was still at her job in Boston. At weekends she took long, compensatory walks in the woods and along the shore, her thickening waistline safely hidden beneath sweaters and a winter coat. Until the previous Saturday, that is, when she discovered the coat no longer covered the honeydew melon-sized bump in her midriff. She was now effectively under house arrest, a state she wouldn't have expected to bother her all that much. It was the middle of a February cold snap, after all, and she hated the cold. For years, she'd been claiming that the bears had it right: the only proper response to winter was hibernation. But Penny's feelings about hiding indoors all winter fundamentally changed when the prospect went from an abstract idea to an applied reality. She hadn't realised how wonderful it was to live in the world, to be free to go about her daily business. Staring out at the bleak, frozen landscape, she wanted more than anything to be out in it, feeling the glacial air's burn on her face. Seeing Mother wrapped up like an Eskimo, scraping ice off the car, filled her with envy.

There was little in the house to occupy her time and fill her days: the cooking and cleaning, but a pair of women didn't eat much or make much mess. Personal grooming habits could only be dragged out so long. She knitted, she sketched. Ted's lunchtime phone calls were a highlight. 'Just checking in,' he'd say. He was the only one she talked to. Peanut and Ellen couldn't afford to call long distance very often, and the Cape was too far for them to visit on their days off. Ted made the trip often – three times, most weeks – and she was grateful, but he could never stay long, driving down after work and off again before sunrise the next morning.

After Mother left for work, Penny took her engagement ring out of the top drawer of her bureau and slipped it on. When passing mirrors or other reflective surfaces, she waved her left hand so the diamond caught the light. It was improper, she knew, to wear an engagement ring from a man who was still legally married to another, but doing so brought comfort disproportionate to the stone's mere quarter carat size and she needed all the comfort she could get, especially now that Mother had started asking about their plans.

There was nothing to say. Ted's divorce proceedings were as frozen as the ground outside. Abigail's precarious mental state remained the giant stumbling block. Penny couldn't understand why, after all the trouble she'd caused, Abigail was still allowed to wield so much power, but she refrained from asking too many questions because Ted got moody and withdrawn whenever they talked about it. They had such little time together; it was a shame to spoil it.

The long, solitary days provided ample time to puzzle and brood about the situation. It wasn't as if she'd expected him to have got his divorce by now. Still, she would have thought *some* advances would have been made toward ending the marriage.

But then what did she know about mental health or the law? Nothing at all. Being cooped up inside all day was making her imagination run wild. Ted was doing all he could, of course he was.

The baby moved inside her. It was wonderful to think that there was a whole person growing in there, rolling and fluttering. The baby felt her, too. When she touched her belly, the baby kicked that spot. If she moved her hand to a different place, the baby kicked there. It brought a burst of maternal pleasure every time. It was a game. Her baby, who wasn't even born, already knew how to play games – a sure sign of genius, she believed – and she happily played along for hours while sitting in what had been her father's chair. If she buried her nose into the back, she could catch a faint whiff of his hair tonic. What would he say about her present predicament?

'Well, Kitten, isn't this a fine kettle of fish we're in?'

We. He would definitely say *we*, if he knew.

He had managed to get his divorce, but then, Mother hadn't been mentally ill and Penny had been eighteen, whereas little Mindy was still a baby.

Little Mindy. Ted had promised to bring her to visit one day.

Penny looked at the clock and saw she had at least fifteen minutes until Ted's call. Impatient and restless, she stood and began to pace. All the sitting made her whole body tight. Five steps took her across the room, through the kitchen and to the entrance to the parlour. Five steps back brought her to the far end of the den.

Five steps out.

Five steps back and she was at the den window, looking longingly at the bare trees and the scraggly brown grass. The afternoon was clear, blindingly bright. The ground would have no give. It would be hard enough to walk *en pointe* in her old toe shoes.

Placing a hand on the windowsill as if it were a ballet *barre*, she put her feet into first position, raised her free arm in front of her and then opened it out to the side. Slowly, she bent into a *demi-plié*, and then another. The third time she dipped toward

237

the ground in a *grand plié*, rising up on her toes as she descended. As she neared the floor, her body pitched forward; she had to put her hand to the floor to keep from tumbling over.

Twelve years of ballet, and this was the best she could do?

She began again, making adjustments for the way her body's altered shape had shifted her centre of gravity. Gradually, marvellously, her body responded. Her spine loosened; her shoulders rolled back. Her muscles remembered. Her arm knew how to move gracefully; her eyes followed her hands. Stepping on to the braided rug in the centre of the room, she did some wobbly *pirouettes*, happy to be in motion. She could have been thirteen again, with her teacher, Mrs Koenig, that tiny wisp of a woman with her thick Hungarian accent and an even thicker braid of wavy grey hair hanging down her back, clapping out beats, and shouting instructions.

'*Jeté, jeté, piqué, piqué, piqué, piqué, and pas, pas, pas, gr-a-a-a-n-d jeté!*'

She soared through the air in a *grand jeté* and landed in the middle of the living room, directly in front of the picture window. She scurried back to the den with notions of trying a *fouetté* turn when she heard a squeak coming from the side of the house. She froze and listened. It was the spring on the storm door pulling back, followed by three quick raps on the glass of the kitchen door.

'Rose?' called a voice she recognised as belonging to Mrs Baker, the neighbour two houses down. 'Rose, are you in there?'

Panic, cold and dreadful, shot through her veins. The only way out of the den was through the kitchen, directly past where Mrs Baker stood. But staying put was not without its risks. Mrs Baker might decide to walk around to the back of the house, to check that everything was all right, and find Penny standing with her waxing crescent of a belly, plain as day. Her reputation would be destroyed; her mother exposed as a liar. Slowly, quietly, she lowered herself to the floor and crawled on her hands and knees into a corner, where she lay in a ball, face to the wall, still as a possum, her body pulsing with the beatings of her heart and the baby's kicks. She dared not move or turn her head for fear of finding Mrs Baker staring at her through the window. The left side of her body went numb. The phone began to ring long, slow trills. One ring, two rings, three . . . eight rings in all and then the phone fell silent.

The sight of her mother walking in several hours later, a bag of groceries in each arm, brought a wave of ecstatic relief. The blinds could be pulled down and she could sit in the rooms that faced the street.

She put the kettle on the stove for tea. 'I was beginning to worry.'

'The lines were long.'

Penny opened the cupboards at the far end of the kitchen and started unloading the bags. 'You bought mushrooms, good. I was thinking about making an omelette for dinner. I could put onions in it, too, and fry some potatoes . . .'

A day's worth of conversation began to flow from her mouth. 'Sounds nice.'

'Do you prefer cheddar cheese or American?'

There was a rap at the door.

'Rose,' Mrs Baker called, 'Rose.'

Penny was cornered once again.

'Quick, hide!' Mother whispered.

'One minute, Mary,' her mother called back. 'I'm just . . . ah . . . clearing something away.'

Mother opened the door to the broom closet and pushed Penny inside. In the darkness, Penny felt her way to the floor. It was cluttered with shoes. A high heel dug into her bottom.

'Were you home earlier today, by any chance?'

Mrs Baker's sharp voice cut through the closet door.

'Why, no,' she heard her mother reply. 'I've only just got home.'

'That's what I thought,' Mrs Baker said. 'Don't think me strange, now, but I could have sworn I saw someone inside your house today. Penny's not here, by any chance?'

'Of course not,' her mother said with a laugh that sounded impressively natural. 'Penny's in Boston.'

'That's what I thought,' Mrs Baker said, 'but it was so strange, Rose. It looked like you, or maybe Penny, jumping up and down. It caught my eye while I was down at the mailbox at the end of the drive. I was afraid it might be burglars.'

'Jumping burglars, Mary?' Mother said with another laugh. 'When was your last eye exam?'

The kettle sang.

'I was just making myself some tea. I'd pour you one, but I suppose you're busy getting supper on for Gerry. It's nearly seven.'

'Tuesdays is Ger's bowling night. We eat early. I was just setting the last of the dishes out to dry when I saw you pull up.'

There was a slight pause. 'How fortunate,' Mother said. 'Shall we take it in the den?'

Once they were safely settled, Penny could crawl across the hallway to her room.

'Here's better,' Mrs Baker said. 'I can see my house. I didn't lock it before I came over.'

'Of course.'

'Have I told you that Andrea is expecting?'

Penny's ears perked up. Mrs Baker's daughter Andrea had only recently had a baby.

'Is that so?' said Mother. 'Didn't she just have one?'

'Little Jeanie will be nine months old on the 12th.'

'Well, they're not wasting any time,' Mother said.

'They're delighted,' Mrs Baker chuckled, 'though I'm not sure it was planned.'

Little Jeanie wasn't planned either, Penny thought. Born supposedly premature, six months after Andrea's hastily thrown-together wedding.

'I said to her, "Andrea, you're having Irish twins."'

'Hmm,' said Mother.

Mrs Baker chattered on about Andrea's idyllic life in the suburbs, her husband's fantastic job, their beautiful home. One of Penny's butt cheeks went to sleep, and then a whole leg. When she shifted her position to try to get the blood to circulate, the shoe heel dug deeper into her backside. She reached down and pulled it, gently at first, and then harder. It came free with a jolt. Her hand flew upwards, and hit the closet wall and something – a tennis racquet? – began to slide, causing a slow scraping sound. Penny stuck out her foot to keep it from clattering on the floor and it fell square across her shinbone.

'What was that?' Mrs Baker asked.

A bolt of pain shot through Penny. She bit her knuckle to keep from shouting out.

'What was what, Mary?' Mother said.

'That noise.'

'I didn't hear anything.'

'It came from in there.'

Penny's skin crawled with shame and dread. She stared at the door, waiting for it to open. The only thing worse than getting caught hiding in a closet was the prospect of being caught hiding in a closet, pregnant.

Mother laughed and, in a tone that Penny thought admirably light-hearted, suggested that Mrs Baker might want to have her ears examined, as well as her eyes, and before Mrs Baker could say anything else, Mother quickly returned to the subject of Andrea's house. Did it have a garage or a carport? (A garage, of course, an attached one.) Penny sat rock-still until Mrs Baker ran out of superlatives with which to describe Andrea's life and left.

Mother opened the closet door. She looked furious.

'We need to make a change.'

Mother knew somebody who knew somebody with a cottage in the next town over. It was in an area surrounded by summer homes, but fully winterised, and isolated enough at this time of year so that Penny could take walks and get back and forth to doctor's appointments without fear of being seen. It had knotty pine panelling and braided rugs, a stone fireplace and built-in bunk beds in both bedrooms. The furnishings were out of proportion to the size of the rooms and their frayed opulence suggested cast-offs from a grander, main residence. The kitchen knives were dull, there were more lids than pots, and the plates were chipped and mismatched. The draught was so bad they had to stuff newspapers around the window casings to keep them from rattling. But it was charming and Penny was happy there.

There was a bookcase full of paperback romance novels for her to read, tales of forbidden love that somehow always managed to come right in the end. As there was no phone, she wrote letters to her former roommates, and to Mrs Rizzo. She drew still lifes and beachscapes. She talked to the baby and played the patting game, which had evolved. Instead of kicking, the baby nestled its bottom into the space beneath her hand. She took long walks on the beach. At night she could see the lights of her home town, and boats coming in to the town dock, the enormous hotel looming on a bluff. The world had carried on, leaving her behind.

Ted's visits continued as before, though it added another fifteen minutes to his journey, each way. He was looking worn out, the poor dear. His back had begun to slope. She made elaborate meals on the nights he came, always in the hope that there'd be something to celebrate: news of progress in his divorce.

It had yet to materialise. Abigail was still in the psychiatric hospital. Whenever it seemed she was close to being released, whenever Ted's lawyer talked of finally serving her with papers, she'd suffer another setback. Every time.

Like clockwork.

It was uncanny.

'How long can it go on like this?' she asked Mother.

'How long is a piece of string?' Mother replied.

'You don't suppose . . .' Penny began, but she couldn't finish the phrase. She knew that there were men out there who led girls on with false promises, but men like that didn't stick around once the girls got into trouble. They didn't give the girls engagement rings; didn't drive hours out of their way, three nights a week just to buck up their spirits. Of course Ted was doing everything he could to get his divorce.

On a Wednesday night Penny prepared beef brisket with scalloped potatoes and broccoli. The night was black outside their windows. Inside, a blue haze of cigarette smoke hung over the dining table.

Mother took out the whiskey and poured glasses for herself and Ted.

'What are your plans?' she asked him.

'Well, I hope . . .'

'Hope is not a plan.'

He took a swallow of whiskey and grimaced. 'I know.'

'I phoned the agency,' she said. 'They can meet us next Thursday afternoon.'

Chapter Thirty-Seven

Mrs Nichols, the social worker, was a small, sturdy woman, dressed in a formless herringbone tweed skirt and jacket and beige shoes designed for comfort. Her grey hair was pulled a little too severely back from her face but her smile was friendly. She shook their hands, and motioned them into a little sitting area within her office. Penny joined her mother on a small sofa, leaving Mrs Nichols the largest chair nearest the desk. A tea service sat on a small table in the centre. Mrs Nichols poured a cup for everyone, and passed around a plate of cookies.

'I understand, Mrs Goodwin,' she said, 'that you are interested in knowing more about the services we offer.'

She began to speak about the screening process for prospective couples – interviews, house visits and background checks. 'We take only the very best,' she assured them – and then she described the thought and consideration they put into matching babies to these very best people. It was clear that she had given this talk before. The message was, 'We're professionals. You can trust us.' Mrs Nichols never spoke of 'giving up' the baby, but of 'release for placement into adoption', as if adoption were the state to which babies naturally gravitated if not firmly held by their mothers. The final decision was, she said more than once, entirely Penny's to make.

'Now, Penny,' Mrs Nichols said, flipping open a stenographer's notebook and taking out a pen. 'Tell me a little bit about why you've come here today.'

Earnestly, if not eloquently, Penny conveyed the story of how she and Ted had fallen in love, his complicated marital situation, and his wife's illness and hospitalisation.

'And so am I to understand that you are still in contact with the alleged father?'

Penny's face flushed. Alleged?

'Of course!' she said. 'He calls every day and sleeps at the house three nights a week.' She hoped that didn't sound tawdry.

'So often?' Mrs Nichols asked.

'It lifts her morale,' Mother said. 'His support and affection ease the anxiety.'

'He stays in the spare room,' Penny said. 'There are bunk beds.' She didn't want Mrs Nichols to get the wrong idea.

'Of course,' Mrs Nichols said. An awkward pause followed and then the social worker turned back to Mother. 'You believe these affections are sincere?'

What a question, Penny thought. 'He's going to pay all expenses related to the birth,' she said. 'He's already given me a hundred dollars.'

'I do,' said Mother.

'How does Ted feel about our meeting today? Is he supportive of releasing the baby?'

'He wants to keep it as much as I do,' Penny said. 'But we're trying to be realistic, given the situation. We want to do what's best for the baby.'

'I see.'

'He is trying very hard to get his divorce,' Penny added.

The nod that Mrs Nichols made suggested scepticism. Penny rushed to explain Abigail's angry parents, the fight for custody of Mindy, the private detectives.

'I see,' said Mrs Nichols, scribbling away. 'It would be helpful, for the purpose of collecting the necessary information, if we met with Ted directly. Do you think he'd be open to that?'

'Of course,' Penny cried. 'He wants to be involved in everything.'

Mrs Nichols looked up from her pad and smiled and Penny

thought that it must be unusual for the fathers to be involved. Most men, she suspected, left the girls high and dry.

'We'll need a doctor in this area,' Mother said.

'Of course,' Mrs Nichols said. 'I have a list of doctors that work with us.'

Mother leaned forward, as if to speak in confidence. 'We would prefer a Protestant.'

'I completely understand,' Mrs Nichols said.

Chapter Thirty-Eight

Ted was sitting in the living room in the house in Elm Grove. It was the middle of the day and the sun was bright. The television was on and he was watching a programme in colour from the comfort of his favourite chair. The new sofa was in its place in front of the coffee table. Abigail called to him; he got up and went to her in the kitchen. She was standing at the open door, her body outlined in sunshine. She took a step back and there was Penny standing on the blue and pink flagstone stoop, holding a baby wrapped in a white blanket. She was smiling and lifting the baby up as if she expected him to take it. He opened his mouth and screamed.

'Jesus, Ted,' Abigail cried.

His eyes popped open. He saw in the darkness familiar shadows, the dresser with its mirror and, beside it, the chair on which rested Abigail's old housecoat.

'You about gave me a heart attack,' she said.

'I'm sorry,' he said, gasping for breath. 'I guess . . .' – his heart pounded in his ribcage as if he'd just run a mile – 'I guess it was a nightmare.'

'What was it?' She reached out to caress his head and quickly pulled it back. 'You're soaked.'

She went to the bathroom and got towels.

'Here, put one beneath you and one on top of you. I'll change everything tomorrow. What scared you so?'

'I . . . I don't know,' he replied. 'I can't remember.'

He thought he might have called out Penny's name, but he

certainly wasn't going to ask. He didn't sleep the rest of the night.

And he really could not afford to lose any more sleep. Nights in Elm Grove were supposed to be a chance to recharge his batteries. He had never been so tired. The bags under his eyes had bags. Early spring was his least favourite time of year: the thaw. The last of the snow departed, leaving behind potholes, crooked fences, dull, brown grass and lots of mud. At Sunday lunch, last week, the sorrowful groans and thunderous rumbles of Waskeegee Pond breaking up could be heard through the sturdy walls of the Hatch family home. Ted was sure it was Danny calling to him from beyond the grave, signalling his doom.

'Did you take a hundred dollars out of Mindy's college account?' Abigail asked a few days later.

'Oh, yeah, I meant to tell you that,' and he laughed as if remembering an amusing incident. 'I must have grabbed her bankbook out of the desk by mistake. Didn't realise it until the teller handed it back to me.' The ease with which the lie rolled off his tongue troubled him.

'What did you need a hundred dollars for?'

'Young executives.' It had become his stock answer, and he worried, some, that he had become over-reliant on it.

'I thought the company paid for everything.'

'Sometimes we pay and then hand in the receipts. I meant to put it back. I just forgot to bring the passbook with me last time I was at the bank. I'll do it this week.'

Another lie. He didn't have a hundred dollars; worse, he'd soon be needing much more. When the baby came there would be hospital bills and agency fees and who knew what else. His commissions were down now that he was spending less time on the sales floor and the team wasn't hitting its targets, killing his chance at an executive bonus. Monthly payments for the mortgage, cars and now the television ate most of his salary. Every month, there was some unexpected expense – Abigail's tuition, or Becky, or the refrigerator repairman – that prevented him from setting anything aside. He couldn't catch a break.

'What's wrong?' Abigail asked.

'Work,' he replied.

This was at least partly true. There were things at the store that he ought to be doing – paperwork, for one, but also relationship-building, chasing down commercial contracts, things he had let slide because he was driving back and forth to the Cape three nights a week.

He hardly ever slept in the same bed two nights in a row. The nights he went to see Penny were always short and the bed – though better than the sofa at Rose's – was narrow and hard. He always woke with a crick in his neck. His mood alternated between impatience and dread. The end was in sight, but first they had to get through the birth, and then the awful business of giving the baby up. That was going to be the worst for Penny. She had ballooned into the unattractive stage of pregnancy, puffy everywhere, with an itchy belly. She cried easily and kept nagging him to make an appointment with the social worker, something he'd so far managed to avoid, and which he planned to keep on avoiding right up until the end. The very last place he wanted to spend his precious time was being grilled by some blue-stocking about how he'd got a nice girl in trouble and why it was he couldn't do the honourable thing and marry her.

Penny had become quieter and more pensive. He brought fashion magazines to distract her, get her thinking about the future, but she hardly looked at them. Instead she knitted: tiny bootees, a sweater and a hat, all in white. She showed him satin ribbons in blue and pink and explained how she would thread them through the clothes once the baby was born and they knew whether it was a boy or girl. She had stopped asking about Abigail and the divorce, but it was clear that she was always hoping for good news and it was painful to watch the brightness in her face dim over the first five minutes of each visit. She begged him to bring Mindy.

'I will,' he told her. 'Soon as I can come down on a weekend.'

'Of course,' she said, wiping a tear from the corner of an eye.

It seemed such a small thing to ask of him that he resolved to give it to her, if at all possible.

Early one Saturday evening in late April, he had his chance. Abigail's professor called. Apparently there had been some kind of mix-up, something about references and the bibliography and it all needing to be sorted by Monday morning. Could she come in on Sunday to help?

Of course she could.

'I'm sorry, Ted.'

'Don't be silly,' he told her. 'He needs your help.'

'Yes, but I feel awful. We hardly get to see each other as it is, what with me and my school work and you off at your training three nights a week.'

'It's only for a couple months.'

'And now we're losing a whole Sunday.'

'We'll make up for it later.'

Ten minutes after she left, he helped Mindy with her coat and led her to the car.

'How would you like to go for a ride?' he said. 'To the seashore.'

He doubted Mindy knew what the seashore was but she seemed enthusiastic enough about the prospect of going there. She was great in the car, sitting up on her knees in the back, leaning to look out of one side window and then the other and then out the back.

'Daddy, look!' she exclaimed, pointing to the tugboats pulling a ship through the canal.

Penny and Rose were delighted with her. Rose gave her a mug of milky tea and a plate of vanilla cream cookies. Penny conjured a paper doll from a cereal box, a black pen and a box of pastels.

'She's darling, Ted,' Penny said as she stroked Mindy's strawberry-blonde curls. They went for a walk on the beach.

'Swimming?' Mindy asked.

'The water is too cold right now,' Penny said, bending down to get to her level. 'But if you come back in the summer, we can swim. Would you like that?'

Mindy nodded.

'I hope so. I would like for us to be good friends.'

When they got back to the cottage Ted said they ought to be getting along.

'Don't forget your doll,' said Rose, handing it to her.

'No, really,' Ted said. 'That's not necessary.'

'Nonsense.'

'It's too pretty. She'll ruin it.'

'What do I care?' Penny said. 'I'll make her another.'

'Honestly, she has so many dolls.'

But Mindy had the doll clamped tight in her little fists.

He drove back along the coast and stopped at a roadside shack for fried clams and soda pop, looking out at the sailboats, the fishing boats and the gulls until Mindy's eyelids became droopy. She slept most of the way home, sprawled across the back seat, hair tangled from the wind, ketchup stains on her face. Before carrying her to the house he searched the backseat for the doll, but it was nowhere in sight. He decided she must have dropped it at the clam shack. It would have blown away before either of them noticed it was gone.

Chapter Thirty-Nine

By unfortunate coincidence, David's book was entering its final, critical stage at precisely the same time as final papers in his three classes were due. In the ten days he had left to complete the final edits on his manuscript, he also had to read and grade sixty-five undergraduate papers on the Boston Massacre, the First Continental Congress and the Bill of Rights. Such a heavy workload provoked a small crisis in confidence that Abigail, in addition to preparing final papers and exams for her own courses, was left to soothe.

'They're going to tear me to shreds,' he said, sipping his seventh coffee of the day. 'I'm nobody from a nothing school. Who am I to wade into the debate of great historians?'

'You're someone who's done the research and made discoveries,' she said. 'Your argument is solid.'

'I'm not sure, Abigail.' He raked his fingers through his unkempt hair. There were dark shadows under his eyes.

'I am,' she replied. 'You neatly sidestep Beard's and Bailyn's philosophical dispute and stick to the facts: the colonists considered themselves British subjects, with the same rights and protections as their cousins in England, including "no taxation without representation". So when the Crown slapped taxes on sugar, stamps and tea without their consultation, let alone their consent, the colonists understood that, in the eyes of the Crown, they had become a revenue source to be tapped at will. That's why they revolted.'

'You make it sound so logical.'

'*You* make it sound logical. I'm just paraphrasing. Few Americans really cared about ideas,' Abigail said.

'Then as now,' he sighed.

Abigail stood to hand him back his manuscript. 'My favourite part is when you write about the Founding Fathers' desire for a weak executive. That should be your next book.'

'Or maybe yours.' He put his hand on the manuscript but didn't take it from her. 'You have the makings of an excellent historian.'

'My father wants me to go to law school.'

'You'd be great at that, too, I'm sure, but would you like it?'

'I like law, what I've read of it, that is.'

'But law school is a viper's nest. People wouldn't be kind, the men especially, I'm afraid.'

'That wouldn't bother me,' she said. 'I'd miss history, though.'

'And I know that I'd miss you.'

Her face flushed. 'That's very sweet of you to say.'

The next thing she knew his lips were on hers. It was an awkward, bumbling sort of kiss, made more so when he threw his arms around her and clasped her to him. The manuscript got crushed between them. At first she stood passively, frozen in place, but when it seemed he was about to stop, she started to kiss him back, not because she enjoyed it, per se – it was overly wet and tasted of stale breath and coffee – but because as long as they were still kissing they didn't have to deal with the repercussions of having kissed. As long as they were kissing, nothing had changed, and so she hung on as long as possible, until he quite literally pushed her away. The manuscript fell to the floor and she dropped to her knees to retrieve it, grateful for the distraction. He turned and walked quickly out of the office, closing the door behind him, only to return, moments later, taking up a position against the wall, his face flushed, unable to look at her.

'I'm sorry, Mrs McDougall. What I did just now was inexcusable.'

'No, it's fine,' she replied as she scrambled to her feet.

'Unprofessional. Should you wish to lodge a complaint with the school against me—'

'That won't be—'

'I can't think what overcame—'

'Necessary.'

'Me. I mean, of course I know. I mean, look at you—'

'It's all right, Professor—'

'Gorgeous.'

'Crocker, there's no—'

'And brilliant.'

'Need to—'

'Wonderful.'

'Say more.'

She held out the manuscript. 'Would you like me to go over the last chapter one more time? I can take it home and get it back to you tomorrow or Friday?'

'No – I mean, yes – that is . . .' He put his palm to his forehead, as if checking his temperature. 'Only if you want to, Mrs McDougall.' It appeared to take great effort to look her in the eye. 'I'm sorry I lost control. Please know that I meant no disrespect. I value you immensely. I promise that, in the future, my feelings, and my hands' – he looked away – 'will always be kept in check. You needn't fear.'

'You are a gentleman.'

He winced, as if she were being cuttingly ironic.

The right thing to do, as she knew full well, was to cease all communication, do no further work on his book and, going forward, avoid his classes. But he was one of only two American history professors in the department. She'd have to change majors, which was out of the question. Why should she? It wasn't as if she had gone running at him. Why, come to think of it, should she stop working on the book when it was a source of so much enjoyment and fulfilment and when they were so close to being done, anyway? David had made a mistake, it was true, but he'd apologised and promised it would never happen again. She was sure he would be as good as his word. She took the manuscript, leaving the office with her usually cheery farewell, as if nothing out of the ordinary had happened. Nothing *had* happened, she reminded herself on the drive home, in direct response to the voice in her head that whispered that a good wife would quit school before placing herself in such a compromising position.

She walked over to Becky's to collect Mindy in a state of confusion, and full of an urge to confess. Fortunately Becky was on the phone, walking around the kitchen tethered by the long cord. They signed their goodbyes. Abigail took Mindy's hand and they headed home, with Mindy skipping and flitting and humming a made-up song as Abigail's head bubbled away. Why hadn't she slapped his face? That would have been so simple and yet the thought occurred to her only now. It must be because she was in shock. It was so unexpected.

The voice inside her head said it was no such thing. She had seen his attentions to her grow and done nothing to stop them. It wasn't an exaggeration to say she'd encouraged him, led him on, even if she hadn't exactly meant to, at least, not in any romantic sense. She was blinded by her own infatuations: with his mind, his grasp of history and the many things he could teach her. Her blood ran cold. She was the worst kind of woman – a tease.

How could she do such a thing when Ted had been so supportive, so helpful? She was a terrible wife, a terrible mother. She turned to look at Mindy for what, she was ashamed to acknowledge, must have been the first time since picking her up because she hadn't noticed she was holding something in her other hand, a cardboard figure.

'What have you got there?' she asked.

It was a paper doll, a bit tattered and smudged but obviously handmade and beautifully detailed. The face had rosy cheeks, blue eyes and curly strawberry-blonde hair, just like Mindy's. Its paper dress was stylish, red with white polka dots, and bows on the shoulders, the hemline swished as if in motion. Becky was amazing.

'Did Mrs Johnson make this for you?'

Mindy shook her head no. 'See-sore ladies,' she said.

'Who are the see-sore ladies?'

Mindy shrugged her shoulders. 'Daddy friends.'

'And they made this for you?'

'Yes,' said Mindy. 'Fat one made.'

'The fat one made it?'

'Yes. Fat one doll. Old one cookies.'

Chapter Forty

The soles of Penny's shoes made scraping sounds on the painted floorboards of the cottage as she paced back and forth, waiting for Mother to return from carrying her suitcase to the car. The case contained all the things Penny would need for her hospital stay: a nightgown and slippers, make-up, brushes for her teeth and hair, toiletries and a change of clothes for after. They drove with the sun rising through the rear window.

'It's for your safety,' Mother said.

There was no phone. Mother was at work all day. Her doctor and the hospital were an hour and a half's drive away. If labour came on fast or, heaven forbid, there was a problem, she would be alone. If she didn't die, she'd have to go to the local hospital where there were bound to be people they knew – a prospect that, it went without saying, was worse than death. Inducing her ten days before her due date was only prudent.

'Besides, you must be ready for this to be all over,' Mother said. She spent much of the early part of the journey praising the wisdom of the doctor's decision – 'sensible', 'wise', 'the only thing to do, really' – and the more she talked about it, the more certain Penny was that what her mother really meant was that *she* was ready for it to be all over.

Not that Penny blamed her. She was well aware of the sacrifices, large and small, that her mother had made on her behalf these past months, when many parents would have washed their hands of their daughter or, at the very least, shipped her off to foster parents or a home for unwed mothers. Mother had stood by her. She had taken time off work to bring her to her doctor's appointments and to meetings with the social worker. She had allowed Ted to visit and stay over, which had made the situation more bearable. Words could not express her gratitude. Still, she felt she was getting robbed of ten days with her baby.

'I'll be right here,' Mother said, as they wheeled her away.

They attached a bracelet to her wrist that had a second, miniature bracelet for the baby. It seemed impossibly small. They stuck an IV into her hand. She watched the clear liquid drip into her veins, knowing that it contained a drug that would cause her pain and ultimately take her baby from her. She feared labour; she wanted to be pregnant for ever.

The pain started hard. Out of nowhere, she felt as if she were going to split in two. She was sure that this could not be normal. The story of Abigail's death in childbirth haunted her thoughts, even though she knew it had been a fiction.

'Am I going to die?' she asked a nurse.

'No,' the nurse replied. 'But it will feel like you will.'

The delivery room was full of harsh overhead lights. In the pause between contractions they shifted her on to the table. Someone came from behind her and slipped a mask over her face.

'Breathe deeply,' said a voice of authority. The doctor.

Penny put a hand on her belly.

'I love you,' she whispered and waited for her baby to kick back. The lights moved in and out like waves. She was slipping. She was going to slide right off the table. There were so many masked faces.

'Count backwards down from ten,' the doctor said.

'Ten, nine, eight . . .' The edges of her vision turned dark. She was sinking into the table.

'Seven . . . six . . .'

Her field of vision shrank. She was travelling backwards through a long dark tunnel. The bright lights and masked faces receded into the darkness: a harvest moon, a full moon, a star, a pinprick and then nothing. Afterward, she could never remember whether the baby kicked back.

She woke in a different room, alone, her arms tied to the bed rails, like a prisoner. She wanted her mother, but was too scared to call out. She stared at the ceiling, her eyes tracing the blossom-like splotch of a watermark on the tiles as she waited for someone – anyone – to come, staring for so long she began to wonder whether they had forgotten her. She looked at her wrist; the baby's bracelet was gone.

In almost any other situation, the cost of a private room would have been an unthinkable luxury, but Ted and Mother agreed that Penny should not be expected to share with another new mother. Seeing their joyous celebrations would be too painful, conversation between them too awkward. Besides, as Mother noted, it was a small world. The alias under which Penny was registered would be useless if they ran into friends or acquaintances. Best to limit the number of people with whom they interacted to as few as possible. And so after she'd stared at the ceiling in the recovery room for what felt like ages, she was brought to the eighth floor to stare at the ceiling of her private room. Mother had things to do – paperwork for the hospital, a meeting with the social worker and a call to work. A nurse informed her the baby was a girl. The desire to see her gnawed at her insides. She felt it in her arms and in the space behind her eyes. She had not anticipated this. People said if she didn't see the baby, she wouldn't get attached. Out of sight, out of mind. But she was already attached. How could it be any other way, given that they'd been sharing the smallest of spaces these past months? And now that they were apart Penny felt completely empty.

'I wonder what she looks like,' she said to Mother when she came in.

'Best not to think about it,' Mother replied.

'I know,' she said, drawing out the 'o' and staring down at the blanket. 'I hope she has Ted's eyes. Do you think she does?'

'It's too early to tell. Babies' eyes take a few weeks to settle.'

'It would be lovely to hold her. To count her fingers and toes.'

'That's probably not a good idea, dear.'

A horrible thought struck her: that her baby had a defect of some kind and they didn't want to tell her.

'There isn't anything wrong with her, is there?' Her throat went dry. 'She's normal, isn't she?'

'Yes, yes,' said Mother, reaching out to pat her hand. 'Completely normal.'

Staying in bed was a struggle. She had pictured herself lying flat, wrung out by the effort of childbirth, barely able to lift her head up off the pillow or raise her voice above a whisper, but within a few hours of delivery she had an urge to run around the block. She was sore, it was true, but that was the same no matter whether she was lying down or standing up. What she needed was a walk. She could take the stairs down to the fifth floor, where her baby was being kept (for her privacy, they said), and to the glass wall of the nursery. Nobody would ever know. She was sure she would recognise her baby the instant she saw her. She got up and was looking for her robe when a nurse came in and ordered her back to bed. A little while later her mother came in with an artist's sketchbook and pastels.

'I thought you might want to draw.'

Penny drew Mother reading in a chair. She drew the red-brick smoke stacks of the city's knitting mills, visible from her window, a beachscape based on the area around the cottage where she had taken her walks these past weeks, and her old apartment in East Boston. Mrs Nichols admired her drawings when she came by to visit.

'Have you seen her?' Penny asked.

Mrs Nichols nodded. Penny hesitated, unsure whether asking about her baby violated the out of sight, out of mind, convention. But curiosity was stronger.

'What is she like?'

Mrs Nichols smiled as kindly as ever. 'She has a large quantity of dark hair, quite long, and I believe she has your chin.'

Penny lifted her fingers to her chin, a body part she had never given much thought to before that would, from this day forth, be the first thing she saw whenever she looked in a mirror.

'You understand, Penny, that you may see baby any time you want.'

'Oh, she doesn't want to do that, I don't think,' Mother said. 'You know how the imagination runs away from a woman at times like these. She's got it into her head that the baby has a problem.'

'I understand perfectly, Mrs Goodwin, and I'm happy to report that all tests indicate that baby is anatomically normal. An excellent specimen. And I mean what I say, Penny. If you change your mind and decide you want to see baby, all you need do is ask. Tell a nurse and baby will be brought to you directly.'

'Thank you,' Penny said, feeling not thankful at all. Longing for her baby was painful enough without the added burden of responsibility for avoiding her own temptation. When she was little, the Bakers had had a pet beagle named Jet that Mr Baker trained to be obedient. He took great pride in this because beagles are notoriously difficult to control. Jet was not allowed to do anything without his master's permission. Not even eat. Every night Mr Baker filled Jet's dish while the dog sat on the other side of the kitchen, watching. Jet had to wait for a signal from Mr Baker before he could approach and Mr Baker took his own sweet time about it. Poor Jet would stare dolefully and whimper pathetically, toenails clicking on the kitchen floor as he moved his paws frantically without leaving his designated spot. Penny couldn't stand to watch and yet at least the dog was allowed to eat, eventually. For Mrs Nichols to dangle her heart's desire in front of her eyes while knowing full well that she would be compelled to decline it seemed the cruellest trick of all.

After the social worker left she went back to sketching, drawing, at first, without much thought as to what she was doing. Her hand moved with quick, impulsive strokes. An image started to take shape: the interior of a house, with an open layout and with windows that went up to the roofline to let in light. The furniture was angular and modern. There was a slate fireplace in the centre and a coffee table in front of a sofa that looked vaguely Scandinavian, hardwood floors and a plush throw rug; a wet bar in the background, and beyond that, a dining room. It was a room she had never seen before. The picture was halfway done before she understood what it was: it was her home, hers and Ted's together, the one they would share someday soon, once his divorce came through. Surely they deserved to be together now; surely they had earned their happiness. And they would have Mindy and other children, boys and girls, a great band of them and they would roam the neighbourhood together and be known collectively as the McDougalls. 'Those McDougalls!' people would say with the kind of exasperation that was really admiration because no one had ever known brothers and sisters to get along so well.

She turned to a fresh page and drew a yellow kitchen full of light, open to a dining room with a large metal and glass table. A space-age-looking chandelier hanging above it. She filled subsequent pages with children's bedrooms – a girl's, frilly and pink; and a boy's, with straight lines and lots of space for sports equipment; and a third, a double, with two of everything, for twins of an indeterminate gender. They wouldn't be the wealthiest in the neighbourhood – or perhaps they would be, though nobody would know it because they weren't show-offy types – but everything they did would have a distinctive style, a panache. They would be known for their kindness and generosity; love would infuse their home. And when Ted came to visit later that evening, she showed him her drawing and he smiled, with tears in his eyes, and promised it would be just as she had drawn it. He brought her an enormous bouquet of long-stemmed pink roses and what looked like a shop's entire selection of women's magazines. He kissed her, took her hands in his and told her that she was brave and that he was proud of her.

'She's a girl!' she said softly.

He put his arm around her and gave her a sad smile. 'I know, sweetheart. Your mom told me.'

'I want to call her Lily.'

'If that's what you want, princess.'

Ted had shown little enthusiasm for discussing baby names in the run-up to delivery, so his acquiescence was all the encouragement she needed to plunge further.

'We can see her. All we have to do is ask the nurse and they'll bring her to us. Mrs Nichols said—'

'Sweetheart, you know that isn't a good idea. Anyway, she is probably down for the night by now. We don't want to unsettle her. They'll want to get her into a routine.'

'Have you met with the social worker?'

'I haven't had time, princess. I came straight here to see you.'

'You have to meet with her, Ted. Mrs Nichols needs your family history to decide where to place the baby. Please, Ted. She has a whole list of questions to ask you.'

'I've told you everything already. I'm Scotch-Irish.'

Penny sprang forward. 'It's much more detailed than that. Please! Imagine if Lily ended up with the wrong family! She could have a miserable life and we could prevent it. Besides, we owe it to Mrs Nichols. She is doing us a favour in letting you come to visit. Normally the hospital doesn't allow the . . . the . . . fathers.' She couldn't say 'alleged' to his face, but without that modifier the whole thing lost its meaning. Of course fathers were allowed in to see their babies. All these words, this terminology, this splicing of fathers and alleged ones, mothers and natural ones, every one of them designed to lower her standing in the world.

'I'll call her in the morning,' he said. 'I promise.'

Chapter Forty-One

Ted rescheduled his meeting with A.T. Shipping, but didn't tell Sally and left the office just after noon as if that were where he was headed. It troubled him. He wasn't afraid of getting caught – he'd just say there was a confusion with their diaries, blame it on the secretaries – but he knew it would hurt his chances of making the deal. Last week, when Penny told him the doctors wanted to take the baby on Monday, he had padded his schedule with fictitious meetings and sales leads, freeing up time so he could spend it with her at the hospital. Cancelling the only legitimate bit of business, at this late hour, would damage the store's bottom line and his reputation as a rising star. It was a self-inflicted wound, an own goal, at a time when he could least afford it. Sales figures for the last quarter weren't what he'd hoped. Mike Cook was coming next week to discuss the strategy they'd agreed to implement six months ago and Ted, running flat out trying to manage the Penny situation, had barely looked at the thing. But he was not going to worry about any of that now. He'd make up for it next week. Next week would be better. Next week all of this would be in the rear-view mirror and he could finally focus his energies on his job. He wouldn't have minded the sacrifice if it were to spend more time with Penny, but it was to meet with the social worker, a woman he didn't trust and whose only knowledge of him was that he was a scoundrel and a liar.

He got to the agency on time. Mrs Nichols looked surprised when she opened her door and saw him sitting in the waiting room, flipping through a gardening magazine. Most men in his situation probably didn't have the guts to show their faces. Score a point for him.

She was tiny, her head barely reached to his shoulder, and plump, wearing a suit made of some lightweight knit and sensible shoes. Her pale skin was dotted with tiny blue veins that she'd tried to conceal with powder. He was not fooled by her gentle demeanour; her grandmotherly smile did nothing to alter the sense that he was back in elementary school, preparing to get a thrashing from the principal for having dipped Helene Proux's braid in his desk inkwell. Now was the moment he would be called to account for his shameful behaviour. If he could have run, he would have, but Penny wanted him to make a good impression and it was his duty as a father to make sure that his baby went to the very top of the list of desirable babies. Even if he never saw her – and he would do everything in his power to make sure he never did – he intended to do all he could to make sure she had a good life. Mrs Nichols led him to the sitting area as if for an informal chat, an informal chat in which one person asks all the questions and writes down the other's responses. The only logical place to start was with contrition.

'Let me just say, up front, how sorry I am that this meeting is necessary. I should have got my divorce sorted earlier. It was wrong of me to mislead Penny about the state of my marriage. I let my personal shame and fear of losing the love of my life prevent me from being honest and I deeply regret it.'

'And what exactly is your marriage status, Mr McDougall?'

He sensed moisture collecting on his upper lip as he reiterated the things he'd told Penny. She raised a sceptical eyebrow only once, when he mentioned the private investigator his in-laws had hired to watch him, and appeared less than wholly convinced by his explanation of the inherent barriers of serving divorce papers on a woman committed to a psychiatric hospital, slowly repeating the phrase, *in another state*, but she didn't question it.

'It's admirable of you to take responsibility, Mr McDougall, but I haven't asked you here to assign blame. I'm focused on what's best for baby.'

Ted didn't believe her, but he nodded along as if he did.

'Many, many parents come to our agency looking for children to adopt,' she explained. 'And the sad truth is that there are far more deserving parents than we have children available to place. The more I know about your family background, the better the chances of finding a good match for baby, if, that is, releasing her for placement into adoption is Penny's final decision.'

He was happy to sketch his genealogy for her, to discuss the ethnic make-ups of his parents and grandparents, the schooling they'd received and the work they'd done or, in the case of his mother, did. Mrs Nichols was impressed to hear that both his maternal grandparents were living and had their faculties. For his paternal relatives he supplied the ages and causes of death. She was very curious about medical problems; he tried his best to provide the right amount of maladies – enough to satisfy her curiosity – fill blank spaces in the file, without raising concerns that might make the baby unadoptable. He took pains to demonstrate his own excellent health. Before launching into the dramatic saga of his father's final illness, he was careful to highlight the doctors' conclusions that the heart problems that preceded it were due to a childhood bout of rheumatic fever and not a hereditary defect. He spoke at length about his mother's career.

'You seem very proud of your mother's professional achievements.'

'I am,' he replied. 'Rightly, I think. Her achievements are impressive.'

She smiled sweetly and made a faint humming sound that he took for agreement.

'Do you think spending so much time with Penny these last few months has been beneficial to her?'

The change-up caught him off guard and confirmed his worst suspicions.

'I hope it has,' he said, as his underarms went damp. 'That was my goal, at least, in doing so. It hasn't been easy, reworking my schedule. I've put a lot of miles on the car, travelling between work, my daughter and Penny, but it's worth it. I know how difficult this is for Penny and, as I've said, I'm aware that I bear the majority of the blame.'

'How will you feel if Penny comes to resent you if, as planned, she releases baby?'

'Terrible. Distraught,' he replied, partly because he knew those were the right answers and also because he was sure that he *would* feel that way – what was all this running himself ragged for if not to keep Penny from turning against him? – and yet, as the words were leaving his mouth he wondered how terrible such an outcome would really be. Much as he would miss her, he loved the idea of having **his** old boring life back. 'But I know that it is a possibility.'

'Would it have been harder, do you think, for you to consider releasing baby had it been a boy?'

She was always underlining that the adoption was not a done deal; they could choose otherwise. Ted liked that she didn't make assumptions with a baby that did not belong to her; nonetheless, the thought of Penny keeping it made his temples throb.

'Not at all,' he said. 'I do think that maybe a girl is harder for Penny. She is such a dainty, feminine person.'

His jaw tightened when Mrs Nichols asked how his family would feel about him marrying Penny, and he was forced to admit that none of them was aware of her existence. Behind Mrs Nichols's passive eyes he pictured the wheels of her brain churning: wondering what sort of man fathers a child with a girl he hasn't introduced to his mother?

And then the interview's focus turned to his personal history. He repeated everything he had told Penny, without the slightest worry that he would leave anything out. They could have cross-referenced the most minute detail. He knew it all in his bones. That's how real it felt. He began to relax; to enjoy himself, even.

Through Mrs Nichols's notes, Penny's Ted was made real, a flesh and blood person with an heir. The things he told her today would be included in the baby's records and kept for all time, sealed like a top-secret file. They would become part of this baby's history, part of the folklore that the parents who raised her would pass on; documented proof that he had gone to college in Colorado on a football scholarship, that he had dodged avalanches as a member of ski patrol and worked for the CIA in Vietnam. By the time he walked out of Mrs Nichols's office he felt ten feet tall.

Chapter Forty-Two

Penny's post-delivery euphoria lasted three days. She slept little and drew a lot. Her mother brought her some pink and white yarn and she set to work knitting a blanket for Lily. On the third night she dreamed that Lily was still inside her. She felt her moving and kicking. She woke in tears. When Mrs Nichols came to visit she grilled her for information about Lily – her progress and development – and when the smiling social worker replied, placidly, that there had not been much change in two days, she burst into tears. She cried again when the doctor raised the possibility of discharge the following day. She was sick of this stuffy room, the smell of disinfectant and overcooked vegetables. She yearned for fresh air. But leaving meant leaving Lily behind. If she didn't see her in the next twenty-four hours, she never would.

'But, dear,' Mother said. 'You always said you didn't want to.'

'I was wrong,' she bawled.

Mother sighed. 'It's up to you,' she said. 'Mrs Nichols says it's your choice.'

When the nurse came to take her breakfast tray, she asked to have Lily brought to her. She said it so quietly, a whisper, really, that she was a little surprised when the nurse returned a short while later, pushing a little wooden crib. The baby was sleeping on her back, her head tilted to the side. Her hair was dark brown, almost black, and her little squished-up face seemed to be pondering great thoughts. Penny put her hands on her heart.

'Hello, there, Lily,' she murmured as tears tumbled and her nose ran.

The baby's arms twitched.

'Fighting tigers,' said Mother.

To Penny it looked more like she was reaching for something and, with a shock, she realised that the thing Lily sought was her. She had recognised her mother's voice and, with a start, she realised that *she* was the thing Lily was seeking. The baby had recognised her mother's voice, and wanted her. Lily needed her every bit as much as Penny needed Lily.

'I'd love to keep her,' she said, looking first to the nurse and then to her mother. 'That would be wonderful.'

'If only,' Mother said. Standing rigid, unyielding.

'You can hold her, if you want?' the nurse asked.

Penny's arms went out to receive Lily but, almost imperceptibly, Mother shook her head, and Penny forced them back down.

'If I do I'll never let her go,' she cried.

She walked slowly around the crib, inspecting Lily from every angle, thinking that she would draw her later. When she got to the far side of the bars she saw that someone (a nurse?) had attached a piece of masking tape to the far side of the bars on which was written in green marker, five words that turned her blood cold: *Do not show to Mother.*

After the nurse wheeled Lily away she curled into a ball on the bed. She wrapped her aching arms around a pillow, buried her face in it and cried, undisturbed, until the pillow was soaked through. When her cries became wails, and she began tearing at the pillow with her teeth, Mother called for the nurse, who called for a doctor, who gave her a shot that made her sleep.

She woke the following morning with Mother at her side. Thankfully, she did not say, 'I told you so.' She helped Penny dress and did her hair. Penny was careful to keep her tears to a minimum while signing the boarding agreement that placed Lily into foster care. A temporary arrangement, Mrs Nichols stressed. 'To give you the space you need to decide what is best for baby.' Mother handed her the flowers Ted had brought on the first day.

They were a little tired and wilted, their necks bowed, but they filled her hands. The car's vinyl seats burned the back of her legs. They rode with the windows down. It blew their hair in all directions.

Penny prayed for Abigail's recovery so that Ted could serve the papers, the adoption could be put off, and Lily brought home. She was prepared to live with him until his divorce came through. That's what she'd tell him, the next time she saw him. She didn't care whether she went to hell, didn't care if people called her a whore; all she cared about was being a family.

Chapter Forty-Three

At the Goodyear store, Ted was in a querulous mood all morning, barking orders and berating his salesmen for errors real and perceived. He was edgy and temperamental until around noon-time, when he grew quiet and pensive. It was such a long road that they had travelled; he was terrified of stumbling at the last hurdle. He calculated extra time for packing and discussions, questions and answers, and then the drive back to the Cape in the slow lane. At three in the afternoon he closed the door to his office, took a deep breath and dialled the number to Rose's Cape house. When Rose answered, the anxiety that had been dammed up inside him burst and he felt joyful relief fill his veins.

'I'm so proud of you,' he told Penny. 'You have been very brave. I wish I could have been there with you.'

'When are you coming down?' she asked through muffled tears.

'Soon as I can, princess.'

As he walked to his car he whistled. He bought Abigail a bouquet of daisies and when he got home he tossed Mindy in the air.

'Big sale today?' Abigail asked.

'Nope,' he said, pulling her close and kissing her on the mouth, out on the front lawn. 'Just happy to be home.'

The Young Manager's Training Programme that had provided the necessary cover for the three nights a week he spent at Penny's was redeployed to allow two uninterrupted weeks at home in Elm Grove. The timing was perfect. The weather was fine – late spring and not yet too hot. Abigail's professor had sent his book off to the publisher. She was named to the Dean's List for the second semester running, and had a few weeks off before her summer courses started. They took evening strolls around the neighbourhood; they saw a movie at the Shoppers' World Cinema, had barbecues and played horseshoes in the back yard. They went to bed early. The mountain of paperwork he'd let pile up at work gradually shrank.

He called Penny every day at lunchtime. Her voice was small and broken. Always, she asked, 'When are you coming?'

He made plans to drive down to the Cape the following Friday but when the Johnsons invited Abigail and him for drinks that Saturday evening, he told her that Mindy had come down with a fever and pushed it back to the next week, Memorial Day weekend. Abigail and Mindy were heading to Wilsonville Thursday morning; Ted would follow after work Saturday evening, which meant his Friday night was free.

It was the worst possible time to head to the Cape. The traffic out of Boston was slow and the back-up to the bridge was over five miles long. His left leg got tired playing the clutch and he was already thinking about how he'd need to be off at first light the next morning to get to the store and then drive north to Wilsonville after work. The odometer on the Corvair had just passed twenty-one thousand miles; he was running her into the ground.

The traffic on the Cape side of the bridge was just as bad. It was creep and beep all the way until he quit the Mid-Cape at Exit 10. The centre of town was buzzing with people and the sounds of a new summer season, but Rose's house had the aura of a funeral parlour. He was surprised how much pregnancy weight Penny had already lost, and equally surprised that the effect wasn't pleasing. She was pale; skin hung in bags under her eyes and from her neck in a way that aged her. Her hair was thinner and had lost its lustre. She prepared a simple cold salad for dinner that she barely touched. On the short walk they took in town she shuffled like an old woman, leaning heavily on his arm, except when they passed a baby carriage and she popped to life, craning her neck, Gumby-like, to see the baby inside.

'Your baby is darling,' she said to a woman. 'How old?'

'Three weeks,' the woman said.

Penny's eyes gleamed with manic intensity. The woman gripped the carriage a little firmer. Penny asked the baby's name, only to lose interest when the mother replied, 'Joseph.'

All the energy went out of her and they lumbered back to Rose's house. He searched for topics he thought would interest her – his struggles at work, funny things Danny had done, even stories about Mindy – but the only thing she wanted to discuss was Lily.

'I'm seeing the social worker next Tuesday.'

'Will this be the last time?'

'I'm not sure. I think there might be one or two more.'

'Jesus!' he cried, louder than he intended. 'Why won't they just let you sign the papers already?'

'It's complicated, Ted, they have to be convinced I'm sure about my decision.'

'How many times have you told them your decision? You've never wavered once, so far as I know, over the five months you've been talking to them.'

'Three.'

'What?'

'My first appointment was in March; it's been only three months.'

'Fine, my point is, isn't that enough? In my book, three months is enough.'

She replied in a voice so quiet he had to lean over and put his ear inches away from her mouth.

'Mrs Nichols thinks it would be nice if you came.'

'You know I can't do that, sweet pea. I'm flat out. I haven't even been able to visit you.'

'I know, Ted, but she thinks it might be helpful if—'

'Helpful? Helpful for what? Helpful for who? You know what I think? I think that social worker is a nosy little busybody who enjoys hearing the juicy bits of other people's business.'

'Don't, Ted, don't,' she said. 'She's trying to do her best for Lily. She needs the whole story.' And then she turned on the waterworks.

But he'd heard enough. He had tried, God knew, he'd tried his best for months and months. He wanted this to be over. His patience snapped. 'The whole story!' he thundered. 'What do you mean by "the whole story"? I told her the whole story. Are you insinuating that I've been telling lies?'

'No, Ted, never! She needs to be sure that we've considered all the options.'

'What other options? What other options are there? You know darn well there aren't any other options.'

'Well.' She was wringing her hands. 'She says that maybe if you were to come to an arrangement with Abigail's father, agree to give him visitation rights, a weekend a month, for example, and—'

'And you're okay with this social worker telling me what to do?'

'She says that it might reassure him and—'

'That's awfully clever of her. Gee, maybe I should have consulted her earlier.' All composure was gone, he was striding back and forth across the parlour like a deranged Perry Mason. 'And I suppose I should just cheerfully sign away part of my parental rights?'

He expected her to capitulate, to simper and make nice. Instead she jumped to her feet, her hands curled into angry fists.

'Yes!' she cried. 'So that I don't have to sign away *all* of mine!'

He grabbed his jacket and marched out to the Corvair. The wheels spun as he pulled away, kicking up pebbles and sending dust in all directions. He watched her face in the rear-view mirror, gaunt and grief-stricken and thought, *That'll teach her.* He didn't know what he was doing, or where he was going. The vessel in his head pumped like a piston in an engine. He was going to bust a blood vessel, just like his dad. He was a good guy; he wasn't a skunk. Why did she do it? Why did she push him so hard? Drive, just drive. He hit the highway, slipped the stick into fourth and let the car run. There was hardly any traffic heading off the Cape. With his foot near the floor and the needle pinned at ninety, the throb of blood in his head began to soften and slow.

Chapter Forty-Four

On any other Wednesday afternoon during the past fourteen weeks, Abigail wouldn't have been home to take the call. She would have been in statistics class, and afterward studying at the library or maybe doing research for David instead of on her hands and knees, scrubbing six weeks' worth of mould and soap scum out of the bathtub.

'I am looking for the McDougall residence,' said the caller, a female, in a tone of affected professionalism.

'Yes,' Abigail replied, guessing it was the folks Ted had been talking to about expanding the patio.

'I see. And with whom am I speaking?' the caller asked.

'Mrs McDougall.'

'Mrs *Edward* McDougall?'

'Yes,' she said. If it was the patio people, they needed a new girl. This one was too high-strung. She hadn't even identified herself. 'Who's calling?'

'Are you the mother of a two-year-old daughter named Mindy?' The girl's voice had jumped an octave and turned brittle.

'To whom am I speaking, please?' Abigail demanded, as the first, tiny spasm of alarm pricked the top of her spine.

The girl made sounds of a drowning sheep.

'Have your husband call this number when he gets in,' she said, and proceeded to rattle seven digits off in a great, desperate rush to stay ahead of the oncoming tears, which she did, just, and then she took a deep breath and exhaled before leaving some parting words of advice: 'You had best look into his activities.'

For some minutes after, Abigail stared at the phone, stunned by both the caller's gall and her choice of words. 'Activities' could mean almost anything.

Was Ted in trouble? Did he owe people money?

She picked up the phone and began dialling his number, but then changed her mind and instead called information for Goodyear's regional corporate headquarters. Once connected, she asked to speak to the head of the Young Manager's Training Programme. A chirpy receptionist promised to put her right through. Abigail held for some time.

'I'm sorry, ma'am,' the receptionist said when she returned, 'what did you say the programme was called?'

'Young Manager's Training Programme – that's what my husband calls it, at least. It probably has another, more official name.'

'And it meets on Monday, Wednesday and Friday nights?'

'Yes.'

'In a hotel?'

'In Braintree, I think.'

'Thank you. I won't be a moment.'

Several moments later, she came back on the line.

'I'm awfully sorry, ma'am,' she said. 'No one here has heard of a training programme fitting that description.'

'I see,' Abigail said. She swallowed hard. 'Thank you.'

It was a gorgeous, warm day and yet she felt suddenly cold, as if the marrow in her bones had turned to ice. She took a cigarette from an open pack Ted had left on the kitchen table and lit it. Her lungs coughed the smoke back out.

Mindy came into the kitchen. 'Mommy no smoke,' she said.

'I smoke sometimes.' Abigail inhaled (and coughed) again.

'Hungry,' said Mindy.

'What do you want?'

Mindy turned her head coyly. 'Cookies?'

Abigail took a box from the cupboard and shook a pile of cookies on to a plate that she handed to an incredulous Mindy.

'Hang on,' Abigail said, and poured a glass of milk. 'Want to eat in front of the television?'

Mindy hesitated, suspecting a trick question.

'Go ahead. You know how to turn it on, right?'

Mindy gave a vigorous nod and carried the plate and glass into the living room with prodigious care. Abigail made herself a cup of tea and sat at the kitchen table with her hands wrapped around the mug.

An after-hours training programme?

Three nights a week?

She left her tea on the table, went to the liquor cabinet and poured three fingers of vodka into a glass; ice cubes and a splash of orange juice were token afterthoughts.

'Stupid,' she muttered. 'Stupid, stupid, stupid.'

The passbook for Mindy's bank account was in the desk. The money was still missing. He wasn't even bothering to try to hide it. She covered her face with her hands and clawed at her hair. How long had this been going on? Were the neighbours whispering about it, laughing about it, behind her back? Was she a laughing stock *and* a freak?

She shuddered. The ladies of Elm Grove would be sympathetic. They'd shower her with kindness, as they had Janice, bringing their casseroles wrapped in tin foil, plates of cookies and cakes. They'd brew pots of coffee and tea and sit here at this table with their heads tilted, brows gently furrowed, lower lips protruding slightly. They'd pat her hand and say, 'there-there', hovering for gossip like turkey vultures circling above fresh roadkill.

'What did she expect?' Carol or Frannie or even Becky would ask. 'Off at her classes all day, in New Hampshire every weekend.'

'While he does the dishes.'

'Folds the laundry.'

'Man's a saint.'

Her mother's language would be gentler, and yet would arrive at the same conclusions. Hadn't she already tried to warn her?

Proud Abigail – the smart one – was so vain and overconfident that she accepted, without question, a story containing more holes than Swiss cheese. She had no interest in questioning it because it left her free to spend more time studying, more time with David.

She squirmed in her seat. Schoolgirl crushes are made of air and pop like soap bubbles, leaving behind astonishment, swiftly followed by embarrassment. She had seen only the brilliance of David's mind, the breadth of his knowledge and his tireless commitment to scholarship. Now there was only the snaggletooth grin, shabby clothes, corny jokes and goofy laugh. The thought of walking into a room on his arm instead of Ted's made her skin crawl. She gulped down her drink and went to the counter to pour another. In the toaster's smudged and crumb-encrusted stainless-steel surface she caught a glimpse of her distorted reflection. The housecoat! The braids! No wonder her husband had found someone new!

She played absentmindedly with her braids, pondering the girl on the other end of the line, whom she imagined to be long-legged and glamorous. Blonde, with bright red lipstick and a face always freshly powdered; a dead ringer for Marilyn Monroe. She rummaged through a drawer for the kitchen shears and when she found them she began to cut, sawing back and forth in a jagged line because the braids were thick and the shears dull.

She joined Mindy on the sofa. They watched *The Flintstones* and then a succession of soap operas. Abigail turned the shears on her housecoat, renting it to jagged ribbons. Mindy lost interest in the television and went to run up and down the hallway on a sugar-induced tear. Abigail sipped at her drink and swung her braids like a lasso. By the time Ted got home she was queasy, her vision a bit blurry.

'What's for dinner?' he asked.

'Beats me.'

'Jesus, what have you done to your hair?'

Her hand went up to touch the uneven ends. She smiled at the sight of confusion spreading across his face.

'How much have you had to drink?'

'Not nearly enough.'

He sat down and took her hand.

'Did something happen to make you sad?' He spoke with such tenderness. 'Is it about school? The neighbours?'

'It's about your activities.'

'My activities?'

'Yes. The woman who called today said I should ask about them.' She spoke slowly to try to keep from slurring. She regretted those drinks. 'She wants you to call her. The number is in the kitchen.'

He came back holding the piece of paper. 'Honey, I have no idea who this is. I have never seen this number in my entire life. It could be a new client, I guess.'

He looked so sincere that Abigail began to doubt herself. 'Since when do clients call our home?'

'Must be a mix-up.'

'Why would a new client ask if we had a daughter?'

'They asked if we had a daughter?' he asked and the mask fell, but only for an instant. 'I already told you, I do not know this number. It's probably kids from the neighbourhood doing prank calls.'

'Ha! I checked the phone book. That exchange is on Cape Cod.' And while Ted talked of the nature of pranks, and how kids say any old numbers that come into their heads, her brain took two loose ends and made a bow.

'The see-sore ladies!' His face shifted in and out of focus. 'How could you, Ted?' she slurred. 'How could you take my daughter? My daughter,' she growled. 'To meet . . . *her*.'

'You're drunk, Abigail. You don't know what you're saying.'

'I know there is no Young Manager's Training Programme.'

'Of course there is, sweet pea.'

She so wanted to believe him; wanted him to be right, but she shook her head no. 'I called the corporate office.'

Time seemed to slow down. In that moment her drunkenness

cleared and she felt perfectly lucid, aware of everything that was happening and yet focused entirely on Ted, whose shoulders eventually slumped and then he fell to his knees.

'Forgive me,' he whispered.

She ran to the bathroom and threw up.

Chapter Forty-Five

Mrs Nichols was smiling her customary smile: warm-yet-professional.

'Penny, Mrs Goodwin,' she called, holding the door to her office open for them. 'Come in; please, come in.'

She had swapped her trusty herringbone suit for a grey linen shift; a pair of open-toed sandals with small heels had replaced the sensible beige lace-ups. The heat, Penny supposed or, perhaps, the subject of today's meeting called for something more festive? The thought made her stomach lurch.

'So nice to see you both.'

Mrs Nichols ushered them over to the sitting area, but not before Penny spied the small pile of papers lying face down on the desk. They took their habitual seats. A warm cross-breeze blew in through the open windows. Had circumstances been different, had those papers not been on the desk, it would have been a cheerful place to be.

'Tea?' Mrs Nichols asked, lifting the china pot that, as usual, was set on the little table between them.

Penny took a cup out of politeness. She declined a cookie.

'You're a little less pale today, Penny,' Mrs Nichols noted. 'Are you feeling any better?'

Penny stirred her tea, the spoon chiming out an uneven rhythm against the cup. 'A little,' she replied, compelled, despite herself, to answer in a way that pleased.

Mrs Nichols took a dignified bite of a cookie. Penny watched her chew and wondered how many teas the social worker consumed on any given day: one with every unwed mother and every adoptive parent. Was it five? Six?

'Managing to eat?' Mrs Nichols asked.

Penny removed the spoon and laid it in the saucer. She cleared her throat. 'Not really, no.'

'Milkshakes,' Mother explained. 'A little toast from time to time.'

'You look thin, dear.'

That was being charitable. Twiggy was thin. She was well on her way to emaciated. Her cheeks were sunken, her eyes looked too big for her face. The sundress she was wearing had been almost too snug last year. Today she could grab a fistful of loose fabric from the bodice.

'It's understandable, isn't it?' Mrs Nichols chirped. 'You've been under considerable stress and, of course, you received an unexpected shock, didn't you? When the body goes into shock it doesn't want food.'

Penny nodded. From the corner of her eye she saw her mother nodding as well and felt a quiet rage. Steam from the tea wafted into her face. She wanted to hurl the cup at the wall just to see it shatter, imagining the tea-coloured stain bursting on the yellow walls; instead, she placed it on the table.

'Dr Warburton tells me he finds you normal, apart from the weight loss. He gave you some tranquillisers?'

Penny nodded slowly.

'Are they helping you to sleep?'

'They knock her out,' Mother said.

It wasn't a good kind of sleep. It deadened the senses and slowed her reactions. It created a woolly barrier between herself and the rest of the world. She wanted to bang on it, but could not make her arms move; when she tried to scream, no sound came out. The world mistook her slowness for docility, saw her paralysis and called it serenity.

'Good. That's very good.'

If only she'd loosen that knot of silver hair at the back of her head, just a bit, Penny thought, she'd be so much more attractive.

'Sleep is essential to recovery.'

'How is she?' Penny asked.

'Fine,' Mrs Nichols replied, smiling again. She never missed a beat. 'Developing normally.'

'Is she eating?'

'She has a good appetite.'

Penny leaned forward in her chair, eyes wide with interest. 'Yes?'

Mrs Nichols put down her cup, shifted in her chair, still smiling.

'You do understand, dear, that there hasn't been much change from the last time we met, a few weeks ago; even less, I'm afraid, from when we spoke on the phone the day before yesterday.'

'Is she sleeping well?'

'I believe so.'

She stared at her intensely, willing her on, and she kept staring even though she could see that it was alarming the old lady. Poor Mrs Nichols, she really did want to help. Of course she did. She imagined herself as a kind of fairy godmother, placing babies into the arms of deserving couples; sweeping the mistakes of the young unmarried women safely under the carpet. How satisfying to spend one's days washing away sins and setting the world to rights; how noble. It was almost godlike. Penny's pain upset the narrative. Nothing in Mrs Nichols's professional arsenal could stem the longing she felt for her baby; no words could take away the pain of losing her. Her arms ached from not holding Lily, deep in the tissue, deep in her bones, and no amount of rest and sleep, aspirin and warm baths, not even those damned tranquillisers, could stop it. When her daughter was inside her, Penny could distinguish a happy kick from an unhappy one; she understood that Lily liked fresh asparagus better than liver, preferred Bach to Herman's Hermits, and Lily, likewise, sensed her moods. There was a bond between them. But six weeks of separation had obliterated all that. At this moment she had no idea whether

285

her daughter was happy or sad, sleeping peacefully or screaming her head off, being doted on or neglected. Did Lily miss her? Did she blame Penny for abandoning her? Penny could not know. She would never know.

She was aware, suddenly, that her mother and Mrs Nichols were watching her, waiting, it seemed, for a response to a question Penny hadn't heard.

'I beg your pardon.'

Mrs Nichols smiled. 'I said, dear, you haven't heard from Ted, I suppose?'

Penny shook her head.

'Ted, of course, is not named on the birth certificate. It has been my experience, however, that the lack of legal standing is not always sufficient deterrent, particularly when it comes to grandparents.'

Yes, Penny thought, recalling all the trouble Ted's in-laws had caused him, before remembering it had been a lie. She'd had a similar experience a few days ago, while reading a magazine article about the CIA's shady role in Vietnam. Who knew whether Ted had even been there?

'I do feel the need to press the point a little, I'm afraid. Sorry if this is painful for you, Penny, but it is vital that we get all of this absolutely straight before we proceed.'

'She understands,' Mother said.

'Do you feel that your relationship with him is over? Clearly and irrevocably?'

'I'll never contact him and I'm certain he'll never contact me.'

'Very well. But what if he did contact you? Let's say – just for the sake of argument – that he phoned or came to see you tonight, or next week? How do you think you would react?'

'I wouldn't take his call. I wouldn't let him in.'

'Are you sure?'

'Yes,' Penny declared, certain that this was the correct answer, the one that Mrs Nichols wanted to hear. Whether it would be the course of action she'd actually take should the hypothetical play out in real life, she had her doubts. She missed the safety of his arms, and the way he made her feel beautiful and womanly; she missed the dream they had shared. Were he to appear on the other end of the phone line, or the other side of the screen door, she suspected she would walk through fire to get to him.

'I think, Penny, that you have matured considerably as a result of this experience,' said Mrs Nichols, still smiling.

How little you know, Mrs Nichols, she thought.

'And now, I'm afraid there is the small matter of the bill,' the social worker added.

'Yes, I've brought my cheque book,' said Mother.

'And Ted?' Mrs Nichols asked.

Penny shook her head. 'Only the hundred dollars.'

Mrs Nichols tut-tutted. 'I'm sorry, Penny, that things have ended so badly for you. Now then, following our phone discussion two days ago, I had some papers drawn up. If you're still of the mind that releasing baby into adoption is the best option, we are ready to proceed.' She got the pile of papers off her desk and handed them to Penny.

'I'll give you a moment to look them over,' she said and she quit the room, closing the door behind her.

Penny stared down at the papers, unable to believe that it was really coming to this. Her eyes glanced over the text.

I, Penelope Ann Goodwin, willingly and voluntarily waive all custodial rights to my child, Lily Beth Goodwin . . .

It was brief, straightforward and, Penny thought, a complete lie. She was not willing; this was not voluntary. She turned toward her mother.

'Do I have to?'

'You know there isn't any other way.'

'We could raise her together.'

'Honey, how could we possibly—'

'We'll move to Boston, some place where nobody knows us. We'll both get jobs and take care of her together.' Penny's heart began to race. The blood flowed through her veins and she felt warm for the first time in weeks.

'Honey, please.'

'I'll work nights in a factory and look after her during the day.'

'You're being emotional, dear, you're not thinking straight.'

'Please, Mommy.'

'Stop talking nonsense,' her mother snapped.

That was when Penny realised that all that talk about it being her decision, her choice, had always been just that – talk, empty words, tepid, used air. The fix was in from the start. There was no way she was going to be allowed to keep Lily. They gave her the illusion of control because it made what they did in this office and in the homes for unwed mothers seem less mercenary, a little less like stealing. The agency talked about creating families when, in reality, their business was breaking them apart.

'Darling,' her mother said, in a softer tone, 'if you take her home, no man will ever have you. This way, you'll have a fresh start.'

'I don't care,' she said, but that was a lie. She wanted a fresh start; she just couldn't believe one was possible. Forevermore she'd carry the grief of losing her baby, and the guilt of having 'released her'. Sure, she could go back into the world, rejoin polite society, but she would always know that she was a fraud, her respectability a sham.

'You don't want the kids at school calling her a bastard.'

'We'll say I'm a widow – that my husband died in Vietnam.'

'The truth will out, dear.'

'Then why have we bothered spinning this great web of lies all these months?' Penny asked.

Mother had been gentle and understanding but it was clear that her patience was wearing thin. 'Think of Lily,' she said.

Yes. Lily. She must not put her desires ahead of her daughter's chance for a wonderful life with two parents who could give her so much more than Penny ever could: piano and ballet lessons, maybe even her own horse, ensure she was the girl invited to all the birthday parties instead of the sad pale social pariah with worn-out shoes and the wrong sorts of clothes. It was selfish to force Lily to share in her shame.

Mrs Nichols returned with the receptionist who, she explained, would serve as witness. Penny wondered how many times the secretary had performed that service. She wished she could ask her how the other mothers behaved: Did they cry? Did they make futile self-justifying speeches about how much they wished they could keep their babies? Had any been courageous enough to refuse?

The pen felt strange in her hand: such a simple instrument for such a dramatic event. A few squiggles of ink on a page meant she would never bake a birthday cake, make paper dolls or Halloween costumes for Lily. A stocking with Lily's name on it would never hang on the chimney next to Penny's. When her daughter called *ma-ma* for the first time it would be to someone else. A stranger. Lily was being quietly sawed from the family tree so that she could be grafted on to a new one. She would get a new name and a new birth certificate. With this pen, Penny was erasing herself. She might pass Lily on the street someday, sit next to her on the subway or at a doctor's office, and never know it.

She was sure that her hand had trembled, that she had failed to apply sufficient pressure to the paper, but when she stepped away she saw, with horror, that the signature at the bottom of the paper was indistinguishable from how it appeared on a letter or a cheque. Just like that, she had said goodbye to Lily when she had barely said hello. What sort of woman gives her baby away to be raised by strangers? A monster, she must be a monster.

'I am obliged by law to inform you, Penny,' Mrs Nichols said, still with the same pleasant smile, as if they were discussing the weather or brands of laundry detergent, 'that if you try to seek out or make contact with the baby, you will be arrested.'

Chapter Forty-Six

Whatever one said about him – and Ted was well aware that, were his actions widely known, plenty could and would be said about the poor decisions he'd made – there was one accusation he would not stand for: the suggestion that Ted McDougall had taken the easy way out. Not many men would have put so much time and energy into an earnest, if ultimately futile, attempt to avoid hurting two women he respected and loved. What was he supposed to do? Just walk away? Drop Penny like a hot potato? Now *that* would have been the easy way, the coward's way. Common decency demanded that he see things through to their sad conclusion – the way Travis has to shoot Old Yeller at the end of the movie – because that's what it means to be a man. His biggest mistake had been in taking so long to admit he was licked. Months after the average man would have packed it in, raised his arms in surrender and slunked away, he kept at it, convinced he could find a way to square the circle, and, by God, he'd nearly done it.

Words alone were insufficient to describe the terror he felt when he returned from work that day and found Abigail staring blankly at the TV, hair chopped off like some demented novitiate nun; Abigail, who'd been fine at breakfast that morning, sitting there with scissors in her hand, a pile of rags on her lap. His first thought was that he had done this: that in having imagined a crazy wife and nurtured the idea of her these past several months he had somehow brought her into being. In that sense, finding Penny's mother's phone number written in Abigail's neat hand had been a relief. It *was* his fault, but his wife wasn't crazy, only a little drunk and justifiably livid. There wasn't time to ponder the obvious question – how the hell had Penny found him? – his sole objective was to keep Abigail calm, at least until he got the scissors away from her. It was horrible watching her throw up, the way the retching continued long after her stomach was empty; the way she'd curled up on the floor like a wounded animal, shaking all over. He had no idea she cared so deeply for him.

'Are you going to leave me?' she asked.

'Of course not,' he replied, unable to imagine anything more ridiculous. Leave Abigail? Why, he'd sooner cut off his right arm. He depended on her, would be lost without her and even if that weren't the case, Ted McDougall wasn't the sort of guy to walk out on his wife and child. He wasn't Stan Gold. He helped her up, wiped her face and brow with a damp cloth, tucked her into bed and brought her a cup of warm broth to drink.

'You need to keep up your strength,' he said.

Stoic Yankee that she was, Abigail was soon back on her feet, carrying on as if nothing had happened, but he knew she was hurting. She'd lock herself in the bathroom to cry, running the water, mistakenly believing it drowned out the sound. She'd emerge with red eyes and blotchy skin. His indiscretions had broken something in both of them. He began to worry that she might leave him. His appetite evaporated. He lived for weeks on stewed fruit and dry toast, the only things he could swallow. His face turned gaunt. Clothes sagged around his shrunken frame. He was in a state of perpetual anxiety, phoning home several times a day, flying into a panic whenever Abigail took more than three rings to pick up.

And yet, oddly, sex was the best it had ever been. Odder still, Abigail often initiated it. In sleep, he clung to her with a drowning man's desperation, so tight she had to kick him because she couldn't breathe.

She withdrew from her planned summer classes and they spent evenings together, resuming their after-dinner walks around the neighbourhood. The first of the Phase II split-levels were complete and new neighbours were moving in: arranging furniture, hanging drapes, choosing colour schemes. He looked on with envy.

On Saturdays after work, they drove up to the cabin, arriving in time for dinner and a paddle around the lake in the boat. Once Mindy was in bed they'd sit out on the porch, a sandal-wood coil smouldering on the table between them to keep the mosquitoes away. They talked about everything except that which weighed most heavily on their minds, sipped beer and took turns pointing out constellations. Sometimes, they skinny-dipped. Sunday mornings they attended services at a tiny rustic church and then went back to the cabin where he made pancakes with whipped butter, hot maple syrup and sides of bacon. Through these moments of simple companionship he gained a deeper appreciation for his marriage vows. He felt he understood, now, what the whole for better or for worse thing was about, and that, after years of pretending, he had at last become a grown-up.

'I'll do whatever it takes to make it up to you,' he promised, 'whatever you want.'

Her reply surprised him, although it probably shouldn't have.

'I want to go to law school,' she said.

Such an easy wish to grant, when what he longed for was a chance to prove his gallantry and devotion.

Penny featured little in his thoughts. He regretted that fate had left her holding such a short end of the stick, but his first priority had to be repairing the damage to his marriage. Toward the end of the summer he considered calling, but it was easy to talk himself out of the idea. No point opening up old wounds. Inelegant as the break-up had been, it was necessary and inevitable and by now, of course, obvious. There was nothing he could do for her at this point. She was well shot of him.

That's what he told himself, and that's what he believed, until one Tuesday in September, when he went to a regional sales meeting in the southeastern part of the state. Driving along the route he'd last travelled to meet with the social worker, and visit Penny in hospital, repressed thoughts of their friendship flooded in. He could only be ashamed of his behaviour, particularly at the end – storming out in a hypocritical fury in response to questions that were not only perfectly justified but also not much different from ones she'd been asking for months.

The meeting was a waste of time. A representative from corporate gave a presentation about all the fabulous things the company was doing so the salesmen could mention them in their pitches, when appropriate. They were the kinds of things Ted could typically get excited about – like launching a satellite into space, building a computer interface for technical workers, and Jack Brabham winning the World Driving Championships on Goodyear tyres – but today he could hardly pay attention. That was partly due to the speaker, a spiffy young suit with a flat delivery; college boy, for sure; probably some big shot's kid. Mostly, though, it was because he couldn't stop thinking of Penny. Poor, sweet Penny. The last time he'd seen her, she was standing in the middle of the road as he pulled away, looking like she was about to crumple to dust. He hoped she hadn't. He really hoped she hadn't. He'd left without saying goodbye; without saying sorry. What a heel she must think he was. The burden of the thoughts grew so heavy that when the signs to Cape Cod appeared on the drive home he felt he had no choice but to follow them.

There was a touch of fall in the bright late-afternoon air. The town's gift shops, seasonal hotels and summer houses closest to the coast were boarded up for the season. It was austere, practical, all frivolity gone now that the tourists and summer people had left. It occurred to him that Penny might be gone, as well. He wasn't sure whether this prospect disappointed or relieved him.

She was there. He spied her through the kitchen window, standing over the stove, and his heart skipped a beat. He knocked, and when she turned towards him, he felt the same old longing.

She was, of course, stylishly dressed, with a crocheted cotton sweater that she'd probably made herself over a tank top, dungarees rolled up above the ankles. Her hair was longer, in a bob that fell to her chin. Her skin bore the golden traces of a summer spent at the beach. Though relieved not to find the painfully thin, pale and breakable creature from last June, he was nevertheless a little taken aback at her having recovered quite so well.

'I'm surprised you let me in,' he said, as he entered the parlour and took a seat on the couch that had so often doubled as his bed. His arms hung clumsily at his sides. He ought to have brought her something.

'I'm a little surprised myself,' she replied, perching on the edge of a hardback chair beside the picture window, back as straight as a washboard.

Rose went to make tea.

'I wasn't sure you'd still be here,' he said.

'I'll be going back to Boston soon.'

'She's got a job with those computer people,' Rose called back from the kitchen with maternal pride.

'Wang Labs,' Penny said reluctantly.

He nodded. 'Just caught you, then.'

'Yup,' she said. 'Lucky you.'

'I . . . I meant to come earlier,' he said. 'You've been on my mind a lot.'

She nodded.

'I don't know what to say. I know there's no defence. I am utterly ashamed.'

She nodded again. Apparently, she wasn't going to make this any easier. He asked about the baby and when she told him he shook his head, sorrowfully.

'I wish there had been another way,' he said.

Her eyes flickered up and to the left, as if drawn to something outside, a passing cardinal or an oriole, before fixing on him with devastating directness. 'Wasn't there?'

'I wanted to help you get through it,' he spluttered. 'If I had told you everything you wouldn't have let me; you wouldn't have wanted anything to do with me.'

'You gave me false hope.'

Such a small voice. He had to make her understand. 'I told you I couldn't get my divorce in time. I never promised I could fix things.'

'You're right,' she said, defeated. 'It was my fault for believing you wanted to marry me.'

'Penny, sweetheart,' he cried, his heart breaking. 'How can you ever doubt that was what I wanted, what I want to this day?'

'You're still married, aren't you?'

He lowered his head and nodded.

'You left when I needed you most.'

'I was angry and confused,' he said. 'I would have come back in a day or two, if you hadn't called my house. How did you get my number, anyway?'

She laughed as if he were a dummy for having to ask. 'Your secretary gave it to me.'

Damn Sally, he thought. Starting tomorrow, he'd find a way to fire her.

'I've missed you, Penny.'

Her hands began to tremble, she looked out the window, and he saw that his first impression had been completely wrong. She was not recovered. Nowhere near it. The fresh, Annette Funicello innocence that used to light up her face had vanished. He hadn't noticed until now because she was still such a damn attractive woman, possibly even more so than before. The sadness in her eyes made her mysterious; it filled him with the desire to comfort her, to make her smile. Tragedy had transformed her from a pretty girl into a truly beautiful woman.

'How about we go dancing some time, when you get back to Boston?' He hardly knew what he was saying. 'I'll take you to the Ritz; for old times' sake.'

She made a strange noise – half chuckle, half sneer – and smiled, but not in the way he'd hoped.

'Don't do this,' she said, her voice cracking. 'Don't you dare do this.'

If only he could take her in his arms, but the straightness of her back, the tilt of her chin, told him she wouldn't let him. 'You are the love of my life, Penny Goodwin,' he said, the words catching in his throat.

'No, Ted,' she replied, inhaling nosily and wiping her nose on the back of her hand with uncharacteristic gracelessness. 'You are.'

He got back in his car, bereft at the thought of never seeing her again. He didn't blame her for doubting his love. How could he, after everything he had put her through? It was the God's honest truth, though. He knew it when he said it. The longing in his throat that grew with each passing mile confirmed it. In saying goodbye to her he was saying goodbye to the best part of his life, the best part of himself, and Danny was deader than he'd ever been.

She would be fine. Some young hotshot technology exec would snap her up out of the typing pool. A few years from now she'd have a big house in Newton or Wellesley, a successful husband, beautiful children, days spent meeting girlfriends for games of tennis or lunches at the golf club. This whole tragic chapter would be a distant memory. He alone would carry the torment to his grave.

On the approach to the bridge, he slipped the Corvair into the passing lane and put his foot on the accelerator. The early evening sky was full of pinks, yellows and oranges, a carnival of colours, reminiscent of the halter top Penny had worn on his first visit to the Cape. The gods were mocking him.

He returned to Elm Grove determined to be a good and faithful husband to Abigail and to turn the Lynn store around. And in the years that followed he worked hard at both, with some success. The store was never profitable the way he thought it would be, the way Curtis's store was. Truth be told, it was a dog of a store in a dying city. Curtis and Mikey had played him for a sucker, luring him to beg for a worthless prize. He made enough to pay the bills, for the most part, including Abigail's law school tuition, and Mindy's babysitter, but not enough for a housekeeper and so he took on some of the cooking in addition to washing dishes and folding laundry. This wasn't much of a stretch as his days working at the diner in Wilsonville had made him a half-decent short-order cook, but to the ladies of Elm Grove, many of whom were returning to school or taking up part-time jobs, it was the same as walking on water.

'Ted McDougall is a man without fault,' Carol Innes proclaimed during what turned out to be the last ever neighbourhood party, for Memorial Day 1972.

Abigail's smile seemed to say that she knew of a fault or two. She never brought up his past indiscretion, never threw it in his face, not even during their fiercest arguments (usually over some impulse purchase he'd made at Shoppers' World – a camel-hair coat, a gas grill, a riding mower), and yet, somehow, it was always hanging in the air over his head. On the invisible ledger where his moral debts were tallied, it seemed he could never do more than clear the accruing interest.

Probably because he never entirely let go of Penny, not in any literal (physical) sense – Penny was firm on that – but thoughts of her took up considerable real estate in his brain. He felt the need to call her every once in a while, to see how she was getting on. She usually hung up as soon as she knew it was him, but just hearing her voice, just knowing she was out there, filled a hole within him, and sometimes, particularly if he phoned late at night, or if Peanut and Ellen were away on overnight trips, she'd talk to him.

She hated Wang, hated office work, and eventually quit for a job dressing mannequins at a department store. She wouldn't say which.

'I always liked playing with dolls,' she said. It was, he knew, a reference to Lily. Whenever she spoke, however briefly, it was always about Lily.

'My arms ache,' she cried to him at 3 a.m. on the morning of Lily's fifth birthday. 'Every day they ache from not having held her.'

'She's in a loving home,' he replied.

They were like the lone survivors of a shipwreck, a plane crash, or some other catastrophe, forever bound by an experience only they could understand.

Not for one second did he question his decision to stay with Abigail. All that free love, counter-culture mumbo-jumbo would be the end of us, he was sure. Society needed rules in order to function and any man who wasn't willing to sacrifice his own happiness for that of his family was not fit to call himself a man. These were the beliefs on which he was raised and he clung to them, even as the stories of illegal bombing campaigns in Cambodia, and the Watergate break-in made clear that the country's leaders weren't above breaking a few rules themselves, when it suited.

He loved Abigail, admired her; was nothing but proud when she made law review. She had her pick of jobs at any of the big Boston law firms, but when she said she wanted to go back to Wilsonville and join Linc's practice, Ted dutifully put the Enchantress on the market. By then, life in Elm Grove wasn't what it had been. Some neighbours, the Gills and the Jenkses among them, had moved to bigger houses in wealthier suburbs. The families who replaced them weren't as congenial. Most were fleeing soaring crime rates and the prospect of racial integration in Boston public schools. The Ladies Culture Club disbanded – fizzled out would be a more apt description. No one had time. Janice was running the ladies undergarments department over at Jordan Marsh. Becky was teaching third grade at the new elementary school. Carol worked as a secretary at the hospital. Things were changing so fast. Inner-city crime was inching out to the suburbs; divorce was ripping through the neighbourhood like a measles epidemic. Even Shoppers' World, the Main Street of the future, had become passé in a decade, eclipsed by the Natick Mall. It wasn't enough to have a covered walkway to keep the rain and snow off a shopper's head. People needed full enclosure. They needed music and a food court. Ted sold the Enchantress for a tidy profit to a bigot from Charlestown, and considered himself lucky to escape, even though an assistant manager's position half an hour away in Keene was the best that Goodyear could arrange by way of transfer. It was a step back after five years running his own show, but he smiled and said thank you very much, certain that the setback was temporary and, anyway, Abigail's earnings would more than make up for any reduction in his own.

They bought a big old Victorian not far from Main Street, with a turret, high ceilings, rooms on three floors, fancy lattice-work and a barn-sized garage out back. It was a home of distinction, custom-made and built to last, and so it surprised him that he was so often nostalgic for his shitty little tract house in Elm Grove. Ticky-tacky box though the Enchantress was, it was his ticky-tacky box. He could take pride in knowing that he'd paid for its four walls and everything inside it. He missed the man he was when he'd lived there, the one who had stories to tell and whose potential seemed infinite. In Wilsonville, he was his father's son; brother of that poor kid who fell through the ice and drowned; Linc Hatch's son-in-law; Abigail's lesser half.

Her career was taking off. Clients were coming from the cities of Keene and Nashua. There were rumours around the court-house that her name had been added to the list of potential appointees to the bench. In the beginning, she earned about the same as he did, but as her reputation grew, so did her billable hours. Meanwhile, his career seemed permanently stalled. The manager at his store was around his age, as were the managers of all the Goodyear stores in the vicinity. Unless one of them dropped dead from a heart attack, he'd be an assistant manager for ever. Ninety per cent of his sales were retail, walk-ins to the showroom floor, like what he'd done in that first summer he was working for Curtis. He didn't get invited to sales conferences or regional meetings. It had been years since his last business dinner, unless he counted the ones in which he accompanied Abigail. These weren't business dinners, per se, but banquets and galas, given by important foundations and societies, where the conversation was about things he didn't understand like tort, which either definitely did, or didn't, need reforming, depending on who was present, and motions in (or was it out of?) *limine*. He felt increasingly irrelevant. Worst of all was Danny's marker in the cemetery, lying a few feet away from his father's, an incontrovertible fact in need of regular tidying. He got a pain in his gut each spring when the pond ice broke up.

Mindy was more like Abigail every day. Ask her what she wanted to be when she grew up and she'd reply, 'a lawyer or a politician'. Nine years old and she called herself a feminist. Well, why shouldn't she? Why shouldn't girls have dreams as well as boys? One of his greatest joys was taking her for doughnuts Sunday mornings at Joellie's Bakery. They'd get there early, sit at the counter on stools that spun, exchanging jokes and playing games, Mindy sprawled across the seat on her belly, arms and legs in the air like a skydiver. The doughnuts tasted of vanilla and cinnamon and released little puffs of steam when he broke a piece off to dip in his coffee.

He adored his daughter, which is why it hurt so much the morning they were playing 'name that state capital'.

'Florida,' she said and he mistakenly replied, 'Miami', an error that was apparently grave enough to necessitate a pause in twirling.

'Tallahassee, Daddy,' she groaned.

It wasn't her disappointment that wounded, it was the sense of resignation in which that disappointment was wrapped – as if she couldn't expect any better from a knucklehead like him – and he found his thoughts turning to another daughter, one he was sure would have always held him in awe.

He had been convinced that not seeing Lily was the best option and, who knows, maybe it was, but the not knowing was its own kind of torture, tossing up a million unanswerable questions, enough to fuel a lifetime of late-night conversations with Penny. He began to think of these as a constant in his life, something that – for better or worse – would always be there and so he was surprised when, during a phone call that took place a couple weeks after Nixon resigned, she announced that it would be their last. She was engaged. She wouldn't tell him the lucky guy's name but, when pressed, admitted that she'd been seeing him for some time. He was divorced, with young kids and an ex-wife with a history of mental instability.

'For real,' she added, a little snidely, he thought.

He forced a laugh that he hoped sounded good-natured – no mean feat given his heart had just been stomped on.

'Does he know about Lily?'

It might have been the first time he'd said the name out loud. Normally he preferred to use pronouns or simply 'the baby'. Penny hesitated, giving him hope that this one piece of her would remain exclusively his.

'He does,' she replied.

'Does he make you happy?'

'Of course.'

'That's great,' he said, conscious that he was straining to sound sincere, which was odd because he *was* sincere. Of course he wanted Penny to be happy; it was what he'd wanted all along.

There was no point asking for specifics he knew she wouldn't divulge. With minimal sleuthing, he discovered the date, time and place of the ceremony. There was nothing to it. He just phoned around churches and banquet halls near Rose's house on the Cape, charming the receptionists with stories about having misplaced the invitation or worrying over where to send a gift or telegram. People enjoyed being helpful and women, especially, would go to remarkable lengths for a hapless man who threw himself on their mercy. He really ought to have been a spy.

He hadn't the slightest intention of interrupting Penny's big day. He parked a discreet distance from the church. The binoculars he brought – the ones Linc kept at the cabin for birdwatching – provided an excellent view of Penny when she exited the car. Of course she looked beautiful and stylish and, to his great sorrow, radiant. He was tempted to slip into a back pew to watch the ceremony, but resisted. He didn't want to make a scene.

Besides, it was a long drive home to New Hampshire, long and sad. He had never felt so empty. At a dive bar in Fitchburg, he stopped for a highball and asked a pig-faced girl to slow dance. While the soles of their shoes made out-of-sync sticky sounds on the dirty floor, she let him slip his tongue into her mouth and then his hands into her pants. With shockingly little effort, he persuaded her to join him in the back seat of his car, where he could have sworn he heard her squeal, though it was probably the sound of her bare butt cheeks rubbing against the vinyl seats.

Afterward he felt remorse but also powerful in a way he hadn't for a long time and he was soon drawn back for more. He chose seedy bars and nightclubs in the grittier towns of northern Massachusetts – Chicopee, Holyoke, Pittsfield – where there was no chance of running in to anyone he knew. In his flares and platform shoes, with his sandy-brown hair waving in the breeze, people said he looked like Robert Redford. Thanks to Women's Lib, there was no shortage of girls game for a quick fuck in the back seat of his car, against the wall of a back alley, or even in a not-so-quiet corner of a discotheque, where the strobe lights gave their gyrations a weird, slow-motion effect. It brought euphoria in the moment, but self-loathing always rode shotgun on the trip home. Each time, he swore was the last, until the next time. He was adrift, rudderless. On a humid night not long after the Bicentennial, when leaving the parking lot of Chickie's bar in Pittsfield, after having screwed a little blonde in a bathroom stall while her unsuspecting husband sipped Pabst Blue Ribbon at the bar, he turned west instead of north and kept going.

Epilogue
April 2008

Penny stared into her open closet as if into an abyss. For the first time in memory, possibly the first time ever, she couldn't decide what to wear.

She had been at it for hours now and time was running out. The bedroom was strewn with clothes that she feared made her look haughty instead of elegant, frumpy instead of relaxed, uptight instead of polished. And dear Larry was of no help, responding to each one with a heartfelt, 'Looks great.'

Her indecision befuddled him and understandably so. Assembling outfits was, after all, how she'd made her living for forty years, working with some of the best boutiques and department stores in Greater Boston, and now she couldn't pick an outfit? The frustration was written across his face: *Jesus, it's just lunch.*

Only it wasn't.

She pivoted in front of the mirror, inspecting herself from every angle, ignoring the queasiness building in her stomach. Was pairing the long denim skirt with a dress shirt and suit jacket a playful fusion of professional and casual, or an unforgivable crime against good taste; a whimsical fashion *do*, or a gauche *don't*?

The answer, she decided, hinged on footwear. She kicked off the pumps and laced up a pair of ankle boots, cringed, and then switched to knee-high ones in brown suede with square heels. She felt like a teenager, and not the carefree, whole-life-ahead-of-them, idealised figment of the senior citizen imagination, but the self-conscious, self-loathing gremlin of reality. Her arms and shoulders ached.

'Classic or boring?' she asked her husband.

'Relax, honey,' he said, skipping straight to the heart of the matter. 'She's going to love you.'

She nodded, feigning agreement. It was easier that way. Larry knew the whole story and was sympathetic, a source of unfailing tenderness and patience every year when, like clockwork, her spirits sank in the week after Mother's Day, but he couldn't really *understand*. No one could. Moreover, his unconditional love for her made his judgement suspect.

'This is what you've always wanted,' he reminded her.

Which was precisely the problem. It couldn't be this simple. Stories of this kind didn't have happy endings. A tickle appeared in her throat; she attempted to clear it.

'If you want me to stay . . .'

'God, no,' she barked. The last thing she needed was to have him hanging around, filling the space with his oversized personality. 'But please don't leave until she gets here.' Her voice sounded husky, as if she had a cold coming on.

He followed her into the kitchen and scrubbed a cucumber, washed and then spun dry the lettuce without her having to ask. She took the chicken salad out of the fridge, the fancy kind, with almond flakes and dried cranberries, and cut slices from the sourdough loaf they'd bought at the Portuguese bakery this morning. There was cold cucumber soup to start and for dessert, a home-made Victoria sponge with strawberry jam and whipped cream. She cast an eye over the dishes assembled on the counter, unable to imagine swallowing a bite.

'Do you think I made too much?' she asked, trying, once again, to clear whatever it was that was stuck at the top of her throat.

'The perfect amount,' he replied, making no mention of her altered voice. Could it be a figment of her imagination?

'The white wine is chilling in the fridge; there's mineral water and ice tea.' She was talking out loud to herself, running through a checklist. 'And diet soda, too, if Lily prefers—'

She stopped in her tracks and shot a panicked look at Larry.

'Jen,' she said. 'If *Jen* prefers.' What if she called her by the wrong name?

'It's a perfectly natural mistake,' Larry said.

The phone rang and he went to the other room to answer it. Penny's heart fluttered; her mind raced – thoughts of car accidents, a last-minute crisis of courage, or change of mind. He came back and handed it to her.

'Your mother,' he mouthed.

'Hello?' she croaked.

'What's wrong with your voice?' Mother asked.

So she hadn't imagined it. She tried again to clear it. The top of her throat felt rough. 'I don't know,' she said. 'I was fine when I woke up.'

'You sound like a frog,' Mother said with a chuckle.

'I'm glad that you find this amusing, Mother.'

'Oh, for heaven's sake, don't be a stick-in-the-mud. I'm calling to wish you luck.'

'Thank you.'

'Don't feel you have to tell her everything,' her mother said. 'Past is past.'

'I've already decided,' Penny replied, forcing the words out because it felt as if her vocal chords were shrinking. 'I'm going to tell her everything.'

'Call me after,' Mother said.

'Last-minute words of advice?' Larry asked.

'You know how she gets,' Penny said. 'It's not for my sake.' Anger mixed with the dryness in her throat, giving her voice a squeaky edge. 'She's afraid she'll come off looking bad.'

Larry wiped the counter down with a sponge. 'She did what she believed was right,' he said. 'You both did.'

'Did we?' Her voice was fading.

'Of course.'

Her arms were made of lead. 'I think we did what was easiest.'

'You can't possibly call what you've been through all these years easy.'

'Of course not,' she replied. 'But I didn't know that then.'

She set the small table on the three-season porch with silverware and her great-aunt's china, examining the bright yellow cloth and light blue linen napkins that echoed the bouquet of irises and daffodils in the vase at the centre. As with everything she'd done today, she was having second thoughts about it. Too much blue and yellow? Were the irises too tall? Was this the wrong room? Had it been foolish to invite her here?

The house was on a cliff overlooking Cape Cod Bay. It was a wonderful house, the likes of which Penny never dreamed of owning until a few years back when, out of the blue, a developer offered a remarkable sum for their thoroughly unremarkable home in a suburb of Boston. It was the land the developer wanted. He tore the house down and replaced it with a McMansion.

Penny loved this home, but she worried, now, that it made her look materialistic and show-offy – the kind of person who valued things more than people. It seemed she could do nothing right. She searched for words to express to Larry the tumult in her head and in her stomach, but what came out of her mouth was a platitude in a squeak: 'What if we have nothing in common?'

'What do you want from her?' he asked.

Penny closed her eyes. 'Forgiveness,' she whispered.

'There's nothing to forgive. She's said so herself. Everything you wanted for her she's had.'

'I know that's what she *said*.'

'How long are you going to beat yourself up?' She closed her eyes and took a breath.

'How long is a piece of string?'

The doorbell rang; Penny made a nervous jump.

'It's going to be fine,' Larry said. 'You'll have a nice lunch, and you never have to see one another again if you don't want to.'

The words, meant to reassure, nearly caused her knees to buckle. With difficulty, she lifted her leaden arms and made shooing motions with her hands.

'Okay, okay, I'm going,' he said, heading for the back door while Penny went to the front on wobbly legs.

Her throat was sandpaper and her heart in the midst of a fantastic drum solo. How should she greet her – with a hand-shake? A hug? A kiss on the cheek? She was afraid of coming on too strong, but also of holding back and appearing cold and aloof. Oh, sweet Jesus, why hadn't she thought about any of this before? She checked her face in the mirror, gave herself a smile of encouragement, and pulled the door open.

And was astonished by her own astonishment. It seemed that in some deep recess of her brain she had been nourishing a fantasy that time could be erased, or at least suspended, and that what waited for her on the other side of the door was not this slightly plump, middle-aged woman with Tina Fey glasses, crinkles at the corners of her eyes and brown hair flecked with grey, but the tiny infant she'd last glimpsed fighting tigers in a hospital crib. How foolish! The child had grown; the dream was dead. In normal circumstances, the weight of such a realisation, the loss it implied, would have destroyed her, but right now the woman was looking up at her and smiling the most beautiful smile. She was a whole, living, breathing being, close enough for Penny to touch, and her arms were now opening wide as Penny's, likewise, began to lift, rising on their sudden, unbelievable lightness.

Acknowledgements

Thanks to my agent, Caroline Wood, for believing in this story from the beginning; to my editor, Eleanor Birne, for her insights and encouragement, and to the whole team at John Murray, whose hard work and attention to detail made *The Good Guy* better. Any faults or errors are mine alone.

I am grateful to E.O.C., social worker at Child and Family Services of New Bedford in New Bedford, Massachusetts, whose detailed notes concerning my adoption provided the inspiration for this story, and to Susan Dineen and my birthmother, the late Lynne Casale, for sharing their experiences of mid-1960s' unwed motherhood.

Several writers took time to read and comment on the manuscript at every stage of its development and I'm obliged to them all, particularly Julian Hussey and Fenella Mallalieu; also Ann Pelletier, first reader, true poet, and forever friend.

I am indebted to the wonderful tutors on the Bath Spa Creative Writing MA, especially Tessa Hadley, who supervised the first draft of this manuscript.

Thanks to my parents; to Flemming for being supportive in this as in all things, and to Austen, Mitchell, Elliot and Sam for simply being.

From Byron, Austen and Darwin

to some of the most acclaimed and original contemporary writing, John Murray takes pride in bringing you powerful, prizewinning, absorbing and provocative books that will entertain you today and become the classics of tomorrow.

We put a lot of time and passion into what we publish and how we publish it, and we'd like to hear what you think.

Be part of John Murray – share your views with us at:

www.johnmurray.co.uk

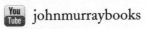 johnmurraybooks

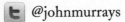 @johnmurrays

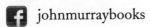 johnmurraybooks